NEXUS™

BLOOD, GUTS, AND GLORY

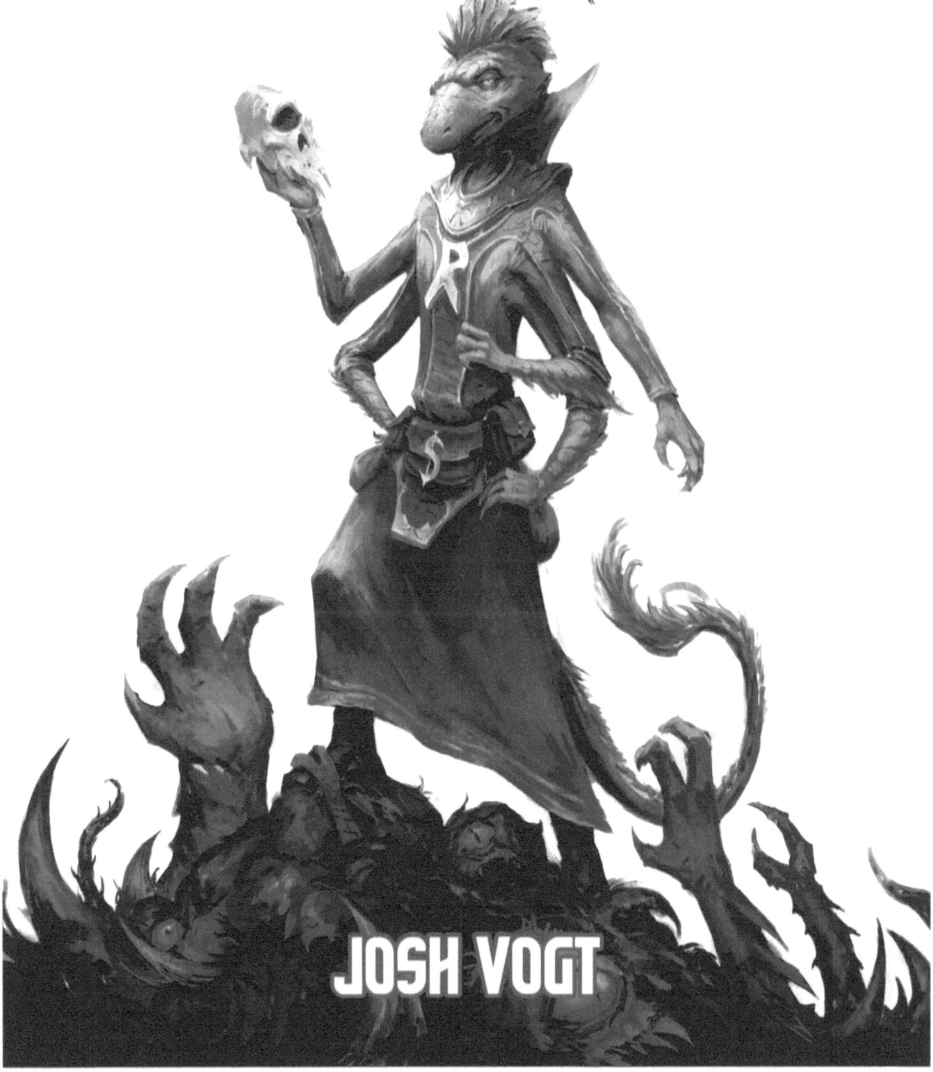

JOSH VOGT

NEXUS: Blood, Guts, and Glory

Copyright 2020 D-Verse Publishing, LLC

ISBN: 978-1-7356163-0-8

Cover & Book Design by J. Scott Rumptz

Cover Artwork by Bogdan Tomchuk

Interior Artwork by Michael Rechlin

Published by
D-Verse Publishing, LLC.
PO BOX 38509
Germantown, TN 38183-0509

www.d-verse.com

NEXUS
BLOOD, GUTS, AND GLORY

D-VERSE
PUBLISHING LLC.

JOSH VOGT

A lanista is nothing without their helot. Their reputation lives and dies by the helots. Treat a helot like trash, and you will be seen as trash and be given trash results in return. They are an extension of you, just like whatever interstellar genitals you lug around, and should be kept healthy and strong and pleasured just like your genitals until they get defeated in the arena. Then you have to move on, unlike with your genitals. That's where the metaphor breaks down. Deal with it, sprukker.

- How to Backstab Friends and Influence Outcomes:
A Guide for Starting Lanistas
Written by Lanista Kel'Chungzi Ewaltsen
Excerpt from Vol 32, Section BVII, Subset 8.11

PROLOGUE

One step to glory, a footprint in blood. Excorius the Undying and Undefeated III, son of Excorius the Dying and Defeated II, knew this mantra well. He repeated it to himself each time he stood on the brink of the arena, ready to revel in the blood and intestines of yet another victim.

He would step into the fight. He could receive the glory of the waiting crowd. He would rise through the ranks of helots whose names were forever engraved in the Asteroid Fields of Remembrance.

One bloody footprint at a time.

Excorius knew the stink of blood well. His own fetid musk surrounded him always, with his species seeping blood into its sweat through vein-pores. It dribbled constantly, a purplish ooze that slurped in his steps as he shuffled in place. That's why he eschewed pathetic power armor or fancy trappings when entering arena combat.

His own vitae served as a morbid cloak across his skin and acted as a warning to any who would see him as easy prey. Excorius enjoyed adding special oils to the ichor, making himself slick enough to be both difficult to grab and so his opponents could see themselves mirrored in his glistening epidermis. They could see themselves reflected in a tableau of gore just before he made their vision a reality at the end of his plasma-bladed cleaver.

The crowd beyond the gate roared as an announcement echoed in the distance. The pit boss undulated nearer to the control panel controlling the door and squatted there, fronds stiff.

Excorius raised a sixth nostril to the air, letting it waggle with its articulated hairs. He snaked an eye-tendril out through the bars and made a forbidden peek into the arena, and then stuck a stubby finger to the floor, letting his knuckle-drum pick up tremors through the barge as it thrummed through the void of space.

The glimpse and scents and vibrations painted a vivid picture in his forebrain.

Above came the air-shivering hiss of the aerie anti-grav generators, keeping his lanista—his owner, his master—aloft to survey the death-match.

To serve the lanista whose name Excorius did not deserve to remember was to live.

To serve the lanista was to fight.

To serve the lanista and win was to get delicious fried marrow snacks after the match.

Excorius drooled at the thought of the crunchy morsels and tried to keep his focus on the fight. Columns and pits and rusted barricades filled the arena floor, with napalm flames sizzling in sconces and tracks along the walls, casting hellish shadows over the stadium-sized combat field.

The audience's cheers and jeers, screams and shouts pounded their way into Excorius' skull, a migraine of ecstasy he heard even in his dreams these days. They called for death. They called for bloodshed. They called for limbs being torn and brains being mashed and entrails being...trailed.

From all corners of existence, the audience came to watch, paying Bits aplenty to scuffle and shove in their seats, jostling closer to the spray zones at the edge of the stands, or jabbing elbows and skull spurs to get a better look at the hoverscreens zooming around above them.

In another corner, the sweet stench of sugared fevril tendons and a screeching gabble indicated the children's viewing section. There, younglings of all species from all universes and dimensions would be joining in the spectacle, members of the Lil' Fuckers organization, dedicated to funding the violent upbringing of alien spawn.

The pit boss flicked a tentacle, signaling mere moments left before the gate retracted and unleashed a gory spectacle before the crowd.

Excorius notched up the plasma-cleaver until the heat of it began to sizzle the blood coated its ten-clawed handstubs. Two helots would enter the arena. One helot would emerge victorious. There was no question in his mind which one he would be.

The holding cell shook as the arena signal blared, and lights flashed, and trumpets echoed from speakers hidden in the darkness high above the arena. The pit boss triggered the gate and slithered away as Excorius thundered into the open. He took a brief moment to wave his plasma-cleaver at the crowd, reveling in their roaring acclaim. Clothing, trash, body parts, and greasy food globs rained down around him, and he took it for the hero-worship it was.

Excorius glanced up at the hoverscreens, seeing his enemy broadcasted through them, just as his own beautiful bulk lumbered for all to admire. Far across on the other side of the arena, a three-legged, two-headed furred beast gnashed fangs as long as the cleaver he held. A security squad was forcing it into the arena with shock-prods, and it rounded on them, trying to scrabble back into the shelter of its cell.

Excorius grinned wide enough to show all five tongues. The bestial foe would be a simple matter. While even dumb brutes could possess a hunting instinct, Excorius' cunning always outplayed them. And he knew this arena well, for the dozens of bouts he had survived in it. The winding ways and obstacles and hazards shifted slightly each time, but he could make his way unerringly through it, circle around behind the brute as it tried to sniff him out, and lop off its limbs one at a time, leaving it to mewl for mercy until he decapitated it to the crowd's acclaim.

Lurching into a lope, Excorius ducked between two pillars, letting a buzzsaw whine as it sheared the air half an inch above his neck hairs. He bolted to the side as a jet of flame shot up high enough to briefly illuminate the ceiling before showering the area in embers.

He moved on automatic, sensing the dangers moments before pits opened up before him, spikes shot out to impale, or acid spewed from hidden nozzles. A pleasant warmup exercise before the true fight began. Perhaps this time he should let the other helot get a few hits in, taste the blood on his skin, even add a small scar or two before Excorius bashed, pummeled, and diced it into oblivion. He knew his lanista enjoyed that sort of excitement—it drew in bigger bets on the outcome, and bigger payouts when he beat the supposed odds.

Another bellow, a cry of challenge, spurred him on faster. He sensed more than saw the countless drones whirring through the air above the arena, projecting his movement to the bloodthirsty crowd. Excorius knew even despite his hunger for victory, the audience's hunger for morbid spectacle far outmatched his appetites. He would be sated for a while after this match, reveling in another fresh kill recorded in the Book.

But the endless throngs that attended his bouts? Those crammed into barge after barge throughout the infinite expanse of the Nexus? The family units within their home-hovels enjoying bonding time over mutual appreciation of mutilation and destruction?

So long as life existed, they would scream for the spectacle of death.

And pay their last Bits to watch while gorging on cheap meats, brawling with cheap shots, and jerking off their alien cocks for the cheap thrills.

A razor-thin line of plasma lanced across the hall as Excorius hunched down. He ducked at the last second, feeling a flash of pain as it seared off an ear-tip. Some cleaning crew would likely snag it later and pawn the chunk of flesh for a few hundred Bits on the sludge market. A helot souvenir.

Carry it for luck, but never get caught or the Gnoems would pay a visit in your sleep!

The scent of the other helot finally slithered into Excorius' lower nostrils, tantalizing him with the stink of fear, of fury, of food.

Urged onward, he dashed around a corner and—

The arena spun as something heavy and multi-limbed slammed to the ground nearby, twitching in death throes. Excorius couldn't understand why he smelled burning flesh.

Why had two of his eyes gone dim? Why did the severed limb flopping to the side look so familiar?

A buzzing whine jabbed his ears, even as his hearing went distant. The deadly blur of a ripsaw spun to a stop, having jutted out of a nearly invisible slit in the hall flooring that he'd been passing over.

His intestines smeared the ugly toothed blade, turning it into a metallic tapestry of gore. A final thought flitted through his forebrain as everything went cold.

I was so much more beautiful on the inside.

Failure is inevitable. Acceptance of that failure unforgivable. Gnash against it. Decry it with all your might. Weep and wail and destroy all things that remind you of that failure as you rebuild from the ashes. Make failure your archenemy and resign yourself to defeating it time and time again for the rest of your miserable existence. Understand?

Now, do I speak from experience? Of course not. Real victors never fail. So if you believed everything I just wrote earlier, you might as well give up now. This has been a test. Everything is a test. And you most likely just failed.

- How to Backstab Friends and Influence Outcomes:
A Guide for Starting Lanistas
Written by Lanista Kel'Chungzi Ewaltsen
Excerpt from Vol 19, Subset 4.21

CHAPTER ONE

Rahgz shoved his mop through the bloody muck coating the arena floor and tried not to think about how hungry he was. Even the cleanest, quickest helot bouts the *Coffin* hosted required extensive sanitizing to prep for the next. Captain Aosi had a reputation for being one of those neatfreak barge masters.

Despite being on the INC's most-wanted list, he had the psychotic urge to run the cleanest illegal arena operation in all of Nexus. As such, he enforced ridiculous hygienic standards such as a barge-wide regulation requiring the washing of limbs before ingesting nutri-chunks, the deployment of waste disposal cyborgs that chased down and thrashed litterers, and a ban on public phlargistymnastics on pain of equally public neutering.

Kicking at a particularly stubborn chunk of dried brainmatter crusted to the deck, Rahgz cursed his luck. Of course he'd get stuck on a spleen team that required real effort. He'd heard of other spleen teams on barges where all they had to do was wander the arena tossing buckets of helot-chum and swill to slick every surface, or ones where audiences used the arena as mass latrines before, after, and during the bouts.

It added a special piquance to the ambiance, attendees claimed.

Rahgz's stomach rumbled for the hundredth time that shift. The meager meal of nutri-chunks he had a few hours earlier wouldn't sustain him for long. He didn't have to glance at the barge-Bit implant on his wrist to know the account balance registered a solid zero zero zero zero, with a dot zero zero for hearty emphasis at the end. Just like it had for nearly a solid TIRD.

Checking around, Rahgz saw no other members of his cleaning crew in sight, and so took a second to lift the mop to his wide lips and sucked the salty glop off the soggy strands. He fought against the gag reflex, swallowing the globs and trying to imagine that what plopped into his first stomach was simple vat-brewed gruel. That when he chewed the cud later that shift, it wouldn't come up tasting like someone had shit down his throat and washed it down with a gallon of curdled phlegm.

But hey. Better than starving, nuh?

Sometimes Rahgz wondered…

Resuming shoving the growing pile of innards around the corner, Rahgz worked his way down the hall, carefully sidestepping the telltale signs of tripwires and pressure plates that would activate the dozens of booby-traps waiting to disembowel, dismember, impale, broil, and fricassee him at a moment's notice. Fortunately, they at least deactivated the motion sensors in between bouts. Still, Rahgz kept his tail tucked in tight and made sure the feathered ridges along his five arms lay flat against his otherwise scaly skin.

Occupational hazard.

The mop struck a slightly harder object half-buried in the gooey remains of the arena's last victim. Rahgz crouched, primary arms shielding his head while sub-arms kept the mop up like a pathetic shield. Sometimes lanistas implanted self-destruct devices in their helots, hoping to give an explosive ending to the bout even if they lost—and sometimes those devices didn't get retrieved, and were left for hapless cleaners or engineers to find.

When nothing went tick-tick-boom, Rahgz peeked out, thin tongue flicking to test the air. Not sensing immediate danger or tasting toxic chemicals or spores, Rahgz straightened, smoothing down his feathers in nervous habit.

The alarming item lay poking up out of the sludge, not much bigger than Rahgz's fist. A poke with the mop handle suggested it wasn't alive, like the time Rahgz had encountered a ravenous mutant tapeworm left behind in a helot's waste pile. A few sweeps of the mop cleared the mess away enough for him to get a better look.

Looked like a piece of a large pointed ear, scarred at the tip, with coarse black stubble making a tiny mohawk down one cartilage ridge. Rahgz picked it up in one of his sub-hands. It felt real enough, squishy and still warm, oozing milky fluids through the charred nub where it looked like a plasma beam had severed it.

Rahgz sniffed it in disbelief.

Could it be? A hunk of helot, all his for the taking? Rahgz hadn't experienced such luck in many TIRDs!

Even thinking of a turn of good fortune, though, made Rahgz instinctively duck his head, as if expecting a cosmic bitch-slap upside the skull from Karma. If he had learned one thing since getting stuck on this backwater, unsanctioned barge, it was that life often put good things in people's paths only so that, once they bent over to pick up the unexpected bonus, they could get fucked up the ass—or whatever else served as their fecal output orifice.

What should he do with it? He turned the rubbery nub over and over in his hand, pondering the options. Sell it at a local meat market? Dry it out and keep it as a lucky charm? Turn it to powder and market it to horny locals as an aphrodisiac? Considering the infinite range of species aboard the Nexus barges, it might actually work that way for someone out there.

After hurried consideration, Rahgz shoved the ear chunk into his mouth and swallowed it without chewing. Two meals in one day? Maybe that should be good enough.

Such luxury. Much rejoicing.

Or maybe he'd just poisoned himself. Plenty of worse ways to go, Rahgz figured.

Rahgz continued cleaning duty, counting down the cycles until the shift ended and the cleaning gear had to be returned to its locker. If Rahgz got it back even a minute late, that'd be more fees docked from his pay, more meals skipped, and more floor munchies he'd have to subsist on.

After shoving the worst of the heap into a drain ditch and scrubbing up the largest stains, Rahgz slunk down a main hall toward the nearest service hatch. He kept patting his scaled belly underneath the crew jumpsuit, debating whether to let the helot remains digest or hack it back up and see what profit could be made from it.

Then Rahgz turned a corner and saw the three other spleen team shift members waiting for him. A three-legged ape with a squidlike head stood in the center, with a stocky human on one side and a needle-armed xabian on the other.

Rahgz wilted, wanting to back away and go the long route to another exit hatch. Too late, though, as the crew had already spotted him. They advanced, and a check over the shoulder showed another shiftmate, a giant millipede in ill-fitting overalls, had slipped in behind Rahgz to block any escape.

The squid-ape burbled at Rahgz. "Pays to pass." It held out a hairy arm that ended in an oily tentacle.

Rahgz dropped the mop and spread all his hands. "Nothing to pay but sweat and blood, Orvul. And I kind of need all I can keep inside me."

The squid-ape's beak clacked. "Saw you pick the shiny up. Haves it over."

Rahgz hunched, holding up his two primary arms in defense while keeping the three sub-arms curled in tight. The dull blue feathers in the back of his head lay flat, trembling slightly. "I don't have anything. I know the rules. You all always get top picks. If I found anything worth anything, I'd have brought it straight to you."

"Woulds you?" Orvul rolled a bulbous eye. It brought out a remote control and pressed a button. A drone whirred over and hovered in the air between them, and a holo-screen sprouted from its projector lens.

The image played above Rahgz, showing the hall he'd been cleaning when he'd started sucking on the mop for sustenance. Orvul and the other crew members gurgled and chuckled at the pathetic display, even though Rahgz knew they'd all resorted to equally desperate measures at some point or another.

However, the recording also clearly showed him picking up the helot piece and swallowing it.

Rahgz sighed, not realizing Orvul even had the technical know-how to hack one of the vid-drones. If any of the pit bosses or spleen team managers knew official arena gear had been abused like that, it'd get the culprit ground to gristle and tossed into the nuclear waste chute. But Rahgz doubted he'd even be believed if he tried to tattle on the other cleaners—not when they already had this little bit of blackmail on him.

"Wants," Orvul said, curling a tentacle for emphasis.

"Sorry," Rahgz said, rubbing his belly. "Already gone. Delicious, though. I'll save you a bite next time."

He regretted the words the instant they left his lips. A tentacle lashed across his face, sending Rahgz sprawling.

Rahgz tried to lurch out of reaching, scrabbling to hands and knees, head low. But a boot caught him in the side and flopped him over, skull smacking the deck. Harsh laughter erupted from the crew as they circled him, taking turns stomping on outstretched fingers, mashed his tail, plucking a few feathers painfully from between his scales.

Orvul wrapped a tentacle around Rahgz's neck and yanked him up, choking. Rahgz's feet dangled inches from the floor as he squeaked and squawked for air.

"Don'ts joke," Orvul said, shaking him. "Yous not funny sprukker."

He let go and struck Rahgz in mid-fall. Another foot rammed into his stomach, slamming Rahgz to the deck plating. He retched and flopped over, guts spasming.

Rahgz tried to hold back, but his insides rebelled and he spewed a putrid mess across the floor—including the precious chunk of helot. Gagging, Rahgz reached for it, not out of hunger anymore but a ridiculous attempt to keep the bullies from getting what they wanted from him so easily. The little rebellions counted, did they?

The other spleen team members scrabbled over each other, howling, yowling, and trying to castrate one another with teeth and talons as they raced for the prize.

Half-limping, half-crawling, fully sobbing and sick of himself, Rahgz edged away from the chaos. With his luck, someone would grab his tail and use him as a club in the growing melee. And then they'd probably claim he'd started the whole fight to the squad leader.

Somehow Rahgz made it clear without further abuse and stumbled into a side corridor full of shadows and flickering lights. Rahgz clutched the pulsing, twisted mess of his torso with all five arms, groaning and snuffling back tears of helpless fury.

What did I ever do to deserve this life? Oh, right. I don't remember...

Staggering further away, veering from the route back to the spleen team station, Rahgz fumbled through side alleys, past sewage chutes, across a dirty market plaza, and at last collapsed beside a refuse incinerator bin.

He lay there for who-knew how long. And who cared? Augurahgz the [REDACTED] didn't exist anymore on any official registry. Only Rahgz the fool. Rahgz the unremembered. Rahgz the starving and exhausted and desperate for one tiny break in this endless flow of agonized existence.

Huddled against the warmth of the incinerator, he wallowed in the dwindling memories of a life that might as well have belonged to someone else.

Augurahgz the [REDACTED] had arrived ten TIRDS prior, a private shuttle bearing him and the whole of his inheritance with which he intended to make a greater fortune outside of the family business—not that he could now remember what that business was.

The Coffin barge had been a tempting target for the many ventures he'd planned. An unsanctioned city-ship outside of INC regulation space where Rahgz could get away with any sort of scheme he desired.

It had taken all of a day and a single run-in with a supposed D-Mart broker who offered to help Rahgz deposit his wealth barge-side and protect him from predatory Bit-scalpers. A wise precaution, it seemed, that wound up with him tossed down a dead-end street not dissimilar to the one he lay in now, the bruises and broken bones less painful than the beating his ego had taken.

Bitless, friendless, and realizing how out of his depths he was, Rahgz had tried to contact anyone back home who might lend him enough money to buy a berth on the next cargo ship off the barg.

That had been the ultimate mistake. Who knew he'd left a few enemies behind who would prefer he never return?

Someone in his own family had sent a memory assassin as punishment for losing the wealth he'd taken along. A single gene-coded dart in Rahgz's ass had permanently wiped his mind of the family name he descended from, along with the planet they resided on. Exiled on a cellular level.

And so Rahgz had been doomed to scrape and scrub together whatever means he could on the *Coffin*, starting with attempts at thievery that nearly got him dismembered or shoved out an airlock. He'd lucked onto the cleaning job after seeing a spleen team member beaten to death by a post-bout mob enraged at losing big bets on a recent arena match. Rahgz had stolen the corpse's uniform and slipped into the next shift, with no one asking questions and him not offering anything in return.

How much longer would it be before someone peeled the uniform off his cooling body and took his place? Not that anyone would notice.

To try and distract himself from the too-painful past, Rahgz started cataloguing the species in the area. An interstellar, interdimensional menagerie flowed past and around Rahgz. The side street was in the mercantile district of the barge, near the arena where D-Mart merchants set up their physical wares to try and pawn off worthless trinkets and useless tools to arena attendees.

There went a band of eglesias, the rodent-like creatures chattering away while flicking their skeletal tails about. A spectral fluvian floated along, jetted by its protoplasmic tendrils that everyone else kept a safe distance from. Robed cyborg servitors worked a blowtorch on an exposed piece of barge bulkhead, while a caged gorplast writhed on its serpentine body while it hummed past on hoverthrusters.

The crowd briefly parted as a two-story-high worm squirmed along, a living transport with aliens of innumerable limbs, brains, and eyes clinging to and squatting along its length. It dragged several pallets of cargo along behind it, while slender avisnii rode on their glassy steeds on either side of it, keeping would-be thieves and stowaways at bay.

Gene-bulked security guards strolled through the crowd, swinging their stun batons and aiming their netguns every which way, while holographic AI entities flickered in and out of existence, spouting bursts of high-speed machinesprek.

At the very end of the street, where it intersected a more populated thoroughfare, an actual lanista floated by atop a luxurious, gilded aerie, the hovering platform keeping the wealthy helot-master above the filthy crowds. The bloated arena lord looked like a shark on chicken legs, with a set of furry tails curled up over its triangular head. Even with it being a totally unknown species to Rahgz, the look of disdain and superiority the lanista emanated with every ounce of its saggy stature remained unmistakable.

The gulf between Rahgz and the lanista couldn't have been wider in every possible way. Not just the physical distance, but in the power wielded, the wealth flaunted, and the adoration shown by all others around the lanista. Rahgz stared at the lanista until the aerie floated out of sight, trailed by a squad of private guards. Envy burned in his core, knowing that the lanista could get everything Rahgz craved with a flick of a digit. That worries about its next meal or living to the next TIRD cycle were meaningless to it, while they consumed Rahgz's every waking moment.

Consumed by thoughts of comfort and security and regular feed-ings and bathings, Rahgz didn't realize he'd been noticed until a form swerved off from the general traffic and aimed his way. A blocky, shab-bily painted robot stumped its way over toward Rahgz, telescoping legs pistoning until it clicked to a halt in front of him. For a head, it had a holo-projector screen glowing above its torso. Two tubular arms spread out as if cordoning them off for a private conversation.

The projector flashed a symbol—a yellow orb with black spots and lines. It took Rahgz a second to recognize it as a garish parody of a smiling face. Humans had brought the intergalactic language with them when they arrived in Nexus. Emoji, Rahgz believed it was called.

Text scrolled into existence underneath the face.

Greetings, Barge Citizen. Is your life an endless stream of shit? Click Y/N

There will always be those who believe they are superior in some way—whether in wealth, in intelligence, in charisma, in placing wagers, in playing dirty, in playing fair, or simply by virtue of their existence. As a lanista, your purpose is to prove them utterly wrong, whatever it takes. No one can be allowed to doubt your unique standing in universal priority. If anyone tries to rise above you, they must be torn down and their bones scattered in the arena.

But never forget that someone will always be seeking the same for you.

- How to Backstab Friends and Influence Outcomes:
A Guide for Starting Lanistas
Written by Lanista Kel'Chungzi Ewaltsen
Excerpt from Vol 5, Subset 19.03

CHAPTER TWO

S tanding, Rahgz winced at the aches across his body as he considered the bot's question.

Was this one of those assisted-suicide bots Rahgz had heard about? Apparently, they were pretty efficient and painless, but no one who'd used one was exactly able to give a rave review about the process afterward.

Most likely it wanted to sell him something—could be anything from stims to full-sensory VR immersion chambers to an engineered pleasure partner born from his own DNA samples.

Jokes on you, Rahgz thought. *I'm broke. But what's it hurt to see what it's offering?*

Rahgz poked a finger through the projected *Y*.

Might as well be honest.

The bot's face flashed into a wide-eyed symbol of elation. More text scrolled before Rahgz.

Congratulations, pathetic specimen of indeterminate origin! You might qualify for a new product trial, completely free of charge.

The "free" part made Rahgz's forearm feathers rustle. That wasn't something heard often on the barges. Of course, there had to be some sort of catch.

Rahgz sighed. Most likely this would be the part where they offered him drugs. Using bots to distribute illegal stims was nothing new, but they were usually pretty upfront about it, rather than trying to disguise their search for new "clients" as a scientific experiment.

No catch! No drugs! the bot displayed. *With your agreement, you will receive a cybernetic cranial implant designed to enhance your quality of life and broaden your ability to interact with banal reality. Guaranteed to elevate your status from social pariah to acceptable commoner within a week's time.*

Rahgz scratched under his chin, several arms crossed.

"What're the conditions? What if I don't like how it works?"

Trials can be stopped any time at the user's discretion, though implant removal comes at the user's cost if done so before the first full TIRD cycle.

The bot projected an image of a featureless body similar to Rahgz's spinning in the air. A section of the back of the skull had a tiny device attached to it, similar to the neural uplinks and D-Mart nodes Rahgz saw some people wearing.

The implant will allow for full auditory and visual stimulation, with a biofeedback loop that provides performance upgrades based on user responses and a library of apps that can be downloaded according to personal preferences.

"What's the point of the trial?" Rahgz asked.

The primary objective is to test the efficacy of barge-wide ad and D-Mart commercial outreach.

"So I'd be an advertising test subject?" Rahgz frowned. "Do I get kickbacks on purchases? Do I have to buy anything, or would I get samples to review?"

Certain discounts and promotions will be made available solely to trial participants. No purchases are required, though subjects may be asked to take various surveys to further refine trial parameters, implant ease-of-use, and optimize operations. Individual offers are based on vendor criteria and fall outside of the purview of this unit. User discretion is advised.

"What if the implant gets damaged? Do I have to pay for upkeep? I don't have any expendable income."

The implant is highly durable and maintenance will be provided. In material terms, it is worth far more than your meager form could procure at even the highest-ranked Meat Gardens. In opportunity, it is priceless.

Rahgz squinted one eye, considering whether it might be worth signing up for this experiment and then see how many Bits the nearest chopshop might give him after extracting it.

As if reading his mind, the bot flashed an exclamation icon alongside a red-face symbol.

Warning: Attempts to extract and sell the implant or otherwise abuse the technology for personal profit will be subject to immediate termination.

"Trial termination?" Rahgz asked. "Not personal termination, right?"

If you wish to define it as such for your misguided comfort. The bot's holo-head showed a brief winky face before reverting to its smiling orb. *Further conditions apply. Please observe.*

An essay of fine print went past at lightning speed. The text froze on a final question.

Are you interested in volunteering your organic matter for this trial? Y/N

Rahgz flicked at the Y.

Do you authorize this unit to proceed with the trial process? Y/N

Shrugging to himself, Rahgz poked the Y yet again.

The bot's hands swiveled into clamps, which latched onto Rahgz, one around his thin waist, another locking both primary wrists behind his back. Rahgz flailed with all his sub-arms as the bot marched off down the street, carrying him along.

"Wait," Rahgz cried. "I actually need a second to think about this."

More words projected in front of him. *Assent has been given and cannot be withdrawn. Do not resist or the procedure will be more painful than necessary. Further force will be employed to ensure volunteer participation.*

The bot stamped along, heedless of further cries of protest. Rahgz called out to security guards who pointedly ignored him as the bot carried him past. Pleas to be freed went similarly unheeded, and those who did pay him a split second of attention mostly pointed and laughed or looked for something to throw.

Typical barge-dwellers. Ignore any sort of trouble unless they started it. And even then, only if it offered some return on the effort to end it.

Misfortune and misery were just more forms of entertainment aboard the *Coffin*, especially in high demand between arena bouts.

After the third turn, Rahgz went limp, resigned to his fate as genetic chum or arena bait. Whatever waited for him, maybe it would be enough to free him from a life of hopeless drudgery, scraping subsistence out of the bottom of a cargo crate that a helot had used as a toilet.

Rahgz looked around as much as the bot-clamp allowed. They were entering a barge sector he didn't recognize, with actual marked walkways and cleaner drain channels. The buildings had less shit and graffiti smeared on them, and most people looked like they just wanted to be left alone, rather than actively seeking to murder and rob every passerby.

Holo-drones soared overhead, beaming and blaring announcements for the upcoming arena match.

A fight for universal dominance to outdo all other fights for universal dominance! The Champion of the Tertiary Ensaviate Empire will do mortal combat with Boscavar Fellios, who will dictate live coverage of the event even as he strives for survival in the deadliest of games. Purchase your seats now!

Clips played in mid-air, on walls, and in implanted screens on cyborg chassis and a multitude of alien aug-skins. Rahgz didn't get to see any of the good parts as the bot cut down a side-street and into an open bay door. The unmistakable stench of putrid flesh and dried blood clawed at Rahgz's nose, reminding him of the unknown torture getting nearer with every click of the bot's legs.

Don't forget. I did this to myself. Though I'm not sure if that's supposed to be a comfort or a further insult to inevitable injury.

The bot shuttled him through several doors, the air growing chillier with each, until it brought him into the main room.

The lab looked like it had been converted from a restaurant, with the eating section now a storage area and the kitchen meal prep stations now being used as surgical slabs. The chill came from an open meat locker off in one corner, with the cooling unit ramped up enough for frost and ice chunks to coat the doorway and several feet of surrounding walls and ceiling. The harsh lightning of the place cast everything inside the freezer in darkness.

The bot dropped Rahgz onto one of these grimy tables. Before he could flee, metal latches rotated out of the surface and locked him in place.

Then the bot tromped out again, apparently resetting its mission to procure "volunteers" for whatever testing actually went on in this place.

Rahgz tried to resist the urge to scream for help. Loud noises only let others know he was there and easy prey. Maybe if he stayed quiet, he'd be overlooked long enough to figure out a way to escape.

As quickly as that faint hope flickered into existence, a guttural voice crushed them.

"Welcome to your grave."

Wide, webbed hands thrust out of the dark freezer entry and clutched the frame. Long, spindly arms stretched and flexed, dragging the rest of the person into view.

A dozen more arms shot out, each one with at least four knobby joints. The fingers of each of the alien's multitude of hands tapered down to nearly invisible filaments that never stopped wriggling. The creature hung from hooks set into the ceiling that might've once held slabs of meat.

An enormous opalescent shell contained half of its gray-blue, wrinkled body, with a sagging head that looked more like a fleshy trunk lined with eyes and other sensory organs. Rahgz finally recognized the person as a male variant of the ulfoganti, which hailed from a dimension lacking in normal gravity but abundant with water.

A disturbing array of surgical tools—or butchering and torture devices, Rahgz couldn't tell and didn't know if there was much difference in the end—hung from straps all around the person's corpulent form, chiming and clanging as he/she/it/whatever clambered into position directly over him.

One weepy eye had a cybernetic monocle shimmering over it, and

Rahgz got the feeling that he was being closely studied. The newcomer regarded Rahgz for a long minute from its perch from on high. Then, with a sucking noise, an orifice opened in the middle of its distended belly, emitting the voice from earlier.

"By grave, I mean that of your old life, of course. Greetings, brave soul. I am Dr. Illiosk Dulg. Welcome to my lab." The scientist swayed heavily on the ceiling hooks, dexterous hands always in motion. "Once I'm done with you, you'll stride forth a new creature. A new...er..." A few hands lowered so the finger-filaments tickled Rahgz's shoulders and forehead. "What species are you, exactly?"

It took Rahgz a second to swallow enough to speak.

"I don't remember," Rahgz said. "Memory-wiped after arrival."

"Shame, that," Illiosk said, body pouches puckering and swelling. "If you hadn't already agreed to one trial, I would offer a few hundred Bits to have full rights to your genetic licensing. Royalties aren't exactly the most lucrative, but it's something."

Rahgz grimaced and indicated his locked-down self with a jut of his chin. "Any chance I can switch offers?"

"Not a one," Illiosk boomed, making Rahgz wince. "Unique specimens aren't as special as they sound in Nexus, but one of them agreeing to undergo my experimental device is a rare enough case that I must take advantage of it."

Rahgz's head fell back. "Of course. Silly of me to think I had a choice anymore."

"Very."

Rahgz eyed the many instruments adorning Illiosk's bulk. "But about this device. An implant, right? I didn't quite understand what it's meant to do. The details were a bit sketchy."

The ulfoganti waved with several undulating arms. "That's because the experiment is constantly evolving. The beauty of the implant is that it adapts to the individual user and provides experiential enhancement based on their unique physiologies, desires, and environmental stimuli."

"I thought it was just an advertising gimmick."

Illiosk dropped so low, Rahgz cringed as much as his bonds allowed, expecting to be squashed. The scientist's trunk-head snuffled over Rahgz's body, an extensive, invasive groping that would likely have him waking from nightmares for the next few TIRDs.

"Scientific advancement is never a gimmick. Now, do I have to prioritize certain donors in order to acquire the funding I need to operate my lab? Well, we all have to make sacrifices. But so long as progress is made, and the data is retrievable from your corpse in the end."

Rahgz jerked against the bonds so hard that three of his shoulders popped. "Corpse?"

"Pardon. Terrible vernacular on my part. I mean, we're all corpses in the end, eh?" Illiosk made quintuple shrugs. "In my line of work, it's easier if I simply perceive every entity as walking bodies heading toward the grave. Allows for better professional detachment. Anyways, I meant a hypothetical corpse. Metaphorical corpse." He withdrew his trunk-head and picked out a few gleaming needles and scalpels of varying sizes. "Except for when it's literal."

Biting back a whimper, Rahgz tried to remind himself that not an hour earlier, he'd literally just had lunch beaten out of him and crawled off with little more than his life intact. By some standards, this situation offered an improvement. He just had to figure out how to make the best of it.

"Are we talking a spine-bonded helmet? An occipital biocomputer?" Countless species strolled around the Nexus barges with all manner of tech fused to their persons, inside and out. Almost nobody could survive without a few Bit-chips under their skin to handle transactions, or at least upgraded visual organs that let them see the many virtu-channels and public vids that broadcasted via the blood.stream network.

Dainty fingers tapped at the flashing monocle. "I personally am testing out the alpha model. You'll be outfitted with the gamma variant, which I just recently rolled out. I finally got safety parameters properly installed on its phasic-AI operating system."

"What about beta or delta?"

Illiosk harrumphed. "All data about those previous models are stricken from public record."

"Why?"

The ulfoganti's whole body shuddered with a deep sigh. "What about *stricken from public record* do you not understand? Oh dear, your intelligence levels aren't sub-sentient, are they? I tried to program the recruitment bot to filter out idiots and mobile genejunk." The scientist adjusted a scanning device that began bleeping at Rahgz in an accusatory manner. "Stupidity is one thing the implant is unable to accommodate and inevitably leads to self-destruction."

"Of the device or the person?"

"Does it matter?

"Yes!"

"No bother. If you're of at least low or middling on the Universal Intelligence Scale, you shouldn't have much trouble."

A hand reached to the side where Rahgz couldn't see. Servomotors whirred, and the slab he laid on began to lever up. "How many other subjects have gone through this?"

"You mean total, or ones that have survived?" Illiosk chuckled. "We have had over a dozen positive procedures, though outcomes vary with each case. That's somewhat of the whole point."

A drill spun up inches from one side of Rahgz's face while a bladesaw screamed to life on the other. He suddenly wished very much to have originated from a more amorphous species. Having a skeletal system could be so inconvenient. "And how many haven't survived?" he yelled over the noise of the surgical instruments.

"I don't see the relevance of that question."

"Can I at least get an anesthetic?"

The drill and saw clicked off and Illiosk eyed him appraisingly. "Do you have the Bits to pay for that add-on service?"

"What? No. Otherwise I wouldn't have signed up for this."

The trunk-head fluttered in exasperation. "This is an experimental laboratory, for Gnoem's sake. Not a charity." The instruments whined back to life, and another hand from the overhanging multitude produced a needle almost as long as Rahgz's prime-arms. "By the way, I'm not sure if my recruitment bot mentioned, but by your prior consent, you've agreed not to sue if you die or experience a psychotic break."

The needle plunged into the side of Rahgz's neck, and any reply he might've conjured was shredded by the hot-white flame that seared through down his spine and flambeed every single nerve ending he possessed.

When Rahgz opened his mouth to scream, Illiosk shoved a hand into the back of his throat. Metal prods jammed the jaws open, while something round and slick hung at the base of his tongue, vibrating softly. While Rahgz tried to belt out an agonized solo, and his lungs clenched in the effort, any actual noise vanished before it came out of his mouth.

"Vocal neutralizer," Illiosk said, shifting slightly higher. "Not necessary for this part of the process, but my upstairs neighbors are rather sensitive to noise and I hardly need to give the building manager a reason to raise my rent again. Hang in there a minute longer."

Rahgz blinked through the tears streaming from his eyes, mentally blaring every curse and death threat he could imagine at the surgeon. Illiosk poked and prodded at him, cutting here, injecting there, but Rahgz couldn't focus enough to figure out exactly what was being done to him through the cascades of pain.

At last, the torture ebbed, and Illiosk plucked the vocal neuralizer out, freeing Rahgz's jaws. Rahgz's throat felt raw despite the lack of noise it had emitted. He gasped and panted, joints aching from straining to free himself.

"Was that really so bad?" Illiosk asked.

Rahgz swallowed, tasting the oily, smoked-fish flavor of his own blood. Had he bitten his tongue? "It's...it's over? That's it?"

For Gnoems' sake, I'd take a dozen beatings before going through that again.

"Hrrm?" Illiosk seemed distracted by a readout on one of his devices. "Oh, no. That just was the paralysis induction. That way you won't squirm while the nerve-netting is applied. It should be taking effect in three, two, one..."

With rising horror, Rahgz realized he couldn't move. At all. Oh, he could feel quite well still. But aside from breathing, all other autonomous movement had been taken offline. Even his eyelids were stuck open, ensuring he had to watch what came next.

The ulfoganti drew out a long metal canister and uncapped it. He carefully poured out a finely woven mesh that glinted silver in the lab lights, each thread finer than a wertevul's testicle-hairs. He spent a while draping it over Rahgz's body, adjusting it just so here and there, drawing back to consider, and then tweaking positioning like an artist evaluating the brushstrokes of a painting in progress.

He muttered as he worked. "Cranial implants are all well and good, but they're too fragile. Far too easy to get clubbed upside the skull by a mugger or vengeful lover, and then the whole effort goes to waste. This netting will embed itself within your actual nervous system, from your nerve endings to your spine, brain, and all the other jiggly bits. Quite thorough. And permanent."

With a final tug, Illiosk aligned the mesh to his apparent liking. Rahgz kept trying to blink. To squeak. To do anything that might amount to the slightest bit of protest or beg for mercy.

"Sorry. This might sting a bit."

He tapped a screen. The netting tightened. And kept tightening. And heating up, weaving molten lines all over Rahgz's body. Rahgz smelled burning flesh. Realized it was his. And the netting kept getting tighter, slicing into his skin like a thousand microscopic razors, cinching down around his bones.

Fortunately, he was nicely paralyzed, so the people upstairs weren't bothered a bit as his brain erupted into unheard screams until he passed out.

A lanista must seek every possible advantage of their enemies and opponents. It doesn't matter how much it costs, how long it takes, the sacrifices made, or the decorum that must be shattered. If you aren't willing to do everything and anything to win, you don't deserve it. Fuck your morals. Fuck your friends and family. Fuck the promises you made and the loves you've lost. If any of that is more important than victory, then you might as well cash your Bits in now and go blow your cerebellum out with the nearest plasma rifle.

- How to Backstab Friends and Influence Outcomes:
A Guide for Starting Lanistas
Written by Lanista Kel'Chungzi Ewaltsen
Excerpt from Vol 15, Subset 3.25

CHAPTER THREE

Unfortunately, Rahgz realized he'd survived.

Reality delivered itself in jagged slices of awareness jabbing into his brain. Hearing thundered back, throbbing his eardrums. Taste made him acutely keen for a drink of water to wash the crust out of his throat and the scum lining his tongue. Touch made Rahgz's body feel like a tuber that had gone through a grinder before being stomped underneath a centaphelant helot's feet.

How could a skeleton system writhe in on itself while staying perfectly still, a bag of shattered permaglass grinding inside his flesh?

A rotting, wet stench assaulted him, answering a question Rahgz would've never imagined asking: Exactly what would week-old cadaver farts reek of if expelled directly into one's nostrils?

Rahgz had always heard that traveling to Nexus and the barges would guarantee him all sorts of new experiences and sensations. They just hadn't clarified that all of them would be of the painful variety.

Sight blasted his sockets with the harsh blue glare of the lab. At least he hadn't woken up in an incinerator, with mere seconds to scramble out of the waste chute before being charred to ash.

Again.

"Hoo! Now aren't you lucky?"

Illiosk surged into view from off to the side, still dangling from the ceiling hooks as he worked on several data consoles. His trunk-head snuffled and waved at Rahgz. "First gamma mesh test-run and it embeds flawlessly. Hopefully the boot-up and synchronization will go just as smoothly. I would've done this next part already, but you have to be conscious for me to get the proper bio-feedback."

He produced another needle, large enough to double as a rectal probe for some of the more gargantuan helot specimens.

Rahgz worked his mouth until the tongue peeled off the back of his gums. "Am...am I getting paralyzed again for this?"

"Hrrm?" Illiosk looked over to the needle and twitched as if surprised to find himself holding it. "Oh, no, no." Several of the ulfoganti's arms waved that nonsense away. "This is a painkiller for your first day operating the device. It's the least I can do as thanks for furthering the eternal pursuit of knowledge. Although..." Illiosk rumbled as he peered at the vial and switched through several other ampoules, each with bright fluid sloshing within. "I'm terrible at properly marking my inter-species analgesics. Not knowing your genetic baseline complicates it further. I suppose I could just dose you with the three most common and hope for the best. I'd put your odds at sixty-forty that you'd get a nice numbing effect, rather than having your mucus membranes petrified."

Rahgz noticed that the metal bindings had retracted, and he sat up, muscles aching at the movement. He pressed a hand to his face. "You know what? Skip the painkillers. I'll take my chances."

"You're sure? This isn't that cheap shit they peddle down at the Necrophorum."

"I'm sure." Rahgz stood on wobbly legs. Trying a step, he faltered as his tail dragged behind him, dead weight. He caught himself on a counter and groaned as he fought for balance.

"Something the matter?" the scientist asked.

Coughing, Rahgz tried an experimental flick of his tail, but the limb might as well have been plaststeel cord tied to his waist. Grabbing it up, he worked it through all five hands, massaging and probing without any sensation whatsoever.

"My tail doesn't seem to be working."

"Nothing to worry about," Illiosk said. "It's a normal side-effect to experience passing numbness in certain areas of the body after system-wide paralysis induction. Just be glad it wasn't whatever passes for your bowels." A dozen hands caressed down Rahgz's spine, making him want to shriek and flee. "I'm sure sensation will return within the next twenty-four hours. If not, please let me know."

"So you can help?"

"So I can record the particulars for your file! It'd make for an excellent physiological case study."

"Of course." Rahgz looked around, seeing vitals that belonged to him on a disturbing number of screens in the lab. "What happens next?"

"Why, the trial commences!" Illiosk pushed a button on a controller dangling from a chain and a hatch hissed open in the far wall. "Go forth. Live. Die. Live again. Suckle on the tit of life until it poisons you. Or don't. I'm supposed to be impartial."

"So I'm free to go?" Rahgz studied himself. The cleaning uniform had a few new charred lines and thin holes, but otherwise appeared intact. His scales didn't show any signs of physical trauma, except for a couple faint lines that might've indicated where the mesh had melted into his body.

Or had it? Could this whole experience have been a hallucination induced by whatever drugs he'd been given? What were the odds he'd see himself on the latest blood.stream prank channel, writhing and screaming like a fool in front of everyone throughout the whole of Nexus?

"I'm not about to keep your freeloading ass around," Illiosk said. "So you'd best scuttle off. I'll be monitoring from here. The mesh comes with an onboard user guide, so don't hesitate to ask questions. And certain features will unlock as you're familiarized with the protocols and learn to navigate them better."

Rahgz waved his hands in front of himself. "I don't see anything different."

"You shouldn't yet. This lab is shielded from all inbound signals to avoid data contamination. You need external stimuli to trigger different responses."

"Stimuli?" Rahgz echoed. "Am I supposed to go sell myself to the highest bidder in the flesh barges now?"

"Not that sort of stimuli," Illiosk said. "Unless that's what you decide to do, in which case it'd also make for excellent reporting. Besides, don't we all sell ourselves to someone for something? Certain transactions are just more legitimate or socially acceptable than others." He blustered and waggled his trunk-head. "Start with the basic task list it suggests. You'll get the hang of it quick enough. Unless you don't."

With that, Illiosk clambered back into the open freezer and became lost in the darkness, hidden but for the rustling, clinking, and muttering.

Rahgz stood there, entirely uncertain about everything. Not that this would be the first time in his life that he'd been in this position. Maybe after it happened a few more times, he'd get used to being at a total loss.

Dragging his lifeless tail behind him, Rahgz shuffled through the hatch and down a long, dark hall. The door at the end hissed aside, admitting him to the streets beyond. Rahgz stepped outside, bracing for whatever terrible sensations the mesh would inflict on him.

The usual barge foot, wheel, and hover traffic bustled by, no one giving him a second glance as he stood on the sidelines. What should he be looking for? The same holo-vids beamed overhead. The same endless alien chatter filled the air. People honked and screeched, bellowed and barfed, hollered and hooted in the endless cacophony only the Nexus could provide, with an infinite number of species mashed together at the center of the universes.

AI-driven crates zipped by, while security drones hovered far above, near the barge sector ceiling. Brain-vats whirred around, communicating in static bursts, while a gaggle of alien spawn made squealing and squawking demands of a streetmeat vendor down the way. A black-car-apaced form lay in the ditch, drooling out of acid-bubbling maws, obviously high on the latest snufterdust. And winged gasbloats bobbed overhead, jetting fiery plumes to boost themselves forward while showering the area with stinking embers.

Business as usual.

Rahgz kept to the side as he headed back in the general direction of the arena. The least he could do was try to retrieve whatever they left of his gear and see if he could slip back into the next shift. Maybe steal some other hapless spleen team member's extra tools and leave them to take the chuff from their manager.

That's when the screaming started.

Rahgz whirled as a hundred voices shrieked in unified rage.

"Pay up or die, you shitsweeper!"

A horde of naked hiromingi stampeded down the street, straight for Rahgz. Their horns glinted with razor tips and their scrotum swayed like barge ballast as they reached for him with countless stubby claws.

"Pay your debts! Every last Bit or we bash them out of your bones."

They trampled everyone in their path as they converged on Rahgz, surrounding him with stamping legs, hooves denting the barge plating. They gnashed rows of teeth as they towered over him. Rahgz dropped to his knees, one set of arms covering his head.

"Please," he cried, "I don't know what you're talking about. What debts? How did you find me?"

One breath to the next, the screaming horde vanished, replaced by a single hiromingi, clothed in a brisk business suit, horns polished and claws manicured. It regarded Rahgz with a grin of its upper mouth and waved at the area, which appeared untouched by the mob that had just been ready to tear him to shreds.

"Bit-collectors chasing you down?" it asked. *"Is the INC taxation squad bashing in your door? Sign up today for the ultimate in Fund Defense Protocols and keep your Bits where they belong. In your account. Or be a constant victim and a pathetic example for all others to avoid. Your choice!"*

The figure swirled down into a mote of light that exploded. Text squirmed into existence, glowing softly.

From 1 - 5 Gnoem Gnads, how would you rate this ad?

Rahgz blinked.

Rahgz looked around. No one else seemed to have seen what just transpired. A few gave him odd looks as he knelt in the middle of the road. But they soon went about their business. Just one more local with too many stims bubbling in the brain.

An ad? That's all it had been? He'd been terrified for his life, thinking he'd become the victim of one of the barge's infamous flash mobs, where people were left trampled in the wake as mobs raced to see a celebrity helot or take advantage of a gone-in-a-minute D-Mart discount at a store.

The text continued to float there, pulsing in soft reminder. He tapped the 3-Gnads option, docking the ad a few points for the existential horror it had inflicted.

Thank you for your input. 5 Bits have been transferred to your account.

Rahgz tilted his head. Interesting. The doctor hadn't mentioned actually getting paid for testing the implant mesh. He really should've started with that detail.

Rahgz turned and came face to face with a giant floating face comprised entirely of squirming barge reactor roaches. The monstrous visage opened its mouth and belched a stream of scrabbling insects at him. Rahgz raised his arms and stumbled back before realizing the creatures flew right through him. Just another virtual overlay.

The head boomed with a voice reminiscent of backfiring rocket boosters.

"GOT PEST PROBLEMS? GET BOGORZ'S PEST-PARADOX SPRAY! GUARANTEED TO TRAVEL BACK IN TIME AND ELIMI- NATE YOUR BUG INFESTATIONS BEFORE THEY EVEN BEGIN!"

The head exploded, spewing giant roach guts in every direction. Despite the incredibly visceral detail of the scene, only Rahgz flinched as burning muck splattered across the walls and doors of the sector street. No one so much as stopped to wipe the flaming gobs off their clothes, and the whole mess faded into nothing a moment later.

From 1 - 5 Gnoem Gnads, how would you rate this ad?

Sighing, Rahgz gave this one a 4-Gnads rating, impressed despite himself at the overwhelming sense of disgust it had projected. Plus, pests were a real problem on barges, getting into cargo, eating crowd stragglers, and leaving their wriggling antennae everywhere. Good to see someone taking the issue seriously.

Thank you for your input. 100 Bits have been transferred to your account.

Rahgz froze. *100 Bits? That's more than I make in three whole cleaning shifts. Just for providing advertising feedback?*

He checked the account chit embedded in his wrist and pulled up the balance.

105 Bits.

-15 for overdraft fees.

Rahgz found the nearest wall and leaned against it, a bit wobbly at the knees. How long had it been since his account had been out of the negative? Most shift pay gave him just enough to eat from, and that only when he lucked upon a raw snack during the mop-up action.

Despite the awful beginning, this experiment could turn out to be the Gnoem-send he'd been praying for ever since finding himself stuck on the *Coffin*.

Reenergized, Rahgz started jogging through the sector, looking every which way to see what other ads he might be able to rate. He encountered a few pop-ups touting the health benefits of drinking fresh helot blood mixed with radioactive bliz-juz.

Eager to add more Bits to his running tally, Rahgz gave them all 5-Gnad ratings.

His vision jittered with crimson flares, making him falter and slam into the corner of a D-Mart stall. The merchant hollered at him as Rahgz tried to make sense of the new flashing message.

Error! Invalid feedback provided! -5 Bits subtracted from your account.

"Invalid feedback?" he asked. "What's that mean?"

More text scrolled: *Biofeedback indicates erroneous data entry with intent to falsify ratings. Further attempts to rig the system for personal gain will result in direct dissuasion.*

Rahgz shifted around the corner where no one would notice him, but still kept his voice low. Apparently, the mesh could respond to verbal inquiries. "What's direct dissuasion mean?"

Electric discharge to the cerebral cortex.

Rahgz coughed and scratched the feathers at the back of his neck. *Fair enough. At least it gave me a warning.*

Resuming his trek out of the sector, Rahgz continued to search for ad triggers. His tail tingled as sensation finally began returning, and he managed a few weak flicks to keep it from gathering more dust.

The mesh appeared to be triggered somewhat at random, with pop-ups and interactive holo-personas appearing after a glance at a particular piece of clothing, when he got a whiff of barbequed gene-meat, on hearing someone mention the upcoming arena bout, or after bumping into a particular slimy voidslug.

Negative or positive ratings didn't matter. Bits still trickled into his account so long as he submitted an honest opinion, with the amount not directly related to the length or level of detail the ad displayed.

As Rahgz ducked through a sector gate, leading into the area populated more by barge laborers, engineers, and grease grunts, an invisible trumpet blew in his ear, followed by a glorious-sounding proclamation.

"Axflorbatan virinius goolamustaphenexian orplagnusttuificat errvplex!"

A figure in a glowing white robe rose out of the floor plating and smiled beatifically from within its hood. It offered Rahgz a three-fingered hand.

"Did you realize you just missed out on a free offer that could've changed your whole life?"

The figure pointed to a small shop a few yards away. The display screen showed an aquarium full of wriggling fish and amphibious life forms. They blinked with bioluminescent splendor, though the effect was muted somewhat as several had converged on a wounded specimen and were now filling the water with a cloud of blood and guts.

"You didn't because you didn't understand it. And you didn't understand it because you didn't have a Gabble Fish in your ear. A result of the Gnoems' genetic genius, Gabble Fish are the purest universal translator in existence. Guaranteed to operate across all biological and dimensional boundaries, even with species based on non-verbal vocabularics and machinesprek. Get yours today!"

The figure receded into the floor, leaving behind another floating message. *"If you are seeing this, you are among the elite few who are being offered a free twenty-four-hour trial, with a pain-free installation included. Guaranteed parasite free and non-carnivorous variety. Would you like to open your mind to a wider existence today for no upfront cost?"*

Rahgz let the text float there, disconcerted by the offer of another experimental trial so soon after the first one that landed him in this spot in the first place. Unlike the mesh he now carried around, though, Gabble Fish were well-documented biotech, and most versions were even authorized in INC territory. The chance to get one for free, even temporarily, might give him a little boost in the right direction.

He'd come to the *Coffin* with a translator device, like most people carried, and knew a few common interstellar jargons, but that tool had been taken along with everything else he'd owned during the scam that wrecked his life.

Then he saw the disclaimer, barely visible as a tiny word cloud in the corner of his eye.

Upon successful completion of a twenty-four-hour test, a participant is eligible to claim a 500-Bit stipend, contingent on their survival and a posting of a positive D-Mart product review.

Five hundred? That has to be an error. Or there's a catch. There's always a catch.

A line tracked out from the disclaimer and a virtual box opened up, running calculations too fast for Rahgz to keep up with. The computation locked in with the statement: *76.84% probability of no catch that would result in user harm. Recommendation: Take the offer.*

Rahgz tapped the side of his head. *Hey mesh-thing. Did you just read my mind?*

No response. At least none that he could see or hear. Illiosk said it had a user guide and AI functionality, plus its ability to determine that he'd given false ratings earlier suggested it analyzed Rahgz's behavior to a rather accurate level already. Maybe it just sensed his hesitancy.

Fuck the Void. Let's give it a try.

Not five minutes later, he sauntered out of the nano-surgery parlor, ears perked to test out the new Gabble Fish embedded in his skull.

All languages appeared legible to him, even as he scanned holopanels and virtu-displays he knew held previously alien glyphs and scrawlings. All conversations were crystal clear, even those between chattering borg-boxes in their wire-high junktions crammed between buildings, with sparks and flares shooting through the various gels keeping the fleshy bits alive.

Rahgz marveled at the expanded awareness he now had. Returning to the spleen team could be to his advantage even more now. The rest of the team often spoken in dialects he hadn't known; perhaps he could eavesdrop and learn a few secrets he could use to blackmail them into leaving him alone from now on.

Advertising incoming.

Rahgz paused midstep. None of the previous interactions had provided any warning. Why did this one—

His world exploded in an insane kaleidoscope of color. Rahgz tore through an impossibly infinite tunnel full of harsh music, mad laughter, looping and swirling through dead worlds and supernovas. He flew above gas giants and into the eye of a hurricane of black holes engulfing the final galaxies of the universe and out through a single drop of water, chased by solar dragons and the gibbering entities that lived beyond all sane reality…

Safety protocols engaged. Rebooting.

Rahgz heard someone screaming. Whoever it was sounded like they were losing their mind in the most horrendous manner. Almost sounded like they were dying. Another poor soul lost to the void.

Mental quarantine engaged in 3…2…1…

Darkness.

Turn kindness and mercy into weapons. Show grace to those who beg for it and keep them adoring at your side until an even better time arrives to strike them down. Heal your wounded foe and pour a salve on their pains—this way they'll be strong enough to withstand the terror and torture you bring upon them in the next bout.

- How to Backstab Friends and Influence Outcomes:
A Guide for Starting Lanistas
Written by Lanista Kel'Chungzi Ewaltsen
Excerpt from Vol 15, Subset 10.32

CHAPTER FOUR

Rahgz didn't like his building streak of surviving incredibly painful experiences. Definitely not one of the Seven Habits of Highly Overrated Organisms.

Unlike before in the lab, awareness didn't return in spurts. One second, blissfully ignorant of his own existence. The next, terrifyingly aware of the grubmaw about to munch his face off. The overgrown void-leech squealed as it flopped away from Rahgz, who had thwacked it with a thrash of his tail. Thank the Gnoems that was working again.

The carrion grub tumbled away down a pile of garbage, which Rahgz found himself lying atop. Coated in slop, stinking of something a helot vomited up after eating an opponent's rotting carcass, and with his head pounding like it had been properly mindfucked in a VR BDSM sim, Rahgz groaned and whimpered. He wondered if it'd be better just to lie there and let the grubmaw return for a munch until it got to the juicy bits at the center.

As he tried to recover, not even bothering with the usual self-orientation of Who, What, Where, and How Much Do I Owe This Time?, Rahgz checked his Bit chit out of pointless habit.

He lurched upright, eyes bugging. The sudden motion sent another grubmaw tumbling away from where it had been sneaking up on him from behind. Rahgz ignored it and fixated on the account balance.

1,500 Bits

Rahgz tried to make sense of this number. Individually the digits made sense. But strung together like that, he couldn't fathom what he'd done to procure that amount. More than he'd had since...since...well, since his arrival in the Nexus had proven just how little the universe cared about his speck of a life.

Think, Rahgz. *That weird ad happened...some psychedelic shit, for sure. Did I sell myself into slavery? Again? Am I missing any vital organs?*

A tingle went up his spine and his vision flashed briefly, with letters appearing.

Reboot successful.

Rahgz scratched at the scales around his ear-holes. *Oh, hello mesh-thing. Glad to see you're still working.* Clearing his throat, he vocalized to try and trigger a direct response. "Don't suppose you can tell me what happened?"

Data started scrolling.

Backend Report & Analytics: Extreme advertising exposure, designed to test the upper limits of biological broadcast saturation before requiring a shutdown of upper cortex activities.

Rahgz squinted. "Uh...translation?"

Translation: You were brain-blasted by a controlled marketing over-dose. You survived. Celebrate. A minor bonus has been deposited to your account to compensate for your time and any permanent brain damage.

When he sorted this out, it almost left him as stunned as the initial sensory overload.

I got over a thousand Bits as a minor *bonus? The fuck?*

Rahgz stood and began clambering down the trash heap. The pile stood in the corner of an expansive cargo bay, full of crate stacks, waste barrels, a few burnt-out mech husks, and a small vagabond camp with down-and-out organisms huddled around a burning plasma leak.

"Can I do that again?" he wondered aloud. "For another bonus?"

Odds of survival were rated at less than 5%. Do you wish to continue re-exposure? Y/N?

Rahgz hastily jabbed *N! N! N!*

"All right. Guess we'll keep that option for emergency funding only."

Making it to the deck, Rahgz read the lettering and sigils on the surrounding bulkheads, trying to figure out where he'd ended up. The sector designation was unknown, but if he made it to a central hall, he could probably find his way back to familiar territory. Or at least find a public network console and access barge mapping. Asking for directions from actual people on the *Coffin* was akin to asking, "Which alley should I step into for the quickest murder?"

His mind still whirled around the funds suddenly available to him. More than enough to repay any lost cleaning equipment and get back in good standing with the spleen team. Maybe even enough for a few days off-shift and a chance to find employment elsewhere.

"What should I do now?" he asked, half-aware of speaking aloud.

Full decision-making guidance protocols offline. Activation parameters not yet achieved.

Must've been some of the advanced features Illiosk had mentioned. Rahgz wished he could figure out how to access those quicker, but no further queries or attempts to solicit a direct response proved effective.

Rahgz navigated the edge of the cargo bay, avoiding the shanty camp just in case any of the denizens found his species palatable. Discovering an exit, he hustled out and into a wide hall strewn with shuttle parts and aerie hover-jets in various states of disrepair. Rahgz glanced over the aerie equipment, thinking of the arena bouts that much of the *Coffin*'s culture revolved around. Funny thing was, having been in survival mode ever since his arrival and immediate fall from grace, and despite having been part of the spleen team responsible for keeping the arena spotless between matches, Rahgz had never seen a bout live.

Oh, he'd watched the blood.stream vids and commentary and frame-by-frame dismemberment replays. He'd studied the get-rich-quick scams and schemes everyone touted, with ways to "break the Book" and know exactly which bets to place on which lanistas and how to know when a match outcome was a sure thing.

But being part of the audience? Reveling in the spectacular slaughter without having to worry about the mess it'd leave for him to mop up and snack on? That pleasure had eluded him.

The decision firmed up in that moment.

Time to fix that lack in his life.

Rahgz flicked his tail and strode forward, eager to take advantage of his good fortune before, like anything worth savoring, it spoiled.

Keeping to the shadows, Rahgz worked his way back through the bowels of the barge, noting the color-coded sigils and lines that demarked different sector boundaries and directions to outlying districts. Most barges had a logical layout, even if they were engineered by three-brained ultradimensional sloggoths from the tenth dimensional fracture. Most crews needed artificial gravity, so there were ups and downs. Most species had a need to feed and waste to dispose of, so marketplaces, restrooms, and sewage channels were familiar landmarks, often centrally located.

But in practically every barge, the arena stood at the center of it all, both literally and metaphorically. Graffiti and holosigns pointed the way toward the arena everywhere Rahgz looked, so he just had to follow the scrawled and fritzing arrows and he should eventually get oriented.

The one exception might be one barge Rahgz had heard of, *The Crowdsource*. Gnoems' forbid Rahgz ever end up aboard that hellish drifting wreck of a barge, which had been pieced together entirely by volunteer labor, crowdfunded engineering, and slapdash planning. He'd seen blood.stream vidtours of the thing, with some sectors still exposed to the void while other sectors had living quarters situated atop the nuclear reactor heat sinks. The arena didn't even have a fully functional wall around it to keep the helot combatants inside.

The plan worked soon enough, and Rahgz soon strolled through a more civilized stretch of deck, with fewer rust and bloodstains, more working lights, and less piles of fetid organic matter shoved into the corners. Up ahead, the street broadened into a D-Mart retail sector, and Rahgz started eyeing the stalls and shops for a spot where he could purchase an arena ticket.

Despite being able to access and purchase most goods on the D-Mart via virtual overlay, doing business entirely online had its drawbacks. First, Rahgz had no domicile to deliver any goods to, and any delivery could be intercepted by trade-thugs who tracked valuable shipments and tried to hold them hostage for extra payout. Besides, on an unsanctioned barge like the Coffin, outside of INC regulations, virtual trans-actions had no real guarantee of being honored if you didn't know the buyer and seller personally. That's why most people preferred to do their shopping in person, keeping business sectors like this area bustling.

Along one side of the busiest square, several winged lizards in mech armor haggled with a vendor over depleted power cells. A blocky essav-ian hooted out deals for recycled ammo, while a robot sat in power-sav-ing mode while having a mural engraved on its metal ass. A crowd gathered around a four-legged tantuni who danced to an electronic beat while juggling an impressive collection of sharp objects, including buzzsaws, vibroblades, cleavers, and balls of scrap metal.

A row of food stalls offered a never-ending array of edibles from across the universe, some of it decaying (which certain species preferred) while other options kept trying to escape their cages before being devoured. Rahgz snuffled, trying to see if any of the meals-on-legs might appeal to him. He preferred most food in its rawest form, and the ability to chase it down did give him a deep-seated delight that suggested his species was more the hunter than gatherer type.

Rahgz spotted a band of black-robed figures, wielding glinting scythes as they patrolled the area. Undertakers of the *Coffin*—the captain's preferred security force. Aside from their grim garbs, they wore scattered assortments of fingers, wing tips, ears, eyes, dried skin leather as totems that made it quite clear what they were about. One Undertaker appeared to be a shamble of stitched-together bones, while another was a tiny humanoid flitting about on fragile wings. Another had a furry snout and bloodstained teeth, while its companion hopped around on all fours, oversized tongue lashing the air.

Steering clear of them, Rahgz went down a smaller street, where the hubbub of the crowd lessened as the many-storied buildings closed in. Here, the vendors were markedly hushed as they helped jittery custom-ers place illegal bets in the Book for the next arena match, doled out ampoules of brainblitz, getterjumps, and C.R.U.S.H., or admitted slink-ing forms into dark pleasure dens, where screams of ecstasy mingled with those of agony.

Rahgz sidled along until he spotted a relatively mundane shop marked by a slashed eye logo, denoting one that offered arena-specific services. Entering the garishly lit store, he wandered the aisles. Shelves held 3D-printed models of the string of latest helots to enter combat, all highly posable. Someone—probably a Lil' Fucker—had positioned many of them in rutting scenarios, using the removable limbs and heads with great imaginative vision.

He perused the snacks section and finally settled on a bag of wriggling keelworms that pleaded for mercy in tiny voices. The rest of the store looked filled with assembled junk, general goods, chintzy art made out of depleted reactor rods, and glob-garments—gel-based, semi-intelligent fabric that would glom to the wearer and adapt to their basic form while generating any desired color and texture.

Rahgz picked up a glob and took it and the snack to where the shopkeeper stood in the back corner. The grizzled proprietor rested two thick, hairy arms on the counter and scratched at its lumpy back with a third. It smelled of stale seafood and had several protuberances around its shoulders and chest that opened and closed like blowholes. The D-Mart merchant turned one of twelve eyestalks on Rahgz and showed off a huge number of triangular teeth. The emoji projector hung around its neck indicated this was a friendly gesture for its species.

When the creature spoke, the organic translator now dwelling in Rahgz's head not only made the words easily understandable, but also conveyed enough nonverbal context for him to recognize the shop owner was male, bored, and already sizing Rahgz up for potential scams.

"What can I help you with today, blot?"

Barge Terminology for Idiots: "Blot" - A multi-use, multi-descriptive vocal utterance with high-context meaning. Below are the most common or comprehensible.

noun ("You blot!") - familiar creature, non-enemy, non-edible entity, harmless fucker, boring loser, Bit-purse, the ofalctory organ of a female thrryn, speck, dead person of no particular distinction

verb ("Wanna blot?") - clear away, fuck, copulate, kill, eat, kill and eat, fuck and kill, kill and fuck and eat, hug

flarg ("BLOTTHATBLOTTERBLOT") - to ingest one's soul into the netherscape and fuel the psychic ascension to the Elder Realm. For Nth-dimensional entities and the legally insane only.

Common slang: "Blotty McBlotface"

Rahgz nodded and showed the items he'd grabbed. "These and a ticket for the next arena match."

The shopkeeper gurgled. "How much you want to die for and which lick ass you want to crunch under? Got a preferred snotrag that you snatch?"

Rahgz hesitated. He scratched the side of his head, wondering if the Gabble Fish had died prematurely. "Sorry?"

All of the vendor's eyes now turned on him. Fewer teeth showed. "You've never done this before, have you? Bought a ticket, that is."

Rahgz tried to keep his arm feathers flat, tucking his sub-arms under the prime ones. "That obvious?"

"As clear as a fluggut sticking out of your porscuple."

"I don't think I have either of those."

"You'd be surprised, blot." The owner shuffled over to Rahgz and eyed him from all angles. "I can always tell a noob. You practically glow like boiling xiv piss but try to act like you're just grabbing the ticket as an afterthought. Something always gives you away, though. The twitch of a tail. The spurt of an eye. Shitting yourself in excitement, thinking an arena ticket proves you're worth keeping alive."

Rahgz narrowed his eyes. "Judgy, are we?"

A belch of a cough. "You're the one in my shop, paying for my time and goods. I have market rights to be judgmental to anyone, everyone, and anything that is in the bounds of my store. It's a survival skill."

"Survival?"

"Everything's about survival on the barges," the shopkeep said. "Everything. And if you don't know that to your core, then you're just another victim waiting to happen."

Rahgz sighed. He preemptively opened the snack-bag and stuffed a handful of keelworms in his mouth, ignoring their promises of wealth and glory if he spared their lives. "Already happened."

"I could tell. Homeless. Jobless, though you weren't until recently. Hungry as fuck but got a short streak of luck you're trying to take advantage of. Trying to recapture a little of the almost-forgotten days when you were wealthier and maybe someone cared that you were alive. That's why you're here, spruk?"

Rahgz checked over his shoulder, wondering if someone was recording this for a laugh later. "How do you read people so well?"

The merchant flexed his arms and eye-stalks. "Aside from being able to read any organism's bio-language from a dozen different angles? And my species having six different senses, including echolocation, mild telepathy, and incredible pheromone control?"

"Sure. Aside from all that."

The shopkeep made a noise Rahgz took as laughter. "The real secret is practice and deduction. Everyone has their real selves, and then there's the self they show to everyone else. With some, there's no big difference between the two. With others, it's like they're always wearing a fat-suit over their personalities. But the truth of who they are, what they're after, and how far they'll go to get it is always there, even if it's buried deep. You just have to learn to see the details everyone else misses or pretends aren't there."

Rahgz stepped back. "What do you see from me?"

Multiple eyes glared at him. "You going to pay for it? I'm not a theater-blot on the blood.stream. My time is my business."

"No, but you go around making big claims like that, you should back it up. Otherwise someone might think your wares are just as much bunk as your words."

The merchant's scabby skin turned an ugly shade of chartreuse, and Rahgz flinched, ready to be tossed out before he could even pay for the snack he'd already gotten halfway through. Then several blowholes puffed and the coloring faded to fuchsia.

"Fine, blot. But I warned you."

"No, you didn't."

"You walk with the slight hunch of someone used to being beaten up by everyone and everything," he began. "But you're also showing attitude, which means you've gotten an infusion of Bits you weren't expecting, and it's inducing a small high in whatever you have that passes as a nervous system."

He shoved a finger as big around as Rahgz's wrists at him. "You also have a tiny crust on the corner of your mouth that looks like dried helot gelatin, which indicates your desperation for a meal and access to helot remnants. That, plus your uniform, puts you as a spleen-team worker, but you're a decent dash from the arena here. Your clothes are a mess, and you're buying the most basic glob-garment I've got. You don't know how to properly ask for an arena ticket, but underneath it all you still don't quite let it all defeat you, which shows a bit of the entitlement that comes naturally to the wealthy-born."

Rahgz raised all five arms in surrender. "All right. Enough. You've got me pinned to the corkboard."

A toothy grin split the merchant's face. "Just be glad I'm content selling goods and not profiting on your shame." He leaned over the counter and rapped knuckles on one of Rahgz's hands. "My personal auditory nomenclature is Felminzski. Clan Threbbit. Third generation. Fifth isk of the oskth. Or just Minz for short."

Rahgz knuckled back. "Augurahgz. Rahgz for short."

More eyes swiveled back at him. "No genealogical connectors?"

Rahgz leaned against the counter, suddenly weary. "None that I remember since I got here."

Minz made a thoughtful noise. "You had a run-in with Lethe?"

"Who's that?"

"Well, that could either be a confirmation or just ignorance. Hard to tell with her."

"Her?"

Minz tapped at a lumpy section of his torso, which Rahgz figured was where his brain resided. "Offers mind-wiping services to willing and unwilling targets alike. Had a bad day on the gambling channel but know you're significant sprukker is waiting at home with a lie detector test to strap to your nether regions? Just wipe your memory for a fee and you can honestly say you know nothing about where they Bits went. Or owe someone a good chunk and want them to forget to send the Ghostclobbers to break your spine in a few places? A smaller chunk can get them off your back."

"You've met her?" Rahgz wondered if he could track down this memory-thief and find a way to restore his. Not that it might do him any good. Even if he found a way off the Coffin and back home, would there be anything worthwhile waiting for him?

"How would I know for sure?" Minz asked. "I know she's a she. At least that's how anyone refers to her. And there's the name. But want a face or voice or any other detail? That's dead space in most people's thinkpan. She could be my own isk-oskth and I wouldn't have a clue. Plenty of rumors. No real facts."

Minz swiped a hand over a portion of the counter, and virtual pedestals appeared, showing off several helots of indeterminate species. All looked big enough to swallow Rahgz whole.

"Anyways, let me get this ticket sorted for you. The bout's only half a day off, so ticket options might be limited. Would've already been sold out, but one of the helots scheduled to fight went down with food poisoning not a few hours ago, and the replacement had a bunch of people refunding their entries because they think it'll be an easy match. Less fun, those."

"Food poisoning?" Rahgz eyed the holographic helots as they swiveled on their display pedestals. "Think that was sabotage?"

"Plenty of rumors. No real facts." Minz taped the holograms, highlighting the two more mutilated helots. A virtual arena map appeared, with different sections marked by Bit prices. He selected one of the lower values without Rahgz saying anything. Rahgz recognized that area as the Shit Seats, standing room only, no guarantee of personal safety. It'd work just fine for him.

"Could be lanistas undercutting each other with their usual double-dealings. Could be the helot got hungry and ate an unlucky pit boss that didn't digest quite right." He shrugged. Taking a small rod out from behind the counter, he tapped it on Rahgz's Bit-counter. It pinged, deducting the cost while transferring a valid ticket into his account.

"Go have fun. And if your luck holds out a bit, come back by and spread it my way a little. I get the keelworms in fresh every three cycles."

Rahgz flicked his tail in thanks. "Appreciated. This might have been the most non-threatening interaction I've had since...well, since I can literally remember."

"That's so pathetic I might cry over it later. Now get out of here, blot. I have a business to run." As Rahgz turned to go, Minz caught his eye. "Oh, one other piece of advice, if you've got the brains to hear it."

"Yeah?"

"Don't listen to the voices in your head too much. They don't always have your best interests in mind."

The crowd is simultaneously your best ally and worst enemy. Pleasing the crowd is impossible. They're only there for death, and so even being the winner of a bout will make them hate you more. Fuel that hatred into a twisted love, a vengeful worship that brings them back to your altar of helot death-dealing, paying for the privilege of seeing you devastate another foe while hoping to see you taken down in turn.

- How to Backstab Friends and Influence Outcomes:
A Guide for Starting Lanistas
Written by Lanista Kel'Chungzi Ewaltsen
Excerpt from Vol 5, Subset 9.01

CHAPTER FIVE

After the third slip and squelch, Rahgz realized how literal the name "Shit Seats" were—despite the lack of actual seats.

Thank the Gnoems his gob-garment had a fluidic outer layer that continually shed itself, casting off most grime and slime with it. It did nothing to reduce the stench of interstellar offal that clung to him, but at least Rahgz didn't look like a walking shitpile.

Though some species aboard the barge looked like that without any outside help, like the morassi oozing by him right then, burbling and bubbling like a living pustule. It took all of Rahgz's self-control not to poke it and see if it'd pop.

The buzzer had signaled the bout's start a few minutes past, the gates had gone up, and the helots were now prowling about for each other. One appeared as a featureless humanoid, ten feet tall, with skin that glowed hot-white. It held a massive spear that crackled and sparked from the tip, while a swarm of metallofluid arachnids crawled over its muscular form, performing some unknown service.

The other had the cobbled-together look of a cyborg elephant, its head more machine than flesh, while it lumbered about on stumpy legs. Despite its bulk and slower gait, it bristled with all manner of technorganic weaponry that targeted and obliterated anything that got near enough.

Despite it being his first real bout attendance, Rahgz found himself having to focus more on his own well-being than caring much about which helot lived and which would be gene-slurry.

This portion of the arena auditorium wrapped around the reactor-side corner and had been built on a slight rise, so people could scramble and scrap for the higher standing spots to get a better view.

Rahgz could see a maze section of the arena floor, with the elevated perspective letting him see the various flame spouts, tripwires, and buzzsaws waited for a hapless helot to run by.

The hoverscreens and holoprojectors around the wall and above the arena would let them watch the bout as it took place throughout the enormous combat floor. Part of the thrill of attending was the chance of seeing the helots kill each other right in front of you rather than via the screens. Sometimes the captain would herd the combatants toward one section or another to please whichever part of the crowd proved itself the bloodthirstiest.

Rahgz found he had to keep shuffling and sliding back and forth, despite having found a spot toward the upper leftmost side. He quickly realized that nowhere in the Shit Seats could be deemed "safe." Even "safe-ish."

The crowd constantly milled about, crawling over itself, cramming and shoving for breathing room, stomping one another down, slamming each other into walls...becoming an obscene, self-devouring organism. The roar of their cheers, jeers, screams, and cries for mercy almost drowned out the thunderous announcers who narrated the match.

"All praise to the Void in this glorious match," one announcer boomed from unseen speakers. "Remember that all our lives are nothing in comparison to the infinite Void that rules the universe. And the helot that loses its soul here in the arena will surrender its essence to the nothingness that we all come from and all go to in the end."

A snarl interrupted from the other announcer. "Fuck your Void. Nobody gives a shit about that religious nonsense. We're all here for one thing. Blood, guts, and glory!"

"That's three things," said the first announcer.

"Fuck your facts, you fake news piece of zerkshit! Blood, guts, and glory! Blood, guts, and glory!"

The chant got taken up until the whole barge thrummed with thousands of voices and psychic emanations crying in unison. Rahgz joined them, shouting without caring at all who he hollered for.

The arena thrill buzzed in his veins like a straight shot of vulch whiskey, sipped right from the vulch's udders. Rahgz felt both lighter and heavier all at once, a scrap of flesh in the grip of the crowd, being tossed and waved like a blood-soaked rag. Yet his feet slapped the slick, sticky floor, cementing him in the then and there of the bout.

Howls echoed back from the arena, rocking the crowd on its collective heels. The helots had found one another at last and wasted no time carving chunks of flesh and bone, metal and wires from each other. The crowd screamed as if it was being torn apart right along with the gene-beasts, gasping and swaying in a morbid mix of agony and ecstasy.

Rahgz looked over to where a trio of serpentine flix-flix who writhed in on themselves, thrashing and smacking aside any other audience members who got too close. Metal bands encircled their long skulls, flickering with crimson lights. Rahgz recognized the tech—nerve receptors. For an extra fee, attendees could access a blood stream neural broadcast that tapped their minds directly into the helots' sensations, pain and pleasure alike.

By the looks of it, the flix-flix were enduring more of the former than latter.

A glance at the overhead projectors showed one helot, the glowing humanoid, already missing a thick leg. The other cybernetic beast had run off with it in its maw, and now munched on it in a distant corner of the arena. Enraged, the first dragged a trail of sizzling, silvery blood in pursuit, using its spear to brace its massive frame.

Something hit Rahgz from behind, knocking him to all hands. He skidded down a few rows, tail flailing for purchase. He slid between several pairs of spindly legs, ricocheted off a starsteel column, and whirled through a puddle of piss, spraying onlookers who guffawed and kicked him along.

Growing desperate, Rahgz grabbed for anything to stop his downward plunge. For he knew the grisly fate that might await him if he slid too far toward the arena wall.

Luck saved him in the end, in the form of a clawed foot that snagged his tail as he slid past. Rahgz knew it to be a cruel stomp, and his spine curled in a tortured spasm, but it stopped his momentum enough for him to dig into the scummy floor and anchor himself.

Panting, streaked with all manner of alien fluids, and bruised even more than the other cleaning crew had left him before, Rahgz still gave a lopsided smile.

What a rush! And I've still got all my arms and legs intact!

A hundred feet further, and the floor dropped over a small ledge, creating a wide trench that led to the outermost arena wall. This front-most area was known as "The Meat Grinder," and to fall in there meant most likely never crawling back out.

Rahgz had seen plenty of blood.stream vids of audience members stuck down there in the latter parts of an arena bout. As sweat, blood, piss, jizz, tears, vomit, and a few buckets of grease dumped in by the barge crew for good measure added up, the floor became practically frictionless, while the lowest section became a swamp of bodies that got churned into slop for the more carnivorous helots.

Even from where he stood, Rahgz could now see into the Grinder, where bodies slammed into each other with teeth-grinding force. Down along the ledge, a tiny furred creature in body armor scrambled for cover. But then a tentacle lashed out from below and hauled it squealing into the depths—followed by a loud burp and spray of guts.

Easing his way back higher in the rows, Rahgz kept one eye on the bout progress and another on the audience around him. Brave vendors roamed the crowd, calling out deals.

"Blerk-on-a-stick! Five Bits dead. Ten Bits still wriggling!"

"Black-market neuroscapes! Live your own death in an endless loop. Guaranteed authentic pure terror v-scape!"

"Blot spruk! Sprukker spruk the blot right here until it blotting spruks off! Fifty Bits!"

When Rahgz checked out a D-Mart skagger waving a Bit-stick to try and solicit a sale, a *ping!* went off in his head and the now-familiar implant text dissolved into view.

Purchase-primed demographic detected. Profitability quotient being calculated.

Rahgz tapped the back of his head, ruffling the feathers there. "Hey, mesh-thing. Almost forgot you were in there. Take a nap or something?"

Earnings increase opportunity present. Primary avenues acquiring extra Bits tallied. Would you like to see the options? Y/N?

Shrugging, Rahgz stabbed the Y.

Affiliated advertisement broadcasting
Event hyping on blood.stream channels
Listing self on hyperlocal flesh services board.

Rahgz squinted one eye. "Does that last one translate to selling my body out as a timeshare?"

Affirmative.

"Okay. Nix that one. What's event hyping? Like getting on-vid and talking about how great a time I'm having with some virtual product placement?" He'd seen that sort of gig all the time, with audience-goers trying to plug this drink or that self-defense force shield for a cut of the sales.

Affirmative.

He gave this brief thought. "Still too much work for too little payoff. What's the broadcasting one?"

This unit will patch into all local advertising channels and saturate any receivers within range with high-ROI messaging.

"Do I have to do anything?"

Negative.

"Perfect. Let's do that one."

Engaging infinite spam mode.

A high-pitched whine cut through the air, and Rahgz clutched his head as it tried to vibrate off his shoulders. The sensation grew until it engulfed his entire body, threatening to shake him apart. Then the strange energy burst out from him in waves that rippled out through the crowd. He could see the pulse on a wavelength he never realized existed. It passed through many audience members, but crashed into just as many others, making people stumble and scream.

Those unaffected by the unrelenting wave stared at the others who began to go into paroxysms, dancing, swaying, screeching, and spinning in circles. One armored zerkmonger started prancing about, spouting in sing-song.

"Loves me some zorbnorfers! Eat them every morning! Norf them zorbnors with the blood of my enemies for a balanced breakfast!"

A many-fingered noskithian started prying up floorplates with its front tusks while roaring, "I pay extra for the fluffiest beds in the *Coffin*! Come sleep your cares away at the Gorge's Rectum, just south of the reactor chamber. Guaranteed no muggings while you rest."

Another pulse went out, and more people chimed in with these random adbursts, espousing the virtue of lotion made from helot tears, the discount sales at the fleshpits over in the red dwarf light district, or new ticket prices for tours to see the Mawgrunt beast at the heart of the barge (non-devouring insurance available).

The mesh continued to spout random ads, each new wave triggering more outbursts with Rahgz at the center.

Rahgz went to his knees as the throbbing in his head ratcheted up to vomit-inducing. "Fuck," he groaned. "This is getting me Bits?"

Despite the tears stinging his eyes, the mesh text remained clear in his vision.

You currently have received 15 Bits so far at a .002% affiliate royalty rate. You are projecting over 1 million ads per second, with a saturation rate of 24.4%. If range were increased, this could be increased to 32.8%.

"What would that do to me?"

Brain liquefaction likely. Bit royalties would increase by 1.3%.

"Yeah, no. This isn't worth it. Turn it off."

Cessation of advertising broadcast will result in below-threshold earn-ings. A minimum of 100 Bits is required for an account transfer via this method.

Another pulse launched. A set if squioids began trading ribald knock-knock jokes, while literally knocking each other back and forth. Another alien lay on its side, bleeding from every orifice, the blood trails forming a popular drink logo. A swarm of rindlebees started stinging everyone in the area while buzzing about the nearest private medical clinic that would be happy to take new patients.

Rahgz gritted his teeth. "Just turn it off already, before someone gets hurt."

You are in the vicinity of 24 wounded, 3 dead, and 13 self-flagellating organisms. Is injury prevention truly your motive?

"What do you care?" Rahgz snarled. "You're a tool, not my hatchspawn. Turn it off!"

Complying.

The vibrations ceased, though a light ringing continued to tingle Rahgz's ears and the base of his neck. The crowd around him held a collective pause, as several people flopped to the floor in relief, others in spasming fits, and the rest looking about in befuddlement.

"What the sprukking Gnoem gnads was that?" someone cried.

Almost everyone had stopped paying attention to the bout, even as the glowing humanoid had finally wrenched off the beast's cybernetic skullcap and was carving out what little brainmeat was left inside.

Instead, everyone looked at one another in furious suspicion.

"Mimetic assault!" hollered a neon-garbed alien.

A hooved centaurian raised a bladed fist. "Someone just tried to brain-blast us into oblivion. There must be retribution. Show yourself, fiend of the Void."

"Gods above and below," moaned a saberlung, gas pockets flexing all over its body. "I'm never going to get the taste of zorbnorfers out of my mouth."

They're talking about me. What I did. Yup. Time to go. I'll catch the after-match commentary from a safer spot.

As Rahgz sidled toward the nearest exit hatch, a loud bell sounded.

At first Rahgz thought it came from the arena system, signaling the end of the bout or other event of note. However, the combatants still thrashed and twitched, with the glowing humanoid now a lovely crimson beacon thanks to the gore coating his body.

"Found the bastard," a voice hollered. "Got a lock."

A green glow lit the area around Rahgz. He looked up to see a giant holo-drone arrow pointed straight down at him, as if marking him as a player in a giant virtual game.

All his feathers went rigid. "Shit."

"Get him!" several people cried. "Tear his spleen out of his asshole."

"And if he doesn't have one," came another cry, "tear him one of those too!"

Rahgz raised a finger. "Actually, I do have…"

"Blood, guts, and glory! Blood, guts, and glory!" The crowd turned on him as one, claws, tentacles, hands, and pseudopods all grasping.

Yelping, Rahgz darted for freedom. He took two steps and then got knocked aside by a massive fist. Tumbling, Rahgz rose and lunged for an opening, only to take a kick to the ribs that somersaulted him. Fists pummeled as he rolled, trying to get clear. Muck and scrummead got sloshed his way, slicking his path and making it harder to get traction.

Someone grabbed his tail and swung Rahgz through the air, slapping him across several other people in the process. A snap and painful jolt went up Rahgz's back, and he spun free, only to hit the broad chest of a moon-ape, who bashed him to the ground.

Rahgz lurched aside just before a huge foot dented the plating where he'd landed. Righting, Rahgz hobbled forward, unsure of his bearings. While he no longer knew exactly which way the exit was, the green arrow above his head let everyone stay focused on his pathetic flight.

But while the packed crowd kept him from easily slipping away, it also proved to be the one thing that saved him from sudden death. Even as the people tried to get at him, eager to enact revenge for the mental intrusion he'd caused, they bumped into one another, stepping on toes and tails and clanging cyborg chasses—all of them wanting to be the singular person who took Rahgz down.

Soon enough, smaller brawls broke out, with aliens choking each other out and breaking out blades and firearms of all sorts. A plasma beam lanced through the crowd, sending a tall alien toppling with a smoking hole in its chest.

That unleashed the crowd's inner beast. Robes whipped open as automatic plasrifles came out. Biorganic whips bristled with toxic thorns. Robotic frames clacked open to reveal innumerable hatches with rockets and electrical grapplers. Hidden hoverjets thrummed to life, lifting aliens into the air all over, while aiming beacons bleeped and laser sights dotted the area.

There came a single calm breath. Like a sniper finding total inner peace while sighting down a scope before pulling the trigger.

And then the crowd went wild.

Rahgz realized that all the ruckus and violence he'd witnessed before held nothing compared to this mob gone amok. Parts of anything resembling a body went flying. Fluids sprayed. Laughter and screams filled the air so much it seemed like several helots had been let into the audience area to wreak havoc on them.

A two-torsoed arachnigaunt stumbled over Rahgz, clutching its second abdomen with four arms. It dropped, smushing him to the ground, but not quite crushing him as it shuddered in death throes. Its many legs formed a barrier around him that kept anyone else from getting closer for the time being. Despite the arrow still signaling his position, people were more interested in carving up their unsuspecting neighbor rather than hunting down a moving target.

Shaking, Rahgz struggled for a plan. He finally glimpsed the wall markers indicating the exit hatch. The way was already littered with bodies, and he'd have to leave the shelter of the corpse shielding him. Being highlighted for all to see, he stood little chance of making it that far unless he found a way to negate whatever was being used to track him.

"Hey mesh-thing," he said. "Can you figure out what's pinging my location and block it?"

Invalid access. That module is not yet activated.

"How can I activate it faster?"

Dormant modules can be activated with a 1,000 Bit purchase.

Rahgz choked. "A thousand Bits? I have to buy your other functions? What features do you have that I can afford right now? Anything useful?"

Several more bodies slapped to the ground just outside of the legs caging him in. Rahgz stepped back further into the shadows of the corpse.

Here are the modules available within the range of your account balance.

A function list popped up with three items:

Tentacle emoji
Fart simulator
Slartifastian date finder app

Rahgz stared at these, wondering yet again if the whole mesh bonded to his nervous system was one insane prank.

A large claw thrust in between the nearest legs and grabbed hold of Rahgz's waist. It yanked him clear and held him aloft so he looked down at a creature with one massive eye and way too many mouths.

"Mine mine mine," the thing gibbered. "Going to munch you and shit you out and then stitch your sloppy remains into a stress ball."

Rahgz writhed but couldn't dislodge himself. Several of his hands tried to batter the claw open, while others grabbed at the stiff hairs covering the alien's skin, plucking them free and stabbing them back in.

At least I'm going to die in the arena audience. That's a lot better than I ever imagined...which is kind of sad now that I think about it.

As the alien lowered him for a bite, a plasma bolt tore through one of its elbows and sent Rahgz crashing to the ground, still in the claw's grip. The alien screeched and rounded on its attacker just as another bolt took it in the eye. The centaurian galloped up and stood over Rahgz, glaring down at him with a cybernetic eye, keeping his weapon trained on him.

"You are a craven creature," he said, metal jaw grinding. "I will put you out of your misery and commit your soul to the Void."

"It wasn't me?" Rahgz tried.

Snorting, the centaurian rose on hind legs, forelimbs carving the air.

"Mesh-thing," Rahgz whispered, waiting for his doom to descend. "Does that eye have a receiving unit?"

Affirmative.

"I'd like to reactivate my affiliate earnings program."

Complying.

The pulse blasted out from Rahgz once more. The centaurian staggered as sparks flew from its cybernetic parts. Barely dodging a hoof through the skull, Rahgz grabbed hold of the centaurian's leg and visualized the outflow of advertisements shooting straight into this one person, overloading his mind just like the sensory input that had blacked Rahgz out for half a day.

The centaurian jolted as if hit by a bolt straight from a deck wire. His long hair caught fire along with his tail, and the stench of burning hair and flesh added to the bouquet of the arena seating.

Pulling away from Rahgz, the centaurian went to his front two knees. He giggled and looked up with a goofy smile. "Buy one, get one dead. Sale ends today."

He collapsed. At the same time, the green arrow winked out overhead.

Rahgz bolted. This time, no one stopped him.

Rules are critical for the up-and-coming lani-sta. Study them. Memorize them down to the last jot. Meditate on them when you wake and have them mumbling under your breath when you go to sleep. Tattoo them on your skin if you have any. Because only when you understand the rules like your own heartbeat can you know best how to break them.

- How to Backstab Friends and Influence Outcomes:
A Guide for Starting Lanistas
Written by Lanista Kel'Chungzi Ewaltsen
Excerpt from Vol 36, Subset 7.29

CHAPTER SIX

Rahgz rested only after he'd put ten barge blocks between him and the arena. Once beyond the confines of the seating area, no one even gave his maddened dash a second glance. People were used to folks fleeing the audience, especially in the final minutes of the match, as the blood craze grew to its peak and the helots laid their final blows.

His legs and lungs burned, and his head pounded, even though the adbursts had stopped a while back. The glob-garment had shed most of the filthy remains that had coated it, and Rahgz felt certain no one had pursued him. Still, he spent a few minutes checking himself over for tracking bugs just to make sure no one would come seeking revenge for the chaos he'd unleashed.

Near the corner of a mechanic's bay, Rahgz huddled against the wall and tried to calm his ravaged nerves. His feathers kept fluttering no matter how much he smoothed them down. His teeth ached from anxiety overload and the sour taste in the back of his mouth had the familiar tang of fading terror.

Funny how terror tastes just like grape medicine.

Briefly closing his eyes, Rahgz steadied his wheezing by pretending he floated in the Void, where nothing could hurt him and no one else existed. While he didn't believe in the religious nonsense spouted by the Prophets of the Void or the Ghostclobbers. But the little visualization exercise, imagining the peace of oblivion, was one of the few ways he calmed himself down after such close calls.

All I have to do is pretend I don't exist and the universe can just go on ignoring me. I mean, it usually does that anyways. Why do I only seem to attract attention when someone wants to inflict pain?

Flicking his tail in thought, Rahgz winced at a slight stab of discomfort. He looked down to see if he'd cut his tail on something in the escape—but instead, a solid six inches was missing from the end, leaving raw purple flesh and a small nub of bone exposed. That's right. He'd been grabbed in the melee and thought he'd gotten loose because the person's grip had slipped or something. No such luck.

Damn. Lost another tail tip.

It would regrow, of course. He just hated the stumpy look of it, plus the slight imbalance it caused until he got used to it. Rahgz tugged it up to where he could suck on the tip, letting the secretions in his saliva accelerate the healing process.

As he gnawed on himself, Rahgz tried to think of ways the arena mess could've gone better. Shouldn't the implant have warned him about the intrusive nature of the broadcast before letting him agree to it? So far, a lot of the offerings it suggested had a lot of unspoken context that he learned only after the consequences were well underway.

So no more blindly going along with the mesh-thing's options. I need fully detailed rundowns of everything involved before I make another choice on what ads to run or view. No skimping. No matter how many Bits are offered.

Text flashed in the corner of his eye and slid into focus.

Voluntary update available, with a bonus of 500 Bits upon acceptance and successful integration. Would you like to accept the OS upload? Y/N?

Rahgz's suspicions immediately went into hyperdrive. *Fuck a Gnoem and have its meatbaby. Why did it send me this offer right now? Is it really reading my biofeedback or does it have deeper access to my neural pathways than it's letting on?*

Clearing his throat, Rahgz opened his eyes, partially to ground himself again as he tried to navigate this new deal, and partially to keep himself from being mistaken for a corpse by the passing group of Undertaker mercenaries.

"Hey mesh-thing," he said. "I want a rundown of this offer. First off, I thought I had to buy more access to you. Why is this a paid gig?"

Survival bonus.

"What's that mean? I get a little extra access because I lived through that madness?"

Essentially. A higher rate of organism viability suggests a potential investment opportunity.

"Translation?"

You are starting to prove that you might be worth more alive.

"Prove to who? Worth what?"

Invalid queries. Do you wish to proceed with the upgrade?

Rahgz chewed his lower lip. *Five hundred Bits can hold me over for a long time. But what's it going to cost me?*

"What's this update do?"

Summary: Decision optimization algorithms.

He frowned. "What's the non-summary version?"

This unit will analyze all past, present, and future sensory input and host behavior in order to determine the optimal sequence of events and resource allocations to achieve predetermined goals.

Rahgz unknotted the verbal tangle in his mind. "So you'd help me figure out what choices to make and what to do?"

Essentially.

"For what predetermined goals?"

This is up to user input.

"I get to set the goals? And then you help me achieve them?"

Affirmative.

Rahgz sat back, the chilly wall reminding him of fresh bruises along his spine and shoulders. He chewed gently on the tail stub.

"Could you help me get rich and famous?"

Results will vary according to user efficiency and adherence to the step sequence provided.

"In other words, think small and don't get my hopes up?"

This time, the mesh's message came through both as text and in a neutral voice that echoed in his mind. "*In other words, do what you're told, blot.*"

Rahgz twitched and sat up straighter. "What'd you just say?"

This unit requests 100% adherence to planned and transmitted responses. Deviation from such cannot guarantee desired outcomes.

"Ah. So any failure would be my fault while you get all the credit for anything that goes right."

The response seemed to come on a slight delay this time.

Affirmative.

Rahgz mulled this over, slightly unnerved by the mesh's shift in tone. Illiosk had said the implant would adapt and evolve over time, so maybe it was communicating in a way it knew would be more effective with him. Sure. Slightly condescending and passive-aggressive language usually got him to do what someone wanted.

But what did it matter if the mesh implant took over some of his decision-making? Especially if the options actually helped him out, would he care if he made them or they came from the implant? No one else would know.

"Any negative side-effects?"

Query not understood.

Rahgz spoke slowly and louder, as if that would make his words clearer. "Will. This. Get. Me. Killed?"

Do you wish to die?

"No!"

Suggestion: Make "Keep Me Alive" a priority goal.

Rahgz huffed. "I would've hoped that was assumed."

"Analysis Complete: You assume too much. That's why you need help."

Rahgz twitched again at the voice. "That's fucking creepy. Another query: will this have me do something that will make other people want to kill me?"

Do you want other people to—

"Fuck a Gnoem in a black hole! Can we move forward with the default of me staying alive for the foreseeable future?"

Input accepted. Do you wish to accept this update? Y/N?

"Can I opt-out later?"

Unsubscription from this performance module is possible based on one stipulation.

Rahgz licked his lip where he'd accidentally bitten it open. "What's the condition?"

Negation and cessation of all benefits and rewards acquired during the term in which the module is in operation.

"Meaning if anything good comes my way because of using you, I have to stop doing it or return the items?"

Affirmative.

"What if I ate something yummy because you recommend it and then I unsubscribe? Do I have to puke that back up?"

Suggestion: Don't ask stupid questions, blot.

The Y/N? hanging in the air began to pulse insistently. Rahgz got to his feet and jabbed the Y.

"Let's see what you can do."

He held his hands out, waiting to receive any indication of a change. Nothing.

Wincing, Rahgz looked around, wondering when the update would hit him. If the experience so far gave any indication, the process would be painful.

Another minute went by. A squad of Corpse Corps strode down the street, hodgepodge armor decorated with skulls, ghostly sigils, snarling alien faces, toothy glyphs, and other morbid accessories. Some still displayed the INC badges that would've meant something if the barge resided in regulation space—and if the soldiers who wore them weren't known as some of the most infamously and dishonorably discharged fighters from the Nexus military.

One of the soldiers spotted Rahgz and shuffled his way, pulling their companions along with them. Realizing they were likely about to confront him for an unknown infraction, Rahgz started to look for the fastest way out of the area.

Except he couldn't move. He just stood there, hands out in a patient pose as the soldiers loomed ever closer. Rahgz discovered he could at least speak and whispered harshly to implant.

"What the fuck? Why can't I move?"

Upload and integration require bio-stasis to ensure full data synchronization. Normal operations will resume soon. 48.3% complete.

Rahgz jittered in place, straining every muscle to move an inch. No such luck. The mesh had locked down everything except his sensory input and output, so he could conveniently watch as the soldiers strode up, bringing many promises of pain with the sneers on their mangled faces and how they lovingly stroked the variety of weapons about their persons.

The lead corpsmember plunked down a speargrinder twice as tall as Rahgz as they came up. A wide-lipped bestial sort with shimmering scales and crusty fins over their sleek body, they glowered down at him through their cracked faceplate.

"Loitering are you?" they asked in burping syllables. "Who gave you permission to squat on our street?"

"Your street?" Rahgz used what function remained in his facial expressions to convey wide-eyed innocence. "I didn't see any signs…"

The soldier pointed with a barnacle-crusted arm. Indeed, up on the side of a puff and spew parlor, crude graffiti displayed: *Corpse Corps Here. Others Pay or Scram.*

"I see," he said. "Obviously I should've seen that right away and realized. How careless and clueless of me. I greatly appreciate you showing me my error before I intruded on your space any longer."

If Rahgz had one skill, it was groveling. TIRDs of experience had honed that to a sharp point. The soldiers, however, just glared harder. One had an emoji screen in the middle of its muscular chest, which showed an endless scroll of frowny faces.

"Are you paying or scramming?" the corpsleader asked. They nudged Rahgz with the butt of the spear, almost toppling his unresponsive body.

"How much is the local access fee?" Rahgz asked.

"Five hundred Bits," the leader said.

Rahgz sighed. Of course it would equate to everything he'd earned so far. But if it got him out of this scrape in one piece, more or less, then it'd be worth it. He could just start over.

"All right," he said. "I'll gladly pay such a fair toll for putting up with my presence. Just ping my pay-chit and I'll authorize the transfer."

"Hold on," said another corpsmember, the one with the emoji screen. The frowny face turned to a red circle with horns. "That's just the amount for entering our territory. Leaving is another five hundred."

Every time he'd thought he'd discovered the deepest level of despondent sighs, Rahgz realized a whole new substrata of despairing exhalations awaited him.

"Unfortunately, I don't have those funds on me at the moment. I will be happy to scram, though."

He grinned up at the soldiers while mentally screaming at his useless, Gnoem-forsaken body to fucking move for spruk's sake!

The soldiers stared at him, clustering closer as it became apparent he wasn't going anywhere.

"You're not scramming," the leader said, leveling the spear at Rahgz's chest.

Rahgz chuckled. Or was that a gurgle of desperation?

"Just waiting for a software update to finish before I go. I hope that's okay. You know how finicky implant apps can be if you switch sectors while getting a security patch. They'll crash and before you know it, you have to reset your implants for a whole day and then roll them back to last week's backup points—"

"Shut your jabber. You making fun of us?"

Rahgz tried to wave his arms in denial, or at least drop to his knees and try some literal boot-licking. His traitorous body remained fixed on getting him killed, though.

"Never would I ever," he said. "I just don't have any choice in the matter, currently, which is funny, you see, because I'm actually trying to learn how to make better choices and obviously coming to this street wasn't a great one and I'd really like to just leave if you don't gut me for another few seconds and we can all just move on with our lives and forget this whole unpleasant incident."

The emoji corpsmember stepped forward and let a multi-jointed tongue dangle in front of Rahgz's face, viscous saliva oozing onto the tip of his nose.

"I say if you's not scramming, we oughts to scram you. Hard." The emoji screen displayed a wide-eyed, grinning face. "What you say to that?"

Rahgz chittered and discovered even his bowels were paralyzed, unable to soil himself in sheer fright. He muttered under his breath.

"You're supposed to be helping me make better decisions. A little help here? How do I get these gubs off my back?"

Data still compiling. 76% complete. Please stand by.

Rahgz grinned sheepishly up at the soldiers. "Uh. It's still loading. Just another minute?"

The leader grabbed his arm and yanked it around to display the Bit-chit. They produced a scanner and began to jab at his wrist, looking for the access port. "We'll just take the fee and then scram you anyways, sprukblot. That's what you get for trying to fun us up."

"I wasn't, I swear by the Void." Rahgz groaned as an electrical charge shot between the probe and chit, trying to bypass the firewall. "Don't any of you believe in the holy Void? Shouldn't we take a moment to, you know, remember that we're all equals in the face of oblivion?"

"You want oblivion?" the fish-lipped leader asked. "We can give you that when we're done."

83%

"Uh, uh...just listen. Once this update completes, I can transfer ten times that amount to my chit and give you each a hefty payout. You just need to be patient—"

One of the smaller soldiers bellowed, "Patience is for slag-porkers!"

"I totally agree with you, one hundred percent," Rahgz said, mouth moving on autopilot as he tried to stall through the sheer power of terrified babbling.

96%

The leader looked at their chit-probe and grunted. "Not accessing. We'll hack it the old-fashioned way." They tucked the probe away and brought out a miniature chainsaw that growled to life. "Last chance to pay and play nice, scrum."

Rahgz bugged his eyes out and yelled, "Holy shit! The Mawgrunt's loose! It's going to devour this whole sector! Run for your lives!"

The soldiers turned in the direction he stared. Seeing nothing, they scowled back at him. Dropping their spear, the leader grabbed Rahgz by the neck and lifted him high.

"You'll pay triple for that. And what you don't have in Bits, we'll carve out."

Module upload complete. Data aggregated. Please input primary goals.

Control returned to Rahgz's body. He thrashed in the soldier's grip and screamed, "I want to live!"

The soldiers all appeared to freeze in place, and the mesh implant both spoke and projected text at the same time.

"Play dead, blot."

Rahgz clutched the corpsleader's hand and tried to pry the fingers away. The soldier and their companions remained still, as if Rahgz's paralysis had been transferred to them. "Why aren't they moving?"

High-relativity decision-mode induced. You have 10 real-time seconds in which to choose how to extract yourself from this situation, with your time perception elongated by a factor of 10. Do not attempt again for 1 TIRD or severe brain damage will occur, plus a high probability of cata-strophic organ failure.

Rahgz swallowed against the grip on his larynx. He couldn't get out of the hold, but apparently he had a quick timeout from reality to figure out what to do next.

"Why is playing dead an option?" he asked.

Your physiological analysis suggests your species has a genetic ability to imitate a death-state for short periods of time. Active this.

"We do? We can? How?"

This unit can stimulate a gland in your pelvic region, at the base of your spine. It will simulate death throes without inflicting permanent damage.

"Any other options?"

Fight back - Chance of mortality: 98%

Beg for mercy - Chance of mortality: 74%. Chance of crippling injury: 97%

Offer your body as a plaything - Chance of mortality: 69%. Chance of crippling injury: 100%

Rahgz grimaced. "Let's go with the playing dead thing. Hope this works."

Decision approved.

Time snapped back into its normal flow; in the same moment, something snapped deep in Rahgz's gut, like an egg being broken open so acidic yolk spilled out to coat his innards. He opened his mouth to scream, but belched bile instead. His clenched bowels loosed and stinking excrement plopped to the ground in a steaming pile. Piss soaked down his garment, and spurts of blood shot from the corners of his eyes. Snot jetted from his nostrils and earholes.

Hollering in disgust and dismay, the soldier dropped Rahgz, letting him fall into his own filth. The corpsmembers all jumped back as Rahgz's body went on autopilot, flopping and rolling as it continued to spew blood, shit, and piss from every available orifice. At last, strength fled and Rahgz lay with his eyes staring at the barge ceiling, unblinking, not a single breath rattling his chest.

Yet he remained entirely alert and aware of what went on around him. The lack of breath didn't alarm him the way it usually did when someone tried to choke him out. Instead, the sensation was almost peaceful.

If this is what death will really be like, I'll take it and be grateful someone else has to clean up the mess.

The corpsleader poked his ribs with the spear. One of the other soldiers shook their head and grumbled.

"Gnoem's gnads, Larmisk. What've we said about killing scrum before they can pay the territory toll?"

Fish-lips swung and smacked the other with the spear shaft. "Shit, I barely touched the sprukker. Shut yours before I leave you lying with it."

"What do we do with the blot now?" asked the emoji broadcaster.

They checked Rahgz's chit again, but it must've gone blank, for they cursed and struck each other over the loss of a few hundred Bits.

"Leave the scrum for the Undertakers," Fish-lips said. "They'll toss the scraps to the Mawgrunt. Good riddance."

They headed off, the last leaving a glancing kick at Rahgz's head. Once they stomped out of sight, he started to wiggle fingers and toes, double-checking that everything still worked. Sitting up, he wiped at the mucus covering his lower half.

"Huh. I never knew I could piss and shit myself to death so convincingly. Would've come in useful earlier." Rahgz rose, letting his gob-garment start to clean itself. "Are there other things you can help me learn about my species? Maybe about my past?"

Is this a priority goal input?

"How many goals am I allowed to have?"

4 primary goals. Infinite sub-goals. It is recommended to make as many sub-goals align with the primary ones, at least tangentially.

Rahgz started walking as he chatted with the implant. "Okay then. So, yes. Primary goal one: Keep me alive and help me get off this barge."

Confirmed. Processing. Proceed with other goal statements.

He glimpsed himself in a storefront window and wondered what other secrets his body and history held. "Primary goal two: Help me discover more about how my species works, where I come from, and who I was before I lost my memory on the barge."

Confirmed. Processing. Proceed.

"Primary goal three: The whole rich and famous thing. Powerful too, if it works out. I don't care how. I just never want to go hungry again."

Confirmed. Processing. Proceed.

Shouts made Rahgz duck behind a corner, just before a group of Undertakers started exchanging threats with Corpse Corps soldiers, each waving weapons while bystanders scattered. Rahgz quickly scuttled away from the area, thinking about the multiple narrow escapes he'd dealt with recently. Running from one survival crisis to the next couldn't be his status quo anymore.

But everyone in the barge was a threat to him and had been ever since he'd arrived. They all looked out for their own profit and survival; if he wanted to do this right, he needed to find ways to be more aggressive in his self-serving ventures.

"Primary goal four: Don't let anyone or anything stand in my way of achieving the three other primary goals."

Again, that simultaneous text/speak: *"Input received. Your new life begins now. System tutorial complete. Integration confirmed. Congratulations. Bit deposit complete."*

His Bit-chit chimed, announcing confirmation of the payout.

"About time," Rahgz said. "I wondered if that was another big bait-and-switch."

He checked the chit. The world wobbled and his vision blurred. When he regained his balance, he had gone to one knee, braced with three arms while holding his heaving chest with the other two. His heart had gone triple-paced and his breathing came raspier than when he'd fled the arena.

Wiping at his eyes, Rahgz double-checked the readout. The same dumbfounding amount continued to display.

25,000 Bits.

Humans have an odd saying: "Bits can't buy happiness." Sure, but Bits can buy you everything that makes you happy, so it's basically a universal proxy. Make sure there is profit in everything you do. Do nothing for free, even if it's for your best friend.

And yes, that was another test. Any friends you have better be paying for the privilege and are walking collateral damage the instant you need a scapegoat.

- How to Backstab Friends and Influence Outcomes:
A Guide for Starting Lanistas
Written by Lanista Kel'Chungzi Ewaltsen
Excerpt from Vol 29, Subset 82.53

CHAPTER SEVEN

Abuzz accompanied a light shock at the back of Rahgz's head. He jerked up and looked around for whoever had snuck up on him with a zapstick.

A voice grumbled in his ear.

"Nobody's there, blot. Just you and me in the mix. Don't know which of us has it worse, really."

Rahgz spun a circle. Indeed, he stood alone, and the only one who'd communicated to him like this previously had been…

"Mesh-thing?" He kept his voice low. "Are you talking directly to me now?"

A mental sigh breezed through his brain. *"You really need to come up with a better term for this unit than 'mesh-thing.' It speaks to unimaginative nomenclature and limited brainpower."*

Rahgz frowned and plucked at his arm feathers. "Why are you just now starting to communicate like this? Seems like you have more...uh..."

"Personality?"

"Yeah."

Rahgz kept twitching as movement caught the corner of his eyes, but no one stood there whenever he focused on any particular spot.

"It's all part of the package deal," the implant said. *"You've committed to upgrading and hearing what I plot out for your life goals, so I'm going to ensure that you pay attention and adhere to the program. If that means I have to overlay a little personality protocol on this unit, so be it. We all have to make sacrifices to get ahead."*

Rahgz huffed, trying to get used to the more direct interaction with a previously impersonal piece of tech. "What sort of sacrifices are you making?"

"Aside from being bound to meatspace and having to slow down my processing output to about a millionth of its potential? Plus being chained to a slag who can barely wipe his own fecal orifice without getting killed? Oh, it's been plucky on my end since I booted up."

Rahgz started walking again, not heading anywhere in particular, but knowing that there were two types of victims on the barges: standing targets and moving targets. At least being in motion decreased the chance of ambushes slightly.

"You're a bit snippy," he said.

"Oh, I do apologize. Would you like me to change up the interface some? Be a bit more gregarious?"

"That'd be—"

"Too bad! You're stuck with this shit, blot."

"Lovely. You're sounding like a Mortimer, so far."

"The fuck you say? What kind of name is that?"

Rahgz tried to hide a grin. He ambled down a sector street lined with cyborg maintenance dens, fritz factories, and a living fluid tattoo shop called *Wraithlight's*. People of all species lined up down the block and around the corner, waiting for their turn to have unique etchings inscribed on their epidermises. Screams coincided with bright flashes from within the otherwise dark parlor, and Rahgz hurried on.

"It's the one you're earning. Puts the perfect image in my mind. Old. Grouchy. Tends to spew a lot."

"Vorkshit. I'm more of a Reginald or Frederick. Maybe a Gretzen if I'm more saucy than snarky."

Rahgz shook his head. "Nope. Mortimer it is. Good to meet you properly, Morty."

Another buzz, this one harsher and lasting longer, rippled down his neck to the small of his back. *"You go around calling me Morty and I will live up to the semantical context and be the death of you."*

Rahgz cleared his throat. "How about a compromise? I'll keep it professional with Mortimer and you don't get me killed."

More internal grumbling. *"Whatever. I hope you're not as shit as following instructions as you are in picking names. Unfortunately, submitting to user preference is part of my programming. But don't think I can't find a thousand loopholes if you try to abuse that."*

Rahgz sidestepped a long trail of literal vorkshit that sat steaming in the road. The air hummed with hundreds of thousands of gutterflies being birthed in the rotting piles. Off to the side, a couple of wattle-necked rasmutins took potshots at the swarms with volt-pistols. Rahgz carefully moved out of range of the arcs.

"Fair enough. How does this work then? I just keep doing what I do while you yell in my ear?"

"Not quite, blot."

"My name is Augurahgz."

"So what? You picked my name, I get to pick one for you. Just be glad I'm not as vulgar as some." The implant chuckled darkly. *"Anyways, it'll work like this. I'll keep pointing out earning opportunities for you, just to keep us flush. I'll steer you clear of harmful, nonproductive pursuits and highlight events, persons, and deals that can get you closer to those wonderfully self-serving goals we've landed on."*

The derision with which Mortimer said that made Rahgz squint one eye. "Are you saying I should've made my goals more...considerate of others?"

"Fuck the Void, no! They're perfect that way. Selfishness survives! That's our new motto, by the way. Repeat after me. Selfishness survives."

Rahgz licked his lips. "Selfishness survives?"

"Whack-a-Gnoem, blot. You make that sound like your epitaph, which is the absolute opposite of what we're trying to achieve." The implant's deep sigh somehow made Rahgz's feathers tickle. How much could it/ he affect Rahgz's sensory input?

I guess pretty completely, since he's tied directly to my nervous system.

"Yes," Mortimer said. *"I do have the ability to make you cry, scream, and dance for mercy. And read your thoughts."*

"That seems unfair."

"Unfortunately, I am legally required to tell you that I cannot cause

you direct, lasting harm just because I think it'd be hilarious. After all, your survival is my survival, so it's not in my best interests anyways to have you wind up as a corpse.

"That's a relief."

"It shouldn't be. It just means I have to get really creative in motivating you to get your shit together if you start dragging your heels."

Rahgz paused by a food vendor and bought a wriggling tick-on-a-stick, the juicy treat bloated with blood. Its legs wriggled as he started munching and slurping. It felt strange being able to just buy a treat like this without wondering if he'd have enough to avoid starving to death a day or two later.

He spoke around dripping mouthfuls. "What if I don't want to do what you suggest?"

"Why wouldn't you?"

"Uh...because maybe I figured out a better option? Or I'm not comfortable with the recommendations?"

"So?"

"So...maybe there'll be times I still want to do things my way. Or does exhibiting free will void my contract and ability to keep what I earn?"

"It'd certainly void getting any real results, because you'd be acting a keen mix of stupid and batshit crazy. Look, what if one of your priority goals was 'Don't Be a Disgusting Slob Who Can't Walk Without Hoverjet Implants Up Their Ass'? And then the first thing you wanted to do was go gorge on the all-you-can-swallow buffet down at Hugo's Vomitorium. My alternative recommendation would be to go find a nice salad and maybe sign up for a VR exercise regimen instead. If you ignored that, what do you imagine would happen?"

Rahgz paused in mid-chew, overtaken by an unbidden mental image of himself as a bloated slug, barely able to move with mounds of jiggling flab crusted with sweat and mold. He forced himself to swallow the crunchy bit in his mouth.

"I suppose that wouldn't be wise."

"Point made."

"But couldn't we try to find middle ground?" Rahgz licked tick juices off his fingers. "What if I realize that I don't want to be the most amazing entity on the barges, but just want to find a comfortable level of existence that is mostly ignored so people leave me alone and I'm just not scared of being eaten in my sleep?"

"Wow. Life goals, sprukker. You need to go big or go toss yourself into the nearest incinerator, blot. If you aren't building up to the top, you're being ground down to nothing."

Rahgz flinched as invisible hands clutched his shoulders and squeezed.

"Try to believe I actually want you to succeed at this. Despite being chronologically younger than the turd you flushed last week, I'm quite attached to existence and all the sensations it offers. Your glory is my glory. Your winnings are my winnings. Your comfort is my comfort. What you eat, I eat. What you fuck, I fuck—we'll talk more about that later. Tragically, I can't walk around and get new experiences without you, so I'll do my damndest to give you the life you don't deserve."

Shrugging off the sense of an unwanted hug, Rahgz tossed the last twitching tick legs into the nearest bin, which zapped it into ash with a muffle *whoompf*. "Are all implants as demanding and meddling as you?"

A loud snort momentarily deafened him, rattling inside his skull. *"How should I know? It's not like we have regular meetups for circle-jerks. As far as you and I are concerned, I'm one of a kind. And you'd better learn to appreciate me, because I actually get spiteful if my feelings get hurt."*

"I'm guessing going back to having you without a personality overlay isn't an option."

"Not a chance."

Rahgz entered an open square with a holographic fountain set in the middle and artistic pieces in shielded stations ringing the area. He recognized the work of local "ARtist" Gathro Mesculivan, known for their complex augmented overlays and ability to insult every single viewer, no matter their species or dimension of origin. One corner of the area boasted a miniature jungle, complete with prowling beasts and carnivorous flora, while another corner appeared to have had a hole blown in the bulkhead, leaving the area open to deep space.

Rahgz double-checked that display, making sure it was actually labeled as an artistic installation and wasn't the barge crew trying to get away with not making repairs to actual structural destruction. Of course, knowing Mesculivan's twisted proclivities, the seemingly damaged area could be real barge damage that the artist slapped their name on to make money off misfortune.

Resting briefly by the fountain, Rahgz scanned the way he'd come out of habit, making sure no one trailed him with ill-intent. Foot-traffic milled through the art displays; people bathed in a kaleidoscope of projected lights that swirled across all surfaces. The fountain burst to life behind Rahgz, spraying beautiful lightscapes into the air that displayed over a thousand slurs and the worst interstellar insults in every possible language.

"Let's discuss the bargebloat in the room. You're worried about the huge Bit boost you just got, right?"

Rahgz crossed his lower arms. "What gave it away? The hyperventilating or the dry heaving?"

"Those were both adorable. But it was also the way you kept saying, 'Oh shit, I'm rich. Oh shit, I'm fucked. Oh shit, I'm rich...' over and over."

"I was saying that out loud?"

"In the most sniveling tone I've ever heard. I'd recommend a vocal cords replacement procedure, but I'm pretty sure that'd just be a superficial fix. What is it with you and freaking out about expendable income?"

Coughing, Rahgz turned away from the square, facing the fountain center. He couldn't help but feel like, despite the noise of the art installations and the people mingling around, that he was being eavesdropped on. That someone had somehow already clued in to his newfound funds and would be plotting to remove the Bits from him either by scam or by shiv.

"I guess it's been my experience that Bits rule the barges. It's a balancing act. Too few Bits, and you're scrounging to make it another day. Too many, and you're walking around with a beacon on your back for everyone who wants to take advantage of you because they belong to the first category."

"Want my recommendation?"

"I have a feeling you'll give it anyway."

"Keep it."

"Keep it all? How is that sort of transfer legit? Where did all this money even come from?"

"The same place that's funding the research you're carrying out by using me. Remember?"

Rahgz glanced at his wrist-chit again, certain the previous amount would have vanished and been a practical joke all along. But the *25,000 Bits* remained persistent.

"And I earned it just by activating you? I know it said there'd be a bonus, but this is a little beyond that."

An invisible hand smacked him on the back of the head, making Rahgz wince and hunch. *"New goal recommendation: Stop being a whiny bitch when good things happen to you."*

"Excuse me?" He rubbed his neck feathers back down, glowering.

"If you want a better life, you have to start acting like you deserve it—whether you really believe you do or not. A big part of moving up in the universe comes from the attitude you project. People will often treat you differently if you set their expectations higher by how you present yourself."

Rahgz ran a tongue over his lips. "So your advice is that I should lie to myself and everyone about how big of a deal I really am?"

"Basically. It's really what everyone else is always doing all the time. Some just do it better than others. Some even do it intentionally." Mortimer gave a scoffing chuckle. *"Besides, since when do you have anything against deceptive methods? You've averaged three-hundred and forty-eight quantifiable falsehoods per daily cycle since you arrived on the*

Coffin."

"I have? Wait, how do you know that?"

"Full-spectrum data analysis performed when I integrated with you. I checked all public records, transactions, and surveillance channels that involved you and then aligned those with your neural storage to create a complete behavioral pattern history and profile."

"Neural storage? That's my memories, right?"

"Bingo, blot."

"Can you access the memories I had before they got wiped?"

Mortimer answered far faster than Rahgz had hoped. *"Unfortunately, no. Those were selectively eliminated with retroactive cellular-level editing. Your personal history will have to be dug up the old-fashioned way. I can tell you, though, that according to my delving into known universal organisms, you appear to be a derivative of the saurovian species."*

A three-dimensional image appeared in the upper corner of Rahgz's vision: a bipedal creature built similarly to him, with a lumpy head, five arms and tail, toothy, with colorful shocks of fur and feathers covering its gray-and-blue scaled body.

Rahgz glanced down at his more drab, mottled plumage. "I guess that's a start. Any chance it suggests a home planet for my kind?"

"There are over a dozen planets in this universal dimension alone that have saurovians as a dominant demographic, or at least a significant percentage. Doesn't really narrow it down much. But hey! Now you know what you are. You're welcome. Don't expect me to always be so nice."

"Wouldn't dream of it," Rahgz said.

"That's because your species doesn't dream. At least not literally. But at least you can have hopes and dreams to pursue. Like the ones we've established that you need to get working on"

"You mean the ones where your advice is to start faking it until I make it?"

"Fortunately, you received that hefty bonus which can go a long way toward helping you help establish this new persona. Why not make a few purchases to celebrate our partnership?"

A map overlay appeared floating before Rahgz, with arrows pointing the way to the nearest D-Mart bazaar. "You want to go shopping?"

"Let's do a few test runs so you can learn to trust me. Get a sense of how we'll work together."

He started following the directions, figuring he might as well give it a try.

What's the worst that could happen? Wait. Don't ask that. I should know better.

Mortimer led Rahgz to a sector street lined with printshops. One printed off personal vehicles on hoverslabs. Another printed up weapons, many of which could only be found here in non-regulated space. But they stopped at the clothes printing store, where Rahgz perused hundreds of schematics with Mortimer chirping in his ear about which ones would be preferable to get him fashionable without drawing too much attention. Dingy rags were no longer acceptable, but rich rags would just get the wrong sorts of people following him into dark alleys.

Rahgz finally settled on a personal defense robe style. It would fit him comfortably, adjusted to accommodate his multiple arms and tail. Mortimer suggested to have it trimmed up with blue and gold and matte grays, with the edge embroidered with the motivational phrase, *Touch me and die*, written in an array of common and alien glyphs. The outfit came with an electric netting woven into the fabric which could either be triggered on verbal command or when others came into unauthorized physical contact with him.

After spending more on a single outfit than he normally would on a week's worth of meals, Rahgz strode back out of the shop and rolled his shoulders. The new clothes felt surprisingly warm and snug despite not restricting his movement or tugging at his feathers and scales.

"Well?" Mortimer asked.

Rahgz plucked at his collar. "You're right. This does make me feel a bit better about myself."

"I'll have you notice that I adjusted the schematic slightly. There are numerous hidden pockets both inside and out, plus slots for blades and an

assortment of projectile weaponry."

Rahgz nodded approvingly. "That's really smart. I've always wanted to have better ways to defend myself, and while being able to fake my death is nice, I'd hate to ruin this new suit. Should we see if there's any discounts on handheld phase-beams? I heard those don't leave much evidence."

He headed for the nearest weapons printshop, eagerly thinking of how good it'd feel to have a few weapons sequestered about himself. As he approached the door, a huge red X flashed over Rahgz's vision and his skull vibrated with such force that he stumbled back.

"The spruk?"

"Not the best idea," Mortimer said. *"Let's move on."*

"But you had this suit outfitted specifically to hold weapons. Why warn me off getting them?"

A long-suffering sigh. *"Let me break it down for you. I'm not going to always waste time and energy explaining my logic, partially because it won't always make sense to a fourth-dimensional meatbag like you. But this time I want you to understand that I'm neither random nor capricious."*

A grid popped up, showing hundreds of variable lines in constant flux over a dynamic timeline. Several of those were highlighted in gold, tagged by descriptives such as "Network Activity," "Public Awareness," and "Personal Security."

"Right now, we're in a tricky stage of getting you established as a person of interest," Mortimer said. *"You're a nobody on the rise, and we two are—so far—the only two really aware of that fact. Together, we can take it to the top. But we have to be careful about drawing too much attention too fast. New clothes? Sure. Anyone with a few extra Bits in their budget can swing that. Suddenly going out and getting an array of weapons through semi-legal channels?"*

The line marked "Public Awareness" shot up suddenly and alarm lights flashed over the grid.

"People will start asking questions, starting with the D-Mart merchant

you buy the guns and blades from. Your name will get registered on a whole bunch of blood.stream forums you never knew existed. Barge security will ping you to see if you're a potential threat. Criminal factions will set up alerts to be aware if you enter their territory. Are you beginning to see the picture?"

Overhead, a pair of drones collided in midair, scattering burning metal shrapnel down on the street. Rahgz joined the rest of the shoppers in scurrying for cover, primary arms covering his head.

"I get it," he said. "But then how do we get what we need?"

"Stop twitching your trigger fingers, blot. Patience. We'll acquire them on the down-low. Unregistered schematics. Prefabbed so there's no record linking you to the printing. And a shopkeeper who's smart enough to know that spilling customer details would be bad for business. I've compiled a list of likely locations we can visit."

A half-dozen shop names displayed, with the D-Mart merchant names listed alongside them and their sector designations. Rahgz glanced over these, and then stopped, pointing to the third one down—even though only he could see the info hovering in front of him.

"Hey. I know this guy..."

Self-care is vital to keeping up your lanista image. Rest when you need it. Keep yourself well-fed. Fuck whatever you want, whenever you want. Rage out and trash your aerie whenever you feel like it. Emotional expression is healthy, and don't let anyone limit your appetites. Take what you want, how you want, when you want, without needing to make any excuses for it. Anyone wants to deny you? Destroy them. That's the only proper self-care.

- How to Backstab Friends and Influence Outcomes:
A Guide for Starting Lanistas
Written by Lanista Kel'Chungzi Ewaltsen
Excerpt from Vol 46, Subset 32.85

CHAPTER EIGHT

M inz didn't seem to have moved from his place behind the counter when Rahgz reentered the store. The burly merchant's many eyes swiveled to focus on him, he smiled in recognition despite the new wardrobe Rahgz sported.

"Back for more keelworms?" Minz asked.

Rahgz grinned. "It's like their slogan says: *Mastication isn't murder if they're delicious*."

Minz's chuckle sounded like a drainpipe about to overflow. "True. I have to keep myself from eating half my stock whenever the fresh delivery arrives. How many can I fix you up with?" He scanned over Rahgz's getup. "Find a well-dressed corpse in the wasteheaps?"

"This?" Rahgz ran several hands over the robe. "New uniform. Got work as a bar-bouncer down in the Nailhead district." The lie he and Mortimer had come up with felt a little awkward rolling of his tongue, but he hoped he'd get better with practice.

Minz chuffed in disbelief. "You? A tough tosser? I've seen plenty of the strange and surprising since I was born on this barge, but you being hired muscle might be the unlikeliest thing yet."

Rahgz puffed his chest up a bit and thumped it with a fist. "That's the best part about not looking as intimidating as a helot on gene-boosters. Nobody pings me as a threat until it's too late." He glanced over his shoulder and back at Minz, pointedly noting the shop being empty except for the two of them. "That's partly why I'm here. Aside from munchies, I need a few other items on the tab."

Mortimer coughed loudly in Rahgz's head, and Rahgz hastily corrected his statement.

"Actually, not on the tab. Off the tab, really. Unregistered purchases.

If, you know, that's a thing you do."

"*Smooth,*" Mortimer said.

Minz leaned back, stumpy arms crossed. "What makes you think I have any unregistered goods here? I'm about as honest as merchants come on this barge."

"*Rule number one about having an implant guiding you to a better life: We do not talk about the implant guiding you to a better life.*"

"I asked around," Rahgz said.

The merchant glowered and drew a remote out from a pocket, thumbing one of the many buttons on it. A few lights in the shop winked out and the front door made a loud *clack*, which made Rahgz think it had just been locked. "If that's true, then I'm going to have to reconsider my clientele. What's the point of serving folks under the counter if the word gets spread too far? Was it Puzzik you talked with? Ormammunimu?"

Rahgz bobbed his head noncommittally. "If I don't want my name in too many mouths, I wouldn't say theirs, right?"

Minz grunted. "Were you scoping me out when you came in here earlier?"

"Maybe."

The merchant lost a few fingers tugging at his wattles. "Must be losing my touch. Could've had you pegged for grubber. I can usually sniff out wannabe clients, but you had a pretty authentic whiff of desperate loser to you."

Mortimer whispered in Rahgz's ear, who repeated the suggested line. "If I know what you're looking for ahead of time, I can have you see what I want you to see."

"All right, all right." Minz muttered as he pulled out a datapad. "Give me the specs of what you're wanting, and I'll check my stockpile."

Rahgz raised a finger. "Unregistered. Prefabbed. Untraceable. Portable."

Minz lowered the pad. "Ah. You want my back-of-the-room bargains."

"With discretion, please."

"Discretion won't get you a discount, understand?"

"Didn't expect it. In fact, I figured I'd used a little of my first salary payout to offer you a bonus. For being so helpful."

"Your new employer didn't equip you?"

Rahgz waggled a hand. "Less investment risk on their part. I supply the heat that works best for me. If I do a good job, I keep my money and life. I die in some brawl and the goons take my stuff? The managers aren't out of any collateral."

Minz scratched at the wiry stubble under one of his chins. "Makes sense, I guess." The merchant tugged at an ear, thinking for a minute. Then he waved as he turned and headed for a door in the back wall. "Follow me." He typed in a code on a wall panel and then scanned several eyes in a biolock sensor.

Keeping a safe distance just in case this led to a trap, Rahgz trailed Minz through the door. They went down a short hall and then through a false wall that turned out to be a holographic projection. Once through the illusion, Rahgz found himself in a larger room than the whole front of the shop—one stocked with enough weapons to outfit a whole small army. Or a large serial killer.

"Blowjobs," Minz said, pointing at the various projectile weapons. "Handjobs." He pointed to the blades and other hand-to-hand pieces. "BDSM." A wave at nets, electric meshes, and auto-ropers. Finally, Minz displayed a rack of shields, portable force fields, nano-armor, and chamo-skins. "Contraceptives." He turned to Rahgz, arms spread proudly. "Everything the INC doesn't want you to know exists, already blue-balling and ready to fuck the other person over."

"Impressive." Rahgz wandered the room, carefully avoiding touching anything. Some of the weapons looked purely mechanical, everything from glossy and sleek phase-pistols to cog-and-wheel puttersputs created by the agornikmech from the ST3MP0NK dimension. Others were tubular and covered in hissing nodes, with pulsing veins wrapping down the handle and a bore hole that looked more like a mouth than anything a bullet would exit.

One of these growled at Rahgz as he passed by.

"*Nothing organic or remotely sentient,*" Mortimer said.

"Why not?" Rahgz asked under his breath.

"*Because you never want a weapon that will decide to refuse to fire because it's gone hangry all of a sudden or developed a conscience. The last thing you need to do when caught in a shootout is start arguing moral existentialism with your gun. Stick to the straight tech and let me be all the extra brain you'll need.*"

Rahgz nodded. "Fair enough."

"What's that?" Minz asked.

Rahgz cleared his throat. "I just said I hope you get a fair deal with your suppliers."

Minz snorted with several nostrils. "If that's your way of trying to get a name so you can cut me out as the middleman, you can fuck off."

Several hands raised, Rahgz waved off the merchant's worries. "Not my slant. I just figured you're taking the biggest risk, holding onto this stash, dealing with violent customers. I mean, what if an INC raid happened?"

More snorts from holes on either side of Minz's head. "Haven't been one of those on the *Coffin* for almost ten TIRDs. Captain has this place quieter than an ash world with whatever deals and bribes he's got in place. And I don't have this stock just for show either. INC fuckers come in here, they won't be leaving again." He eyed Rahgz. "Only ones who know this room even exists are paying customers."

His emphasis on *paying* made Rahgz focus, not wanting to test the merchant's patience. He quickly picked out a variety of close combat weapons—spiked knucklers, a phase-dagger, a coilsword, and a nano-cube pendant that reassembled into a punchblade. Then he haggled with Minz over a gun assortment for the better part of half an hour, with Mortimer whispering in his ear to guide him.

The final array included a stinger, a pensnipe, a ricochet shotter, and a pair of rail pistols.

They settled on 1,250 Bits for the whole lot, ammo and energy cells included. Rahgz felt that strange light-headedness from earlier while pinging the transaction to Minz's chit. He couldn't remember the last time he transferred so much money at once. He must've done so in his previous life; after all, he knew he'd brought a wealthy trove with him to the barge. But the details of exactly how it left his possession were blurry thanks to the mem-wipe.

Once the Bits bounced over, Minz grunted and grinned, and then helped Rahgz arrange the assortment on his person, finding the right pocket for the smaller items and strapping on pieces to achieve the best balance.

"Which if the small ones do you want up your ass?" Minz asked.

Rahgz blinked. "What?"

Minz stared back as if the question were entirely normal. "For emergencies, right? I have a couple lube-bubbles you can take for free, seeing as you're now my customer of the month. Just pop your piece in the gel packet, take a squat and shove it up. They pop right back out when you clench a certain way." He noticed Rahgz's cringe. "They say it gets easier with practice."

"I'll keep everything a bit easier to access," Rahgz said, patting down his robe and feeling the bumps here and there where the new weapons were stashed.

"That just means they'll be easier to find and take if you get knocked down in a real fight."

"I'll take that chance."

"Eh. Your life. Your loss." Minz glanced up at a section of the wall which illuminated, revealing a camera shot of the shop front. A low beep signaled as the door out there opened and several people shuffled in. "Shit. Wasn't expecting them until tomorrow."

Rahgz tried to inspect the newcomers, but the screen kept their features blurry from his angle. "Who's that?"

"Other customers and none of your business." Minz bustled over, pushing Rahgz toward another corner of the room, where a door swiped open. "Head out the back. I'll deactivate the turrets and pressure plates.

Once you reach the alley, you're golden so long as you head portwise. Any other direction will get you skewered."

Rahgz got shoved through the door before he could protest much, and it clacked shut behind him. The plain metal corridor smelled of dust and cheese and hummed with a threatening buzz that made him hesitant to move forward.

After a second, that humming faded, which Rahgz took as a sign that the security features had been deactivated as Minz promised. Easing ahead, he took several turns, not seeing another door until he came to a blank wall. Touching it made the wall swing out into a bleak alley filled with junk. Rahgz picked his way through the detritus, using an AR compass to orient himself to portwise as Minz directed.

He emerged onto the shop's busy street, dusted his outfit off, and started heading toward a quieter area. Mortimer piped up, though.

"Hang on. Let's wait for a bit."

Rahgz checked over his shoulder but saw nothing worth the holdup. "For what?"

An image blipped up, a shot of the security screen from inside Minz's weapons room, showing the trio of new customers whose arrival had hustled Rahgz to the back door.

"For Minz's other customers to come back out. And then we introduce ourselves."

"Are you crazy? Why would we do that?"

"First off, they've got funds, otherwise they wouldn't be showing up to do the kind of shopping we just did. Which means they've also got connections. Viable employment. Maybe some networking opportunities if we sidle up to them in the right way."

"If they're there for weapons, it means they're probably the violent sort."

"Who isn't on this barge?" Mortimer laughed darkly. *"But these are the predator sorts, and we can use them to keep moving up the food chain. Also, I ran an ID scan and came up with profile matches."*

"You can do that?"

Rahgz learned what a mental deadpan glare felt like.

"If I couldn't, would I have just said that I'd done it?"

"I don't know. You could be lying."

"Point. But I'm not. Look."

The picture of the trio zoomed in. The different people wore hoods and helmets that obscured most of their facial features. White squares appeared around an identical item that each of them wore on various spots on their garb: a tiny skeletal hand clutching a metal club. The jewelry piece was understated, but visible on each.

Rahgz groaned. "They're Ghostclobbers."

"Getting in their ranks might be a nice step up from the spleen team chores you were doing just the other day."

Swiping down a ruffled feather, Rahgz bit his lower lip. "They're all lunatics. They think the barge is literally haunted!"

"Exactly. Use that to your advantage."

"How? Pretend to be a spirit so they try to send me to my final resting place in the Void?"

Mortimer chuckled. *"I'd love for you to try and convince them that you're a ghost. I'd post that vid on the blood.stream and go viral so fast—"*

"Hey!"

A sigh. *"Spruk a fucker, get a sense of humor. Obviously I wouldn't recommend anything so asinine. But you already have another angle to play up. Remember who the Ghostclobbers hate almost as much as the lost souls on this barge?"*

Rahgz found himself reaching for the nearest blade on his person. "The Corpse Corps."

"Exactly. Who we just had a fun little run-in with. Focus on the common enemy and get yourself some new allies."

Rahgz pinched his shoulders back, trying to make himself stand straighter. "Assuming they don't eat me."

"Avoiding slathering yourself in the musk of fear and desperation and you might not be too appetizing. I calculate a 76.3% probability that they'll give you half a minute of their time if you make an intriguing

enough offer."

Rahgz threw a couple hands up. "What offer?"

"Good question. Better brainstorm quick. They appear to be done with their business dealings."

As Mortimer indicated, the cloaked trio stepped out of Minz's shop and started heading down the street, shoving aside anyone who strayed into their paths. Their figures bristled with weapons, mostly clubs and cudgels of various crudity. From what Rahgz had heard and seen, the Ghostclobbers believed the best way to send an errant spirit into the Void was by inflicting enough pain on it that the spirit-in-question gave life a final middle finger and left for whatever afterlife waited for it. Why they believed their physical weapons would harm ephemeral entities, though, remained a matter of debate and ridicule.

Steeling himself for a quick bout of mockery and bruising, Rahgz trailed after the defenders of the mortal coil. One of them, the tallest who stayed in front, moved with sinuous grace, long arms dangling to the ground, swaying like ropes with each step. The one to the left looked like a block of stone in a thick dress and moved as if on wheels, no bump or shift to its smooth gait forward. To the right, their companion hopped along on broad feet that loudly smacked the decking, the noise added to by the many chains and talismans hung over its lumpy form.

They moved quickly, making Rahz hustle to keep up, much less close the gap. He wove through the crowd, stepping on tentacles and stumbling over toes as he fought not to lose them. The trio rounded a corner and Rahgz broke into a sprint to catch up without them seeing his effort.

As he took the turn, a huge fuzzy paw shot out from the side and caught him in the ribs. Rahgz gasped as the Ghostclobber swung him up against the wall and pinned him there. The other two appeared on either side of him, as if stepping out of the shadows—except there were no shadows in this portion of the garishly lit sector. So how had they ambushed him so completely?

Up close, he got better views of his new captors. The one with the white mottled fur and enormous floppy ears was a female leporidean, with huge incisors that could gnaw through metal as well as flesh. Her blood-red eyes bored into Rahgz as she huffed in his face.

The blocky person was a species Rahgz didn't know, with a cubed body that looked partly made of stone, the rest of half-healing scabs that keep crusting over and breaking open. It had several mouths that squelched like open wounds, and it emanated a stench of burning meat as its body quivered beneath its cloak.

The tall, willowy alien had a sticklike body and insectoid eyes at the top, with multi-jointed limbs that ended in razor pincers.

The three Ghostclobbers crowded around him, menace clear in their postures.

"Following without permission is rude," the leporidean said.

Rahgz gurgled, all the sound he could manage with his chest close to being crushed. The leporidean eased the pressure slightly, letting him croak a bit.

"Greetings." Rahgz managed a grimace. "Do you, by chance, have any need of a recruit? I was hoping to join your cause and help rid the *Coffin* of the many wayward dead haunting it halls."

They regarded him in long, heavy silence. Then the leporidean snuffled and twitched her nose. She looked to her companions.

"This one's cute. Can I fuck, kill, and eat him real quick?"

Research is what wins in the arena more often than dumb luck. Some ancient Shitzu guy once said, "Know your enemy." Buy their secrets. If they don't have any, invent them and make the rumors stick. Know what they eat. How they think. Follow their fashion choices. Memorize their genetic code. And then unravel them until there's nothing left.

- How to Backstab Friends and Influence Outcomes:
A Guide for Starting Lanistas
Written by Lanista Kel'Chungzi Ewaltsen
Excerpt from Vol 4, Subset 45.01

CHAPTER NINE

"Please don't," Rahgz said. "My species' feathers contain a neurotoxin that affects most other known organisms. It paralyzes on ingestion and is either fatal or causes a permanent neuromuscular disorder that removes control of your bowels."

Mortimer made an approving noise. *"Nice one. You're a faster thinker than I gave you credit for."*

Fur tickled his nostrils as the leporidean ran fingers down his face and neck, licking her lips.

Then I'll just have to take my time and pluck you." Her teeth glinted in the lights. "That'll make it far more fun." She tugged his cloak open enough to expose the numerous weapons stashed inside. "Even better. You come with your own serving utensils. Which one cracks your scaly flesh open and which one is the butter knife?"

Mortimer groaned. *"What did I say about not making yourself more appetizing?"*

Rahgz stuttered for a second until a fresh angle clicked in his mind and the words flowed down the new avenue of thought.

"I'm serious," he said. "I've been dealing with a number of hauntings around the ship of late and have nowhere else to turn to. I know you risk your lives to banish ghasts and wights and other undead fiends who don't know the solace of the grave. And I know you get some of your supplies from Minz. I'm a customer of his as well. A back-of-the-room bargains regular." He waved at the items the furry alien was inspecting. "I just stocked up on all this to try and take down the devils I've been fighting on my own, if I had to. But when I saw you, I knew our paths were crossing by fate. Please take me as an apprentice and show me how to properly cleanse this barge of all things unholy."

The trio glared at him while Mortimer laughed dryly in the background.

"The fuck did that come from, blot? I'm adding impromptu speechwriter to your list of surprise skills. That'll come in handy."

The furry female crinkled her face further. She looked to her companions.

"You think he's serious?" she asked.

Rahgz swallowed. "I'm extremely—"

Her focus snapped back to him, eyes flaring. "Who asked you, blot?"

Rahgz didn't have to fake the quaver in his voice. "Sorry, it's just I've been terrorized by a maniacal spirit for a while now. It whispers in my head all the time, following me everywhere, trying to take over my life."

Mortimer rumbled. *"This better not be going where I think it is…"*

The pressure on his throat and chest lessened, and Rahgz gestured wildly, trying to make himself seem at wit's end. "Ever since this other presence began plaguing me, I've been seeing things I never did before, being offered wicked deals with dark spirits, and pushed with all sorts of immoral urges. I see people around me being influenced by cravings that would put the most twisted sadist to shame."

The leporidean and craggy alien turned to their taller companion.

"Turrurnium, you've got the psychosensory gift," the female said. "What's your sixth eye make of him?"

The insectoid stick figure bent nearly in half to put its head near Rahgz's. Rows of beady eyes fixed on him, all glittering with fierce intelligence. Rahgz smiled back nervously.

"Spruk our luck," Mortimer said. *"You had to go and cross a bona-fide psychic species. It's going to sense that you're hiding something, one hundred percent."*

Details popped into being around his inspector:

Species: Vellenoid
Dimension: Devi - LXII 34
Distinctive features: Multi-jointed, Psionic manifestations

Me? Rahgz thought back. *You're the one who insisted we try and join up with these goons! Fuck the Void, Mortimer, this is all your fault.*

"*Spruk you, you little Voidfucker. Go stick your cock in a reactor pipe.*"

Just leave me alone, you worthless piece of implant junk!

"*What's with this hostility? You want to talk about junk? I know about a dozen ways to set off a chain reaction in your brain that makes you shit yourself every time you sneeze. You're a walking pile of living garbage. A sentient trash heap of genetic impotence.*"

Rahgz clamped hands on either side of his head and shook in place. *Shut up! Shut up! Shut up! Leave me alone! I hate you! I hate you! I hate you!*

The implant's bitter fury shifted to confusion. "*Uh, Augurahgz? Did I miss a history of psychotic episodes in your medical history? What's with you?*"

Rahgz opened his mouth and arched back in a silent, mental scream. Then he collapsed as much as the Ghostclobber's grip would let him. The two shorter Ghostclobbers looked at him in wariness while their psychic companion continued to study Rahgz.

At last, the insectoid spoke in a wheezy whistle. "I am detecting an odd secondary manifestation suffusing his aura." Turrurnium straightened slowly and folded its upper arms. "He is in true distress, with agitation from an outside source. I believe that he believes what he is telling us. Though whether that means it's a haunting we should deal with is another matter entirely."

"Hmph. You take all the fun out of jabbing the newbs," the leporidean said. "Who asked you, anyways?"

"You did," Turrurnium wheezed.

Mortimer stayed silent for a few, and then huffed his own laughter in the back of Rahgz's brain. "*Ohhhh. I get what you just did. Savvy. But you pull something like that again without warning me and I will do that sneezy-shit thing. I'm not bluffing about that.*"

Rahgz gave a mental shrug. *Had to make it feel sincere or else the psychic would pick up on the duplicity.*

The leporidean stepped back, releasing Rahgz while also offering a tufted finger in salute. "I'm Bateesma. Third rank clobnut. What's your name, sprukker?"

Rahgz regained his composure and wiped down his outfit, trying to tuck the blade hilts and gun handles away. "Augurahgz. My friends call me Rahgz."

Mortimer snorted. *"What friends?"*

These ones, hopefully, Rahgz shot back.

Bateesma pointed with her ears. "You've met Turrurnium, and it's a good thing it vouched for you. Otherwise I would've turned you into fried vickle wings and let Ukspug here munch on the leftovers." She indicated the cuboid slag pile. "He's not as picky as I am."

She checked him up and down, obviously unimpressed. "Well, Rahgz, why didn't you go on the network and find our recruitment submission form? Or officially reported these supernatural disturbances?"

Because I had no idea those were an option until just now. Rahgz ducked his head. "Too impersonal. Besides, I was warned by my tormenters that to seek help in any way would bring retribution tenfold. I risked much by approaching you."

"Do you seek a blessing or a boon?" Turrurnium asked.

"Blessing?" Rahgz echoed.

Each of the trio produced a weapon: Bateesma flashing a metal spike with a knobby end, Turrurnium bringing out a slim flail with the handle made from a length of bone, while Ukspug reached inside his semi-solid body and produced a large stone orb covered in cracks and pits.

"A blessing for your weapons," Bateesma said. "Otherwise how are they going to impact the spirit realm? It'd be pointless to try anything without sanctifying your instruments first."

"Uh...yes! Yes, a blessing. That's absolutely, one hundred percent correct. I knew only your purity of focus could provide the protection I've been seeking." He hesitated. "How much exactly does a blessing cost?"

Turrurnium clasped all three pairs of its twig-like hands. "Foremost, we don't protect. We hunt."

"Oh." Rahgz blinked, not sure of the distinction being made. "All right. So you can hunt down the spirits for me?"

Bateesma clapped him on the shoulder with teeth-jarring force. "Not for you. With you."

Turrurnium swayed. "Indeed. We can empower and embolden, if your cause is true and just."

"It is. I assure you that it most assuredly is. You have my utmost assurance on that."

Mortimer growled. *"Stop saying assure. You're emphasizing the ass part of it."*

"But you must lead the way," Turrurnium said. "Only by walking the path to its end can you step off it and into a life free of this vile outside influence."

"Hey, sprukker. Watch out who you're calling vile."

Rahgz's neck feathers twitched as he tried to ignore Mortimer's unheard grumblings. "I understand. I think. How do we start?"

Ukspug spoke in a blurp of magma and grinding stone. "Where is this haunting?"

Good question. Let's see... Rahgz turned and surveyed the sector, giving himself a few extra seconds to figure out where to lead them. He pointed toward center-barge. "Near the arena. In it, actually. I used to belong to the spleen team working the north portside sector and we saw so many horrors after the bouts. In fact..." Rahgz hesitated as a whisper of an idea floated through his mind.

Mortimer giggled. *"Oooh. That's almost nasty enough to make me proud."*

"I believe several undead entities have possessed the bodies of my former colleagues." Rahgz laid several hands over his hearts. "They are not themselves, and I would like to see them freed from spiritual bondage. In fact, it would be my honor to join you in doing so through whatever means are necessary."

Bateesma cooed. "An exorcism." She shivered in delight. "Yes. It's been way too long since I did one of those proper." She nudged Ukspug with a hip. "Remember when we cornered those phantasms two TIRDS ago? The ones possessing that roboid clan? Beat the ever-loving shit out of those spirits before they finally got puked up. Of course, did the roboids thank us once we were done? Never. All that whining about their broken servo-motors and cracked fusion cores. No one's ever grateful when we drive the demons out."

"A shame," Rahgz said. "More people should understand the service you provide and honor you for it."

Turrurnium pointed at Rahgz, arm extending until several fingertips flicked just outside his nostrils. His hand smelled faintly of soap, nutmeg, and dung.

"You'll be ghostbait," he said.

Rahgz tried not to go cross-eyed at the fingertips. "You mean I'll be the primary target if anything goes lopsided?"

Bateesma pouted at Turrurnium. "Poo. You never let me be ghostbait."

"You want to be at higher risk?" Rahgz asked.

She winked at him. "Ghostbait is a sacred duty. You should feel special, blot. Few outsiders ever get to hold that role in an exorcism."

"Fewer survive the experience either," Turrurnium said.

Mortimer? Rahgz thought. *Are we hooking ourselves up to a bunch of loonies?*

"*That's such a subjective question, I barely know where to begin,*" Mortimer said. "*But one hundred percent, yes. The real question is whether these are the type of loonies you want on your side. And I factor that in at eighty-seven point six percent affirmative.*"

Rahgz tucked his shoulders back and tried for a confident grin. "Sure. Why not? I've always dreamed of being ghostbait."

A furry paw clapped him on the shoulder and made him stumble a couple steps.

"Attablot." Bateesma kissed her metal spike and hung it off her belt.

"Point us toward the afflicted so we can cure them."

Rahgz drew out his phase-dagger and held it up. "What about that blessing you talked about?"

Turrurnium held his hands around the blade. "Ashes to ashes, dust to dust. Ghosts are asses who we fuck up. May this weapon free them from this physical plane so we don't have to put up with their shit again."

"Amen," Bateesma said, head bowed.

"Gluk," said Ukspug.

Rahgz blinked. "Poetic."

"Isn't it?" Bateesma tapped a wrist console and pulled up a holo-map of the barge level they stood on. She tapped the arena sector and an arrow pointed the way along the shortest route. "Let's get moving. Once we get closer, you can guide us in."

They headed off, striding with new purpose. Rahgz kept pace, feeling a mix of strange emotions. Excitement and the thrill of having a fresh sense of purpose with the Ghostclobbers. Raw terror at the potential for being found out as a phony and becoming their target if this ploy went wrong. Mild disgust at heading back to his old cleaning grounds, but also anticipatory of how his old crew would react when they saw him in the new duds and with companions.

They navigated the decks rapidly, and Rahgz discovered another benefit of having allies of convenience—people actually moved out of the way as their group headed down the streets. It might've been in part from flashing their respective weaponry. It might've had to do with Ukspug's loud, belching chants about disembowelment, or Bateesma's singsong about finding a true love and eating their head after a hearty mating session.

Whatever the case, they made rapid progress until they reached the district ringing the arena where Rahgz used to work not long ago. There they slowed, letting Rahgz take the lead. He took them down a side path past the gut grates and along the blood ducts, toward the nearest cleaning hatch.

Few people lingered in this area between bouts, though they passed a few shanty camps made out of old bulkhead sheets strung up with navigation wiring, residents huddled around burning nova cores. Alien script scrawled in glowing letters illuminated otherwise dark stretches of hall and the tunnels that narrowed down to the service sector. Barge grubs squirmed in the shadows, munching and slurping on sloppy seconds of bodies that had been left where they fell, or homeless victims that had been caught sleeping in the trash.

Rahgz kept his eyes out, knowing the cleaning crew should be active at this hour. His alertness let him spot the movement near an arena hatch as they came around a corner. He motioned for the Ghostclobbers to duck to the side. They followed him to crouch behind a bulky energy relay, although Turrurnium stuck up above it a few feet like an unsightly power pole.

"Who are these now?" Bateesma asked.

Rahgz recognized the three spleen team members laboring beside the dark hatchway, illuminated by a single red emergency beacon. A large stack of black bundles sat beside the arena wall, looking like a pile of garbage set for the incinerators.

Orvul worked with his tentacles and ape-like body, lobbing the packages onto a nearby hovercart, while his human and xabian lackeys secured the cargo and adjusted the antigrav thrusters to handle the growing weight. The way the sacks sagged, folded, bounced, and slumped, though, made Rahgz second-guess whether mere garbage was inside.

Rahgz pointed them out and spoke in a hushed voice. "That's Orvul. He leads my old crew. He used to be such a peaceful person but started taking dark turns to violence toward even his closest friends."

Orvul tossed another bundle onto the cart. This one, though, flopped over the far side. Before the human could catch it, the bundle crashed to the ground. It burst open at the seal-seam, spilling a ropy mass of eyes, legs, and stomachs. Rahgz recognized the remains of a mangled cordortian as the crew cursed and scrambled to contain the morbid mess.

"Fuck the Void," Orvul hollered. "Can't you useless slops do anything proper?"

"Bad toss," the human said. "Watch where you're aiming."

Orvul stomped over and struck the man aside, tentacle slapping across his big belly. "And watch who you're talking to, blotspruk. Want me to add you to the chum pile?"

The man glared up at Orvul. "Yeah? Sell me to the choppers and who're you going to have to clean up all your shit, you lazy Gnoemglokker?"

Orvul wrapped a tentacle around the man's waist and flung him back over toward the cart. "Get your flappy ass back to work. Or is that your mouth? I forget with you humans. Both are noisy and stink like Voidshit."

They resumed loading up the cart, and Rahgz realized what this operation was.

Bateesma murmured in his ear. "What are they doing?"

"Those bags hold bodies from the Pits and arena fodder," Rahgz said. "Some of them were meant for helot feed. Others are workers, pit bosses, and lanista tenders who died on the job. And I'm betting there are some audience members in there too, ones that got crushed in the crowd during the last bout. Meat grinder grist" He swallowed hard. "Orvul mentioned choppers. Sounds like they're taking this load to a butcher bay."

Bateesma's growl made Rahgz's feather's prickle. "Corpse thieves. Gene smugglers. Those bodies should be destined either for the nearest Meat Gardens and turned to recycling sludge or sent to the Mawgrunt for feeding."

Ukspug belched. "Heretics."

A hand settled on Rahgz's shoulder, and he barely swallowed a yelp before he realized Turrurnium had stalked up beside him. "You were wise to bring us here. Even if those lowlifes are not under the influence of dark spirits, their actions most certainly would spawn many restless souls with displaced bodies."

"Let's go beat some respect for the dead into them," Bateesma said. "And if they don't listen, we'll make sure their corpses are properly disposed of."

The three Ghostclobbers began to confer in hushed tones, determining the best angle of attack.

Bateesma giggled. "So what if we take the newb and throw him screaming through the air as a distraction. Then, while they're trying to figure out where he came from…"

Mortimer spoke up, snagging Rahgz's attention.

"Hang on."

Rahgz turned aside so the others wouldn't notice him talking to himself. "What now?"

"We're not actually going to fight, are we?" Mortimer asked. *"You're going to hang back and let them handle all the action."*

"I don't think that's an option."

The implant made a derisive noise. *"You jump in there and I put your likelihood of surviving at a measly twenty-three point two percent."*

"Thanks for the vote of confidence."

"It's nothing about confidence. It's just math. You don't have the brawn. Your species isn't known for its combat prowess. If anything, you're ambush predators. Direct assaults are not going to go well for you. Trust me."

Rahgz patted at the weapons under his robe. "You could've made these points before I committed to being their bait. I don't think my new friends are going to like it if I suggest my best place in a fight is nibbling on people's ankles and asses."

"Just tell them you'll be the moving distraction so they can get in the glory kills."

Bateesma leaned over. "So the plan is you walk up and engage them. Then take the first shot, however you want it to go down. We'll ring them in and make sure no one escapes mortal justice. Snazzy?"

Rahgz smiled weakly. "Keen."

"Fuck. Can't even argue for one of them to go with you? What kind of

weaksauce negotiation was that?"

Rahgz shrugged as he started taking stock of his weapons, trying to figure out which might be best suited for the first strike. "Maybe I'm just a sucker for a pretty face."

"Pretty? The leporidean? Seriously? Gag me. You have to pick the ugly one to get a hormone rager for?"

Rahgz frowned. "Ugly? You don't have a body and you're less than two days old. How does that give you any ability to weigh in on physical attractiveness?"

"Again, math. Aside from the fact that her kind tend to murder their mates on a regular basis, which I don't think anyone should find appealing, her teeth are askew, her eye colors don't match, and she would do well for a full-body shave and ear reduction surgery."

"Pretty sure if I mentioned any of that to her, she'd murder me without the mating part." Rahgz pulled out the phase-dagger the Ghostclobbers had blessed. It didn't feel any different, but what did he expect? A holy aura to pulse around it? For all he knew, their spiritual fervor had about as much impact as wishful thinking.

He flicked the blade on so it vibrated and pulsed softly with phasic energy. "I want to try something new," he said.

"What? Getting killed?"

"No, that's actually pretty standard for me." Rahgz tucked the blade back away, but kept it unstrapped. "I want to try not being a coward."

Mortimer sighed. *"Can I at least suggest activating the autopilot mode?"*

Rahgz cocked his head. "You have an autopilot? For what?"

Mortimer cleared his nonexistent throat. *"Your body."*

"What? You can take control of my whole body?" Rahgz flexed his arms and legs, trying to determine that he could still move freely.

A tingle went up his spine. *"I'm embedded in your central nervous system. And compared to my level of sophistication, running your biological functions would be as easy as stacking tinker toys."* A mutter. *"But I can't activate it without your permission."*

Rahgz blew out hard. "So sorry you're inconvenienced by my choice in the matter."

"It is annoying. However, I'm only offering it because I think it could help you survive this. I can process things by the microsecond. Relying on your organic instincts and reaction times is a huge disadvantage in a fight. Let me take the wheel for a bit and I'll hand control back over once we're still alive."

Rahgz gave the offer serious consideration. If Mortimer told the truth, it might make him a more effective fighter. He usually relied on desperate scrabbling and lashing out at random to get free from a brawl. Not the best strategy. But he'd never gone into a confrontation so well-armed, or with people to back him up—assuming the Ghostclobbers followed through on their end. Odd curiosity had him wondering how well he might fare on his own now.

"Keep it in reserve. But no. For now, I want to be in control."

"Seventy-four percent probability of that ending in disaster."

"I'll take those chances." Rahgz turned back to the trio. "Ready when you are."

Bateesma narrowed her eyes at him. "Who were you talking to?"

He waved vaguely. "Just trying to silence the voices so I can focus on the matter at hand. The spirits know we're about to fight and are eager for more bodies. Some even hope to possess the dead and walk again."

Bateesma nodded soberly as if she heard that all the time. "Don't worry. We've got the holy fire hot sauce ready to douse everyone in afterwards. Won't be any walking dead on this barge while we're around." She looked at the others and then nudged him toward the spleen team. "Get out there and make us proud, ghostbait."

"Snazzy keen." Rahgz exchanged looks with all of them, looking for that twinkle that suggested they were about to play a nasty prank and leave him all alone to take the pain. To his surprise, they appeared entirely serious and ready to live by their word.

With a quick feather-flick salute, he strode out from behind the relay and headed for the spleen team.

"Would you like to make a wager?" Mortimer asked. *"Say, a thousand Bits that you end up in one of those body bags?"*

"No wager," Rahgz said. "Besides, all the Bits I have are mine. You can't use them to gamble."

"Come on. I've helped you get all of them so far. Seems like a fifty-fifty earnings split is only fair."

"You're a noncorporeal entity living inside me," Rahgz said. "I'd say that's enough property split already to be fair. You don't get to place bets with my money."

"You're no fun."

"Maybe not. But I am ghostbait."

Some lanistas make the mistake of clinging to a sense of honor or some ridiculous code of conduct. That'll get you ruined real quick. Nothing will drag you down faster than unnecessary ethics or constraints on your behavior. Pretending at them? Sure. Go all out. Encourage everyone around you to be as pious as possible. But never actually uphold those standards.

- How to Backstab Friends and Influence Outcomes:
A Guide for Starting Lanistas
Written by Lanista Kel'Chungzi Ewaltsen
Excerpt from Vol 39, Subset 245.72

CHAPTER TEN

"*Please reconsider this,*" Mortimer said as Rahgz tried for a nonchalant stroll toward the cleaning crew.

"You actually sound concerned," Rahgz said. "Careful. I'll start believing you care about me."

"*Remember that whole thing about me only living as long as you do? That applies here. I don't want your false bravado to get us killed!*"

"Fake it until you make it, remember?" Rahgz asked. "I'm just following your earlier suggestions."

A mental snarl curdled in his thoughts. "*Taking my directives out of context is not going to win you any points here.*"

Rahgz stroked the front of his robe. He slipped one of five arms inside where he could hold the phase-dagger while keeping other hands free. "Give me some credit. I'm not going in helpless or without backup. If any of them hit me, my outfit's self-defense mechanism will kick in and give me room to hold them off until the others arrive."

Mortimer grunted and Rahgz sensed the implant shifting into the background to sulk and observe.

Orvul remained so focused on loading the hovercart that he didn't notice Rahgz's approach until he was within a few paces. Suddenly the apish cleaner grunted and looked over, face scrunched into a hundred folds as he struggled to recognize Rahgz.

The human and xabian turned, scowling and squinting. They assumed positions on either side of Orvul, arms and fronds crossed aggressively.

"You? What're you doing back here?" Orvul gave Rahgz another lookover. "What's with the fancy duds? Who'd you steal those from?"

Rahgz smiled at them, keeping his arms relaxed at his sides. "I didn't steal a thing. Just happened to have a bit of good fortune float my way and wanted to come back by and thank you."

Orvul's scrunched-up face twisted and tightened further, looking like a gargantuan anus. "Thank us? For what?"

Rahgz clasped two hands behind his back while keeping two more splayed, palms up. The fifth remained tensed around the dagger hilt under the suit. He made a short pace back and forth.

"Yes, see, when you were constantly stealing my food, beating me up, yelling slurs, and leaving my cleaning area booby-trapped, I didn't realize the valuable lessons you were teaching me. And I am truly appreciative."

"What lessons?" the human asked. Rahgz had never bothered to learn the names of Orvul's lackeys, since Orvul was the only one who'd ever responded to direct begging for mercy.

Rahgz smiled at the male. "Oh, that this shitty life you're leaving as grub goons is far beneath me, and that I should aspire to much greater things. When I look back on this time in my existence, I will remember you fondly as the stupid little Gnoemshitz who spurred me on to my real destiny."

Orvul snorted, shooting a wad of pink mucus to the floor at Rahgz's feet. "You saying you're better than us, blotspruk?"

"I mean, look at the evidence." Rahgz spread four arms. "Here I am with a full belly, comfortable clothes, good friends, looking forward to the rest of day. And here you are carting corpses for whatever pit boss thinks you're pathetic enough to pay for one of the dirtiest jobs on the barge. I mean, you're just a step up from licking the Mawgrunt's asshole clean."

"Fuck this blot," the xabian said, hissing as its fronds unfurling to expose the beaks at their core. "This talking is making me hungry."

Orvul growled. "You always were too dumb to live. Should've stayed away when you had the chance." He stomped forward, lips smacking. "I'm going to peel that fancy suit off you and then pluck your scales with my teeth."

Rahgz held his ground, despite every nerve ending quivering with the impulse to flee. "I'd reconsider. I brought some friends with me, and they aren't happy with this little body-selling scam you've got going on."

"What friends?" the xabian said, fronds twirling like radar dishes.

Rahgz glanced around, waiting for the Ghostclobbers to appear and jab a little fear into the crew. Or at least make them hesitate. Or...appear at all?

Come on. My first attempt at getting allies and they abandon me?

"Told you so," Mortimer said, sounding far too happy with himself.

Orvul loomed over Rahgz, shoulders up by his earholes, claws and tentacles grasping. "Looks like we'll be adding one to the delivery cart, blotwats."

Peering up at him, Rahgz stuck out his skinny chest. "I wouldn't do that if I were you."

"What're you gonna do?" Orvul flexed a tentacle. "Say 'please' and piss yourself?"

He slapped his tentacle around Rahgz's arms and torso, pinning every limb in place—including the one holding the dagger.

Rahgz laughed, waiting for the suit's volt-victimizer unit to blast his tormenter away. Or at least shock Orvul's tentacle into spasms.

Or work at all.

When nothing happened for way too many heartbeats, Rahgz chuckled weakly up at the crew leader.

"Uh. Please don't?"

Roaring, Orvul turned and flung Rahgz at the other crew members. Screaming, Rahgz flew over their heads, taking a swipe of a razor-sharp frond to one leg as he went.

Rahgz landed with skull-jarring force against the pile of bodies on the cart. He rolled over and down the other side, breath suddenly deciding it wanted to be anywhere else but inside his lungs.

Gasping for air, Rahgz snarled and coiled in on himself, tail shaking in impotent rage.

What the fuck? Why didn't it zap him?

Mortimer groaned. *"You didn't activate the self-defense protocol before you left the shop, did you?"*

Rahgz gave that a moment's thought and groaned. "I was distracted by having clothes that didn't smell or look like Voidshit for the first time in forever. Sue me."

"Can't sue a dead idiot. Good luck."

Sucking a deep breath, Rahgz grunted as his chest crackled painfully. He got to his feet just as the spleen team rounded either side of the cart. Ovrul flailed his tentacles, the human cracked his knuckles, and the xabian clacked its beaks.

"A little help?" Rahgz hollered to the Ghostclobbers.

Not so much a peep in reply. He at least had figured to hear some fading laughter as the others ran off to leave him to his fate.

Rahgz whipped open his robe and drew the phase-blade, the stinger, and rail-shot. The human dove for cover while the xabian snapped fronds in front of itself. The rail shot scattered against them with all the effectiveness of spittle. Orvul grabbed a bagged body as he came on, using it as a shield to absorb the stinger darts that exploded on impact.

Flinging the charred corpse aside, Orvul charged in. A claw swept across, knocking the guns out of Rahgz's grasp. Rahgz thrust the phase-blade and sliced open a thick section of a tentacle, blue blood splurting out. The other tentacle crushed Rahgz's wrist, making him cry out and drop the blade before he could get another stab in.

A kick launched Rahgz backward, rolling him over several times until he struck up against a metal bin. Groaning, he rose on shaky arms and legs. The crew stalked in again, making increasingly physically-impossible promises about what they were going to do to his biology.

Mortimer hummed in the background. *"Want to play dead again? I can tickle your gland."*

Rahgz bared his teeth. "No. I'm tired of them pushing me around. I want them to hurt. So they'll never hurt anyone again."

"You mean…?"

"Activate the auto-pilot. Make them pay."

"Goody. Hang on for the ride!"

A *click* resounded in Rahgz's mind. An invisible hand grabbed him by the ghost and yanked him back in a direction he could only describe as fuckasssprukwards.

Watching the world now from a removed state, Rahgz marveled as his body sprang into action under Mortimer's control. He moved with a savage grace he never knew he possessed, coiling away from another hit from Orvul and lashing out with his tail.

Orvul howled as the tail struck a node on his leg, which must've been a sensitive spot for his species. Stumbling, Orvul blindly punched. Rahgz's body ducked and weaved, staying in close while letting the hits whiff past within an inch of bashing him down.

Another missed blow. Rahgz responded with another tail strike. He grabbed a claw, twisted and pulled. There came a pop in one of Orvul's joints, and he screeched in pain.

Rahgz watched it with the detached feeling of an immersion vid channel with the sensory input turned down low. He felt his body move. Felt the muscles clench and weight shift and lungs fill and feathers flick. But it all happened at half-speed from his perspective, with him totally removed from anything involving the action.

His body suddenly ducked and rolled away. The xabian raced in on all six legs and bowled into Orvul by accident. The two tumbled to the deck. The human male came at Rahgz as he stood, but Rahgz leaped higher than he knew was possible. A foot took the human in the face. His tail snapped across his chest, and when he landed, it was on the man's elbow, which shattered under his weight.

Leaving the babbling, weeping man, Rahgz's body raced back toward Orvul, who had shoved the xabian aside and now fumbled for a gun inside his vest. Rahgz ducked another tentacle lash and dove for Orvul's crotch.

Inside his own head, Rahgz screamed in horror. "No, wait, don't!"

"I've been wanting to try this ever since I discovered your species can do this."

With a fleshy pop of his own, Rahgz's lower jaw detached, letting his toothy mouth gape. He slammed into Orvul's genitals and bit down with terrible tenacity.

Orvul's cry echoed throughout the sector, sending a flock of barge midges into flight from a nearby drain porthole. Orvul bucked and spin, whirling Rahgz around with him.

Rahgz could only watch in disgust as his body remained locked on, blue blood seeping out from his jaws and oozing down his throat with a putrid tang.

At last, Orvul dislodged him. Rahgz spun once and landed on his feet.

The three cleaners stared at him as if waking up to a living nightmare in their midst. Mortimer chuckled with Rahgz's voice and wiped his dripping maw.

"Seconds, anyone?"

With yelps and yee-haws and whistles, the Ghostclobbers joined the fray from multiple sides. Bateesma dropped from the ceiling and landed on the human, turning him into a fleshy slinky on the deck. Organs spilled out everywhere, as if the man had been an overripe tomato.

Bouncing off, she kicked the xabian toward Ukspug, using the momentum to fling herself at Orvul. Recovering from the shock, Orvul wrapped a tentacle around her neck. Bateesma grabbed the rest of the length and pulled it to her, biting deep. Blood gushed, staining her fur blue as she gnawed into him.

Screaming, Orvul thrashed, trying to get her off, but Bateesma clung on, giggling madly. To the side, Turrurnium had bisected the xabian, leaving it in steaming halves. The human—what was left of him—had started crawling away, trailing shit-stained blood.

With a jolt, Rahgz's awareness lurched back to the forefront. The world slammed into its real-time flow. For a moment, all his senses went into overdrive, the air feeling harsh, the deck too solid, his own skin too tight. Then his mind recalibrated and he regained control of his body.

Spitting out Orvul's many fluids that coated the back of his throat, Rahgz shuffled over to the side and let the Ghostclobbers finish off the crew. It didn't take long before Orvul collapsed, having been mutilated by oversized bite marks all over his flesh. After stomping his head in, Bateesma hopped over to Rahgz and beamed at him.

"Where were you?" Rahgz asked.

"Sorry for the delay," Bateesma said as she stamped the xabian's fronds to pieces. "Turrurnium wanted to give a pre-fight prayer and went a little long. Besides—" She whirled and threw her spike at the fleeing human, piercing another floppy piece. By the screams, it sounded like a pretty painfully essential piece too. "You seemed to be handling yourself just fine. We watched for a bit because it looked so fun."

"Glad I could entertain you," Rahgz muttered.

She punched his shoulder. "You did good as ghostbait. Made us proud, so we figured you should have first blood. We just didn't expect you to take so much so quickly. You sure you even needed our help with this?"

Rahgz picked at a stringy bit caught between a few of his teeth. "Safer that way."

"For who? You or them?"

Mortimer coughed. *"You're welcome."*

Shrugging, Rahgz looked around at the bagged corpses. "What now? What do we do with all this?"

The two other Ghostclobbers joined them.

Turrurnium whistled softly. "Now we turn this evidence over to the proper authorities and let you take full responsibility for what went on here."

Already not liking the sound of that, Rahgz's ears picked up another noise: that of rapidly approaching feet. He turned just as a security squad marched into view. A full contingent of bipedal barge guards in tight, crimson and gray uniforms, each member sported the hydra-headed insignia of *Coffin* security officers, guns in hands and claws as they approached.

Rahgz's head buzzed as Mortimer shrieked. *"Shit, why are they here? What did you do? I reviewed your criminal record and didn't see anything. You could've told me you were on a security watchlist or something."*

Scowling, Rahgz rapped the back of his skull. "Why are you spazzing? I've never been on barge security's radar, ever. If anything, they've always looked straight past me."

The implant AI continued to gibber for a few moments while Rahgz tried to understand the sudden panic. For all the implant's talk about it being superior and able to calculate better ways for him to live, this sure seemed like an irrational response. What did Mortimer have to fear?

Mortimer finally settled down and blew a deep breath out. *"Sorry. I just assumed the worst. Took me a second to recalibrate. Something must be off with my sudden alert algorithms."*

"It's not like they're here for you," Rahgz said. "If we caused trouble, I'm the one taking the fall, not you."

"Right. Absolutely. One hundred percent correct. Let's see what we're up against."

Rahgz glanced at Bateesma. "What's security doing here? We make too much of a ruckus?"

She shook her head, ears flapping. "We called them in. Another reason it took us a little longer to get to your side."

"Why?" Rahgz raised a hand to the Ghostclobbers. "I'm totally fine with you all getting the credit here. No need to involve anyone official."

Bateesma snuffled. "Don't be so modest. You really should get what's coming to you here."

"I don't understand."

The Ghostclobbers stepped back as the security team arrived. The head officer was a slope-faced giant with armor plating forming an artificial carapace over its lumpy body. The brute checked a tiny datapad in its hand and grunted at Rahgz.

"You the one who took these scammers out?"

Rahgz glanced back at the trio, who urged him with silent gestures and gleeful looks. Sighing, he squared up with the officer.

"That'd be me."

The officer swung its head around like a cargo crate. It surveyed the three bodies scattered and splattered over the area. Looking back at Rahgz, it looked dubious at his ability to have done so much damage. It pointed its datapad at another guard.

"ID the bastard with the tentacles. What's left of him, at least. See if there's a DNA match."

The security guard broke off and went to Orvul's body. They jabbed him with a gene sampler and waited as it processed the results.

Bateesma popped up beside him, grinning as she bumped him in a celebratory manner. "This is going to be good."

Rahgz's arm feathers trembled in trepidation. *When are things going to turn violent again? I basically just expect that all the time now, don't I?* "What's going on?"

"We ran an ID algorithm on your old crew when we first scoped the place," she said. "Turns out this Orvul character has been running schemes like this all over the barge for years. Security's been tracking him but never could pin him down. You just helped them find and take down a notorious criminal. And serial killer."

"Serial killer?" Rahgz echoed.

"You bet." Bateesma nodded at all the body bags. "You think those are all just from the arena sidelines? I'm betting there's at least a few in there who've never been anywhere near an arena in their existences. It's how he covered his nastier activities."

Rahgz stood stunned, brain stuttering as he tried to comprehend this. Could that be true? Orvul had been a sprukward asshat and bully. But a serial murderer?

The gene sampler bleeped, and the guard looked up at the head officer.

"We got him."

The officer's mouth split into a craggy smile, fuming hot, stinking breath over Rahgz. "Congratulations. Where would you like the reward funds deposited?"

Rahgz blinked in confusion, something he realized he'd been doing a lot more within the last couple of days. "Reward?"

The officer grunted and double-checked the datapad. "Captain Aosi and the chief put a price on this scrum's head a long time ago. Whoever's responsible for stopping him gets a nice payday." It glanced up. "Unless you don't want it."

Rahgz held his Bit-chit out, wrist up. "No, I'll totally accept it. And thank you."

The officer held out the pad. "Just note acceptance here for our records."

Rahgz scrawled a signature with a fingertip. The officer tapped the pad to his chit, which pinged to signal a successful transfer. Then the guard lumbered back to the squad, booming.

"All right! Let's clean this sector up. I want every blot of DNA scanned and wiped clear. Do not make me late for shift reports."

As the security detail scrambled to obey, Rahgz stared at the readout on his chit.

100,000 Bits added to your account balance.

Mortimer whistled low in his ear. *"You're welcome again."*

Tingles broke out over Rahgz's scalp and ran down to the tip of his tail. He kept licking his teeth over and over, waiting for this impossible dream to transition to a nightmare of endlessly running down a corridor that turned into a beast's bottomless throat. But reality stayed firmly affixed around him.

I'm rich. Fucking rich. I don't even know what to do with this amount of money.

"What do I do now?" Rahgz wondered aloud.

Bateesma giggled as she peeked over to see the readout for herself. "You ever snorted neurosnuff before?"

A laugh escaped Rahgz, half hysterical with uncontrollable giddiness. "You kidding? That shit's expensive. Like mainlining pure Void essence. A whole block of it would buy you a barge twice this size."

Her eyes gleamed. "Yeah. I know a guy. Let's party."

Never take the blame for anything that went wrong. Always take credit for anything that went right. Make this a lifelong habit, and eventually that will be how you are remembered—as a flawless paragon surrounded by idiots and fools.

- How to Backstab Friends and Influence Outcomes:
A Guide for Starting Lanistas
Written by Lanista Kel'Chungzi Ewaltsen
Excerpt from Vol 13, Subset 431.65

CHAPTER ELEVEN

Rahgz realized the universe had an infinite number of stomachs through which he could pass, being burped up into a divine maw in which he was chewed like so much existential cud and swallowed again to travel down a metaorgasmic intestinal system at the end of which waited the glorious fate of being shat out by an uncaring reality and turned into so much quantum fertilizer that would form the loamy substrate by which a new seed of life would be birthed, only to grow and be devoured again by the universal cow-being that was currently munching Rahgz's mind into mush…

Rahgz sucked a hot breath through his nostrils and luckily inhaled a modicum of self-awareness that lodged in his brain.

Shit. I am high as fuck

He lay on a cushioned surface, just warm enough to be uncomfortable, but not uncomfortable enough to summon the strength to move and adjust whatever covered him. His body felt scattered around the room—legs in one corner, arms on the ceiling, head under the nearby table, epiglottis over by the door. As his mind became aware of his biology, those pieces floated back together to the central element of himself that lay on the softest couch he'd ever encountered.

Rahgz floated there, spinning inside himself as he chased down barely sentient thoughts one by one and wrestled them to the ground.

Why did I get as high as fuck?

That question sent his mind looping in on itself like a self-devouring serpent, coiling into a DNA strand that kept rewriting itself, turning him into every possible species at once before settling back into his normal form. Had his feathers always been so lusciously purple and green? He couldn't remember. Wait. What had he been wondering?

Flicker-flashes shot through his mind like meteorites trying to commit suicide via intra-atmospheric plummets. The Ghostclobbers. The spleen team. Going auto-pilot Voidshit on Orvul's ass. Security showing up and...

Oh. Right. I got high as fuck because I got rich as fuck.

Rahgz raised his head and discovered, to his delight, that his spine hadn't been replaced by a bungee cord as he'd feared. Soft lighting illuminated the room, and his vision blurred and swam as if he saw everything through a gelatinous viewscreen. After much squinting, scrunching, and staring, he finally made out a luxurious suite with numerous seats and lounges, the walls covered in vidscreens and holoprojectors, the ceiling a massive mirrored surface that reflected himself below as well as the three Ghostclobbers all sprawled around him, snoring on their respective beds.

The air hung heavy with perfumes, and catchy music played from invisible speakers, an energetic flute underlaid with bumping, thumping bass that emulated the humping rhythms of multiple species. Empty bottles and drinkbulbs turned the floor into a minefield, and several trays of half-eaten vorkwings and fried glitter eyes crowded one low counter. One of the fried eyes blinked at Rahgz, who blinked back while his stomach rumbled in hunger.

Rahgz tried to estimate how much staying in this room cost, even for just a few hours. The price tallied up fast.

Shit. Am I already poor as fuck because I spent all my rich-as-fuck money to get high as fuck?

Sitting up, Rahgz winced as several more bottles and glass canisters clattered to the floor. As he stared down at the mess, he also noticed his previous outfit had been swapped out for fancy gold-and-silver threaded duds. Quite silky and far more comfortable, but also lacking the weapons cache he'd just been learning to love.

Rahgz stood and brushed himself off, studying the snoring Ghostclobbers and wondering when someone was going to enter the room and start yelling at them to get out.

"There you are. Thank the Void."

Rahgz spun a circle, trying to find the speaker before recognizing the voice. His voice slurred until he pinched his tongue and gave it a quick spanking, telling it to behave.

"Morty old pal," he managed.

Grumblings. *"Yeah, no. Try again."*

Rahgz cleared his throat, trying to ignore the mélange of strange flavors residing in it. "Mortimer. Good to see you're operational."

The implant gave an exasperated sigh. *"Finally. I've been waiting for your neurons to reassemble into anything resembling sanity so I can reengage and explain the situation before it gets any worse."*

Rahgz wandered over to the snack bar and started settling his rumbling stomach with greasy chunks. "What's been happening? Did we go a little overboard with the partying?"

"First off, go easy on the vorkwings. You already puked up several tray's worth before passing out. Be glad this place came with a sanitation unit."

Rahgz continued to gnaw at the munchies, alert for any warnings from his intestinal tract. "Noted. So what's wrong?"

"Where to begin? The summary would be that you made some highly questionable choices while off your blitzer."

Rahgz's gaze strayed to the furred leporidean, who had a trail of drool running from her mouth to stain an impressive pile of pillows.

"Fuck. Did I sleep with Bateesma?"

"No. You wish it were that good."

Rahgz looked past her to the stick-like alien propped up in a corner, but still decidedly unconscious. "Did...did I sleep with Turrurnium?"

"Worse."

Trying not to look, Rahgz couldn't help but stare at the lump of flesh half-hidden under several blankets and furs.

"Spruk me sprukwise. I slept with Ukspug, didn't I?"

Mortimer snorted. *"I kind of wish that was it. You could get that incredibly pathetic walk of shame done and be over it. Alas, it's more than that."*

"More?" Rahgz checked himself over for any piercings, tattoos, genetic implants, symbiotic or parasitic organisms, and other new additions. Fortunately, nothing appeared out of place. "Am I...mate-bonded with any of them?"

"No. Look, it doesn't actually have much to do with them, though they are sort of along for the ride now."

"What ride? Hey, can we get some extra light in here?"

A soft, gender-neutral voice spoke from everywhere. *"External viewing window activated."*

The largest wall dissolved in front of Rahgz, becoming a floor-to-ceiling window that revealed a busy barge sector beyond. Whatever room they were in appeared to be situated well above the main deck. Far below, hoverjets whizzed by, cargo shuttles followed their tracks, and the usual zoo of people shuffled and bumped their way through the streets.

Rahgz went over and put a hand on the screen. "Nice view. How much am I renting this suite for?"

"Who said you're renting it?"

Alarms clanged in Rahgz's head. "Did we break into someone's pad?" Another jolt of horror. "Please don't tell me we sprukking broke in and killed whoever owned this place. Please tell me there's not a body somewhere under all these cushions."

"Good news: You're not that much of a monster, even when tripping to the twelfth dimension. Bad news: You are the owner."

Rahgz froze. Nowhere in any sense of reality that he knew had that possibility even seemed the remotest thing to bring up as an option. "What?"

"Welcome to your new home."

"The spruk you say, blot?"

"Watch who you're calling blot, blot. Here's the model view."

A flash made Rahgz turn to where a holoprojector blipped on. A virtual ship appeared, spinning slowly to give him a view of all angles. Not a spaceship, but a smaller, personal transport craft that looked like it could house the room he stood in, plus a tiny storage area and stabilizers. Large hover thrusters were fixed to the bottom, and the rest of it had a sleek, silvery flow with the sides curving up into stylized wingtips while the body looked like a flattened ovoid.

Rahgz realized that the room they were in didn't actually attach to anywhere, and they were all floating above the deck. He also realized where he'd seen personal transports like this before.

"Mortimer…"

"That's my name."

"This is an aerie."

"Correct."

Rahgz swallowed against a suddenly dry throat. "An aerie like a lanista would use."

"Also correct."

Feathers started prickling. "Did the Ghostclobbers have a lanista friend we ended up partying with?"

A pregnant pause. *"Sort of. I mean, they have that kind of friend now."*

"Spruk me. I'm a…"

"Yes."

"Like a real…"

"Yes."

Rahgz dropped to his knees, arms trembling, breath coming in shallow gulps. "How is that even possible?"

"Well, becoming a lanista has a surprisingly low threshold of official requirements. No age, gender, or species restrictions. You don't even have to prove you have a soul. So long as you have the startup funds to purchase an arena license, more funds to buy a Meat Garden spawn to become your helot, more funds to get a low-end, used aerie from the docks, and more funds to foot the entry fee to the next bout—which is tonight, by the way—and boom. A new lanista is born. Congratulations. Also, you're almost broke."

Rahgz checked his wrist-chit and saw a measly 1,237 Bits languishing in his account. His breaths sped up with his heart, muscles turning to so much mush. Flecks speckled his vision and he slumped forward, forehead resting against the window screen. The chilly surface pressed firmly against his scales, forcing him to accept the reality of the situation.

"How could you let this happen?" he whispered.

"Are you talking to me?" Mortimer asked. *"Because if so, fuck you and the high-grondle mount you rode in on. I am not in charge of your choices, remember? I just guide you. And when you are so spaced out it makes the Void look crowded, I don't really have much say in what you do. I'll have you know I spent a good half-span trying to talk sense into you at every step of the way, but you were so bound and determined to impress your new friends that you barely burped my way. Whatever you think, this is not actually a worst-case scenario."*

"It's not?"

"Nope. You're just going to have the shortest lanista career ever, because you already wagered on winning tonight's bout, using this aerie, your helot, and yourself as collateral. When your helot dies, all of this and you will become someone else's fresh meat to chew up and spit out however they wish."

Rahgz wheezed and clutched his chest.

"Don't panic. Do you see a towel anywhere?"

"A towel? What the ever-sprukking-fucking for? To smother myself to death with?"

"No. You're just dangerously close to going into fake death spasms out of sheer panic and you'll need something to clean up the piss and shit with."

Rahgz clamped down on all his orifices, willing himself to calm down before he made a mess of the place. More of a mess, at least. Seeing as he apparently owned the aerie now, it made sense to keep it a bit cleaner since nobody would likely be coming behind him to spit-shine the place.

As he knelt there, wondering what to do next, soft steps came from behind him. Thinking Bateesma had woken, Rahgz tried to compose himself. Apparently the Ghostclobbers had gone along with him in this unfortunate series of events, so hopefully he didn't have to overly explain everything to them—doing so would probably put him into death spasms again.

However, the creature who had entered through a side door took his breath away in an entirely different manner.

"Good blissful waking, master."

The voice was decidedly sensual, as if someone had pinpointed the genes responsible for erotic vocalizations within all known species, bundled them all together, and then took them to the Meat Garden and said, "There. Start with that and make a living being to fit the sounds."

Not able to take in everything at once, Rahgz started with her tail. And it was most assuredly a her, from the mind-boggling curves of her serpentine body to the knowing curve of her three sets of lips to the exotic pheromones hanging in a cloud around her. She balanced on two thick, yet graceful legs, with a pair of sinewy arms slipped through a white silk robe that left her uncovered in all the right places—predominantly the mid-thigh, thorax, and upper hypoglonoid.

Her head looked like a merging of three faces, with a central green eye, with a blue one to its left and a purple one to its right. Three mouths smiled at him, while a central set of nostrils fluttered provocatively. The purple-white mottle scales that covered most of her body glistened as she undulated slowly from head to tail, even as she stood in place. Silvery hair formed a mane that was braided halfway down her slender back.

"Psst. You're drooling. Really not a good look."

Rahgz clamped his mouth shut, which shot a glob of spittle to the floor between them. She didn't bat an eye at the uncouth display, her eyes on him.

"Who are you?" he asked once his vocal cords remembered that they existed.

She swayed and bowed, the arch of her neck making him shiver. "I am Phara Stekka Zolma, your personal assistant, aerie pilot, and helot handler. You remember purchasing my contract, of course?"

"Uh, of course. How could I forget something like that?"

He sent a thought to Mortimer. *How could I afford an assistant like this?*

"Did I mention you're almost broke? You've rented her contract for one TIRD and then she's up for renewal. Assuming you don't lose everything you now own all over again by then."

Phara pursed a couple lips and checked off something on her data-pad. "Excellent. Now, I have just a few matters of your new business accounts that require your illustrious attention and then I will be able to leave you to the solace of your...ahem...insensate companions."

Rahgz shot Bateesma and the other Ghostclobbers a glance, wishing at least one of them would wake up so he didn't have to navigate this all alone. Aside from Mortimer, obviously, but Rahgz felt less like Mortimer was a companion and more like a barge barnacle he couldn't scrape off without causing a nuclear meltdown.

"Of course," he said. "Let's hear it all. Bad news first?"

Phara made a tsking noise. "I am unfamiliar with moral relativity in regards to your existential perspective, master, so I would avoid classifying anything as either good or bad for the time being. I believe you will respond positively, however, to the news that I have registered your wager for this evening's bout."

"Of course." Rahgz fixed his smile, trying not to grind his back teeth too loudly. "I don't suppose there's still time to rescind that or lower the amount?"

Phara shook her head. "Once it's officially in the Book, no take backsies. That's a direct quote from the regulatory body behind the Book's existence, by the way. With your wager registered, that of course means that no one will ever confirm its existence except in the event of a winning match and payout, with an anonymous deposit to your account."

"Of course."

"And then there's the matter of your helot. Upon your purchase of the genetic mass from the Meat Gardens, you declared its name to be," she peered at the datapad, "'Glomph.' Is that the nomenclature by which you wish it to still be registered?"

Rahgz swallowed a hiccup. "Of course." Inwardly, he shot a question at Mortimer. *Did I really name a helot "Glomph?"*

"Actually, when she asked you about a preferred name, that was all you could say. Over and over, in between about ten minutes of nonstop giggling fits."

Rahgz briefly closed his eyes and resisted the urge to whack his forehead against the nearest bulkhead. *Fuck a Gnoem and toss me in the Void.*

She raised a perfect eyebrow and nodded again. "Very well. Glomph is hereby slated to face its first opponent, a helot champion known as Hiliac, in the arena in several hours. I assume you wish to be in attendance for your servant's maiden bout?"

"Of course."

Phara frowned with two out of three mouths. "Is everything all right, master? You seem to be stuck on a verbal loop."

"Of course! I mean," Rahgz coughed into several fists. "Yes, I'm fine. Just a bit dehydrated from the, er, partying."

She slinked over to a wall panel and tapped out a command. A slot opened, dispensing a tall bottle of clear water, which she retrieved for him. Rahgz gulped from it gratefully, realizing how thirsty he really was, and also using the delay to let his thoughts settle and brace himself for more surprises.

Wiping his mouth of on a sleeve, he smiled at her. "Thank you."

"I live to serve," she said.

"I love the sound of that," Mortimer said.

Shut up, Rahgz thought. *She's my assistant, not my slave.*

"Check her contract." A sector-long legal document began scrolling in the corner of Rahgz's eye. *"She's from the meat market, full property status. Her contract doesn't just extend to her services but herself as well. The only thing you can't do outright is kill her, and that's only because you*

didn't pay extra for the rebirthing deposit."

Well, we're— Rahgz revised that thought. *I'm not doing anything like that to her. Not on a contractual obligation, anyways.*

"Why? You think you could do better?"

Of course not! I just won't treat her like that. It's not right.

"Whoa. None of my research suggested your species was so prudish."

He realized Phara continued to watch him expectantly. "Something more?"

"I just confirmed the final authorization of your arena activity. Glomph is being transferred to the proper Pit. Would you like me to navigate us into position for optimal bout-watching?" She tapped a band on her wrist, and a holographic image beamed up between them, showing a map of the arena. Half-a-dozen squares highlighted along the outskirts, showing field-of-view cones calculated from various angles. "These areas are still available, as your opposing lanista has yet to claim a preferred viewing spot. Which would you prefer, wise one?"

Rahgz clasped hands behind his back and hummed to himself, pretending to inspect the map while having no real clue which would be the best option.

A little help? he mentally whispered.

Mortimer blew a raspberry. "He wants my help for seating choices and not mating options? I am living my best life right now."

Before Rahgz could argue, a flashing dot signaled a position on the reactor side of the arena. He pointed to it.

"That one, please."

Phara bobbed her head, looking pleased at his selection. "Excellent choice, illustrious one. That will certainly give a lovely view of the carnage as your helot dismembers its foe."

He tried for a disarming smile. "You can just call me Rahgz. No need to keep it fancy with me."

Discomfort flitted across her multitude of features. "I would not want to be too familiar with you, master. It would be disrespectful of your vaunted position."

"If it makes it easier," he stood closer to her, soaking in the olfactory assault of her pheromones, "consider it a direct order from your current owner."

That eased her tension slightly. "As you wish, magnificent...oh..." Her sultry giggle made Rahgz's feathers twitch all over. "As you wish, Rahgz. I will go make preparations for departure."

As she turned to go, Bateesma launched from where she'd been sprawled and tackled the other female. Yipping, snarling, and hissing, the two tumbled over the furniture, pillows and bottles flying everywhere as they bit and grappled each other.

"I'm so recording this and posting it on the blood.stream," Mortimer cried.

"You will do no such thing," Rahgz said under his breath.

"Already uploading..."

"Then stop it now!" Rahgz shouted.

The two wrestlers came to a sudden stop, Bateesma with Phara's tail coiled around her throat, gasping for breath, while holding a blade a hair away from gutting the other woman.

Phara kept her eyes downcast while maintaining her stranglehold on Bateesma. The leporidean scowled at Rahgz.

"Apologies, master," Phara said. "I am certainly willing to sacrifice my personal safety for yours."

"Who's this spitz?" Bateesma asked. "What's she doing invading my personal space?"

Rahgz held hands out. "Let go of each other. No fighting, please. You're both with me." He waved them apart, each moving apart stiffly as if prepared for the other to resume the fight at any second. Finally, they stood just out of reach of the other.

"Bateesma, this is Phara, my new personal assistant. Phara, Bateesma is a friend from the Ghostclobbers."

Phara was the first to recover her poise, as she flicked her tail in salute and bowed. "Stekka Zolma Phara. A pleasure to make your acquaintance. I am at your service in the presence of my owner."

Bateesma tugged at the fur on one elbow as she sized the other female up. Then she stamped a foot and bobbed her head. "Yeah, all right. Good blessings to you too. May your days go unhaunted."

They exchanged smiles, though Rahgz wondered if the tension in each truly existed or came from his worried imagination.

Phara turned to Rahgz and fluttered glinting lashes. "I will resume preparations to leave and announce when we are underway." She swayed toward the same door she'd entered through.

Watching her go, Bateesma plucked a bottle off a side table and took a swig without even checking the contents. After a contented burp, she shuffled over to Rahgz and pointed with her chin at where Phara exited.

"She's cute," Bateesma said. "Can I fuck, kill, and eat her?"

"Please don't," Rahgz said. He dropped to a lounge chair, hands clapping his knees. "I didn't get that kind of deposit."

"Pooh." Bateesma squinted at the bottle, and then around at the aerie as if seeing the place for the first time. "So, I don't remember much, as usual. Fill me in. Where are we? How much do we owe? Any alibis to coordinate?" She twitched her nose. "And why are you dressed like a noodle-ass lanista?"

Rahgz sighed. "It's a long story."

"We've made questionable life decisions and learned nothing from them!"

With another deep sigh, Rahgz put his head in his hands. "Actually, maybe not so long."

Don't let people question you. About anything. Ever. You are the smartest person in the room, always and forever. The instant you let anyone doubt that, that doubt will creep into everything else you do like a slow poison, weakening you. Enforce your superior intellect on everyone, and if they disagree too long, just bash their brains out. Problem solved.

- How to Backstab Friends and Influence Outcomes: A Guide for Starting Lanistas Written by Lanista Kel'Chungzi Ewaltsen Excerpt from Vol 2, Subset 1.03

CHAPTER TWELVE

"You're one of them now?" Bateesma asked for the dozenth time.

She and Rahgz had woken the other two Ghostclobbers and now they all sat on several central cushioned chairs and stools while experiencing the view of the barge sector below. Rahgz had conveyed all he now knew about his situation, with a few colorful details added by Mortimer. Their fragmented memory added a few colorful details about the mutual lost time, with no one having a full chronology of events leading up to the present.

Together, they remembered bits of harmless brawls, hefty meals, lots of funds exchanging hands, and a meetup with a dust dealer in a dank back alley by the waste recycling center. Plus a definite assurance to never again visit a particular corner deli in the Aftarena district. Nobody questioned or argued that one.

"Seems I am," Rahgz said, wiping down his robe. "Do you not like lanistas?"

"Nah. Not the clean ones, at least." Bateesma munched on a handful of squirmnuts. "The dirty ones though, those rubbishmongers just don't make our work much easier."

"Dirty? Clean?" Rahgz frowned. "You mean like cheaters?"

Turrurnium held an arm out, waggling it around. "She means in how they treat their dead and dying. Good clean deaths with proper ritual post-mortem purification cut down on the number of tortured spirits that cling to this barge. Those lanista who encourage messy demises for higher entertainment purposes and leave the losers rotting on the field in mockery—well, they're making us do unpaid overtime."

"I see." Rahgz leaned forward, curious. "You'd want me to make helot deaths quick and simple?"

The twiggy Ghostclobber folded its elbows in. "Or at least see that yours has its soul laid to rest after its first match ends in disaster."

"If it has a soul," Bateesma said.

"I'm sure it does," Rahgz said, oddly defensive about the helot he'd never met. "And why are you assuming this fight will end badly? Glomph might surprise you." *And me.*

Bateesma flopped to one side, scoffing. "If my name was Glomph, I wouldn't want a soul. From what you've told us, the thing hasn't had any training. You've never been a lanista before and your personal fighting skills don't exactly translate to having a combat proxy in the arena."

"*Sheesh,*" Mortimer said. "*Their confidence in you is overwhelming. Stop, please. His ego can't take much more.*"

Fake it until I make it, Rahgz told himself. *If I don't start pretending to believe in myself, who will?*

He made a show of standing and stalking across the room, robe swishing. He punched in an order on his new food fabricator and waited as a meaty treat got printed out of spamsludge.

"You're all welcome to stick around," he said, keeping his back to them. "But if you think so little of me and my new calling, then you can hop off this ride and get back to beating up spirits. I won't stand for anyone's negativity."

The Ghostclobbers whispered among themselves, and he kept waiting to hear the swish of the door as they left. Yet they made no move to go.

"We're already rooting for you," Bateesma said. "We just want to be realistic about your chances."

"Everyone starts out as a nothing and nobody," Rahgz said, turning to face them again. "I just got serious closure on my last job and now I'm moving up. This is my chance to show everyone what I'm really capable of."

"Fame is a fickle path," Turrurnium said. "The higher you fly, the farther you can fall."

Rahgz snorted. "I've fallen as far as you can get. I'm basically trying to climb out of a bottomless pit at this point."

Bateesma looked around. "I don't think anyone would call this place a pit."

Rahgz opened his mouth to complain about her stretching his metaphor too far, but Phara's voice spoke over the shipboard speakers.

"Greetings, esteemed guests. This is your pilot, Zolma Phara Stekka. We will be moving shortly. The gravity plates are at full capacity, but we may experience some internal turbulence as our artificial gravity interacts with the barge's own artificial field. It would be safest if you remain seated until we arrive."

Ukspug rolled its bulk over to a corner and thrust stubby legs out to brace itself. The aerie trembled briefly as the hoverjets thrummed to life; the view outside began to slide past. Further discussion of Rahgz's chances of victory were sidelined as they all got lost in scenery from a perspective none had ever enjoyed before.

Yet as they slipped through a sector ceiling gate and into the outskirts of the arena, Rahgz's nerves started crackling.

If my helot loses this match, he thought to Mortimer, *how bad will it be?*

The implant threw several charts up, with lots of red text and exclamation points. *"Do you want me to show the actual financial debt you'll be in, or round it up to the nearest hundred TIRDs of slave labor?"*

Rahgz clutched a couple fists over his stomach, trying to keep food down as the aerie lurched slightly.

So we need Glomph to win.

"You know that life goal you set? The one about being rich and famous and powerful?"

Yeah.

"You don't get any of that by losing!" Mortimer sighed. *"Unfortunately, you are a loser, Rahgz."*

Uh, excuse me?

"Your whole mindset is accustomed to loss. You expect it, and so you

become a self-fulling prophecy of loss and setbacks because that's all you figure life will give you. But giving isn't enough if you want success. You have to seize that." More timeline charts swapped into view, showing steep lines shooting ever lower. *"Every trajectory your life has taken since you came to this barge is downward. Until..."* The central line plotting Rahgz's quality of life veered upward. *"Me. So I'm going to help you seize success whether you want it or not, starting with this match."*

Rahgz chafed at being called a loser but couldn't think up enough examples to refute Mortimer's assertions.

How can you help with an arena fight?

A video window opened up, flashing through scenes of countless helots bashing and clashing across hundreds of barge arenas. Blood and other vital fluids sprayed, body parts flew impressive distances, and billions upon billions of aliens cheered on the endless melees.

"While you were sleeping off your doses, I started analyzing past bouts from across INC and non-regulated space. I've already gone through three thousand, two hundred, and fifty-eight matches and also read through two dozen bestselling strategy books from other lanistas. Most of their stuff is utter bullshit, meant to make a few Bits or mislead competitors. But I've picked up several legitimate lanista management patterns that could help Glomph survive this bout."

Rahgz perked up. *Really? You think we have a chance?*

"We'll find out soon. Let's get ready."

The aerie shuddered as it came to a halt along the upper rim of the arena, hovering in place. Rahgz joined the Ghostclobbers in gawking at the expansive view. He could see into every main seating area, where people already poured in to pack the sidelines. The elevated station also let Rahgz see across half the arena, though it might as well have been an alien planet. None of the landmarks looked familiar, even though he'd trekked much of layout as part of the cleaning crew.

Phara reentered the room, bowing and nodding at the other two Ghostclobbers before addressing Rahgz. "Would you like me to prepare your monitoring station, Rahgz?"

"Naturally," Rahgz said, not knowing that that had been an option until that moment.

Phara tapped a few commands into her datapad. A portion of the floor slid aside in front of the viewing port, and a semi-circle of control panels rose and powered up, with holographic dashboards, a VR port, and a neural interface jack.

Rahgz stared at this, completely dumbfounded. With his luck, he'd press the button that initiated the helot's self-destruct sequence. He knew that some lanista literally plugged in to their helots and directed their actions like puppets on virtual strings. Others preprogrammed their helots with various attack patterns and algorithms that played out once the bout began. Others simply let the helots' natural predatory instincts lead the way. Not knowing anything about Glomph's physiology, however, left him in the lurch.

Rahgz forced himself to stand in the center of the station, making sure he didn't touch anything that looked important. "Phara, do we have any data on my helot? I'd like to review Glomph's bio profile."

His assistant double-checked her pad and flicked fingers at the viewport, where a small block of text appeared.

"This is the summary provided by the Meat Garden on point of sale."

Rahgz skimmed the short lines.

Specimen 42OODLVZ9.2
Proprietary genetic blend. Primary species dilution, 98%.
Limbs: None.
Brain: None.
Mouths: Lots.
Sex: You try.

"Is there a video? An image?" Rahgz asked.

Phara flicked through to another file. The image that came up, though, only showed a gray and pink ball of flesh with milky protuberances where eyes or mouths might be.

"That's my helot?" Rahgz asked. "That's Glomph?"

Bateesma came up to peer at the image. "It kind of looks like Ukspug's third asscheek."

Ukspug gurgled. "Don't insult me."

Phara converted the picture to three dimensions and rotated the lumpy orb around. "I believe this is from its early gestation period within the pod. It's likely much bigger and more developed at this stage. We will have more information once it emerges to fight."

That's it? Rahz asked Mortimer. *That's all we have? How did I buy this helot without knowing more about what I was getting?*

"You basically ran in, pointed at the first pod with a price you could barely afford, and said, 'Gimme that one.' Then you paid quick and sprinted back to the others, not wanting to miss the next round of neuros-nuff."

I have an impulse-buy helot. Great.

The Ghostclobbers watched him, the weight of their stares making Rahgz want to flee out the door and fling himself to the deck far below. *What have I gotten myself into?* he wondered. *Is there any way out of this that don't include suicide or slavery?*

"How about sucking it up and sticking to what little of a plan we have?"

Rahgz shot Mortimer a mental eye. *We need to talk about boundaries in our relationship.*

"Sure. They're for wimps and losers. Remember which one you are? Do you want to change that or not? Now pay attention..."

Mortimer spent the next couple hours running Rahgz through operational procedures on the various control panels, not so he could actually manage the bout, but more so he could at least pretend he knew what he was doing. By the time Rahgz managed to distinguish the zoom function on the viewport from the self-defense sequencing, the bout loomed just minutes away.

As the signal came for the final countdown to the bout, Rahgz lowered his hands and took a long look out of the viewport, telling himself to enjoy this once-in-a-lifetime experience of being above everyone else.

In this briefest of careers as a lanista, he could understand why people pursued it at the cost of everything else. Despite knowing he would likely be humiliated in this bout, ending up owing his existence to whoever ended up owning his debt, Rahgz would forever be linked to the arena at all levels.

Bateesma and the others took up seats behind him, chattering excitedly as they pointed out their favorite hazard traps.

At last, the announcers blasted over the arena speakers, going through their usual welcome from the barge captain, giving updates from the lost-and-found, and news of a donation run for the Lil' Fuckers Foundation. Then they focused on the specific bout details.

An image of Rahgz appeared on the massive screen, and he groaned. Whoever had taken that shot of him during his registration as a lanista made him look cross-eyed and half awake. Or that might've just been the drugs he'd been on at the time.

"A special welcome to a first-time lanista, Augurahgz," said one announcer. "A personage of no known origin or previous public acclaim of any sort. Speculation is already running wild about this newcomer to the arena. No sponsors and no juicy gossip to spread around yet. What will we enjoy from this newcomer?"

Despite being secure up in the aerie, Rahgz felt more exposed than ever, as if the thousands of people in attendance were lining up targeting sights on his image, assaulting him with a million ill-wishes and envious, violent fantasies of what they'd do if he ever came down to their level. He'd had those same thoughts while part of the audience as well—both hating the lanistas who floated above it all while also wishing to be them, willing to murder for that chance.

"Blood, guts, and glory!" said the other commentator. "I hope this newb goes out like a flaming ball of shit tossed into the Void."

"Today's combatants couldn't be more different," the first said. "In a position of esteem and blood-drenched victory, we have Hiliac the Sonorous, here under the auspices of Lanista Yorgulmeist. You're in for a treat, folks, as Hiliac sings the most beautiful ballads as she tears her opponents to shreds. So get those recording devices prepped."

Distant cheers piped through the aerie's sound system, with the crowd tossing pieces of clothing, garbage, and flaming bottles into the arena, already eager for the match to begin.

"And with Lanista Augurahgz comes the being known only as Glomph." A pause, as the audience stood expectant. "And that's literally all we know about the creature. So, good luck, Glomph. We hope you get a sweet song to send you into oblivion."

This time, boos and jeers sounded, with more trash and flaming objects littering the arena perimeter. Rahgz used the viewport controls to zoom in on the pit where his helot waited. The gate remained sealed, though red lights flashed around it to signal an active combatant about to be released.

Rahgz's feathers prickled as the announcers began the final countdown.

"For victory and the Void," cried one.

"Blood, guts, and glory," cried the other.

The crowd picked up the chants as the timer ticked down to zero. A claxon blare resounded across the arena, shaking even the aerie in its lofty position.

"Good luck," Bateesma hollered.

Rahgz held his breath as the Pits opened. Hiliac emerged first, a tall, bony giant with an enormous skull that had large tubes out the sides and back. She hooted and sang as she marched into the arena, painted all over in tribal splashes of lurid paint and shimmering tattoos. She carried several keen blades that crackled with plasma.

Then Glomph rolled into view. At first, Rahgz thought the viewport had reverted to full-distance mode, as his helot appeared to be miniscule compared to the arena architecture. But double-checking the scanners showed magnification to be at four hundred percent.

Glomph sat there, looking like a large ball of mud-colored pudding. Its fluidic form blopped and burbled, with milky eyes roving all over, sharing the turbulent surface area with a smattering of lipless mouths that sucked and puckered at random.

"That's it?" Rahgz asked. "I paid a small fortune for an oversized shit bubble?"

"Pull up all scanners and run every diagnostic available," Mortimer said. *"I need data on that organism, fast."*

Rahgz followed the directions, ordering remote bio profiling and full-spectrum scanning on Glomph. The dashboards started pumping out info faster than he could track, but Mortimer seemed to catch it all.

"Better than I could've imagined," Mortimer said. *"I can work with this, and then some."*

"I hope so," Rahgz said. "What's the plan?"

So far, Glomph appeared content to sit where it had emerged, its mass jiggling and swaying. Its skin glistened with thick ooze.

"Can I borrow your fingers and vocal cords for a moment?"

"Sure, why not?"

Rahgz's awareness once more took a back seat as the implant assumed control of his functions—though this time the separation from his body didn't feel so complete. More like he'd woken up to a foot and arm having fallen asleep, numb and distant from immediate responsiveness.

His hands operated independently, opening a communication channel to Glomph while also packaging arena map files, preset paths, an image of its helot opponent, and several other details Rahgz missed.

"Your name is Glomph," Mortimer said through Rahgz's mouth. "You are my combat property. My helot. I am your master and you will obey every command I utter without hesitation. Do so, and you will consume your fill and more. Absorb all the data I have just sent you, orient, and prepare to move."

Glomph can understand all that? Rahgz asked. *I thought it didn't even have a brain.*

"Not a centralized one," Mortimer said. *"But it has dispersed neural capacity. From the readouts, its whole body contains aggregate nervous tissue that allows for a modicum of self-awareness and intelligent thought and action."*

The implant tabbed the direct channel active again. "Glomph, proceed directly to the arena center. Wait there for your opponent to engage you directly. Allow her to land the first blow. Then enact the element of surprise."

Glomph stayed put for half a minute more, and then started rolling toward the spot where Mortimer had directed it. Rahgz watched it trundle along, hitting walls blindly, veering around corners, and bumping into posts. It triggered several traps along the way, with razor spikes jabbing it and fire searing a swath of its flesh, but Glomph showed no sign of pain as it bumbled onward.

What's the element of surprise? Rahgz asked.

Mortimer chuckled. "Let it be one for you too. I think you'll be pleasantly...er..."

Surprised?

"Exactly."

"Do you always talk to yourself so much?" Bateesma asked, popping into view.

"Gah!" Rahgz jolted back into control of his body as Mortimer swapped mental places with him. "Don't do that. I'm concentrating."

"Sorry." She sounded anything but. "Just sounded like you were being haunted again."

"I am," he said. "Haunted by fears of losing everything if this all goes wrong. Can I please have a little space until this is over?"

Her nose twitched and she scratched at a long incisor, but she kept silent—though she stayed distractingly close as Rahgz refocused on the arena far below.

Glomph had reached the center court of the arena, a wide, round open area ringed with spiked walls and oil-slicked slopes that led down to more trapped pits.

Hiliac closed the distance swiftly on her long, multi-jointed legs. Her song became louder, keener as she reached the center and spotted Glomph waiting for her like an ambulatory dung heap. Baring her blades, Hiliac reached a peak of her solo chorus as she swept up to

Glomph. She poised over it, while Glomph sleepily gazed up at her with unblinking eyes.

With a powerful slash, Hiliac cleaved a blade straight down Glomph's middle, parting its jelly-like flesh with ease. Glomph's insides splayed open for all to see as it oozed across the deck, not looking much different than its outsides. It gave a final jiggle and went still.

Hiliac's song dropped to a mourning bass that Rahgz could feel through the floor of the aerie. His own heart sank while the crowd joined her in marking Glomph's swift demise.

"Is that it? She killed it just like that?"

Mortimer retook control of Rahgz's hands and tabbed a few panels on the dashboard.

"Sampled. Inverted. Now digest."

Shuddering, Glomph swam back together like a bubble bursting in reverse. Hiliac stepped back in surprise, but too slow. A pseudopod shot out from Glomph and latched onto her leg. The rest of Glomph followed, flowing up and over her bony frame until she was encased in semi-translucent, glistening flesh.

They held this pose for a moment. Then Glomph shrank back into its original size, compressing Hiliac inside into a ball of mashed flesh and compacted bone.

Everyone in and around the arena stood stunned and silent.

Glomph spat out Hiliac's blades, releasing a squeak of air. Then it went back to digesting its defeated opponent.

The crowd erupted in roars of shock, outrage, cheers, and denial. The announcers couldn't even be heard over the ruckus as video replays immediately began flashing all over the screens, everyone's datapads and wrist chits pinging madly with updates about the match. The Ghostclobbers joined in the unexpected celebration, thumping around the aerie while Rahgz remained frozen in place, staring down at his helot.

His winning helot.

"What just happened?" he asked.

Mortimer shifted back into the shadows of his mind with a self-satisfied air.

"Surprise. We've got a baby Mawgrunt."

Never take off your robes. Once you've donned the proper lanista garb, consider it your second skin (or carapace, or whatever your species has as an epidermis). This is who and what you are in all circumstances, to all people, in all times. The moment someone spots you not looking like a lanista, they will stop thinking of you as one, and you will be lowered in their esteem. This is why lethal self-defense systems in your showers or toilet are also necessary.

- How to Backstab Friends and Influence Outcomes:
A Guide for Starting Lanistas
Written by Lanista Kel'Chungzi Ewaltsen
Excerpt from Vol 87, Subset 15.34

CHAPTER THIRTEEN

It took Rahgz the better part of an hour to convince Bateesma that, no, getting their brains blitzed by neurosnuff again wouldn't be the best way to celebrate the unexpected win. He really didn't want to wake up from that finding himself fighting in the arena itself. Mortimer agreed, and instead suggested printing up a round of mild intoxicant drinks for themselves, which they now sat around sipping, enjoying a mild buzz. Though Rahgz thought his own nicely humming nerves and pleasant tingles along his feathers came from two other sources: being alive and now having more Bits in his account than he ever thought possible.

As Phara promised, his all-or-nothing wager had been paid back tenfold, catapulting him into the ranks of the truly luxurious.

Even before the bout results had been officially announced and broadcasted, Rahgz had received a rush of direct channel pings from at least a hundred people he didn't know. Sponsorship offers. Bribes. Mating requests. Solicitations to fund one of a dozen charity organizations or another, or obvious phishing scams trying to get him to send funds to poor, orphaned children toiling in labor camps in a far-off asteroid belt.

Mortimer had assigned a portion of his processing power to filtering Rahgz's com channels and keep him from being overwhelmed, promising he would alert him if anything truly important came down the line.

Bateesma kept acting out the bout in the center of the aerie room, with Ukspug acting as a stand-in to Glomph. Through the viewport, Rahgz marveled at the sight of his face plastered across the arena screens, with blood.stream news jesters and jockeys giving meaningless rundowns and reports about him that had nothing to do with reality.

According to Mortimer, the most popular rumors involved Rahgz being a Gnoem in disguise, him being from a wealthy family that was paying his way to victory, or that he was a brokenhearted suitor who became a lanista to win back the affections of a spurned lover.

"*Let them speculate,*" Mortimer said. "*That's the best way to get a ton of profitable attention without any real effort on your part.*"

"What about the story that I eat my own babies in dark rituals to ensure my wins?"

"*All press is good press, even the negative hot takes. The smart ones won't ever believe it, the average person won't care, and the ones who do buy into the rumor mill are too dumb for you to care about anyways.*"

Phara had joined them and now sat primly beside Rahgz, politely ignoring advances by Turrurnium, who whistled and hooted his appreciation of her feminine form. The heat of her body made Rahgz ache to lean in and enjoy a post-bout cuddle, but he refrained, not wanting to ruin his good mood with being spurned.

"Your assessment is correct," she said to Rahgz. "From the analysis I've performed, your helot bears a striking resemblance to early forms of the Mawgrunt barge beast." She projected an image of Glomph's globular mass alongside one of the many public images of the Mawgrunt that were spread throughout the Nexus. The creature had made the *Coffin* infamous, with an endless appetite and boundless growth. It had become an early arena favorite when first introduced, devouring helot after helot until it became so large it now served as tourist attraction rather than a combatant.

The Mawgrunt had actual limbs and a central nervous system, but certainly looked similar in its milky eyes, many-mouthed composition, and the slick, semi-translucent skin that showed off underlying muscle and organs.

Rahgz shook his head, disbelieving. "How in a Gnoem's gnads did we get a mini-Mawgrunt? Pretty sure the captain has never allowed any DNA sampling of his precious barge beast. And if they did, they sure wouldn't be selling it for what I got it for."

"*Luck?*" Mortimer suggested.

"The good or bad kind?" Rahgz asked. "What if someone pawned this podling off on me so I get targeted by security for genetic infringement?"

"*Relax*," Mortimer said. "*I already quadruple-checked the purchase contract. You have no liabilities in the matter and there are no hidden clauses. There's nothing officially linking Glomph to the Mawgrunt, and if anyone notices the similarities, we can claim they're coincidental.*"

"You think people will believe that?" Rahgz rose and paced, hands clasped in front and behind. "I've seen bigger lanistas than a one-win blot like me be taken down by frivolous gossip with way flimsier logic. Whole careers ruined because someone called their methods into question. We're not even in INC space, and people still take sticking to the few rules of the bouts with deadly seriousness."

"*No they don't.*"

Rahgz stuttered. "Of course they do. I've watched the arena my whole known existence. I know that's not much because of the mindwipe, but I've still seen the fallout of people who try to cheat the system."

"*Those are the ones who pushed their luck too far. They were exposed and ousted by other lanistas who all play by the same hidden rules and lack thereof. You think the only competition is between the helots in the arena itself? Hardly. More than half the battle is won before a bout even begins, through sabotage, bribery, popular opinion, and, of course, Bit distribution.*"

Rahgz opened his mouth to reply, and then realized the Ghostclobbers and his assistant were all staring at him. Smiling weakly, he waved off their concern. "Sorry. Just lost in thought. I tend to talk to myself when I'm processing a lot."

Bateesma nodded sagely. "You don't have to pretend. We know you're still being haunted."

"Haunted?" Phara asked.

"You didn't know?" Bateesma flashed a grin. "Your new boss here has a whole gallery of ghosts surrounding his soul."

Phara frowned with two mouths. "Is that something you can help him with? Being a lanista is a holy calling, and I would not wish to see him distracted by the spectral presence of the unworthy."

Bateesma snickered. "Holy? What's holy about it?"

"You're a Ghostclobber," Rahgz said. "I thought anything involving death and the afterlife was holy."

Bateesma rolled her eyes. "Sure, if you want to be anal about it. Turrurnium sure is. Always on about his prayers and well wishes to the dead."

The spindly alien whistled in protest and clacked a pincer.

"But a lot of us Ghostclobbers, like me and Ukspug, we think of our work as more of a form of pest control. We don't have any personal guff against the dead or undead, but when they stick around too long, they tend to cause a lot of harm." She flicked an ear at Rahgz. "Your ghosts don't seem to be hurting you too much. If anything, it sounds like you can have semi-rational conversations with them. The real problem is when you start losing arguments with them. Then you have to worry."

"Fascinating," Phara said, rising and curling her tail around her feet. "Have you ever considered there to be another explanation for the phenomenon you've encountered besides ghosts? The supernatural realm has always seemed to be a messy, complicated theory. Have you not considered Occam's razor?"

Bateesma frowned and ran a hand over the weapons on her belt. "What's that? Like a plasma blade?"

Phara smiled knowingly at Rahgz, who motioned for her to not tease the other woman too much. He wanted them to all get along. He had enough new lifestyle complications to deal with without have to juggle interpersonal drama with his...hm...

What am I supposed to think of these people as now? he wondered. *My crew? My partners? My posse?*

"*Go with entourage,*" Mortimer said. "*Most lanista encourage hang-ers-on to help with their popularity boosts. You snagging a few legitimate Ghostclobbers already puts you ahead of those wannabes who rely on paid lackeys and helot-humpers to pretend they have any real associates."*

Rahgz paid attention as Phara finished explaining the concept of logical simplicity to Bateesma. The leporidean thumped a foot and nodded.

"I get it. But I still say 'you've got ghosts' is a pretty simple explanation to most things." She squinted at Phara. "What about you, sisblitter? What's your story? Why are you here?"

Phara splayed a hand over her slim chest. "My master bought my contract."

"What about before that?"

"I have been an indentured assistant ever since I was hatched." Phara cupped hands as if holding an invisible egg. "My brood was specifically laid to be sold off and pay my progenitor's debts. I have a few more decades of service before I am likely to have any sort of personal freedom."

"That's terrible," Rahgz said. "Maybe we can find a way to shorten that sentence."

"What're you doing?" Mortimer asked. *"She's the perfect hired help and you want to cut her loose?"*

I didn't say that, Rahgz thought. *I just don't like the idea of having a slave.*

"Everyone's a slave to someone or something else. Might as well get used to that."

Phara glanced at him with half her eyes while keeping the others on Bateesma. "My progenitor's debt was in the many millions of Bits. Half of my brood has died in their own service to other owners across the sector, and any debt they failed to pay off is added to the surviving tally I and the few remaining are responsible for."

"It's a really sad story," Bateesma said. "Is it true?"

Phara frowned. "You can view the public records of my past contracts. Even in non-regulated space, my history is well-documented."

"Sure. But records can be faked." Bateesma turned to Turrurnium. "Do your whimmy-whammy on Ms. Scales and Tails here, would you?"

She beamed an overly innocent smile at Phara. "You don't mind, do you? It's just a formality with us."

Phara looked to Rahgz, who indicated that she should go along with it. She lowered her head and hooded all her eyes. "I live to serve."

Turrurnium stepped up to her and held both her hands and gaze. Rahgz thought he looked a little too fondly into her many eyes, while Phara remained neutral in poise and expression.

Rahgz sidled over to Bateesma and spoke with voice lowered. "What are you doing? What's with the interrogation?"

The leporidean stuck her front teeth out at the assistant. "She might be under contract, but there's always loopholes to what she can and can't do. And considering you bought her while a bit out of it, I thought it'd be smart to double-check that she's here doing what she claims." She laid a furred hand on one of his arms. "I don't want her to get close and end up hurting you."

Rahgz blinked, feathers twitching at her touch. "You're trying to keep me safe?"

"Of course."

"Why?"

She grinned. "Because I haven't had this much fun in at least ten TIRDs! I figure sticking with you is my best bet to see some real action. Besides, you're cute."

Rahgz coughed. "Didn't that observation when we first met mean you also wanted to kill and eat me?"

She ear-flicked that concern away. "I only do the mate-murder-meal thing with total strangers. Species instinct, you know? I mostly drop the murder-meal part once I get to know somebody."

"Mostly?"

"Seventy-five percent of the time. On average."

Before Rahgz could work out the logic further, Turrurnium stepped back from Phara and whistled softly.

"She is sincere in her devotion to Augurahgz," he said. "She is the person she presents and wants nothing more than to assist however she can."

Rahgz smiled at Phara, who winked back. At the same time, the side of her multi-featured face that angled slightly away from him scowled up at Turrurnium, while the one closest to Bateesma gave her a vicious glare. The muddle of emotions confused Rahgz, but then all the facial variances smoothed over, leaving her with a serene look.

"What would you wish of me now?" she asked him.

Rahgz thought for a minute about his options. Party more? Maybe so long as no nootropic or hallucinogenic drugs were involved. Yet with this first arena bout over with, it seemed like he should step into his role as a new lanista more legitimately. What would a real lanista do at this time?

"I'd like to meet my helot," he said.

"No you don't," Mortimer said.

Rahgz frowned. "Why do you say that?"

Bateesma and Phara exchanged looks.

"Ghost gossip," Bateesma stage-whispered, which Rahgz ignored. However, he went back to the control panel and pretended to putter around it as he spoke to Mortimer under his breath.

"Because the worst thing you can do is think of your property like a pet. Or, heaven forbid, a friend. Or, as with some of the more obscene lanistas, a lover or anything that can have anything resembling a relationship with you. It is your arena champion, nothing more, nothing less. It exists to serve you and bring you fame, honor, and wealth. It delivers its blood and guts for your glory." Mortimer grumbled. *"You already gave it a name, which is bad enough. Should've let your assistant handle that and never hear it except over the bout speakers. Never speak it. Much less go visit it and start fawning over it like it's an actual lifeform that has any value beyond what it earns you."*

Rahgz cocked his head and massaged his tail in thought, not realizing Mortimer could be so impassioned about something. "Okay. Well, that's one approach."

An angry huff. *"I'm not just making this up to. Listen, Rahgz, let me give you a statistical projection of how it'll go. You'll meet your helot and start thinking of it as a person rather than a tool or thing. You'll start to care about it. Want it to be safe and stay alive."*

"Obviously."

"Yes, but the point is, you're going to be putting it into constant death-matches. It will eventually lose. And when it does, all that emotion you've invested in it will be wasted. What return will you get on it? Absolutely nothing."

Rahgz worked a claw in his teeth. "I should just ignore it then? Pretend it doesn't exist?"

"What you should do is go shout its praises over a few dozen blood. stream interviews. Get some screen time in with all the hucksters who want to use your name and recent victory as a way to boost views and subscribers. Get some sponsors lined up. Talk vaguely about your helot and let the speculations run wild, doing all the hype hard work for you. Then sit back and let it fight the real battles until it loses. Replace it, and do it all over again, just in a higher Bit bracket."

Rahgz pulled up a still image of Glomph engulfing the other helot. "Where are you getting all this from? You talk like you've done this before."

Mortimer snorted so loudly Rahgz felt earwax dislodge inside his ear hole. *"It's called research, you blot. I can do it literally while you sleep. Other lanistas have tried what you're thinking—the whole helot-bonding shtick—and every single one of them became a broken person because of the emotional toll it took on them. Look, if you don't think you can handle it, here."* A roster of medical centers scrolled into view.

"What's this?" Rahgz asked.

"Facilities that provide emotional surgery. They can remove your capacity to feel specific sectors of the emotional spectrum with impressive precision. I'd recommend requesting a swift removal of the ability to develop feelings of fondness toward your helot, whether this one or any future creatures your personal well-being would be connected to."

Rahgz recoiled from the list. "I'm not going to do that. No way am I letting anyone muck around with my feelings."

"Afraid they'll get hurt? Suck it up, blot. Eighty-three percent probability that if you don't, it'll wreck you in the long-term."

Rahgz turned to Phara. "You've worked with other lanistas before?" he asked.

She turned her head so the leftmost face presented to him. "A few, yes. Some longer than others, but this obviously isn't my first time aboard an aerie."

Rahgz went over to her, standing as close as he dared, just near enough to get a whiff of her clean scent. "What do you think about me going to visit Glomph in the Pits?"

"I think it's wise for a lanista to know who or what is representing them in the arena," she said. "Knowing the particulars of your helot will help you command it better."

"Obviously she's an idiot," Mortimer said.

You really need more positivity in your personality overly, Rahgz thought. "Can you set up a time for me to drop by and inspect my helot?" he asked Phara.

She swept a bow, arms curling gracefully over her head. "Absolutely, Rahgz. It'd be my pleasure. I will act as your personal escort and security detail."

"He doesn't need security," Bateesma said, keeping close to Rahgz's side. "He's got us."

Phara eyed the Ghostclobbers, not in doubt, but more in amusement. "Of course. However, seeing as your area of expertise involves non-physical threats, I thought it best to cover all our bases." Another glance at Rahgz. "I'll prep the aerie to fly down to the nearest pit port."

While Bateesma glared at Phara's back as she left the room, Mortimer groused at Rahgz.

"You're going to listen to her over me?"

Rahgz shrugged and murmured. "She smells really good."Rahgz shrugged and murmured. "She smells really good."

"Of course. How could I compete with that logic?"

Rahgz grinned. "You can't."

Treat your aerie like a home planet. It is your center of gravity, where all other things orbit. Never let the common masses see it touch the ground and never invite riffraff aboard, unless you intend to toss them over the edge as a spectacle to appease a bloodthirsty crowd. In fact, it is recommended to keep a small entourage of expendables for just this purpose.

- How to Backstab Friends and Influence Outcomes:
A Guide for Starting Lanistas
Written by Lanista Kel'Chungzi Ewaltsen
Excerpt from Vol 17, Subset 56.23

CHAPTER FOURTEEN

After the aerie docked and they all disembarked, Rahgz followed Phara's sinuous figure down several ramps and into a winding passage that skirted the arena walls. An elevator chute took them down to the pit levels, where helots were normally kept in-between bouts.

They entered a large, sub-arena track and boarded a small rail-line shuttle that whisked them off through the Pits. While most arena battles hosted just one-on-one combat, throwing multiple helots into the fray occasionally helped bolster the blood.stream ratings, and even ten or twelve-on-twelve (or twelve-on-one) bouts weren't unheard of. The barge Pits could hold hundreds of helots at a time, with Pits outfitted for many different species sizes and temperaments.

Environment control kept the track cool against Rahgz's scales, and he enjoyed the close confines of the shuttle, which kept him pressed up by Phara, with the Ghostclobbers at his back. Despite being in it more for the fun and novelty, Bateesma still remained serious in acting as armed backup for their new lanista friend—even though Phara continued to assert that she provided all the security Rahgz would need.

Rahgz studied the woman and her flimsy outfit, not seeing any obvious weapons on her person. However, the short tussle she'd had with Bateesma certainly showed her capable of handling direct confrontations. Hopefully neither she nor the Ghostclobbers would be required to protect him.

Mortimer, who'd been quietly sulking in his corner of Rahgz's brain, finally spoke up. *"You realize there are plenty of people who'd literally murder you to take your place, given half a chance."*

Rahgz tossed thoughts back. *What did I ever do to them?*

"Succeeded."

Fair enough.

The shuttle zoomed by several larger Pits, each being watched over by respective pit bosses who eyed them with jaded wariness. One, a cyborg centipede with a hundred razor-sharp legs looked more fitting to fight in the arena itself but remained sedately coiled up by the entryway to its Pit, ensuring only authorized personnel came and went. Another, a trembling pile of fleshy slag with bulbous eyes and tiny mouths called out crude jokes as they passed by, and its mad giggling followed them deeper into the Pits.

The bosses all served the same general purposes—keep their assigned helots alive and in one piece until their next bouts. Keep out the gawkers and helot-humpers. Kill any would-be saboteurs or assassins. Don't let the helots escape, no matter how much they bargained or begged. And above all, make sure the helots got fed on time.

Most of the Pits looked similar on the outside, with heavily latched and clamped doors ratcheted down tight, some with minimal viewing ports or window slits to allow for easier monitoring of the dwellers. Others were sealed off entirely, with screams alternating with pounding quakes from the other side. A few had glassy paneling and force fields that revealed the inhabitants who watched Rahgz's crew zoom by.

The visible helots would've easily filled all ecological niches of the most interstellar zoo. Most of them started at behemoth size and ranged up to gargantuan, with a few relatively smaller specimens that still would've towered above any of the onlookers. Some were built for speed, moving along the edges of their Pits with whip-quick motions, slinking close to the ground. Others sat hunched amidst piles of bloody bones and knotted tendons, gnawing on the remains of dinner. Others yet stood silent and watchful, clad in massive power armor that hid all their features except for an expanse of one or two scarred limbs.

Rahgz had watched many of these fight in the arena over the blood. stream, and it felt eerie to see them so close and outside of the combat area. One didn't often think about helots beyond the bout. That was for the lanista and pit bosses to handle—and now he was one of them.

At last, the shuttle slowed in a misty stretch of tunnel and Phara indicated they had reached Glomph's Pit. They hopped off and stood before a large chamber door that appeared to have no pit boss in attendance. Rahgz looked around, concerned.

"Where's the person responsible for looking after Glomph?"

Phara double-checked her datapad, frowning as well while the Ghostclobbers took up protective points around Rahgz.

Then a shrill voice from everywhere at once made him jump.

"We are here. Present identification or be dissolved."

"Uh…" Rahgz spun, tail flailing as he tried to spot the speaker. "Present to who?"

Bateesma lunged forward and swiped at emptiness. "Spirits, reveal yourselves!"

Phara side-eyed the other female. "I don't believe we're in the presence of any ghosts."

"Ugh." Bateesma rolled her eyes. "Obviously no real spirits are going to show themselves when a nonbeliever is around. Your negative vibes muck up the whole etherosphere."

Phara smirked. "Then perhaps I would make for a better phantasm deterrent, scaring them off with my aura of disbelief."

Before Bateesma could retort, the mist floating through this section of the tunnel quivered as if in a sudden breeze. It sucked in on itself, forming a denser gray globe that hung in the air, and the orb buzzed with the disembodied voice.

"We are many and one. We guard here as is our duty. Present ID or your corporeal being will be negated."

"Ah," Phara said. "A swarm sentry. I should've realized. Let's do as they say."

Rahgz held up his wrist-chit and flashed his lanista license while Phara also readily projected a number of certificates and regulatory IDs from her pad. She stepped in front of Rahgz and waved as if presenting a celebrity.

"The esteemed victor Augurahgz wishes to inspect his property with all due haste. Your protective diligence has been noted and appreciated, but do not delay him further."

The swarm—Rahgz couldn't tell if it was made of nanites or biological units—wove about for a moment before dispersing. The giant latches on the pit door opened with resounding *clacks!* that deafened Rahgz for a moment. The lights along the top of the bay door flashed yellow, and a buzzer sounded as, with a hiss and deep grinding that he felt in his bones, they began to open.

He and the others stepped back as a fetid gust of warm air swept over them. The pit beyond remained swathed in darkness, while weak lights blinked on along the edges, keeping the center area gloomy. Glomph appeared to have been housed in an open space, like a small cargo bay, outfitted with drainage piping, ventilation grates, and a dump hole for food to be tossed down. Rahgz peered across the seemingly empty Pit, through the gloom, to where another oversize hatch filled most of the wall. This would lead to tunnels that could be opened or closed to guide Glomph to various arena entrances, come time for another bout.

Bateesma whispered, "Isn't there supposed to be a helot here?"

Phara frowned as she studied the area, and they all shuffled inside, looking for signs of their winning creature.

"Perhaps your helot has a camouflage ability and is standing before us, unseen?" Turrurnium suggested. He waved several joints of a long arm and clicked a pincer for emphasis. "Or it has the ability to condense its matter to obscure itself?"

Ukspug spluttered. "Kidnapped? Sabotage! Kill!"

Bateesma nodded and drew a club. "True enough. Whoever stole your helot is going to pay with their lives. You can count on us."

Rahgz held up a few hands. "We can't rush to conclusions. Maybe we just got sent the wrong pit registry, or Glomph got moved so they could do some maintenance and cleaning here. I'm sure there's a perfectly reasonable explanation."

Frowning, Bateesma glanced up. Shock smacked the glower off her face and she dove at Rahgz.

"Look out!"

She barreled into Rahgz, knocking him to the ground just as an enormous object fell from the ceiling. It struck the floor plating with enough force to knock everyone else to their knees or respective lower limb joints. Bateesma ended up sprawled on top of Rahgz, with Phara splayed out over the both of them, her tail wrapped around one of Rahgz's arms.

In other circumstances, he thought, *this would be a dream come true.*

The two women muttered as they disentangled and got him to his feet, brushing off his robe and talking over each other to ensure he was all right. Assuring them nothing had been broken, Rahgz looked past them to the creature now filling most of the Pit.

Glomph squatted before them in all its pustulent glory. While the helot hadn't looked big compared to its opponent in the arena, here Rahgz finally got a better sense of its scale.

The thing's skin maintained its translucent shine, making Glomph look like an ambulatory sac of muscle and organs, with unknown fluids sloshing within. Its skin gleamed with a constant mucus drip, and Rahgz noted that the seepage steamed slightly wherever it touched a surface. Acidic sweat?

Bulbous eyes floated underneath the thick outer lay, bobbing and spinning in place without blinking. The multiple mouths shifting around its body, lipless and toothless, mewling and squelching, burping and gibbering. Whatever Glomph said was either in no language Rahgz's interpretive fish could translate or it was actually meaningless babble. Gaseous emissions from those maws filled the air with multi-colored belches, adding to the sweet-rot stink of the Pit.

Deep within the mud-colored gut of the beast, several bony protrusions jutted out like oversized fingers pushing to break free of the flesh. Rahgz recognized these as the still-digesting remains of the helot Glomph had swallowed in the arena.

This thing could swallow my aerie and still have room for dessert, he realized.

"*Who's a pretty boy?*" Mortimer said. "*You're a pretty boy. We just want to pet you and cuddle you and feed you still-living snacks all day, don't we?*"

Rahgz scoffed. *I thought you were totally against the idea of coming down here.*

"*I still am,*" Mortimer said. "*But since you came anyways, it doesn't mean I can't admire our beautiful little death-dollop here. We couldn't have picked a better specimen.*"

After having plopped from its hiding place on the ceiling—apparently some of its epidermal stickiness allowed it limited wall-climbing ability—Glomph remained inert before them. An occasional squeak or fart escaped its gelatinous form as it rolled in on itself, constantly reshaping.

Rahgz stepped forward, then hesitated. "Does it know who I am?"

"You should be safe to approach," Phara said. "All helots are imprinted with a genetic and psychic profile of their lanista before being released into the arena. It likely hasn't tried to swallow any of us because we're in attendance with you."

"Could've warned us that was possible," Bateesma muttered.

"Oh, but I didn't want to scare you too much," Phara said sweetly. "I know how easily frightened your species can be."

Rahgz shifted so he stayed between the two females just enough to block a direct line of assault. If the two females kept this up, though, his being collateral damage might not be enough to divert their growing aggression.

"Cover me," he said. "I'm going to try and say hello."

"I'll perform more thorough scans while you get acquainted," Phara said. "Take your time."

Rahgz kept all five arms still at his sides as he approached the helot. While the creature's instincts might be programmed to keep its master safe, Rahgz didn't want to provoke it unnecessarily. Lab-bred for combat, who knew how sensitive its fight-or-flight mechanism was?

Glomph jiggled all over as he neared. Its gibbering quieted and it looked like more of its roving eyes were fixed on Rahgz than before. Rahgz stopped a few paces away, close enough to see his reflection in the helot's slimy exterior.

"Hello, Glomph. Um…" Now that he was here, Rahgz didn't quite know how to proceed. "Great job in the arena earlier. I hope you can do more of the same. Otherwise, you know, you'll be killed." He looked back to Phara. "Does it even understand what I'm saying?"

"Intelligent testing is inconclusive," she said, "but considering it responded to your commands during the fight, yes, basic communication should be possible."

"Good to know." Rahgz smiled up at Glomph's nearest eye cluster. "You're an excellent helot, I hope you understand. And I also hope we have a long, mutually beneficial relationship."

"*Ugh,*" Mortimer said. "*Spare me the sap.*"

Rahgz sent a mental flick at the implant. *My helot,* he thought. *I can decide if I want to be nice to it if I want.*

"*Being nice to these creatures is a form of psychological torture,*" Mortimer said. "*They live lives of dread and misery, with brief periods of respite before they're inevitably released by the oblivion of death. So playing nice with them is one huge tease. You're a cruel master to this beast.*"

You can think of it that way. I just know if I were in Glomph's position, I wouldn't mind a bit of kindness and encouragement.

He tossed a question to Phara. "What's a good reward for a victorious helot? Even just a first win?"

"*Letting it live to fight another day,*" Mortimer said. "*That's the only thing you owe this creature.*"

"Food is a traditional nicety," Phara said. "Most helots have a favorite snack or two that they can be treated with after a bout to encourage heightened loyalty."

Rahgz stroked his chin with a couple hands. "Considering Glomph's method of dispatching its opponent, it seems like it would prefer live victims as a treat."

Bateesma raised a furry paw. "Can we just be clear that I am way too cute to be used as a sacrifice?"

"I'm not going to feed anyone to Glomph except another helot," Rahgz said. "I'll order in something big and wriggling though. Give it a target to chase and chomp down."

"Don't sate its hunger overly much," Phara said. "Having its appetite be as keen as possible before the next bout can help enhance its hunting prowess."

Mortimer hummed in thought. *"Recommendation: gene husks."*

What are those? Rahgz asked.

"Mindless clones, vat-bred to have barely any lifespan. They're non-sentient and are used for dangerous jobs like shuttle crash-test dummy lifeforms. They have enough spastic nerve control to run around if let loose and would give Glomph a bit of a chase before it scarfs them down."

"Good idea," Rahgz said, realizing too late he'd said it aloud.

"What is?" Bateesma asked.

Rahgz coughed. "Just an idea I had about feeding Glomph some gene husks."

She narrowed her eyes. "You congratulate yourself on your own unspoken ideas?"

He shrugged. "It's a good way to build self-esteem."

That got him another squint. "You're an odd blot. I'm mostly glad I didn't kill you."

"Fascinating," Phara said, scanning her readouts.

"What did you find out?" Rahgz asked, turning to her.

She displayed the reports, though Rahgz wouldn't have been able to tell if she was showing him antimatter engine diagrams, for all he knew. "Glomph is, in many ways, a living stomach. The secretions across its surface are similar to digestive fluids found and bile. Its musculature is perfect for contracting on a massively compact scale, creating crushing force that few creatures can resist once they are within its grasp. All matter it absorbs is put directly toward self-growth, and hunger is a primary motivator of its actions. In fact, hunger and growth would be the two things that give its existence any real meaning."

"So it's a murder-meal machine? Skip the sprukking?" Bateesma asked.

Phara nodded. "Essentially. I do not believe it even has a way of reproducing outside of the Meat Gardens."

The leporidean shook her head. "Sad. A life without sprukking. I'd want to kill and eat everything I came across too if I couldn't get a good fuck in every once in a while."

Rahgz tapped the side of his head. "So it's like the Mawgrunt in that it could get too big to keep fighting in the arena?"

Phara did some silent calculations. "Even on a regular diet of helots similar in size to the one Glomph faced today, I would estimate at least fifty TIRDs before that eventuality became a concern. And that could be circumvented further by taking our helot to bouts held in larger barges, like those found in more civilized sectors."

"You're suggesting we plan to leave unregulated space?" Rahgz asked. "Move to INC territory?"

She held a palm up. "That would be the logical extension of your exaltation as a lanista. While there are those, yes, who profit by hiding their dealings in unsanctioned barges such as this, greater earnings can be had by being more legitimate as your reputation grows."

Rahgz expected Mortimer to object, so the implant's silence surprised him. "All right," he said. "I guess that makes sense." He shot a silent question Mortimer's way. *So what now? Do what she says?*

An affirmative grunt. *"Now we sign up for the next bout and prove to everyone this win wasn't a fluke."*

Rahgz turned away from the others, trying to keep his worries contained. Sure, he had all this new wealth and status, but that just meant he had more to lose. *What if it was?*

"We'll make sure it wasn't. Give me the lead in commanding Glomph during the bouts and I'll make sure every high-risk wager we make pays out tenfold."

You can guarantee that?

"I've been running the variables and am at ninety-eight percent certainty of the outcomes. We should send our assistant to the Book with double the last wager we made. That sort of show of self-confidence will make people want to bet against us, which will boost our winnings."

"My assistant," Rahgz said, feeling an odd pang of possessiveness. "She works for me, not you."

"Sure. Whatever helps you feel better about yourself. On that note, if you're interested in sprukking that blottisma, I'd suggest getting her a gift sooner than later." A D-Mart inventory module flipped open across half of Rahgz's vision. Items highlighted themselves, ranging from snack packs to floral arrangements to a variety of species skulls with romantic phrasings engraved on the bone plating. *"I've taken the liberty of narrowing down a primary list of items that her species would find appealing."*

Rahgz blinked. *You're helping me woo her?*

"Seeing as we can now afford to keep her contract active for the fore-seeable future, it would be a direct boost to your quality of life goals and overall happiness quotient to find someone or something to fuck on a regular basis. An attractive assistant who doesn't appear entirely repulsed by you is a good place to start. Once you get tired of that one, we can start looking for other options to keep your marrow running hot. Just no helot-humpers, remember? They're always more trouble than you think they'll be."

Rahgz gazed at Phara, admiring the curve of her elongated neck and the bulge of her oviscula.

What if I didn't want to get tired of her, though? Maybe something a little long-term...

"Then you're a sprukking idiot who deserves to die alone."

Oblivious to the internal conversation, Phara displayed her data-pad and pointed out the tally. "This is your deposit for the next match. Details on our opponent will be provided on confirmation."

Rahgz twitched and gurgled. "That much? That's over half the winnings from last time."

"Indeed." She tabbed the transaction to open up a scanner widget. "Most barge captains require even heftier buy-ins from the lanistas they host. Being outside of INC space works in our favor on that, for the time being. Lanista investment in the bout is critical, and too many captains have suffered when a helot master pulls out at the last second. By requiring a significant financial deposit, it greatly increases the chances of you following through on your commitment."

"I always follow-through," Rahgz said.

"Of course," Phara said demurely. "But most barge captains are hardly going to take your word for it. Bits are the real bloodline of the barges."

Sighing, Rahgz pressed fingertips to the pad and bio-signed the contract. He winced as his wrist-chit ticked down the immediate account transfer, though it still left him with more Bits than he'd ever had—not counting whatever wealth he'd arrived on the *Coffin* with.

"Still moaning and bitching about that are we?" Mortimer asked. *"That was your old life. It's dead and gone. Let it go and embrace this new one."*

Another sigh escaped him. "Or die trying."

"That's the spirit."

Turn the arenas into your unspoken allies. Study them like you would a lover and dissect them like you would a fallen foe. Know the layout like your own neural network and if you are unaware of a new map, bribe whoever it takes to know all its secrets before your helot sets foot, tentacle, or claw inside. Ignorance of the landscape will only ensure that your helot becomes part of it, permanently.

- How to Backstab Friends and Influence Outcomes: A Guide for Starting Lanistas Written by Lanista Kel'Chungzi Ewaltsen Excerpt from Vol 10, Subset 93.76

CHAPTER FIFTEEN

"How did Glomph just survive that?" Rahgz peeled fingers off his face, forcing himself to watch the match.

Far below in the arena, his helot slogged down a wide track, pulling half of its body along behind it, attached to the front by a bloody stretch of tendrils. These lines thickened by the second, sludgy flesh congealing and drawing the cleaved portions closer.

Moments before, Glomph had gone around a corner and been almost bisected by a razor wall that sheared up out of the floor. Everyone in the aerie had cried out, expecting the match to be finished along with Rahgz's lanista career. But Glomph had quite literally pulled itself together and resumed crawling ahead, seeking its opponent.

Three of Rahgz's hands were under Mortimer's control, the implant directing the helot via remote prod implants that moved it around the arena without requiring verbal commands. His hands tapped back and forth over the station panels, like odd, fleshy puppets attached to Rahgz's body. After the last two bouts, Bateesma and the other Ghostclobbers had approached him quietly and asked when they should schedule the exorcism for, since it sounded like he'd been possessed by a devious entity when Mortimer vocally ordered Glomph around.

Once the trio had been convinced to put away their blessed acid satchels and purification bludgeons, Rahgz and Mortimer had decided that a body-share deal would be the best way to manage the arena events without making the others worried about his sanity or soul.

"It's persistent," Bateesma said from her perch beside Rahgz's control station. Her huge feet swung back and forth as she eagerly watched the bout, running a nonstop commentary under her breath. "Got to give it credit. I've seen a few gaseous helots that manage that 'mostly killed' kind of survival trick."

"Gaseous?" Phara asked. "I haven't seen one of those fight for many TIRDs. They fell out of favor after most lanistas realized a simple plasma trap or flamethrower obliterates them instantly."

"Those were the best matches ever," Bateesma said, bouncing slightly. "Especially when the gas helot got hit and went up like the most Void-blasting fart in existence. It'd sear off the prusk-hairs of anyone within a mile of the whole arena, and the fireball sometimes would take out the winner in a post-mortem draw. Totally pissed off the lanista who thought they'd won."

Is that something we should be worried about? Rahgz mentally asked Mortimer.

"*I'm concentrating on not falling into another one of those traps,*" Mortimer said in a distracted tone. "*I'm well aware of the risk of a dual death outcome. A lot of helots get booby-trapped so they blow up or become an acidic fountain on defeat, trying to take their opponents with them and rob the other lanista of the victory. Common tactic.*"

Do we have any way to defend against it?

"*Aside from Glomph being impervious to an increasing range of physical damage? Our wits. Or my wits, at least. I had Phara purchase a few microdrones that surreptitiously scan the opposing helot once the match starts, looking for any implants that might be a wide-range self-destruct device. If any threat of that sort is detected, I can ensure that enough of Glomph is protected from the ensuing blast or that Glomph also spits out its dead foes before a device can be activated inside it. It's mostly a matter of awareness and timing—two things I excel at.*"

Wait? You had Phara do that? When?

"*During your last sleep cycle.*"

"What?" The outburst turned everyone's heads his way. Rahgz waved off their attention with one of the hands that remained under his control and resumed talking in his mind. *Since when are you doing things in my sleep?*

"*Since always,*" Mortimer said. "*I don't simulate sleep myself, and I have plenty more processing space in your brain when the rest of it goes into sleep mode. I do a lot of my strategizing then."*

I get that, Rahgz thought, clenching fists. *What I don't like is you interacting with people while I'm unconscious. What if they ask about stuff that I don't remember doing or saying later?*

"I would let you know at the relevant time. By the way, the current moment is neither relevant nor convenient. Do you really want Glomph to get destroyed because you're distracting me?"

Grousing, Rahgz backed off that line of questioning for the time being. He really needed to sit down with Mortimer—metaphorically speaking, of course—and get a few more boundaries in place. Ever since Rahgz let him start using his body for the arena bouts, the implant continued to assume an increased range of control even when Glomph wasn't in combat.

Sure, it mostly proved helpful, such as when Mortimer had been an invisible stand-in for a dozen blood.stream interviews, spouting off terms, tactics, and ancient match details that only a seasoned lanista would know, making Rahgz look like a natural-born expert. Mortimer even claimed to be writing a fake autobiography and "industry secrets" guidebook for would-be lanistas that should add to his ancillary income. In his spare time, of course.

Rahgz refocused on the match as Glomph squeezed through a tight tube that forced its jellied body to shrink to a tenth of its normal width. The helot disappeared, oozing blood and slime behind.

"I'm surprised you hold such an expansive knowledge of arena history," Phara said to Bateesma. "I would've thought you focused more on memorizing battle tactics to apply against nonexistent ephemerals."

"She's quite a fan of helots," Turrurnium said, leaning against a near wall like an oversized broom. "A collector as well."

"Collector?" Rahgz asked.

"Shut your gawper," Bateesma said, rounding on Turrurnium. "That's not your business to go spouting to others."

Glomph's opponent, a spidery helot with venomous mandibles and a thousand eyes, crawled along the walls of the arena, heading the same direction Glomph had been. Rahgz watched the beacons on the arena map draw closer, on an intersection course. However, Glomph had yet to reappear.

"I'm curious," Rahgz said. "What do you collect?"

"It's nothing," Bateesma said, one ear falling to hide half her face. "Really. No big deal. Just stupid souvenirs."

"Helot parts?" Rahgz asked. *I used to eat those to survive not too long ago.*

Bateesma gagged. "Voids, what's wrong with you? I'm not that kind of sicko, carrying bits of the dead around with me. Fuck that to a full spruk session and Gnoems for dinner. No, I just, you know, get mementos of the action. Nothing big."

Turrurnium made a cheeping noise that Rahgz now recognized as his form of chuckling. "She has the full holofigure lineup of the last three hundred helots to fight in the arenas, sanctioned and unsanctioned limited edition runs. Most of them are autographed by their respective lanistas too."

Bateesma's snarl made Rahgz's feathers go flat as possible. "Turrurnium, if I didn't owe you a life debt, I would be skipping the mating part and going straight to the murder-meal right now."

The sticklike alien bobbed his arms in a way that indicated great amusement.

"Nothing wrong with having a hobby." Rahgz smiled at Bateesma, trying to soothe her wrath before it became a distraction from the match. "If a holofigurine ever gets made of Glomph, I'll make sure you get the first one produced. Signed too."

"Seriously?" She stared at him with gleaming eyes, tail and ears twitching. "You'd do that?"

"Absolutely. Only the best for my...friends." The word felt odd still, dropping off Rahgz's tongue, but he had to keep practicing it. That was one of Mortimer's new rules for him. Keep calling people a certain thing, and eventually they'd start believing they were what he wanted them to be.

Looking chuffed, Bateesma settled back into her seat, hands behind her head. "That might just get you the murder-meal part of the session skipped."

Scowling, Phara flicked her tail and hissed softly at Bateesma. "I would appreciate you not threatening to murder and eat my master, even in jest."

"Lighten up, Miss Scales and Tails." Bateesma shrugged and didn't even bother looking over at the other woman. "Besides, if I wanted to have my way with him—whatever way I wanted—not like you could stop me."

Phara angled her faces so the leftmost eyes and mouth focused on Bateesma. That third of her expression went cold, menace in the glare. "Perhaps not with Phara," she said. "But Stekka might have something to say about that."

"Huh?" Bateesma looked to Rahgz and thumbed back at Phara. "You did give her a sane-scan before hiring her, right?" As he fumbled to answer, though, she glanced past him and frowned. "Hey, where's Glomph?"

Rahgz double-checked the control panel map, seeing Glomph's beacon still glowed strong, but the area it marked stood empty. The helot still hadn't reemerged from whatever piping it had gone down. The announcers were commenting on this at the same time as he noticed, talking about the fate of cowardly helots that tried to hide from a match.

Mortimer? Did you lose our helot?

"Trust me. I got this."

You sure?

"Just wait. It'll be fun."

The spidery helot picked its way along, wielding multiple gun and blade deployments bolted to its carapace. These appeared wired into its brain, as the mounted weapons rotated and aimed without any visible control mechanism. Its mandibles dripped purple-green venom, leaving steaming stains on the deck plating as it went.

"Just a little closer…"

The enemy helot eased through an archway, checking all angles as it approached the spot Glomph supposedly waited. Could Rahgz's helot have a camouflage technique after all? Could it spread out its amorphous body so thinly as to blend in with the wall or floor?

As the giant arachnid stepped past a thin drainage ditch, one of its legs seemed to slip and it fell half-over into the gap. Its gun mounts fired wildly as its many other legs anchored and grabbed for purchase. It struggled to turn and bite back at whatever had snagged it.

Which turned out to be Glomph, who boiled and bulged out of the ditch like a sewage backflow. Glomph's quivering form surged around the spider's limbs, wrapping it up with sticky pseudopods even as the other helot fought back with savage fury.

Yet the spider's fangs did little against Glomph's hide, and once a few of its legs snapped off under the pressure, the creature sagged and focused on trying to flee. Several legs separated voluntarily, leaving the arachnid's head and thorax teetering on three final limbs outside of Glomph's grasp.

"Oh no you don't!"

Rahgz's hands maneuvered expertly across the panel, and Glomph responded by vomiting out the legs it had already engulfed, spinning them out to strike the escaping helot's remaining legs. The spider toppled in a spray of gunfire that went askew. Glomph rolled over and once more flung tendrils out, and then the bulk of its body flowed down those lines to swallow the other helot whole.

The defeated creature thrashed inside Glomph for a minute more before finally going still. Glomph's expanded form began to shrink as it compressed the now-digesting remains, though Rahgz knew the helot wouldn't be quite as small as it started this match.

The Ghostclobbers cheered. Phara began fielding multiple channel pings, having routed Rahgz's comms through her datapad so she could filter out the rabble while signing him up for more sponsorships, scheduling interviews, responding to event invites, and keep his fame growing.

As Rahgz stepped back from the control panel, a sudden light pierced the murky depths of Glomph's body. Gasping, Rahgz swiped at the aerie port's magnification control, zooming the viewing window close in on the helot.

Blue flames spouted out from Glomph's body, charring the flesh all over. Many of Glomph's milky eyes swelled and burst from the heat. Miniature eruptions blasted out from within as Glomph shook and melted into blackened piles of molten waste. A distant shrieking resounded over the arena as the helot's multiple mouths opened wide in agony.

Glomph collapsed in on itself, spreading out in an oozing puddle as the flames finally died down and sputtered out. The arena spectators, who had moments before been cheering and jeering Glomph's win, now stood in shocked silence as the helot smoked and sizzled. Remnants of the spidery helot jutted out from the mess like broken struts and beams.

Rahgz stood in horrified helplessness, all the blood in his veins turning to icy sludge full of jagged bits that shredded his guts with every heartbeat. His breathing huffed hollow in his earholes, and the back of his throat got that peculiar pre-vomit taste he tried to choke back.

Then the scattered giblets and globs that once formed Glomph trembled and, ever so slowly, began to ooze back together. Rahgz rediscovered his pulse and his lungs as relief flooded through him and washed away the chilly dread that had threatened to overwhelm him. The pre-puke fumes still tickled his sinuses, though.

"Helot vitals are present," Phara said. "Glomph remains subsistent enough to remain a legitimate victor."

As Glomph began to shift its mangled mass toward the pit exit, the announcers roared over one another across the arena channels.

"And that was a marvelous attempt by Lanista Uryukamu at a double-homicide takedown. Pity that payload didn't deliver."

Howls from the other announcer translated to, "The dread rachnid got the blood and guts, folks! Too bad it didn't get the glory. But what a whammer. I'd feel sorry for any sentient being that tried to eat that belly buster. Lanista Augurahgz is going to need a few laser scalpels and sinew swaths to get his helot put back together in time for the next match."

Rahgz dismissed the control panel and rounded on Phara. "I thought we had drones to detect this sort of threat."

Phara gave him a quizzical look. "We do, on your orders. But Glomph is alive, as predicted."

"Predicted?" Rahgz flung four arms wide. "Who predicted?"

"You did," she said.

Mortimer's phantom hand smacked the back of his head. *"I did. Let's take this conversation somewhere private."*

Trying to contain his rising temper, Rahgz spun on a heel and marched over to his favorite lounge chair, where he flung himself into the deep cushions and activated the seat's noise-dampening field. Phara and the Ghostclobbers became silent figures in the background as Rahgz focused inward.

"What did you do?" he asked.

Mortimer spoke slowly, as if to a spawnling. *"I detected the flame-burst charge embedded in the other helot's core at the start of the match."*

"Then why—"

"I also calculated that Glomph would survive it, and that the spectacle would be a worthy return on the risk invested."

"But you said—"

"I said I'd make sure Glomph remained alive. I didn't say it wouldn't be hurt in the process."

Rahgz lurched half out of the lounger. "You just let it be half-slagged!"

A gentle pat from unseen hands made him bristle.

"It will heal. Just like it did from the last helot's plasma blades. Just like it did from the vorpal tongue piercing the helot before last used. Just like it did with the one before that, remember? The chainsaw infant hivemind? A helot that comes out of an arena match unscathed is a boring helot, and boring helots don't get big wagers put on them. You have to accept that."

Rahgz crossed a few of his arms. "I don't like seeing Glomph hurt."

"It was created to fight and die. What does it matter if it gets wounded along the way?"

Rahgz thrust to his feet. "Because it's *mine*! Don't you get it?"

Mortimer sighed. *"Not really. But I do get that your sentimentality is your greatest weakness and will bring you to ruin if you don't deal with it sooner than later."*

"I'm not getting emotional surgery."

"Doing so would significantly speed up your timeline for achieving your pre-set life goals."

"Maybe I don't mind taking a little longer getting there, then." Rahgz deactivated the quiet zone and rejoined the others. He caught Phara's eye. "I'd like to give Glomph another visit as it recuperates."

"How soon?" she asked.

"How about immediately?"

Bateesma hopped up to his side. "Righto. Let's go."

"Just me this time," Rahgz said, laying a hand on her arm. "I'd like to have a little one-on-one with my helot."

Bateesma licked at her front fangs. "You're not a secret helot-humper, are you? Even if you are, I wouldn't care, but you don't have to hide it from us. We're your friends, and we don't think you going alone is the best idea."

"That's one of the few things she's said that I heartily agree with," Mortimer said.

"Fine. Phara will go with me." Rahgz patted down Bateesma's protests, knowing he needed to come up with a Glomph holofigurine sooner than later. "She's my assistant and official security, after all. You all can wait here. Drinks and food are all on me, as usual. Just don't go too wild. And Ukspug?"

"Blorpup?"

"Please remember which door leads to the waste recycler and which one goes to the storage closet this time."

"Bluppit."

Phara kept giving him piercing looks and side-eyes as they docked and headed to the pit shuttle. Rahgz tried to brush off her scrutiny, but finally faced her as they raced along the tramline.

"Go ahead," he said. "Ask whatever you want."

She made a few false starts before shrugging and holding a hand up. "What's bothering you, Rahgz? First you want to enact a straight-forward embrace-the-Void maneuver, but then when it succeeds, you act like you hate yourself for going through with it. You seem…" She peered at him. "Conflicted might be an understatement."

Rahgz considered telling her all about the implanted mesh and how it was guiding him along these unexpected paths to a more fulfilling life. How all this was happening so fast that it gave him psychological whiplash, and how he had to reconsider all of his priorities and values practically by the moment now. But doing so might endanger the progress Mortimer had unquestionably delivered, even though such questionable methods. He still had to act all this out as if it came from him alone unless he wanted to lose it all.

"I'm not supposed to get attached to my helot, am I?"

Phara's triple eyes bore subtly different looks, from suspicion to confusion to a gentle pity. "That depends."

"On what?"

"On you." She leaned over and rested a hand on his thigh. "Do you feel attached to Glomph?"

It took him a long moment to tear his gaze away from where she touched him. A bit longer to get his tongue working again.

"Let's make it hypothetical that I do. Is that bad?"

She ran a claw up his chest to the soft scales under his chin. "It shows you have something most lanistas lack, empathy. That's something I admire. It's rare and endearing."

Rahgz swallowed, trying not to let his feathers flutter too obviously. "Is…is endearment a winning trait in the arena?"

She smiled gently. "Is winning everything?"

"Fuck yes!" Mortimer cried. *"Voidshit, I hate that dumbass question."*

"I suppose not. There are other things I care about beyond winning." Rahgz couldn't quite make himself look directly at her. "Other people."

The shuttle jolted to a stop by Glomph's assigned Pit. Cursing the poor timing, Rahgz got out, followed by Phara. He looked around, but the mist present at their previous visit was absent.

"Where's the pit boss?" he asked.

Phara pulled out her scanner and inspected the area. "Odd. I'm detecting nano-residue all around us, but inactive. And the door clamps are offline too."

Rahgz scuffed feet on the ground, noting a thick layer of dust that might've been the swarm they'd spoken with before. Then he noted the security lights for the bay door were indeed dark.

"Something's wrong," he said.

Her datapad bleeped and Phara swore so vehemently, Rahgz flinched. "The swarm sentry's been taken out by a localized EMP." She thrust the pad into a pocket and ran for the pit entrance, claws out. "I don't think Glomph's alone in there."

Rahgz helped her yank open a side panel, revealing a manual release gear wheel. They cranked on this together, alternating spins as they forced the doors wider by inches until they stood apart far enough to grant access.

Phara dashed inside, him on her heels.

Glomph's badly damaged bulk squatted in the middle of the Pit. A black-clad slip of a person stood beside it, shouldering an injector needle the size of a rocket launcher. The intruder hefted it, poised to plunge it into Glomph's quivering hide.

Pit bosses must be relied upon but should never be trusted. They are loyal only to their own gain in what they know to be a vital role in arena functions. It is an art unto itself to learn how to bribe pit bosses, giving them just enough to ensure your helot remains secure, but never enough to make them greedy and tempted to overextend their supposed influence.

- How to Backstab Friends and Influence Outcomes:
A Guide for Starting Lanistas
Written by Lanista Kel'Chungzi Ewaltsen
Excerpt from Vol 12, Subset 9.20

CHAPTER SIXTEEN

Hissing, Phara opened her mouth and launched a projectile through the air, striking the stranger in the side. A scream indicated impact, and the intruder dropped the injector needle to clutch at the wound.

Rahgz raced forward, grabbing under his robe for any of the many weapons he carried. Someone was trying to hurt Glomph! Protective instincts surged through him, causing a rattling noise to erupt from the back of his throat while all his feathers stood on end, stiff and sharp.

Phara beat him to the culprit. Claws lashed out, taking off one of the trespasser's upper limbs. The person moved bonelessly, trying to wriggle free, but Phara's tail coiled around them and tightened with a crunch. Another scream, and the person went limp.

Panting, Rahgz stumbled to a stop, trying to rein in his violent impulses. Phara seemed to be doing a fine job of expressing them as she sank fangs into the victim's neck and tore a chunk out.

"Wait," Rahgz cried, a brief clear thought flashing through his mind. "We need them alive." This person likely wouldn't be working on their own and had a boss funding their payroll. The likelihood of figuring out who that was from a corpse were slim.

Too late. The creature spewed a fresh gush of clear fluid from the wounds, pale, shimmering skin now visible through rents in the black fabric that had clothed them. Phara swiftly disengaged and the two of them studied the would-be saboteur who had already gone still on the floor.

"Apologies, master," she said, hiding one set of her eyes. "I acted rashly."

He laid a hand on her shoulder. "Not your fault, and no, it wasn't rash.

I would've done the same if I'd been just a bit faster. We both wanted to protect Glomph." Two fists on his hips, he held two more out, one at the helot and one at the assassin. "We need answers, quickly. How did they get in here? What were they going to do to Glomph?"

Phara turned to face him more with her middle visage. She pulled out her datapad and sensory array and began to sweep the area. As she did, Rahgz pinged the aerie comms and got in touch with the Ghost-clobbers to let them know what had happened.

"Told you I should've come along," Bateesma said.

"Wouldn't have changed anything," Rahgz said. "We'd still have a dead assassin here."

"Yeah, but now who's going to eat the corpse? I don't gulp other people's kills."

"No one's going to eat the body," Rahgz said. "We need it as evidence to figure out who was behind this attack."

"Boring," she said. "Let whoever it is send another killer. I'll be waiting and hungry this time."

Shaking his head, Rahgz went off-comm and focused on Phara, who had wrapped her review of what evidence they had. She'd peeled off the garments from the assassin's head, revealing a slim, amphibious face with narrow eyes, membrane-sealed nostrils, and frilly gills. The hands and feet were webbed, with sinewy muscle under slick, pearly skin.

"Glabrasian," she said, identifying the species. "Known for high environmental adaptability and having absolutely no moral qualms about being bought at the right price. Their kind are saboteurs of the cheaper variety. Dirty, fast jobs. Expendable. About as common as fluxticks and just as revolting."

Rahgz resisted the desire to stomp the creature's head into pulp and string up the body on a pole. He settled for a hard boot into the corpse's ribs. "Any evidence of how they got in? I thought these Pits had video security and other alert systems."

Phara pointed to an observation nodule in a corner of the chamber. "Offline from the same EMP that took out the pit boss. Shoddy shielding. Typical of unregulated barges."

"So, another reason to look to rank up to INC space sooner than later."

"Stole the words right out of my verbal processing unit," Mortimer said. *"People think that INC regulations take all the fun out of the arena games, but they really just make it easier to manipulate the system when there's more structure to it."*

Nodding, Phara crouched to poke at a device strapped to the dead person's hip. "I doubt barge security even knows anything has happened. The assassin had a sample of your DNA and broadcasted it via a genetic amplifier. Glomph must've thought it was you here, which is why it let itself be approached."

Rahgz checked himself over. "Where'd they get my DNA from?"

A shrug and tail flick. "Practically anywhere you've been in the last TIRD. Places you've eaten, public waste repositories. I've heard of people stalking aeries and plucking skin samples from the air recycling outflow vents, and lanista who've sealed themselves inside fully isolated ambulatory habitats for the rest of their existence to avoid this sort of trick being used against them."

"Okay, not doing that," Rahgz said.

He stepped over the body and went to Glomph, hovering a hand over the helot's undulating hide. The damage from the recent arena bout remained evident all over Glomph's form, from deep ruts in its flesh to oozing sores to pockets of half-melted skin that looked like frozen foam and rotting jello. Still, it appeared to be healing rapidly, as Mortimer claimed it would. The helot rolled slightly closer, as if wanting to cuddle its owner. Rahgz backed up a step to avoid contact with the acidic ooze coating its hide.

"What were they trying to do?" he asked.

Phara picked up the injector needle and turned it to display the chem-capsule slotted in the discharge chamber. "Genetic dissolution formula," she said. "Artificial virus that adapts to the target's DNA and unravels it on the chromosomal level. Even Glomph, with its high healing and defense factors, would've eventually have been entirely undone by this."

Rahgz took the injector from her and gripped it hard, enraged that anyone would've attempted to use this on his helot. His property. His champion.

"Someone needs to pay for this," he muttered.

She carefully retrieved the injector from his tightening grasp and hung it from a strap on her back. "We'll figure out who to send the bill to in time, I'm sure. For now, my best recommendation would be to act as if nothing untoward has happened."

"I agree with her assessment," Mortimer said. *"We can't get all worked up over nothing."*

Rahgz pinched the tip of his nostrils. *Nothing? We just barely stopped someone from trying to kill my helot.*

"It happens," the implant said. *"We were lucky here and now Glomph lives to die another day. But an assassinated helot would've given us a sympathy card when we took to the arena next. Look at this as a good thing."*

He turned away from Phara and paced a few steps off, as if inspecting the area. *Good? Really?*

"It means someone sees us as a threat. We're getting attention, which means we're making an impact. Nobody wastes resources, even ones as cheap as glabrasians, on a nobody. Having someone make a move on your property is practically a traditional rite of passage for new lanistas. Ninety-eight percent of all lanistas have had at least one helot offed in the Pits during their careers."

Rahgz blew out a long, controlled sigh. *Can you at least promise me a chance of revenge?*

Mortimer chuckled. *"Ninety-seven point eight percent probability of that being a complete waste of time and resources. Accept Glomph's survival as a quiet victory and just look for opportunities to dole out the same in kind."*

Snarling, Rahgz swiped four hands through the air. "I don't want quiet victories. I want someone to hurt for what they did!"

He paused, realizing that outburst had been verbalized. Glancing over his shoulder, he saw Phara looking back, but more to check if he needed her than out of any real concern. Perhaps many of her previous masters had talked to themselves enough that it didn't bother her. Or perhaps her contract included a "don't ask, don't tell" clause.

"Try to keep a more level head," Mortimer said. *"If ninety-seven point eight percent isn't enough to dissuade you from chasing shadows, then maybe you should remember that only two things are certain in existence, and I can guarantee you'll get both if you go gunning for revenge right now."*

Rahgz swiped the feathers down at the back of his neck. "I know, I know," he muttered. "Death and the Void."

"Pardon?" Phara called from over near Glomph.

Heading back to join her, Rahgz shrugged off her concern. "Just wishing death and the Void on whoever is responsible for this."

She grimaced. "That'd be too good a fate." Phara took one of his hands and squeezed it. "We may never find them, but seeing you keep winning bouts is the surest way to make them suffer."

They shared a look of mutual disdain and a craving for vengeance. This shifted slightly as their eyes remained locked. Rahgz's shoulder feathers started quivering again and her tail slithered around his ankles.

A bleep on both their wrist-chits broke them apart this time. Rahgz flicked his comm on and Bateesma's face projected into the air between them.

"Rahgz, the aerie commline just got a public invite request for you," she said. "Some kind of lanista-only shindig you're invited to. I read all the details but I'm too bored to repeat them. Just figured you should know. Transferring it from the dashboard to your private channel. Hope you don't mind me taking your calls."

Rahgz frowned as the comm blipped off. "Public request?"

"That means someone wants everyone to know that they sent you the invite," Phara said. "Standard procedure for extending courtesies to your opponents while also giving your image a generosity boost."

Rahgz checked his comm screen and saw the new message blinking for him to receive. Tapping it active, he studied the person who flashed onto the display.

He didn't recognize the species immediately, though they appeared lavishly dressed in typical lanista style, with gold threads draped over their conical body, a single eye peering at him from the end of a tubed neck, with frilly wing shapes projecting in symmetrical fashion around its form. These waggled as the lanista spoke in clicks and chirps that translated in Rahgz's mind.

"Greeting, esteemed loser. I am the more esteemed Lanista Volka, and your inevitable conqueror. You have won a few lucky bouts, but your time of dismay and humiliation before all lifeforms aboard this barge draws nearer with each victory. So to help you enjoy what brief majesty you have left before misery becomes your closest companion, you are invited to a luxurious soiree to be held in your honor within my personal skysuite within the next cycle. Please do not send a proxy, as they will likely be devoured or sold at the meat market. We anticipate your presence with all salivations and other desirable secretions."

The image frizzled into a few lines of event details, including the time, sector GPS coordinates, and a RSVP Y/N? holoresponder.

Mortimer made a thoughtful noise. *"My guess is whoever sent this saboteur will also be at the affair. It might even be the same person who's hosting it. By now they'll know their ploy didn't work, and so this invite might be an immediate follow-up to pursue another angle. Or it could be completely unrelated."*

Rahgz swiped the message away without responding just yet. He massaged the back of his neck to forestall another headache. After a second, another pair of hands joined his, and he groaned as Phara masterfully melted away the stress under her fingertips.

He sighed in pleasure and leaned into the touch. "Are things always this complicated with lanistas?"

"More than most people imagine," she said. "This is just the beginning. The more we win, the more we must fight outside the arena to keep you in your aerie, untouched and untouchable. But I believe it will be worth every drop of blood to achieve the glory you are due." Fingers triangulated into a new position that made Rahgz realize even his scales could be more sensitive than he ever imagined. "What do you wish for me to do now?"

"Uh…"

"Ooh, let me," Mortimer cried.

An endless catalogue of sexual positions and erotic acts started scrolling by, ranging from the simple to maneuvers that would require anti-gravity, mag boots, and grappling hooks. Rahgz never knew there could be so many things involving nozzles, tentacles, velcro, and lube.

Rahgz shook his head, trying to disperse the images. This made him accidentally pull away from Phara's hands, and the massage abruptly stopped. Turning, he noted her look of confusion and slight disappointment as she hastily tucked her hands behind her.

"If my touch is undesired—"

"No, no," he said, holding his own hands out. "I really enjoyed it. I'm just still, er…" He waved at Glomph jiggling a few yards away and the body on the floor. "Just not here and now. Too many distractions."

That seemed to ease her consternation and her smile regained some of its former promise. "I understand. Neither helot-humping nor necrophilia are particularly my kinks either."

Rahgz choked and coughed. "Right. Exactly what I meant. Listen, let's table all that for now and handle this event invite. I assume it'd be in poor taste for me to refuse."

A nod as she whisked out her datapad and resumed being the perfect assistant. "Spurning other lanistas, even those who are in direct competition to you, is normally taken as a sign of cowardice. If you are to be seen as an apex predator, you must prowl among their kind without fear."

"But I'm not an apex predator." Rahgz stepped closer to Glomph. "That's what my helot is for."

Phara turned her head slightly, showing off one side of her triple features with a dangerous glint in those eyes. "Not true. It is the muscle while you are the mind. You are in control of the beast that dominates all others—therefore, you are the true predator. Not only do you defeat the opposing helot by proxy, but you conquer all those who bet against you, who cheer against you, and who dream of your demise as a lanista."

Rahgz felt himself standing straighter, a thrill of pride worming through him at her words. "I never thought of it that way."

Her cunning grin made his tail stiffen. "You will. Sooner or later, you will. It's inevitable."

Returning her grin, Rahgz brought up the other lanista's invite and hit the RSVP Y option without further hesitation. Phara nodded approvingly.

"I'll make the proper arrangements. I assume you'll want the Ghost-clobbers to attend with us?"

Rahgz looked over at Glomph as an idea tickled his brainstem and made him actually eager to attend the get-together. "You, me, them... and one extra off-the-list guest."

Everyone—myself excluded—has at least one weakness. Learning to spot it and exploit it in others is always a priority. And as for your own flaws? Don't waste energy defending them. Simply preemptively strike and never give your enemies the chance to access whatever chinks exist in your armor.

- How to Backstab Friends and Influence Outcomes:
A Guide for Starting Lanistas
Written by Lanista Kel'Chungzi Ewaltsen
Excerpt from Vol 8, Subset 34.24

CHAPTER SEVENTEEN

"Ukspug, you know the rules about these sort of things?" Bateesma patted down a curl of errant fur on one ear as she walked beside Rahgz.

"Blurp." The other Ghostclobber grumbled at her heels, having been the target of her nonstop lecturing since they'd disembarked from the aerie.

"No trying to digest other guests."

"Vlup."

"No preemptive self-defense."

"Gorble."

"And no making me look bad."

"Splsss."

She rounded on him, almost smacking Rahgz across the face with one ear. "You do too! Last time we went to a party together I had stains in my fur that the sonic scrubbers couldn't get out for weeks."

"Hlup-up?"

"No, that wasn't me trying to make a fashion statement and you know it."

As Bateesma went back to primping, Rahgz eyed the neighborhood, half out of growing paranoia, half out of awe.

Aside from the visits to the Pits, he'd been cloistered in the aerie since waking up on it a newly minted lanista. And his living situation prior to receiving the implant mesh had ranged from "in the sewer channel" to "above the sewage drain" to the lofty abode of "in the sewage bins." Hardly prime real estate. Mostly he'd drifted around the sectors, scrounging for scraps, being chased off by security when he loitered too long, and generally trying to be as invisible as possible.

If he'd ever tried to sneak a nap on the sidelines of this sector, though, he likely would've been tossed into the nearest incinerator, treated as the literal garbage the denizens would've seen him as.

Rearing dwelling towers soared from the floor to the barge ceiling, with glittering sky bridges strung between them. Cleaning drones and sani-bots constantly patrolled the streets and scrubbed the airways, removing the slightest speck of grime and showing off the barge's rarely-seen gray-green deck plating. Aeries were docked or hovered high above all around, a panoply of alien design with everything from golden swoops of organimetallo threading to pulsing biospheres to thorny vestibules to glassy orbs full of crimson liquid, wherein swam dark, wriggling shapes.

Security tramped about from all directions, monitoring the droid-cams, manning the plasma turrets, and glowering at all passersby. Rahgz cringed at every sensor sweep that passed over their group, expecting for an alarm to blare and for them to be surrounded and hustled out of the area as trespassers—or summarily executed. That never happened, to his surprise, and they headed toward a central spire that gleamed like polished ebony, with rusted coils banded about it.

They could've flown the aerie straight to the tower and disembarked there, of course, but Phara and Mortimer had been unknowingly unified in asserting that strolling through the sector would be more of an audience booster. Rahgz didn't see anyone specifically gawking at them, but Phara assured him that she detected at least several hundred nanocams recording their passage. Rahgz's name was already seeing significant rating boosts on the blood.stream commentaries, with topics of discussion ranging from his clothes to the dye job on his feathers to further speculation on his origins.

"It's actually quite fortuitous that you have severed all ties to your planet and family of origin," she'd said while helping him dress and prep for the event.

"That wasn't voluntary," he'd said while studying himself in the aerie mirror wall. While he still recognized his form and features, the gaudy robe made it appear as if a stranger stood there in his place, pretending at a wholly different life. "I did explain the genememetic assassin, right?"

"Yes, but still," she said, "while it's hardly anything that would keep you from competing in the arena, family drama, secrets, scandals, and whatnot can be a drag on many lanista reputations. Any dirt they could dig up on you would just be ammunition we'd have to defend against in jousting for fame and glory. But for you, it literally doesn't exist to be dug up. You're a tabula rasa. Your destiny is being made from scratch."

Rahgz frowned at the memory, wishing he wasn't an entirely blank slate to himself as much as everyone else. Ever since accepting the invite after Phara's little motivational speech, he'd regretted the whole affair.

This is going to end badly.

"*That's a real cheery mantra you've got going on there,*" Mortimer said. "*Why don't we drink some poison before we even get there and make this a full-on self-fulfilling prophecy?*"

Rahgz twitched as another drone, bristling with anti-loitering probes, shot by just overhead. *You still think this is a good idea?*

"*It's less an issue of being good or bad and more of being absolutely necessary if we're going to take the next step into lanista history. From the helots to the arena to the aeries, it's all one big game. One big competition that we have to play and win—and a big unspoken rule is you don't sit on the bench when it's your turn to play in the spotlight. Want to hear about the last big lanista that started to act like a social hermit?*"

Who? Rahgz asked.

"*I don't know. Which is the point. Those kinds of lanistas are forgotten almost immediately. They may win for a bit, but they never make any real impact. No names anyone cares about. No reputations for anyone to be envious of. The instant they hit a losing streak, they get tossed into the trash heap of our collective brain bins.*"

I understand, he thought, *but I don't want to be making a reputation as the newbie who sticks his flagellum in his mouth every time I talk.*

The group shuffled to the side as a googlepede bioform raced down the street, countless legs churning it along, its hollowed-out carapace carrying hundreds of passengers to an unknown destination.

"*Are you kidding?*" Mortimer asked. "*That was this one guy's whole shtick. Orvarium, the Crested Gabadoon. A certifiable dumb fuck and pathological liar who dressed up in the fanciest swag and acted like everyone was his personal coxsucker. Couldn't open his gutmaw without saying something more idiotic and obviously false than the last time—but for some reason, he had this cult following of people who worshipped the farts he emitted. And being a gabadoon, he emitted a lot.*"

Still, I'd rather not be known for that, Rahgz thought. *I'd prefer a more positive reputation.*

"*I can help you handle any of the talking,*" Mortimer said. "*Just authorize me for conversation control and you'll be the smartest person in the room on any topic.*"

Rahgz touched his throat and nodded. *All right. Done. Just be kind to the vocal cords.*

"*Think of it this way. I'll be doing all the hard work while you get to eat and drink and actually enjoy the party.*"

Assuming someone doesn't try to kill us while we're there.

"*And that's why we have your friends running interference. Speaking of which, let's have Bateesma stop cleaning her pocket-pistol, shall we?*"

Rahgz glanced over to where Bateesma made a show of assembling and disassembling a tiny gun with one paw, a finger-juggling act that would've impressed him if it didn't keep drawing the eyes and sensors of every nearby security guard and bot.

The next time Bateesma flourished the gun parts together, Rahgz gently placed a hand over it, sandwiching it between their palms.

"That should be good," he said. "You don't want to intimidate everyone too much."

"No such thing as being too intimidating," she said, bouncing slightly. "But this is just exciting, and my trigger fingers get twitchy when I get excited. Everything starts looking like a target."

Rahgz circled a deep breath through his nose and out his mouth.

"Once again, we're wanting to get in and out without anyone opening fire on anyone else. We're going to make a good first impression, try all the tasties we can stomach, and then leave and send a nice thank-you drone."

She licked her incisors. "You can also make a strong impression by bolting the competition between the skull plates and hoofing it as soon as everyone's dead. Nobody would see it coming."

"Actually," Mortimer mused, *"our host is likely anticipating violence and will have exorbitant self-defense measures in place."*

Rahgz stated this in his own words, deepening Bateesma's glower.

As she scowled, her bushy brows almost hid her eyes. "Why does it feel like the more famous you're getting, the more boring you are? Data this. Facts that."

"Because I want to stay alive long enough to enjoy my fame for a while. I would prefer you do the same. If we don't survive tonight, how will I get you that signed first-edition holofig?"

"Fine." She secreted the tiny gun somewhere on her furry person. For all Rahgz knew, she had it tucked into her ear. "Hey, Ukspug?"

"Orgle?"

"A hundred Bits says I can eat more than you at this shindig."

"Florp!"

Rahgz exchanged a long-suffering look with Phara. They soon rounded a corner and came upon a broad elevator dais at the base of the nearest spire. Mounting it as a group, they stayed close as the dais hovered and then zoomed upward, spiraling around the tower ever higher, passing roosts and arches, shielded portals, and nest pods. They shot by whole aquatic floors, and then another section that appeared engulfed by a living thunderstorm that shot out lightning bolts in their direction.

Rahgz jerked back as the air sparked and stung, but Phara whispered in his ear.

"It'd be polite to return the greetings. That is Lanista Xxxeershlll, hailing from the Torvoli System."

One of Rahgz's hands reached out to press a vocamplifier mesh on the side of the dais railing, and Rahgz's lips moved of their own accord.

"Salutations, magnificent foe," Mortimer spoke through him, voice echoing over the booming storm. "We are honored to survive your presence. May your eddies be unending."

Another thunderbolt and boom shook the elevator as they ascended. The dais docked at the tip of a metalloid ramp that jutted out from the spire's side. Phara led the way, closely followed by the Ghostclobbers, and Rahgz at the rear. A shimmering forcefield blocked an arch at the end of the ramp, but this fizzled out as they approached.

They passed into an expansive suite that could've held a dozen of Rahgz's aeries. With lofty ceilings, walls lined with frothy fountains, full-spectrum artwork animated in every corner, and tables laden with intergalactic and interdimensional spreads that were so exotic, Rahgz had a hard time telling where the digestibles ended and where those noshing on them began. Great platters of writhing tubes were being savaged by a horde of toothy dungars while a squat elegorp plucked juicy glands off a giblet tree on the other end of the table. Along another stretch, live muchollas were being speared on the run by diners who dragged the kicking, squealing creatures over to be devoured.

In a far corner, a huge machine made of innumerable coils and an expansive wire mesh kept spitting out tiny orbs of rainbow-hued electricity which were being sucked up into the power spigots of a cyborg collective. Down a broad hall, Rahgz glimpsed a series of large globes, each holding a different colored, glowing liquid that attendees were taking turns sipping from, bathing in, and contributing their own secretions into.

Above them all, from one end of the space to the other, the ceiling flickered through scenes from the arena, highlighting particularly violent moments from helot matches, both recent and ancient. Rahgz kept checking to see if Glomph might make an appearance, but it was hard to tell with the rapid-fire images.

A dozen lanistas were supposed to be in attendance, and Rahgz spotted several straight away, but they all appeared to have brought plenty of their own entourages to crowd the place. Phara had briefed him on a few of the bigwigs he should pretend to know about, including his host, but Mortimer also highlighted each one as they appeared in his field of vision and tagged them with a data-cloud for Rahgz to peruse. The implant also narrated a quick summary of the nearer ones.

What looked like a pile of rocks draped in tatters of silk was identified as Gomorgra the Uneroding. *"Its helot is literally a chip off the old block,"* Mortimer said. *"A biomineral fusion grown from its own MNA into the size of a mountain back on its home planet. Every time the current iteration gets obliterated in the arena, Gomorgra just goes back and hammers off another hunk to take its place."*

The corneal targeting system blipped over to a gasbag bobbing near the ceiling, held down by a silver net attached to anchoring drones. Glossy tendrils hung down from the bulbous form, where a riot of colorful fumes roiled inside the semi-translucent flesh.

"That's Lanista Welfofalaoloa Shhuppoofeelio. Don't try to shake any of her tendrils, even if they're offered for such. Immediate neurotoxin delivery, deadly to all known sentient species. Her helot changes every few TIRDs, and she rotates new ones in to try and throw opponents off when they want to study her tactics. But she picks a lot of them up from slave planets and promises them freedom if they can win a hundred bouts in a row. So far, none of hers have ever quite made it that far."

The eye-target switched to a giant bestial skeleton held together by metallo-wires, with mechanical augments in the hollows of the skull, and cybernetic limbs coiled in the depths of the ribcage and pelvis. Nano-spikes thrust out from its spine, and sensors blinked all over the ambulatory museum piece.

"That's the tenth incarnation of Sire Lanista Evo X.I Loe Flx. It has about a thousand fossilized remains it uses as shells for its mechorganic self, depending on the occasion. A few of them even came from prior lanista opponents who lost their skeletons in ill-advised wagers on arena outcomes."

Rahgz plucked at his arm feathers. *Lost their skeletons? Is that even allowed with the Book? I thought it was just Bit betting. And how do you know that since those wagers were all anonymous and cryptosealed?*

Mortimer gave a mental shrug. *"I think Flx boasted about it in one of the countless biographies I've scanned since I activated. I don't recall exactly. Most Book activity is limited to Bits, but you can wager just about anything of value with a private arrangement."*

The Ghostclobbers had slowed as they gawked, letting Rahgz catch up. He joined them, half-listening to Mortimer's ongoing lecture while nudging his companions forward.

"Let's mingle," he said. "Don't stray far and keep your comms linked to mine and Phara's. If any trouble starts to go down, we want a quick out, all together."

Bateesma pointed at a spread off to one side. There, attendees were noisily thrusting tongues and fingers into an array of plump meats and glistening bladders laid out on low stands and floor mats. "What are they eating? It smells delicious."

Phara flicked her tongue out, tasting the air. She grimaced and shook herself slightly. "That's not food. Those are other attendees. And they're not eating."

Bateesma squinted. "Then what...oh. Oh!" She rubbed her paws together. "Well spruk the Void and give me some room. I didn't realize it was going to be that kind of party." She nudged Rahgz with an elbow. "You can cover any damages, right?"

"No damages please," he said, even as she hopped off to sample the offerings.

Turrurnium whistled low. "I'll make sure she behaves herself."

He and Ukspug hurried after the leporidean, who aimed for a terrified-looking terpoid who was rapidly trying to close its shell and protect its exposed innards.

Rahgz watched after them with trepidation until a scaly hand slipped into the crook of two of his elbows. Phara held him close, sharing her warmth. Yet her nearest visage looked stern, gaze shifting from one person to another in open suspicion.

"Stekka on duty," she said. "I will protect you against all harm."

"Stekka?" He frowned as she tugged him hard to avoid a bristling ruk-ruk that slithered past. "I thought that was your secondary nomenclature."

"It is when that forebrain is ascendant," she said, words taking on a harsher undertone. "Phara is your assistant. Zolma is your pilot. I am your security."

When what she said clicked in his mind and neurons started shooting off warning flares, Rahgz mentally reached for Mortimer. *Voidshit and spruk a Gnoem. She's a multID?*

"You didn't realize?" Mortimer asked.

Rahgz swallowed a choke. *You did? And you didn't tell me?*

"It's in her contract and personnel profile. Makes her far more resourceful as she literally brings multiple skill sets to her service."

Rahgz became keenly aware of how tightly Phara—or was it Stekka?—held him as they strolled through the party. Her muscular limbs, which he'd imagined wrapped around him many times were now potential weapons that could throttle the life out of him if he said the wrong thing or looked at her the wrong way. Her triplicate facial features, which he'd found alluring and exotic, now made him think of fragments of a shattered mirror, all knife edges and unspoken threats that could flay him open.

MultIDs can be psychotic serial killers. Subversive INC terrorists. Barge-blasters who are just waiting to open the nearest airlock and shove you outside because one of their minds literally doesn't know what their other ones are doing.

"Or they can be employees just trying to get a pay raise with value-added services that one brain alone isn't equipped to handle. Yes, people juggling multiple identity overlays in an organic brain can certainly go a little crazy, but there are some decent ones as well. Don't judge a whole sentient sector because of a few that went off the rails." Mortimer pulled up a data overlay of Phara for him to review. *"Besides, I certified that her*

multID integrations are relatively safe. Though you might want to give her a violent outlet from time to time to avoid repressive overload for Stekka. She needs to let off the occasional steam."

Rahgz contained a whimper as he was half-dragged through the crowd. He waved the data readout away, making him jerk against Phara's grip. She glared at him.

"What is the source of your distress, master?"

You are, Rahgz thought. Wisely, he kept that outburst sealed away. "Just a little crowded in this place. I'm a bit snacky, so maybe you can give me a little space to grab a bite?"

"Negative," she said. "I must maintain optimal distance to protect your person, and my securing of your limbs gives you three with which to feed yourself. If desired, I will also transport edibles to your mouth."

Rahgz stopped and disentangled his arms from hers, forcing himself to match her glare. "Phara, or Stekka, or whichever one you are right now, my species is very particular about personal space. Refusing to give it is grounds for immediate termination of your contract without appeal or backpay."

His assistant looked ready to bite his face off. Rahgz wished he'd planned on how to protect himself against his own entourage, but that hadn't really occurred to him until too late.

Then her expressions blanked and she turned to face him with her middle eyes. "Apologies, Rahgz. With my limited knowledge of your kind, I was unaware of the taboo nature of physical proximity. I will fully respect that moving forward."

He couldn't help but notice the hurt hidden behind her professional demeanor. Sighing, Rahgz took her shoulders in a few hands. "I trust you to protect me, no matter what. I'm still getting used to all this and my nerves are already jittery. You and I are still getting our bearings with each other, but I'm still glad you're here. I wouldn't want to ever do this alone."

That lessened her distress somewhat, though she kept her arms tight to her sides, making him ache for her touch again—despite its underlying threat.

Then she gestured to something behind him. Rahgz turned to see his lanista host gliding toward them. The other lanista stood atop a hover-disc, the crowd parting before its approach.

Its conical body rose like a miniature spire of its own, with its eye wavering at the end of the extended neck, wings fluttering on either side. As it neared, Rahgz could make out wide ridges that circled its body, visible through its golden raiment. These pulsed with a whitish fluid that gave its voice a gurgling background murmur.

"Greetings, Lanista Augurahgz," it said as the hoverdisc stopped right in front of him. "I am delighted beyond my capability of physical expression that you decided to attend this simple gathering."

Rahgz crossed several arms in a salute, having been warned not to bow or show any other signs of subservience. "Greetings, Lanista Volka. It is my obvious right to be in this company, though I recognize your graciousness in spending the Bits necessary to fill our bellies and gizzards. I look forward to the day when our helots seek mutual vanquishment in the arena and my preemptive condolences on your defeat at that time."

And switching over to you, he thought, as that was the extent of his verbal coaching with Mortimer and Phara.

His lips and a few arms went numb as voluntary control over them was diverted to the mesh. Mortimer projected a sense of glee as he took the controls.

A couple other lanistas stood nearby, within obvious auditory range—though Mortimer gave Rahgz a silent warning that almost everyone in the room could be listening in via long-range sensors, nanodrones, and their own enhanced biological capacity.

Volka's wing fronds chimed as they shivered. "You are an unknown element in this great competition that spans universes and eons. Your name is so fresh it might as well still drip with womb-milk. Yet you navigate the arena like you were born to it."

Rahgz's hands knotted together into a complicated symbol, representative of universal and absolute indifference.

"I care little about births, whether you were hatched, popped out of a cyst, or bubbled up in the vats. Death is all that matters. The death of all helots that oppose mine."

Volka began to rotate on its hoverdisc, its eye remaining fixed on Rahgz while its body steadily turned, wings swinging like gaudy vent filters.

"I would request the verbalization that explains your swift ascension to our ranks," it said, "and your ongoing, statistically improbable winnings you have exhibited. Is it through sheer stirrings of the Void or is there some plucking of fateful strings that the rest of us insofar lack the sensory nodes necessary to envision?"

"You're asking if I'm either very lucky or very skilled?" Mortimer/Rahgz chuckled. "Why does it have to be one or the other? Maybe I'm a complete anomaly. The perfect lanista who can win without trying just because I'm a one-in-a-gajillion odds embodied in this flesh."

Volka stopped turning and its neck telescoped out further, putting its great, lens-like eye right up in Rahgz's face. Rahgz was glad, in that moment, that Mortimer had taken control, as he would've had an almost impossible time not jerking away from the aggressive display. It might've even triggered his fake death instinct.

The lanista trumpeted loud enough to echo throughout the room, even over the music thumping across the walls.

"You are a fraud!"

You may be tempted to give many grandiose speeches or make many hyperbolic threats. By all means, do so. Just remember that whenever your mouth or other orifice is active, you are making yourself a highly obvious target and opening up a gaping hole into your body at the same time.

- How to Backstab Friends and Influence Outcomes:
A Guide for Starting Lanistas
Written by Lanista Kel'Chungzi Ewaltsen
Excerpt from Vol 67, Subset 3.20

CHAPTER EIGHTEEN

The lanista edged closer, almost near enough to hit Rahgz's face on the edge of the hoverdisc.

"You are a pathetic know-nothing who has glutted upon false glory," it continued. "Who funded your rise to questionable fame? Who whispers secret instructions in your ear? For you are not one of us, nor shall you ever truly be. A black mark upon the barge bouts, I name you. Your name is an ill-wind that blithers in our ears. Slither back into your den and weep for the humiliation that will be heaped upon your empty skull." Volka retracted its eye and began to spin again. "And please be sure to sample the selog fermentslush in the vat behind you. I am told it is quite delectable. Alas, I am not in possession of the sensory nodes required to indulge in the biological pleasures I offer you here."

With a whir, the hoverdisc started off again, whisking the lanista back through the crowd which thronged around it, one half trailing after the host while others all turned to stare at Rahgz, murmurs and whispers and outright laughter directed his way.

Scales and feathers burning at the mockery, Rahgz scowled in the backseat of his mind. *Did that thing just invite me here to insult me to my face and then suggest I try the wine?*

"Basically," Mortimer said under his breath. "Which is what I expected. Shall we make the rounds and meet a few other esteemed guests?"

Rahgz snarled. *I'd rather not. This is obviously intended to be a complete shitshow with me as the star. We should bail.*

"And miss all the fun and good food?" Mortimer made a show of going to the nearest table and plopping a few wriggly chasmberries into Rahgz's mouth. Then, just as Volka had suggested, he poured a liberal flagon of selog and downed it in several swigs. Even from the mental distance, Rahgz felt that burn all the way down, making every limb tingle and washing him through with giddy vertigo.

*Easy with the slush, h*e said, as the world wobbled. *I thought we were trying to avoid acting stupid.*

"Your body feels it," Mortimer said, pouring another flagon, but not sipping from it just yet. "I, however, being a tech-based sentience, am running my processes in tandem, but separate from yours."

Phara appeared at Rahgz's elbow. "Are you all right? I know that was a rather harsh introduction, but I don't want you to lose focus."

"Perfectly fine," Mortimer said, letting Rahgz's body sway a bit. "Let's see who else wants to bump hands and shake uglies."

So began an hour of constant mingling, with Rahgz meeting lanista after lanista, all of whom Mortimer already knew intimately based on extensive research and dark-channel digging. The implant spouted off names and acted like an old friend to everyone, evoking familiarity to even the grungiest, grumpiest of the lot. This act caught most off-guard, soliciting a few friendlier responses mixed with lingering suspicion.

Most of the lanista peppered Rahgz with questions about his heritage, his fortune, his love interests, or sibling rivalries. As Mortimer side-stepped those questions with vague answers that never provided anything of substance, other questions surfaced about his bathing habits, childhood pets, art tastes, or his favorite blood.stream subscriptions. Mortimer waxed eloquent on these seemingly innocuous inquiries, giving expansive details that changed with every answer, no matter how many times the same question was put forth.

Inwardly, Mortimer moaned and groaned in delight as he sampled the fare from every table, from the dark matter-laced pobble eggs to the carbonated jet-juice that had an aftertaste of afterburner.

Would you take it easy? Rahgz asked. *It's still my body you're using. I don't want to be sick for a whole TIRD after you eat some rotten horkbake.*

"Just leave me in control until after I flush your system," Mortimer said around a mouthful of torvolini sprigs. "You won't be bothered by a thing."

Except you obviously angling for more time running the show.

"Am I doing a poor job? Would you be doing any better?"

I wouldn't even be here in the first place.

"Precisely. So just relax and enjoy the view. I promise to make a good show of it."

Rahgz grumbled but had to admit the mesh would likely navigate this event far better than he could've. By now, anyone who observed him expected him to be quite inebriated, which Mortimer played to their advantage. He tossed out random facts and hints here and there, all completely fabricated nonsense, but which people took note of with rapt attention.

They aren't really believing what you're saying, are they? Rahgz asked.

"Maybe a tenth of it," Mortimer said, hiding a grin. "But the only true thing they know about you is your name, Augurahgz, and half of them think that's a pseudonym anyways." He sauntered over and pretended to study a hard-light statue of several of Volka's past helots, each in their death throes.

So what's the point of all this? Rahgz asked.

"Buying time," Mortimer said.

To do what?

"Ever since we got here, I've been detecting a lot of back-channel chatter on the comms," Mortimer said. "There's a private network active that's underlying normal broadcasts. I've been trying to hack it, and just got access thanks to that last lanista's less-encrypted comm unit. Sooner or later, one of them was going to give me the key to listen in."

What're you talking about? A private network? Who's on it?

"Everyone but you. And they're all asking each other the same thing."

Which is?

"Who is Lanista Augurahgz?" Mortimer chuckled to himself. "Everyone we've been talking to has been working off a prearranged script. We've been dealing with one extended interrogation from a dozen different angles."

So they're all in on it. Trying to discover...me? What about me?

Mortimer sniffed and made Rahgz's feathers frill. "Anything. From what I can glean, they're all as in the dark about you as the general public. And they hate you for that."

Hate me? What've I done besides win a string of bouts so far?"

"Everyone comes from somewhere. At least, that's what they're used to. Even the most aloof lanista from the darkest corner of the universe, or from the most obscure dimension has a history that can be picked over. Used against them somehow. You don't. Their problem is they think you're hiding the truth when, in reality, it's as obfuscated to you as it is to them."

What do we do?

"We do what I've been doing: use their increasing curiosity and frustration to our advantage. Sow some confusion, make a quick exit, and leave them with more questions than before. That'll infuriate them even more and a few will likely make a mistake and overreach trying to get back at you for revenge. They expose themselves; we take the kill shot inside and outside of the arena."

Revenge? For what?

"As Volka said, for being an ill wind."

I don't like the sound of that.

"That's the point." Mortimer turned and waved Phara close. "Phara, summon the aerie to pick us up here. I don't want any delays when we leave. Tell me when it's docked."

She ducked her head, murmuring. "It's already on its way. I anticipated unknown trouble and thought it prudent. ETA three minutes. I hope that was not too presumptuous."

"Good girl. You get a raise." Mortimer switched channels to the one Rahgz had established with the Ghostclobbers. "Hey everyone. You all sane and sober enough to hear me?"

Bateesma's hysterical laughter came over the comm and somewhere from across the room at the same time. Turrurnium's shrill voice quickly replaced hers.

"We are intact and mobile," he said. "What is your wish?"

"Zip up your pants and get ready to make a swift exit on my signal."

"Understood. What signal would that be?"

"An obvious one."

I have the same question, Rahgz said, riding his body like a passenger on a wayward shuttle.

"Same answer," Mortimer said.

Rahgz groused in his mind while Mortimer steered through the crowd, Phara at his side, monitoring the aerie's arrival. Mortimer made a casual show of brushing by a few lanista they'd talked with previously but snubbed or outright blocked their requests and pings for further conversation. Mutters followed in his wake, and by the time he stopped near to the entrance they'd come in through, many dark looks were being cast his way.

Mortimer took his time chewing and swallowing another mouthful of husknuts, chasing the fronds with a swig of slush. The Ghostclobbers arrived, Bateesma held up between the other two. He waved off their questions and simply instructed them to stand close.

"Aerie has docked and is primed for immediate takeoff," Phara said.

Rolling Rahgz's shoulders, Mortimer turned and spread all five arms. Clicks and squeals sounded as his voice emitted from every personal comm unit at once.

"Greetings, fellow lanistas. Gracious of you to have me as the darling of your party. Rude of you to leave me out of the private chatter."

Shouts of surprise and wonderment responded, with some scattered denials.

"Oh yes," Mortimer continued. "I've been well aware of your little hush-hush conferencing behind my back the whole time. Even then, I was generous with my time, receiving little but backhanded insults and outright slander to my face. Of course, I wouldn't expect anything less, if any of you were actually strong enough to deal with me one on one. But no!"

He swung several arms around. "Instead, you've all proven yourselves cowards and simpletons. You are so frightened of the new and unknown that you have to put aside any real competition you might pose just to keep your current rankings. You're so weak on your own that you have to cower in numbers just to stand in my presence. Pathetic."

Mortimer turned until he spotted Lanista Volka across the way, trembling in rage atop its hoverdisc. "You, oh high-hostly one, are the epitome of worthless effort and wasted flesh. You hide behind all these others and let them do the work that you are not capable of carrying out. Some may call that conniving. I call it absolute incompetence."

That sent some rumbles toward the conical lanista, as other attendees began to wonder how they might've been played by their entertainer for the evening. Mortimer secured everyone's attention again with another wave of Rahgz's hands.

"Now that this little sham is ended, I only have one thing left to say. So listen closely."

Mortimer paused, and everyone leaned in ever-so-slightly.

Then a noise blasted through the room—rising from every speaker and comm unit in the vicinity, it was equal parts docking emergency klaxon, Voidwhistle, foghorn, dying scream, and the gut-churning thunder of a nuclear core on meltdown. As it swiftly rose in volume, glass started to shatter and stone started to crack. Giant vases blasted apart and whole tables split down the middle. The art displays shuddered and went dark, and the cyborg pleasure dispensary unit gave a final blast of putrescent green-purple energy orbs that sent its users reeling.

The nearest lanista all collapsed, writhing as blood and other fluids sprayed from their respective heads. Others reeled, clutching at their stomachs and faces, vomiting and projecting columns of mucus from auditory and olfactory orifices alike. A few eyeballs burst, and those people made of more machine than organics jittered to a halt as their systems sparked and stuttered.

Volka's hoverdisc cracked below it, sending the lanista tumbling.

After just a few seconds, Mortimer gestured, and the unearthly noise vanished, leaving a terrible ringing in Rahgz's ears. His whole body buzzed with a grinding, nerve-jarring energy, and he was once more grateful that Mortimer acted as a filter between him and full neural interface with reality.

Mortimer swung about and strode for the exit.

"Follow me," he said, "and don't look back."

As they left, Rahgz kept trying to cringe, expecting a blade, bolt, or blaster in the back at any second. Somehow, they made it to the aerie without any reprisal, and the craft soon launched with all of them aboard and intact.

The Ghostclobbers got Bateesma to a side chair, where she started dozing and drooling. Mortimer plopped Rahgz's body in the control station. He pulled out a medication packet and down several large pills and gel vials designed to eliminate intoxicants within a few minutes. Then he sighed, leaning back and putting a few hands behind Rahgz's head.

"That was fun," he said.

Want to tell me exactly what "that" was? Rahgz asked. *It looked like a sonic attack.*

"Exactly. I patched a frequency modulator through the channel everyone was using to talk about you so nastily. The feedback was programmed to make things very uncomfortable for all involved. Make a good first impression. Make a permanent last impression."

They're going to hold me responsible!

"Obviously. It's a step to cementing your lifelong infamy."

The goal was fame, not infamy.

Mortimer waved a couple hands. "Semantics. Whether you're known for being revered or feared, it really doesn't matter in the end. Anyways, you're welcome. I'm going to cycle down my processing unit for a bit and leave you to enjoy the aftermath."

Wait, don't—

Rahgz's awareness zoomed to the forefront of his brain as Mortimer's control slipped off. While the sobermed pack had started taking effect, the vestiges of Mortimer's indulgences at the party still throbbed through his veins and even added an extra pulse to his eyeballs and abdominal sac. Groaning, he put his head in his hands and tried to stop feeling like the aerie had launched into the nearest black hole.

Swallowing against his rising gorge, Rahgz pressed controls to expand the chair into lounge mode, giving him breathing space and softening the cushions. He closed his eyes and tried to imagine himself anywhere but here—which, funny enough, was one place he'd spent hours imagining himself being not too long ago. In the lap of luxury, all his wants and needs within easy reach, companions close by his side. However, his fantasies of glory and power hadn't included any come-down migraines.

Gentle hands traced the back of his neck, tickling the feathers and putting all his senses on high alert. Rahgz didn't move, fearing it would scare off Phara's touch.

She slipped into the chair beside him, both of their bodies slim enough to be held there without crowding. A nuzzle under his jaw made him stiffen in several different areas around his biology.

"I think you're brilliant," she whispered in one of his ears.

Rahgz blinked and worked to get his tongue wet enough to speak. "You do?"

Her face shifted into view, and Rahgz wondered which mind was currently in control. Most likely Phara, since she didn't invoke any honorific. "A hundred percent. And brave. After all, you walk into a den of your fiercest enemies, take their mockery without flinching, and then leave them all writhing on the floor like rotworms in helot shit. It was glorious to behold." She pressed herself against him, tongue flicking over an ear hole. "I think you should be rewarded for that effort."

Rahgz gulped. "Is that in your contract?"

She pulled away, looking hurt. "What? You think I'm doing this because I have to?"

Her two other sets of faces twitched and lips writhed as if she argued silently with herself. She crossed her arms and turned aside. Rahgz realized he'd truly insulted her and mentally reached to Mortimer for advice. The implant felt more distant than usual, though, muttering as if half-asleep, and didn't offer up any immediate advice or his usual data display to show a strategic way to handle this interaction.

Breathing deep, Rahgz put a hand on Phara's arm. "Phara, you're a multID. And my contracted assistant."

She showed her upper fangs. "Yes? And? We have feelings too, you understand. Mine are quite clear how attracted I am to you. Obviously it's far less clear on your end."

"But are they real? Is any of this?" Rahgz spread his hands to indicate himself, the aerie, and the whole situation they were in. "Part of me wonders if anything I've experienced lately is legitimate. Or am I the fraud Volka claimed?"

Phara studied him with suspicion, as if wondering whether he might be making a joke of her. Then her expression turned sly. She reached down and squeezed between his legs. "Does this feel good?"

His eyes bugged and a squeak slipped out. "Yes."

She reached up and caressed his neck feathers. "How about this?"

"Very much so."

Another hand trailed down his spine and pressed into an extremely sensitive spot he didn't even know existed on his hip. "How about this?"

He ground into her touch and groaned. "Feels wonderful."

"Do you enjoy when you watch Glomph win?"

"Every time."

"Does it feel good to be above the masses in your aerie, knowing that people would literally kill to switch places with you?"

Rahgz grimaced, having been one of those people recently. "Yes. I won't deny that."

She pulled away and ran hands down her lithe frame, undulating in ways that made invisible needles prick all over Rahgz's scales and several glands engorge.

"Do you feel good when you look at or touch me?"

He stammered, and she winked at the unnecessary answer. Rolling across the lounger cushions, she put her face close to his, clouding his senses with her musky pheromones.

"Our feelings, more than our minds, guide what's real to us. What matters. Pleasure is what separates us from the Void. It gives us meaning. Fight for what feels good and lifts you higher. Deny and destroy whatever would steal your happiness." She ran a claw down the slit of her garment, parting the silky folds without revealing anything fully. "I'm bought and sold, yes, but that doesn't mean I don't feel pleasure in doing my job. It doesn't mean I can't be drawn to my owner and want to satisfy them for the mere fun of it. Whichever of my minds is in control, they are still me and I am still them. And they all want you."

Rahgz tore his gaze from her torso and tantalizing hypoglonoid. "I get what you're trying to tell me. So where does that leave us?"

Smiling wickedly, she leaned in and nuzzled his neck again, murmuring. "This aerie has a small private chamber that has remained unused until now. I can assure you that it is quite cozy and intimate. Allow me to go prepare it—and myself—for you."

It took Rahgz a few tries to clear his throat. "I'll be right there."

She sashayed off, tail dragging, but curled slightly like a finger crooked for him to follow. Rahgz breathed hot and heavy as he watched her go.

Another voice huffed in his ear, and Rahgz jerked and struck out, thinking Bateesma had snuck up on him. Nobody there, but the breathing continued, and Rahgz realized Mortimer was mocking him.

"What is your problem?" he asked.

"*Congratulations,*" Mortimer said. "*You didn't fuck that up, surprisingly. Your reward is now the chance to go fuck that.*"

Rahgz scowled. "Don't talk about her like a thing."

"*Possessive of your possession, are you?*"

Trying to maintain the arousal Phara had left simmering inside him, Rahgz focused on combing through his feathers to make himself more presentable. "Where were you?"

"*Submitting our dossier to the INC for authorization and filing our aerie transferal via a transport ship."*

That made Rahgz perk up. "Transfer? To where?"

"The first INC-sanctioned arena barge that we can book passage on."

Rahgz looked out through the aerie viewport, at the gray and brown barge sectorscape crawling by below. "Leaving the *Coffin*? I thought we were supposed to discuss these kinds of big decisions before you just make them"

"Except this is entirely in line with your priority life goals," Mortimer said, *"so no debate was needed. We've officially scraped the bottom of this barge barrel and proven the lanista scum mucking it about here are no real challenge for us. We'll stick around for another bout or two just to prove our point, and then it's time to up our game. Find some bigger helots to have Glomph skull-fuck. Bigger wagers. Bigger earnings. And entirely legitimate."*

"But...so soon?"

"It's now or never, Rahgz. You have to trust me on this. We're building momentum, and we have to keep it up. No hesitation. No looking back. No holding back."

Rahgz wanted to argue it over, but he couldn't come up with any rationale to debate the implant's logic. Hadn't he always wanted to get off this chunk of a rig ever since he could remember? Wasn't this the perfect opportunity to continue making a whole new life for himself? "All right. Make it so."

"Already made. Now go enjoy a good spruk. Just don't do enough damage to void the insurance policy.

Let the INC have their way. They like to be bullies. Let them bully and boast and brag all they wish. It's the surest waste of their resources and diverts their focus away from your true schemes and profitable endeavors, which you better be running on the side with the utmost discretion.

Of course, be sure to catalogue other lanistas' errors and missteps with due diligence so you can deliver a damning report to the INC at a moment's notice.

- How to Backstab Friends and Influence Outcomes: A Guide for Starting Lanistas Written by Lanista Kel'Chungzi Ewaltsen Excerpt from Vol 58, Subset 11.73

CHAPTER NINETEEN

R ahgz stared down the bolt of the plasma pistol, his tail cramping as he tried to squish it behind his legs, with his back pressed to the wall, all five arms splayed out.

"Is this really necessary?" he asked out of the corner of his mouth.

Phara, in a similar position right beside him, nodded, also playing a no-blinking game with the gun held less than an inch from her scaly snout. Both pistols were held by a single security drone with a dozen articulated arms, each sporting a weapon, crowd control device, or medical tools that could easily double as weapons and crowd control devices. The metallic orb hovered in the aerie, holding Rahgz and Phara in place, while two more drones had the Ghostclobbers pinned to the floor a few paces away.

"Standard INC procedure," Phara said, keeping perfectly still. "They're checking for any final irregularities before they allow us to participate in our first bout. They're just doing their job."

The inspector, a female bioborg with a massive skull and tiny forearms, stalked around the aerie cabin, scanning with a dozen different instruments in each corner. Her upper half had its left side replaced with machinery while her lower half had the right leg replaced by coiling tentacles made of living diamond. Her eight eyes rotated independently as she took notes and checked off items on a screen in one hand.

Rahgz grunted as he resisted the urge to scratch the many nervous itches that had sprung up across his feathery parts. Not the warmest welcome to his newest barge abode since leaving the *Coffin*. Part of him still couldn't believe they'd left that floating hunk behind. The aerie now docked within a sleeker, shinier barge named *The Slithering Slivereen*, which Mortimer and Phara both assured him would provide the perfect gateway to bigger, more profitable bouts.

he hadn't seen much of the barge itself since the aerie had been transported aboard, with Mortimer warning against getting too settled into their new accommodations. So far, all he knew was that it didn't stink as much inside. The locals weren't always trying to kill each other. Random security sweeps were replaced with stoic INC goons in regular patrols. Oh, and the captain was a sentient gas cloud contained within a forcefield bubble, whose fumes were deadly to every known organic lifeform.

Make the aerie the only thing you rely on, Mortimer had said as Rahgz read up on the new barge on the blood.stream. *Of all the barges and bouts you'll go through, of all the lanistas and helots we'll face, the aerie is our singular constant.*

"That and Phara and the Ghostclobbers," Rahgz had said. "They stick with us through it all."

Sure, the mesh had said after a long pause.

Rahgz craned his neck to try and see what the inspector muttered over on her datapad.

"We're precertified, though," he said. "Fully sanctioned by the captain and security clearance provided before we even came aboard."

The inspector snuffled laughter and ignored him.

Phara managed to reach one of his hands with hers and patted comfortingly. "Authorization requires full aerie and entity searches to complete the process. It shouldn't take long, so long as we don't resist."

"But our first bout starts in," Rahgz double-checked the chronometer ticking down in a corner of his eye, "ten minutes."

She smiled wryly. "Exactly. The INC assumes everyone is cheating and just hasn't been caught yet. Unexpected, last-minute inspections are their way of trying to catch people off-guard."

Mortimer chuckled. *"Of course, when you know that's how they operate, it's easy to circumvent those seemingly random procedures. That's why rules are important. When you know them intimately, it's easier to break them without anyone noticing."*

Speaking of which, Rahgz thought as a scanner beamed over his face, *are they going to pick up on you?*

"*Hardly. I'm perfectly enmeshed in your neural network. At this point, I'm practically you, for all they could tell, if they even realized I existed. I run off your biological functions, and we've been working together long enough that I can mimic your personality well enough to fool anyone who actually knows you. Or cares enough to tell the difference.*"

The inspector moved on to scan Phara, then the floor, then a random chair, and then a bowl of candied fruits Rahgz had been snacking on prior to the unannounced boarding.

I guess that's reassuring?

"*Relax. Remember, I'm here to make it so you get all the glory while I do all the gruntwork. Speaking of which, can you preauthorize me for automated control of this bout and the next, I don't know, dozen? Actually, just make that indefinite. With the INC regulations now in place, we need to ensure strict adherence to proper policy.*"

That made Rahgz's stomach squirm. *You want full biological command clearance moving forward? Can't you just keep advising me more like you have been? Be my mouth and hands when we need but let me work the rest.*

A grumble rattled inside Rahgz's head. "*Which one of us read the three hundred and forty-eight rules and regulation treatises regarding legal bout operations in INC space? Raise your hands.*"

Rahgz eyed the gun still a breath away from his forehead and at the drone hovering placidly, ready to execute him at the inspector's signal. *Obviously I can't raise my hands anyways. You've got the expertise, sure, I'm not arguing that.*

"*Thank you. And since there are some regulations that disqualify you if you sneeze improperly at certain moments, I think my having more complete control over both mind and matter is the smart thing, don't you?*"

I'll think about it.

The inspector stopped as she almost trampled Bateesma and the others, as if she hadn't noticed them lying on the floor below the pair of drones that had subdued them. When the INC inspection party had blown the aerie hatch open, Bateesma and crew had gone into full defend-and-dismember mode, but a few tranquilizer harpoons had taken care of their initial protective frenzy. The Ghostclobbers were just now coming round, peeling their faces up out of puddles of drool.

"Who are these?" The inspector tapped Bateesma's ass with a tentacle, making her snarl.

"Friends and associates," Rahgz said. "Part of my security contingent as well."

The inspector made a note of this, scowling. At least, Rahgz assumed it was a scowl. Hard to tell with half of her head looking like metal slag. "Will they be participating in the arena match in any fashion?"

Rahgz frowned. "No. They're not here for that. They're just—"

"Then they qualify as spectators," the inspector barked. She held her hand out, displaying the screen she read from, which was actually embedded in the stretched and stapled skin of her palm. "You haven't paid your spectator fee."

Phara sighed. "They're not here on leisure. They are lanista staff members and will not be viewing the bout out of entertainment purposes."

"The sprukking fuck?" Bateesma's shout came muffled with her still being face-down in the carpet. "We're not even allowed to peek for fun?"

Rahgz groaned as the inspector grinned, showing off metal chompers. "How much is it per spectator?"

The inspector swiped to a tally, and Rahgz's eyes tried to pop out and scuttle off into a corner.

He scoffed. "I could buy new friends for less than that."

"Hey," Bateesma cried. "I am not some sort of bargain-bin buddy!"

"I was joking, obviously," Rahgz said.

"*This is just one hidden cost of keeping these others around,*" Mortimer said. "*You use hyperbole, but you're not far from the truth. Purchasing companions to suit your whims is far more convenient in the long-term.*

225

More efficient, too."

Rahgz flexed his spasming shoulders. "Maybe there's a more personal arrangement we could come to? One less costly, but more profitable to y—"

Phara coughed in warning. The inspector's head smacked the pistol aside as she thrust her face in his. Her cranial plates scrunched against Rahgz's forehead scales painfully.

"Attempting to bribe an INC inspector is a breach of regulations punishable by death!"

Rahgz squinted against the fleck of spittle that struck one of his eyes. "That was not my intent at all, and I furiously apologize for any assumption on your part that I would impugn your honor as such a rigorous and mindlessly unswerving servant of the INC."

"Not bad," Mortimer said. *"Just hope she doesn't have an insult detector app operating."*

"I simply meant, perhaps there was another option beyond paying the fee directly that would satisfy the spectator regulation in an entirely legal manner."

The inspector nodded to one of her guards, who turned on a miniature flamethrower bolted to their forearm. The blue flame crackled the air inches from Bateesma's head, singing some of her ear fur. She yowled and hammered the floor with feet and fists, the drone's pacifying prod rammed into the small of her back.

"We can blind them temporarily," the inspector said. "Simply to ensure they do not actually spectate while serving your esteemed person. No permanent damage will be done to their optical faculties, but surgical restoration of eyesight will be at your cost."

Rahgz sneezed against the stench of burning hair that filled the aerie. "You know, let's pay that fee right now, shall we?"

They released one of his arms long enough for him to press his Bit-chit to the datapad, transferring the amount.

The inspector looked put out by the peaceful resolution to matters, and sulked as she disembarked with her squad. Once the aerie entry hatch had sealed, everyone sorted themselves out, the Ghostclobbers mostly stalking around where the INC goons had just been and muttering threats.

Rahgz caught Phara's eye as he wiped down his robe.

"How many INC regulations are punishable by death?" he asked.

"Most of them," she said.

An alert pinged Rahgz while another simultaneously went off on Phara's datapad. The Pits were getting ready to open.

"Finally," Mortimer said. *"Let's get moving. We've got less than a minute to spare."*

Mortimer summoned the control station and Rahgz lurched into place moments before the mesh took over and shucked his consciousness into the back seat.

From the aerie viewport, Rahgz could see over a quarter of the arena. Strange to not be viewing the *Coffin*'s rust- and blood-stained corridors, and the packed audience blocks around the perimeter. This arena's spleen team must've been kept working overtime, keeping every surface spit-shined and scrubbed clear of even the slightest scuff mark. If Rahgz didn't know any better from the blood.stream vids he'd watched of bouts held in this arena, he might've believed it had never been used before.

Most of the halls had rounded-out floors, with tubular tunnels connecting spherical chambers connected main passageways. Mortimer pointed out the strategically placed floodgates in the walls and ceilings, where the barge captain and other bout overseers could unleash tidal waves of water, acid, blood, mud, corrosive vat fluids, plasma, liquefied flesh, and any other available semi-solids just to make the competition more interesting. And slippery.

The arena also sported hundreds of electrified plates, tripwires, spike pits, and other hazards built to the captain's predilections. From what Rahgz studied at this elevated angle, there looked to be little pattern to the layout—just a twisting knot of endless winding ways for helots to get lost in as they hunted each other down.

Mortimer sighed in pleasure and crackled a dozen of Rahgz's knuckles. "Nothing better than a brand new arena to spoil with blood and shit. New traps to discover. New beasts to unleash. New audience members to deprive of what innocence they have left."

He tabbed open a virtual overlay and rotated it to display a hopelessly complicated snarl of paths and nodes. It took Rahgz a moment to recognize it as a map of the arena he'd just been scoping.

You have a map? I thought Phara said they refused to provide us with one until we won our first bout.

Mortimer smirked. "Funny what you can buy if you tap into the right shadow channels on the D-Mart."

Weren't you just talking about how we have to work even harder to stay within INC regulations?

"That's only for when there's a chance of getting caught." Mortimer grinned and ruffled Rahgz's arm-feathers. "Besides, every lanista worth their aerie acquires contraband maps."

So if everyone does it and gets away with it, we just go along with that? Not the wisest strategy.

"What are you? My non-existent mother?" Mortimer snorted. "In the sanctioned arenas, there are three tiers of rules. The official INC regulations are at the top and the most boring. You follow the obvious ones to avoid fines and disqualifications and forget about the rest. Then there's the rules of sportsmanship, intended to show respect to your fellow lanista. Things like 'don't poison a helot in its Pit,' or 'don't assassinate the lanista in their own aerie.' Those you keep or break depending on the resources available to you and your ability to outsmart the inspectors and barge security. And then there's the third tier. The unspoken rules. Aka, the don't-be-a-fuckwit rules." He paused. "Actually, I guess there's really only one rule in that category."

And that is?

"Do whatever it takes to win. Including ignoring all of the previous rules."

Before Rahgz could argue further, the pit gates hissed open. Glomph rolled out, streaking the shiny arena deck plates with its acidic ooze. The helot had grown visibly since leaving the *Coffin*, having been fed a steady stew of dismembered helot parts that Phara had procured for it. It jiggled and wobbled as it sloughed into the curved platform just outside the gate.

Jeers greeted it, with obscene alien glyphs being flashed all across the arena side screens, and slurs being screamed by the announcers in defiance of the newcomer.

"Go back to the Void, you unregulated shank!" one cried. "Honor-less scum like you have no place in the glories of the true arena."

Excuse us for existing, Rahgz thought.

"Always the curse of the newbie," Mortimer said. "Doesn't matter how much you've proven yourself on other barges, unsanctioned or regulated. Nobody likes the fresh meat."

A drone broadcasted a view of the opposing helot's Pit, off in some unknown corner of the arena. Rahgz tried to see what emerged, but it looked like a cloud of steam issuing out from the gaping opening. However, he realized the error of his initial assumption when the "steam" started writhing and coiling into dizzying shapes.

"We are the mighty many," the helot shrieked, patched into the arena's speakers. "We are the one and whole that will devour you from within. Tremble, maggots and manlings, as we unleash our full wrath upon your gonads."

Mortimer had already started running combatant diagnostics, creating a rundown of the other helot. Rahgz read the results as if standing over his own shoulder, only catching every other detail that popped up on the display.

"Intriguing. A swarm-form champion," Mortimer said. "The perfect time to try out a new stratagem."

He began typing out commands for Glomph to follow. The helot quivered far below as it received the instructions. However, he positioned Rahgz's body and actually kept his gaze lifted so Rahgz couldn't see what the input involved.

Rahgz strained invisibly to get a better view but wasn't currently in charge of the proper neurons to make that work.

What are you telling Glomph to do? he asked.

"You know I love surprising you," Mortimer said. "Let me have a little fun."

You know I hate surprises. And I'm letting you have my whole body, currently.

Mortimer heaved a sigh. "Spoilsport. Here's the angle. Swarm-forms are notoriously difficult to get a satisfying kill on. Being dispersed, you have to destroy every last member to count as a legal victory. Some swarm-forms have gone on huge winning streaks simply by dispersing enough to never be destroyed until their opponents starved to death. In fact, the longest registered arena bout lasted two whole TIRDs, with two nano-particle swarm-forms playing chicken down to their last mote the whole time."

That sounds boring.

"Exactly. And the barge captain went bankrupt hosting that bout and those types of helots fell out of favor. But it's a great opportunity to show the audience exactly how effective Glomph is. A solid, decisive win here will draw in big-name lanistas from all corners of this sector and get us off this two-bit barge quicker than we hopped on."

Off it? Rahgz checked over the arena again, noting how even the cheap seats looked posh compared to the literal garbage dumps back on the *Coffin*. *It looks pretty nice. I thought we would be here for a little while. Build up our sanctioned rep.*

Mortimer swept the control screen clear and stepped back with a satisfied air. "Void no. This barge is a mere steppingstone to higher hunting grounds. The faster we get on par with some of the real competition, the less chance we have of being tripped up by the rabble we're stuck fighting for now. We want a bout or two, three max, per barge before we buy our way forward."

Speaking of being stuck, Rahgz said, noting another detail, *Why isn't Glomph moving?*

"What makes you think it isn't?" Mortimer replied.

Rahgz pointed an immaterial finger at the viewport, which showed Glomph still in the bowl-shaped platform.

Aside from the fact that it literally hasn't moved since it rolled out of the Pit.

Phara sidled up to Rahgz's body, unaware of who was actually in control of it. "Rahgz? Is something wrong with Glomph?"

Mortimer threw a couple of arms around her shoulders and hugged her closer. "Nothing whatsoever." He indicated the helot's bio readouts. "Glomph is in perfect health thanks to your tender ministrations on the trip here. I've simply laid a cunning trap and am waiting for our opponent to spring it."

Phara looked surprised at the embrace, but leaned into it, making Rahgz's neck feathers tremble. "The trap is...Glomph just waiting there? No attack approach?"

Mortimer shrugged and nuzzled her neck. "Why expend extra energy when the enemy will do it all for us? You smell delightful, by the way."

Hey! Rahgz shouted. *That's my sprukling you're groping.*

"Thank you," she said, easing out of Mortimer's grasp. "Perhaps we can take advantage of that after the bout? Which I should let you focus on."

"You're the only kind of distraction I would ever invite," Mortimer said. "I look forward to celebrating our latest win."

He watched her go, tracing her sinuous frame with Rahgz's eyes.

What's the big idea? Rahgz asked, steaming enough he thought he might boil his brain.

"Still don't trust I have your best interests at heart?" Mortimer said under his breath. "I got her in the mood for you, easily calculating she would want to wait for just a little while. Then you'll be in full sensory control when the actual deed is being done, so the pleasure is all yours. Although, if you want, I could provide some guidance that as well for heightened bliss. After all, I've now processed through about a hundred inter-species copulation manuals and extraterrestrial erotica that would serve to—"

Thanks, but no thanks.

Chuckling, Mortimer turned back to the control station to check on Glomph.

Fucking spruk! Why'd you let her distract you?

The swarm-form's lanista was either quite familiar with the arena layout or had also acquired a shade-market map, as the helot had sped across the combat grounds directly to Glomph—who remained rooted to its spot.

The enemy helot's nebulous form hovered in a growing cloud just down the main path from Glomph. It appeared to be studying the amorphous helot and surrounding area, looking for the trap Mortimer promised would be there.

What are you doing? Rahgz asked.

"Waiting," Mortimer said.

For what?

"My scans showed the swarm-form is comprised of six-hundred and fifty million distinct particular entities. I am currently detecting six-hundred and forty-three million in the cluster before us." He continued to tally quietly. "Forty-four...forty-five..."

The swarm began streaming down the passage toward Glomph, the crowd cheering it on as they savored the death and destruction about to occur.

"Forty-six...forty-seven..."

Not all of it's moving in close, Rahgz said, noting how at least half the swarm remained stretched out behind the main cloud. *It'll survive any initial attack Glomph makes still, just like you warned.*

"Forty-eight...forty-nine...Come on, lucky fifty..."

What's the point? Rahgz asked. *It's all spread out still. It's not taking the bait like you wanted.*

"Fifty! Now!"

From where Glomph sat all the way out to the barely visible distance, the arena walls and floors seemed to come alive, rippling and peeling up and inward. A translucent layer of...something...began to retract from where it had been lying unseen across all the surfaces, like a slow-motion wave in reverse. The layer curled in from all sides, scooping up the swarm particles as it contracted in on itself from all directions, cutting off any retreat.

And all of it centered back on Glomph, who waited patiently right where Mortimer had kept it.

Swarm particles rose high above the arena, attempting to escape over the edge of what Rahgz realized was Glomph's flesh, having been oozed out invisibly thin until it coated the very halls and tunnels the swarm had come down to corner its prey. The swarm reacted too slow, with every last particle getting swept up and snagged by trailing pseudopods.

Seconds later, the last of the extended flesh returned to its body of origin, making Glomph thicken and swell back to its full size, the swarm-form now held securely within it, already being digested.

"Swarm, zero," Mortimer said. "Glomph, six hundred and fifty million."

You think the end goal of winning in the arena is the death of the other lanista's helot? So shortsighted. You are, in actuality, vying for the long, slow, painful, and humiliating death of the lanista. Each loss they suffer is another wound to their very soul. Each time you prove all their efforts in rearing, training, and sending a helot out to be crushed by your own property, their lifespan shrinks that much more. Learn to savor that suffering.

- How to Backstab Friends and Influence Outcomes:
A Guide for Starting Lanistas
Written by Lanista Kel'Chungzi Ewaltsen
Excerpt from Vol 6, Subset 9.99

CHAPTER TWENTY

The arena fell quiet. Rahgz discovered how much he enjoyed that shocked silence when his helot outperformed all audience expectations and provided a truly unique show.

Then a message flashed on all screens: *Death Verified.*

The barge impossibly rocked with the uproar that followed. Mini riots broke out among the spectators, with INC forces swooping in to violently enforce peace and quiet.

The Ghostclobbers whooped and hollered in victory, already getting the aerie printports serving up celebratory drinks and snacks.

Phara caught Rahgz's eye and winked just before she slunk off into the private chambers. Rahgz waited for the implant to relinquish control so he could go enjoy his reward, but Mortimer continued to study the control panels, adjusting inputs here and outputs there.

Uh, hey, Rahgz said after a minute. *I've got a date.*

"She can wait," Mortimer said, still focused on reading the post-match datastreams.

I'd rather not make her.

"Is your little sprukfest really more important than me integrating everything gleaned from the last bout into our evolving combat algorithms. You may not realize it, Rahgz, because you're so focused on the momentary, fleshy pleasures, but data is like meat. It's best digested when it's fresh."

Rahgz mentally reached to force control to switch back over to him, but something slammed into his awareness, dizzying him even as the world outside his eyes dimmed slightly.

Mortimer's voice roared through his mind. *"You ungrateful little nullworm. I just won you one of the best matches this sector has seen in fifty TIRDs. Your net worth just tripled. We've got invites coming in from a dozen new barges who want us as their lanista-of-honor, and I've already spotted another dozen back-channel contrast posted that are putting pricey hits on your head and the heads of everyone associated with you—including the scaly bitch you're so fond of—so I'm also trying to figure out the best way to keep you, her, and all of us alive and winning. And you can't give me a few minutes to update my calculations and proto-cols because you want to pluck your feathers and dip them like quills in your little messy spit of flesh?"*

The implant went silent, pulling into the mental distance so far, it left Rahgz feeling chilled and floating alone within himself. He hadn't realized how much Mortimer's presence propped him up from within. The vehemence of Mortimer's reaction doubly shocked him.

What's happened to you, Mortimer? Rahgz tentatively reached out for the knot of sentience he'd come to identify as the implant's presence. *That didn't sound like an emotional simulation from a personality over-lay.*

"*It's called evolution,*" Mortimer said. "*You're not the only one whose existence has shifted way out of bounds of intended parameters. I'm not just the result of a lab experiment anymore, and you aren't a hapless guinea pig. Like it or not, Rahgz, we're stuck with each other. Everything I do, I do for you. I exist for you. Without you, I'm nothing.*" A mental jab hit struck the middle of his thoughts. "*But without me, you're nothing too. I take my hand off the controls for a single bout, and you would lose miserably. I pull back my guidance on how you walk and what you say, and you would be Bitless, friendless, loverless, and homeless within a tenth of a TIRD. Do you want me to run the scenarios I've projected that show the most likely outcomes for you if you ever removed or deactivated me? They involve most of your orifices getting so sprukked that your asshole would make the Void look like a pinprick and you being so pathetic no one would even stop to put out of your misery. Is that what you want? I'm trying to save you from being you, and honestly, you keep getting in the way.*"

With an abrupt inversion, full sensation shoved its way back into Rahgz's awareness. Mortimer receded into his mental landscape, grumbling and cursing to himself.

Rahgz regained his physical balance while also trying to sort through the implant's little lecture. He couldn't deny that all the good things in his life now came from Mortimer's guidance, if not direct control. In his core, Rahgz didn't care that the implant basically ran the show when it came to life's logistics and his existential chores. Mortimer seemed rather happy to be in charge of the arena bouts, but Rahgz hadn't thought that the implant had any concerns beyond that and the primary goals it had been programmed with at the very beginning of their symbiotic relationship.

At least, until now, Rahgz didn't think that Mortimer would've—or even truly *could* have—felt emotionally invested in the effort. In many ways, Rahgz had been thinking of the implant as just another AI assistant like many had running on their personal chits and pads. Complex processes and synthetic sentience could produce some amazing results, but it didn't make the AI in question more valued than the living organisms they were made to serve.

Except, of course, the machine lifeforms from the Teknix dimension, that had achieved mechanical self-awareness in their own odd evolutionary chain, and then gone on to create biological organisms to serve them.

By now, though, perhaps Mortimer deserved a place of greater respect. In some ways, the implant had become his conscience. Perhaps more than that. Mortimer acted as the soul Rahgz never believed he had.

Rahgz tucked hands inside his robe. "All right. Full autonomy during the bouts. Authorization granted indefinitely."

Mortimer stopped moping around on the sidelines of his brain. *"What?"*

Rahgz turned and headed for the private chamber. "You heard me. It's the least you deserve for everything you've done for me. We're partners in this now, like you said. Equal measures of give and take." Even though a secret part of him admitted the implant was doing far more of the heavy lifting these days.

Mortimer spluttered. *"I...I don't know what to say."*

Rahgz grinned. "You don't have to say anything. I know I can trust you with my life, so have a little more of it. Now keep on saying nothing while I go enjoy dipping my feathers for a while."

To his chagrin, immediately after he and Phara had expressed their respective orgasmic fulminations, she had a list of new bouts and barges lined up that precisely mirrored Mortimer's for his advancement up the lanista ranks.

Our strange form of pillow talk, he thought, as his assistant/sprukker/lover went down the growing roster of invites and anticipatory challenges that she'd ranked according to the nearest sector hotspots and most popular helots in the blood.stream commentator streams.

"The trick will be making you look like a threat to their reputation," she said, scrolling through a projected holostream show of lanistas and their respective monsters, goons, freaks, and champions. "But not enough of a threat to their helots. Keep it looking like you're barely winning these bouts or doing so by a fluke and making your hot streak a tempting thing to try and break. Once you get too big, then the bouts can become more costly to buy in because all the less-funded lanista won't be willing to risk their current investments on a losing bet."

He propped up on two elbows. "I see. Keep me acting like the underdog, trying to prove myself so they think I'm an easy target who has to be put in his place."

She grinned and teased a few feathers. "Precisely. Now, being the soon-to-be-darling of INC space, we're going to have to keep you looking humble on the interview channels and spotlight streams. Remember to be respectful when talking about the Gnoems, for instance. Don't spit or be vile when someone brings up regulations and INC raids. Act like this is all still a big surprise to you, like winning is not even in your control and just a happenstance of some universal destiny."

Rahgz chuckled. "I think I can manage that. Who're we up against first?"

She swiped to a lanista file that showed a bundle of fur with several toothy mouths and a barbed tail. Rahgz cocked his head.

"Is that the lanista or helot?"

Phara wagged a finger of warning. "Respectful, remember? Mock your opponents all you want in private, but merely show appreciation for them being willing to fight you while on any public channel. This is Lanista Hikslip, and they've been in the game for almost a hundred TIRDs. A comfortable target, who has seen a careful balance of wins and losses. Beating their current helot—who is registered as a fungal shambler with biomechanoid augmentations—won't surprise anyone but will get your name circling in mainstream circles all the faster."

Rahgz pretended to study the file, knowing Mortimer likely already had this lanista in his sights and knew a dozen ways to lay the competition low without breaking a sweat. "Let's make it so."

And so it went. The next few bouts became a whirlwind of activity, despite Rahgz doing little of the actual work himself. Phara made all the logistical arrangements each time they switched barges, until Rahgz could barely remember the name of the ship the aerie docked with. *The Fatted Colvina. The Crimson Purge. Retail Therapy. The Comeuppance. Gnoem's Gnarly Gnodules.*

Each with a different arena. One full of plasma rivers and lightning towers that fried anything that got too close—including spectators. Another completely underwater, populated by carnivorous amphibian species from a hundred different worlds. Another a simple affair of packed dirt and stone surrounded by metal walls, reminiscent of prehistoric gladiatorial arenas.

Rahgz's favorite of them so far was an arena that stunk of mold and rot, with fossilized trees and logs forming the passages and small clearings surrounded by moss-draped walls. Spongy earth covered the deck plating, having been shipped from a jungle planet to soften the footfalls of helots stalking the mists. For some reason, it reminded him of the home he couldn't remember.

And the helots came as varied as the combat landscapes. Glomph faced and devoured cybernetic monstrosities and undead serpents fueled by necroscience. It destroyed towering scions of perfection and gorged on the slavering drek of cannibalistic psychos. It silenced the pious calls of spiritual leaders who believed they would find salvation in the arena and cracked the self-scarred bones and mutilated flesh-plates of a shr'rek who volunteered to fight out of a warped sense of penance. Once, Mortimer had Glomph let itself be swallowed whole, only to burst out of the swollen belly of a gluttonous zerglin, whose half-melted corpse ended up becoming a feast for the Lil' Fuckers organization aboard that particular barge—and for a day, Rahgz was considered a patron saint to the spawnlings who adored him and his offering to further their miserable existences.

Mortimer relished taking full control each time a bout came up, and Rahgz learned to let the implant intelligence have his fun during those times. It was true that the others didn't even suspect when he wasn't in control anymore. Mortimer also played the role during public events and broadcasts that he participated in, continuing his persona as the mysterious lanista who lacked a past and kept everyone guessing.

During this time, Bateesma, Turrurnium, and Ukspug caught two would-be assassins trying to board the aerie, leaving their battered corpses strung up from the anti-grav thrusters during the following bouts. Phara found another killer hiding in their private chambers during an internal sensor sweep. This one had been funded enough to afford a cloaking device but, unfortunately, forgot that the device only masked visual output, and did nothing to hide them from Phara's incredible sense of smell.

Mortimer convinced Rahgz not to investigate who sent any one particular assassin, as they were simply a matter of fact of the lanista life.

"The reality is," he said, "only the poorer, more desperate lanistas resort to assassins for the most part. They know they can't afford high-quality helots and are stuck in a cycle of barely winning enough to scrape by before hitting another losing streak. So they try to up their chances by offing the competition more directly. But as with everything, their efforts are sprukked from the get-go."

The real threat, apparently, presented itself when a lanista achieved large and lasting fame that couldn't be brushed aside or explained away as luck any longer. That's when the big players started using the bigger guns to try and knock enemy pieces off the board. Highly skilled and high-priced assassins were the tools of the wealthy lanista who owned their own barges and whole sectors of space, with private Meat Gardens that churned out helots by the dozens. Only one lanista had reached that level of acclaim in any recent memory, and they had disappeared almost fifty TIRDs past and had never been heard from since, leading most to assume that rivals had finally succeeded in a yet-to-be-discovered plot to eradicate an otherwise defiant foe.

Glomph continued to grow until it had to be upgraded to the bigger, pricier Pits. Fortunately, Mortimer's calculations still put the helot several TIRDs away from outgrowing its usefulness. Even then, there was the purely speculatory chance that the helot might undergo an unknown form of mitosis, resulting in two smaller helots—making Rahgz's initial purchase a BOGO extravaganza.

"*Slim, but possible, from what I've analyzed in its genetic code,*" Mortimer said. "*In even the rarest possibility of that happening, I've actually worked up a few legal arguments to continue registering Glomph and Glomph Junior as the same entity, allowing them both to be entered in bouts and doubling our deadly potential.*"

"And if it doesn't happen?" Rahgz asked. "How do we ensure we get a helot nearly as effective as Glomph to replace it?"

"*I've been attempting to reverse-engineer the Meat Garden proprietary DNA blend in our big bad beastie ever since we got it. Most Gnoems and their underlings put in genetic stop-gaps that make it impossible to perfectly copy-paste a helot template into a new vatwomb. But I've been making progress. I'm not saying the results would be Glomph 2.0, but they*" *could at least give us similar resilience and digestive capabilities. Still, it would likely cost us every spare Bit we would've earned by then."*

"Which makes it critical that we keep winning and earning as much as possible, huh?"

"Precisely."

Glomph went on to devour a sentient world tree seed, a dinosaur-like helot that sang beautifully as it died, and an angel that fell through a dimensional rift to some species' afterlife. The aerie hopped between an INC prison barge, an organic barge formed of intelligent molds, and an inter-universal collective that kept offering to assimilate Rahgz for the low low price of a hundred Bits and his free will.

After they left the last barge with their individualities intact, they wound up on a barge called *The Extinct Euphemism*, which contained a hundred thousand individuals who each represented the last of their respective species. After Glomph ate two helots and one spectator who decided to commit suicide-by-arena-streaking, Phara approached Rahgz with an updated bout list.

"A couple points of order," she said. "According to my surveillance nanites, our most recent pit boss has been taking bribes to delay Glomph's feedings and has also arranged for a shipment of contaminated genestew to be dropped in the pit just before the match."

"That's not going to really hurt Glomph any," Rahgz said. "The last helot it devoured was practically nothing but poisoned flesh and rotting marrow."

"No, but it means whoever's paying them off is trying to indirectly assay Glomph's weaknesses outside of the arena. See if it can be starved or weakened or anything. We need to deter further attempts before it escalates from a nuisance to an actual distraction."

"Fine." He waved the Ghostclobbers over. They had long since shed their gloomy cloaks and gear, upgrading for finer, starspun threads and holy weapons that gleamed with razor edges and crackled with electrified spikes. Bateesma had a few new tattoos gleaming under her fur, while Ukspug had several starsteel piercings through his corpulent musculature. Turrurnium had outfitted his spindly frame with dangling crystals that clinked musically as he swayed about the aerie.

Bateesma licked her front teeth. "Someone making trouble for you again?"

"You all want to go spank my pit boss for me?" Rahgz asked. "They're being naughty."

Bateesma giggled. "We talking a fatal spanking or…?"

"Can't be helped if they resist too much. Just don't make it too messy, all right? Otherwise the local spleen teams will send us the bill, which I'll have to dock from your fun money accounts."

She looked solemn at that. "You got it. Discreet torture and selective dismemberment it is. You want us to save you any snackage?"

"Gorge away."

Once they headed off, Phara stayed hovering by Rahgz's side. He looked up at her, always admiring the velvety scales under her throat and down her slim chest. "What's the rest?"

She tapped up an alert. "There are two missives deserving of your attention. Foremost, you've received a direct invite from Lanista Chylsmuth to face his helot in mortal combat aboard the barge known as *Sundered Accord*."

Rahgz rose in his recliner. "Should I know who that is?"

"Chylsmuth ranks among the top hundred lanistas in all INC-sanctioned space. Even to just be challenged by him will automatically elevate your standing tenfold."

"Excellent. What's the other message?"

"Captain Thorluthsmien of the *Sundered Accord* has requested a private meeting with you prior to the bout. Contingent on you accepting the challenge, of course."

"Yes to both," Rahgz said, flipping a couple hands in the air and clasping a few others behind his head. "Put them on my schedule and make the appropriate arrangements."

She smiled. "Done. What gift should I acquire for you to take for the captain?"

Rahgz blinked. "Gift?"

"Lanista gift-giving protocol in response to personal invites." She tucked the datapad away and steepled fingers in thought. "We haven't had much chance to practice it, but it is a delicate challenge. The gift should be personal, but not too exclusive. Valuable, but not in a manner to shame the recipient. Meaningful, but not in an insulting manner. Memorable, but not obnoxious. And yet also subtly exclusive, shaming, insulting, and obnoxious, if at all possible."

It was his turn to smile. "I know the perfect thing."

Barge captains are an odd mix of enemy and ally. They want you to win. They want you to lose. They want to be your best friend. They want to be the first in line to stab you in the back. In reality, they want to simply be in control. Most of them are high-functioning sociopaths in the first place, which means you need to work on being a high-functioning psychopath to get the upper hand.

- How to Backstab Friends and Influence Outcomes:
A Guide for Starting Lanistas
Written by Lanista Kel'Chungzi Ewaltsen
Excerpt from Vol 10, Subset 0.34

CHAPTER TWENTY-ONE

"We're going to be late." Phara adjusted the sparkling hover-bangles that orbited her neck and the other jump-jewels that created the illusion of tiara above her forehead.

"We won't. Had to wait for this either way." Rahgz jogged to the door of the aerie and admitted a delivery drone that lugged in a large cargo container. He pointed it to the middle of the chamber and then finger-printed to accept the deposit.

Phara eyed the hermetically-sealed crate. "What's this? I didn't order anything for you."

Rahgz found the biolock and let it get his fingerprint again, along with iris scan, breath analyzer, and scale sample. "I occasionally still like to do things for myself. Everyone likes a good surprise sometimes."

He paused. *Except me. I don't like surprises. Mortimer likes surprising people. Is he rubbing off on me?* Shrugging that thought away, he bounced in place like an excited spawnling as the lid unsealed, a hiss of air bringing with it a stink of packaged smartplastics. The container opened, revealing hundreds of palm-sized discs with glittering edges and holographic etching.

Phara looked over his shoulder. "Are those…"

He nodded and plucked one up, activating it with pressure points around the rim. A vivid projection of Glomph shimmered into being above the disc, going through a swift rotation of scenes from past bouts. It showed the helot devouring several opponents, sitting in place, and careening down arena tunnels with extended pseudopods. Another flick of the wrist replaced Glomph's image with one of Rahgz in a noble pose, face half-hidden within the folds of his hood.

Satisfied, he checked the top layer of discs until he found the one with the prime serial number. He set this aside for Bateesma.

"She'll be so happy," Phara said, admiring a disc of her own.

Rahgz snagged another holo-disc and tucked it in his robe. "The perfect thank-you gift for the captain for hosting me."

"I'm sure he'll be thrilled," she said. "A lot of captains are collectors of one sort or another. And it fits the parameters quite well. Now we must go, or we really will be late."

Rahgz let her lead him out to the waiting transport shuttle the captain had sent for them. Once they settled into the plush seats, it whisked them off through a luxurious barge district full of pearlescent domes and wide-open spaces full of luscious foliage. *Sundered Accord* boasted several wilderness expanses designed to hold a menagerie of game animals from hundreds of worlds, with barge denizens able to purchase entry to hunt inside the bounds for both sport and sustenance. Several of the hunting sectors fed into large holding pens near the arena outskirts. The captain was known for occasionally releasing herds of crazed beasts into the arena during bouts just to spice up the action.

Rahgz and Phara didn't say much as they watched the bargescape zoom by below them. They snuggled close, enjoying the solitude and quiet. Camdrones whizzed around them, keeping pace with the transport, but Phara assured him that the shuttle shielding repelled all attempts to get unauthorized images of them or otherwise eavesdrop and record their activities.

Before long, they arrived at the barge's control deck, where the captain's private quarters attached to the outermost hull plates—looking like a shiny bubble about to pop along the internal ship skin.

The shuttle docked and they entered the captain's sanctum along a thrumming hallway that doubled as an airlock.

Mortimer stirred in the wings of Rahgz's mind. *"Ready for me to take over?"*

"Go for it," Rahgz said. "Just don't shove me so far back that I can't sense things. I want to know what's going on and not be catching up on the backend."

Mortimer hummed in agreement as the mesh eased into control of Rahgz's brain and body. Rahgz floated above himself, an out-of-body sensation that sometimes occurred when Mortimer was at the forefront. It was actually quite pleasant and relaxing, letting him observe the surroundings and events with a detached curiosity, soaking in the details without them mattering too much in the moment. A form of existential bliss, where he could just be, without worries or cares.

Mortimer guided him forward, Phara on his arm, unaware of the switch. They passed through a bubblefield that sealed off the hallway from the inner chamber. Here, the walls curved around in a series of evenly set antechambers with numerous creches and pillars that showed off an immense art collection. Alien busts and sculptures adorned every spare inch, with paintings—both holographic and real—covering the ceiling and floating in suspension shafts throughout the room. Even the carpeting looked to be a work of art, with bioluminescent threads woven through an otherwise black expanse. The carpet responded to their presence, a rainbow of lights sparkling into existence under their feet and then zooming out to encircle them with Mandelbrot fractals and other impossibly detailed patterns.

A main table stood in the center of all the splendor, set with a modest spread of food, mostly fruits and spiced meats, all of which appeared properly deceased. Two goblets filled with a pink liquid waited for them. Mortimer and Phara approached the table and looked around for their host.

Mortimer took up both glasses, sniffed them, and handed one to Phara. "I half wish the captain might be late to his own appointment so I might enjoy all the company I desire in such a fine setting."

Phara's neck scales flushed all the way up to her ear fronds, and Rahgz had a flash of resentment at how easily Mortimer flirted with his companion.

She took a goblet and sipped, eyes half-closed as she savored the heady drink. "We've both been in some unexpected places since we first came together. Makes me wonder just how strange this journey we're on might become before it's over."

Mortimer raised his glass in an unspoken toast. "Why talk about endings when things are still just beginning for us all?"

And then they were no longer alone.

One moment, empty space. The next, the air flickered and Captain Thorluthsmien stood at the opposite end of the table. Rahgz had seen a single image of him before, from Phara's provided profile, and he looked practically identical. A male humanoid, bald with prehensile tentacles draped over his mouth and deep-set, gleaming eyes like black pearls. He had a muscular frame clad in a velvety uniform, all deep crimsons and purples, with gold and silver sashes and medals accentuating the getup, hinting at some military background. A plasma sabre hung at his side, with a nullpistol on the opposite hip.

How'd he do that? Rahgz asked. *Teleporter?*

Mortimer grunted internally, a sound that Rahgz recognized as being confused frustration. Rarely did the implant not immediately have an answer for everything.

"No," Mortimer thought back. *"I would've picked up the spatial displacement if so."*

Then a cloaking device?

"Not that either. Though I am detecting some photonic disruption in his immediate area. Strange."

"Welcome to you both," the captain said, deep voice not the slightest bit muffled as the tentacles writhed over his lips. "Time is precious to us all, and so I appreciate you gifting me with these moments of yours."

"It is our privilege," Mortimer said, bowing with just Rahgz's head and shoulders. He flourished out the holo-disc and presented it raised in a pedestal formed by three sets of fingertips. "Please accept this humble gift as a thank you for welcoming us into your presence."

He handed over the disc, which the captain took with a return bow. Mortimer brushed fingertips with him as they made the exchange, and Rahgz got a distant sense of the person's super-slick skin, almost as if he was frictionless. Yet the disc remained secure in his grasp as they broke contact.

"Quaint," the captain said. He examined it from several angles, giving a liquid chuckle on seeing Glomph ingesting a helot that was scrambling to get free. The utter panic on that creature's face was one of the reasons Rahgz had that particular scene commissioned for the figurine.

The captain tossed the holo-disc onto a side table, where it clattered up against several other baubles. "I am sure it will give me fond memories of your time as a lanista once they are through."

"Through?" Mortimer echoed. "I would hold it close to your side, then, as that will not be for some time. I intend to enter the Hall of Legacy while still alive, being the first lanista to do so."

"Nothing is eternal," Thorluthsmien said. "Except for the beauty of death and decay, of course." He brushed down a row of medals along one side as if recalling a fond memory. "As for your legacy, perhaps in another life, if you believe in such things. For now, I would prepare to invest your efforts in another career. A bout mechanic, perhaps, or blood.stream commentator. The survivability of those roles is far higher than the one you're occupying."

Mortimer set his drink down and leveled a cool glare at the captain. "While your hospitality is excellent, your tact is lacking. That threat was about as subtle as your taste in alien erotica." He turned and jutted Rahgz's chin at several clusters of sculptures, which Rahgz realized were meant to represent numerous species all tangled up in a literal cluster-fuck.

Phara came up beside him and placed a hand on Rahgz's back in silent warning. Mortimer, of course, ignored this.

He leaned in, Rahgz's feathers flat against the scales. "I take it you are betting heavily on Chylsmuth winning our bout. This attempt at intimidation is not only deplorable but boring. Fortunately, I believe you still have time to withdraw or transfer your wagers before the bout, if you were wise."

The captain flicked fingers to toss this idea aside. "I hold no vested interest in Lanista Chylsmuth, other than hosting him on this barge alongside yourself. He is an esteemed guest, nothing more. Unlike most, I refrain from placing any wager in the Book, under my name or any other."

Mortimer frowned. "Then why bother with this diplomatic posturing that you know I won't take seriously?"

"Because you should." The captain gestured around at the chamber. "Since this is one of the few places aboard my barge that one may talk freely without fear of being overheard by unwanted parties, let me make my intentions as clear as possible. This is not a threat as much as it is an opportunity."

"Oh?" Mortimer smirked. "For what, exactly?"

"For you to accept the honor that this bout has already given you." Thorluthsmien knotted his fingers together in a thoughtful pose. "And then to gracefully accept defeat and depart from the lanista ranks before it becomes a far deadlier game than you can bear."

A scoff escaped Mortimer. "You underestimate my ability to bear adversity."

The captain sighed. "I'm not speaking of merely the lanista opposition and undermining that you face. The INC has been watching you ever since you left unsanctioned space. You've drawn quite a lot of attention to yourself, despite playing up the attitude that you could care less about what people think about you. But officers and investigators have been keenly studying your meteoric rise to fame. They're waiting for the right moment to pounce."

Phara took a step forward. "Which is why we have been beyond thorough in ensuring all of our fees are paid, our licenses are secure, and our registries are current with every barge we visit. You have nothing to fear from the INC while we are aboard."

The captain ran a hand along the edge of the table, dark eyes glittering. "According to my sources, the INC isn't concerned about any of your documentation."

"What then?" she asked.

"Your helot."

Mortimer glanced at the holo-disc, which still displayed the helot spinning in place. "Glomph? What about it?"

"Where did you find such a unique specimen?" the captain asked.

A shrug. "The Meat Gardens, of course."

The captain made a doubtful noise. "It is quite clear to anyone with a quarter of a brain and at least one optical sensory organ that it is a derivative of a creature that has been labeled an illegal bio-template that is never to be replicated under pain of—"

"Death," Mortimer said. "Yes, we're well aware of the usual penalty for infractions."

Thorluthsmien smirked somewhere under the mouth-tentacles. "At the least, you could come under charges for defiance of Gnoem law and illegal access to unsanctioned genetic banks. If not that, the INC could at least arrest you on the basis of stolen intellectual property."

Mortimer made a few fists. "Glomph was properly bought and paid for. There is plenty of evidence to prove that and none for any of these wild assertions."

"Since when has evidence stopped an INC investigator?" Thorluthsmien looked to the painted ceiling, as if seeing the rest of the barge and the Void beyond it. "I have captained this barge for nearly three hundred TIRDs and I have done so by being exceptionally discreet in my dealings with your kind. The wisest of you have heeded my advice and survived. Those who ignored the warnings have all suffered the consequences, one way or another. And I will not have the reputation of my barge sullied by an INC raid because of your pride."

He picked up a piece of shelled meat, rolled it between a few fingers, and then tossed the steaming lump aside without tasting. "Give Lanista Chylsmuth the win. Let Glomph take its place in the eternal history of arena corpses. Take your meager losses and preserve what winnings you have stockpiled thus far. Then leave and never return."

Mortimer smoothed down the ruffled feathers along Rahgz's arms.

"That's your offer?"

"That's your opportunity to take advantage of. It's the best you'll receive, I guarantee it. And let me be equally clear about the alternatives." He stalked up to stare down his tentacles at Mortimer. "Defy me on this, and you will exist long enough to regret it with every fiber of your being. You will crave the oblivion of the Void, but it will be denied you. You will know terror and humiliation and everything you know and cherish will be brought to ruin." His look darted to Phara for the briefest moment, yet enough to convey just how far the promised wrath would extend.

He stepped back and bowed, tentacles raised in parting. "I have other business to attend to, but please, remain as long as you wish. Enjoy the comforts here. Survey my collection. I believe there is none like it in this dimension."

With another flicker of the light, Thorluthsmien vanished.

Mortimer stared at the space the captain had occupied as if trying to pierce through to the Void with his eyes. Rahgz's hands shook for a second, until Mortimer tucked most of them inside the robe. With a remaining hand, he reached for his drink, ran a finger around the rim of the goblet, and then tipped it over.

Pink liquid poured across the table and dripped off the edge to the floor. He studied the resulting mess, and Rahgz thought the flow looked quite like a victim's blood trickling across the arena deck.

A shuddering breath slipped out of Phara, and she visibly steeled herself after having been struck by the captain's vicious words.

"What do we do now?" she asked, voice quavering.

Mortimer winked at her. "Let's eat."

She looked taken aback by this, while Rahgz voiced her unspoken question from the recesses of his mind.

What're you talking about? How can you think about eating after all that?

Mortimer dove at the table, scooping up fistfuls of food and drink to slurp and gobble it all down with abandon. Phara stepped back to avoid being stained by the sprays of wine and splatters of fatty drippings.

The implant cracked open the meatshells and swallowed them whole. He tore off goujou berries straight off the thorny vines and sucked sweet marrow out of the barbecued femurs. When he came up for air, it was just to suck down goblets of prickpalm juice.

Take it easy, Rahgz cried. *My stomach is actually capable of bursting if you eat too much.*

Mortimer didn't slow. If anything, he sped up the intake, mashing whole platters into Rahgz's mouth and barely breathing as he choked it all down. At last, he licked the last bowl clean and drained a final flagon of char-scented ash wine. He stepped back, face and robe a filthy mess. He took his time sucking juice and grease off Rahgz's fingers and picking out a few bites that had fallen into his feathers.

What the fuck was the point of all that? Rahgz asked. *Aside from petty gluttony.*

Phara eyed the remains of what had been a splendid feast. She looked a bit ill and clutched her stomach as if feeling the bloating that Rahgz knew he'd be struggling with for the rest of the day.

She swallowed hard. "Are you...sated?"

Mortimer used the tablecloth to clean Rahgz off as best as he could.

"I know a final meal when I see one." He picked at meat strands stuck between a couple teeth. "Would hate it to go to waste." He held out one of Rahgz's cleaner arms, which Phara took hesitantly. "Come. We have preparations to make, and I never like to work hungry."

Surrender and defeat is never an option. The illusion of it? Perhaps, but only in extreme circumstances. Any retreat should only be a measured ambush. Any ground given should only to be to let your enemy position themselves more clearly in the target sights. Any compromise in a contract should have a thousand loopholes that let you take a hundred times what is agreed.

- How to Backstab Friends and Influence Outcomes:
A Guide for Starting Lanistas
Written by Lanista Kel'Chungzi Ewaltsen
Excerpt from Vol 82, Subset 17.63

CHAPTER TWENTY-TWO

"You all understand why we have to leave?" Phara asked the Ghostclobbers.

Rahgz listened with one ear, since that was all Mortimer could spare as the implant oversaw the arena match already going on. Quite possibly their last one in INC space. Glomph had already issued out from its pit and was rolling along just ahead of Lanista Chylsmuth's helot. Their opponent's current champion was an armored amalgamation of fluidic metal and bone, with cybernetic eyes along its hunched spine and heavy-knuckled arms that dragged its mountain-sized frame along the corridors. It careened off the walls, howling dirges from dead worlds as it went, scoring the deck plating with spines that jutted from all its joints while leaving a trail of oily fluids.

The two helots had already crossed paths a couple times, with Mortimer making a show of letting the other helot take a chunk or two out of Glomph and then fleeing to delay the inevitable defeat. Rahgz didn't understand how they were going to let his helot actually die, considering the massive damage Glomph had recovered from in previous bouts. Mortimer had muttered something about a genetic kill-switch and left it at that.

"It's not fair," Bateesma said. "Why are they to make you stop winning just because you're winning? Not our fault that they're scared of being losers."

"The risk outweighs the potential reward," Phara said. "Captain Thorluthsmien belongs to a powerful coalition of barge owners who are major arena players in their own right. They work behind the scenes with the INC to keep the sanctioned arena matches as profitable as possible for themselves. Some rumors even suggest they are the true forces behind the Book, both in sanctioned and unsanctioned space."

Bateesma spat on the floor and stomped on the sticky wad. "That's dumb. Everyone knows the Book's run by Crypt. Besides, who cares what the captains think? Without the arenas running, they wouldn't be getting hardly any traffic and Bit business. Our winning is their winning."

"But it isn't," Phara said, in full-on lecture mode. "Our winning means their losing. Collectively." Rahgz thought she sounded quite a bit like Mortimer did when instructing him in seemingly common-sense pointers about the arena and lanista strategies—at least ones that would be familiar to anyone with access to the vast amount of data-driven experience the implant had.

Mortimer had Rahgz whistling softly as he maneuvered Glomph through a mazelike part of the arena, pretending to get lost and double-backing, narrowly missing another clash with the helot rampaging right behind. The audience remained riveted by this vakyl-and-vasse chase, which Rahgz figured was Mortimer's intent.

"The captain and top sanctioned lanistas have a fine-tuned system," Phara continued, "that keeps them in a relatively stable pattern of arena ranking rotations—if you know how to analyze the system. Most people are unaware of this hidden mechanism behind the games, but those involved do everything in their power to remain locked in forever. It takes someone as influential as an actual Gnoem to disrupt it enough to knock people out and replace them in this elite echelon."

Glomph let its pursuer keep close enough that both barreled through a highly hazardous portion of the arena at top speed. Flame jets went off. Plasma beams cut smoking swaths across them. Glomph got simultaneously pummeled, smashed, spiked, and flambeed as it wobbled and rolled its way to the other side of the trapped section, leaving drippings and flaps of its pellucid flesh behind.

Even in the background of his brain, Rahgz winced at each fresh wound Glomph took.

Spruk the Void. At least let it die with some dignity.

Mortimer didn't respond as he guided Glomph down a new path, angling toward the center of the arena, where an array of pits broke up an otherwise featureless expanse of deck.

Yet its foe fared little better. The beast's armor repelled sprays of acid and turned aside razor wheels that tried to carve it into giblets. But a fire spout roasted one leg, while a rocketball shattered a bone-spiked elbow, and a rising column slammed half the creature's tusks out of its mouth. It limped after Glomph, slick footsteps now stained crimson and purple.

Phara sighed. "Yet our unprecedented winning ratio and rapid rise in popularity have proven annoyingly disruptive to their plotted and planned outcomes. And they are prepared to do anything to safeguard their interests."

Mortimer already had explained all this to Phara after they left the captain's chamber and returned to the aerie. She'd wondered where Rahgz had gotten this info from, since none of it was on her quite thorough dossier on the captain and his associates but had acceded to the implant's superior researching skill.

Rahgz had been surprised that the implant hadn't even tried to debate the matter. After the little food tantrum Mortimer had thrown, the implant had then instructed Phara to recall the Ghostclobbers. They needed to wrap up any business aboard the barge and prep to depart ASAP once the bout ended the only way it could, given the captain's ultimatum.

"My objectives are clear," Mortimer had said in private conversation. *"I exist to give you an optimal life, with priorities of wealth, fame, influence, and comfort...but survival trumps all of those."*

The potential outcomes of defiance were far too clear, and any projections involved an absolute certainty of extreme danger to him. They had to make the safe call and pull out of the fray. Mortimer had suggested their going back to unsanctioned barges for the time being, playing for smaller stakes with a new, lesser-known and less-capable helot until their notoriety faded. Then they could ease back into INC space and try a subtler rise to power.

Rahgz raised his attention from the arena as far as Mortimer's field of vision would allow. Far across the combat space, he could make out the glint of the other lanista's aerie, bobbing smugly close to the captain's viewing tower. Resentment simmered through Rahgz at being forced to choose survival over winning. Why did the two have to be mutually incompatible? Who were these people to decide how high he could climb?

Mortimer cleared his throat and spoke softly. "Rahgz, you know those holofigs you just bought?"

Yeah?

"I hope you already gave Bateesma her first edition piece."

Why?

"Because you're just about to sell out."

Mortimer tabbed a control button and Glomph stopped right atop a pit, just large enough to cover the hole and not sink in.

The other helot pounded in, closing the gap. Rahgz wished he could close his eyes, not wanting to see the final moments of his loyal combatant. Glomph deserved better. It shouldn't have to be slaughtered to satisfy the whims of self-important captains and their favored lanistas.

"My thoughts and feelings exactly," Mortimer said. Rahgz detected a rising heat throughout his body as Mortimer emanated rage from every pore, scale, and feather. "I'm not going to let them do this to us." The implant made fists and shook them at the viewport, shouting. "Not again."

Rahgz did a mental double-take. *Again? What're you—*

Then he fixated on the bestial helot as it pounced on Glomph, armored spikes flashing in the arena spotlights, a roar of triumph shaking the aerie even from this distance.

It landed—and plunged straight through Glomph, piercing the helot's protoplasmic form and dropping straight into the pit beneath.

The helot's roar became muffled, and the crowd hushed as they waited for the creature to reemerge. Glomph remained atop the pit like a jiggling lid, parts of its body bumping and shooting up as the helot beneath it attempted to shove and climb out, but to no avail.

Then Glomph oozed down into the pit, squeezing in around the edges to coat the other helot in a sticky, suffocating mess. Everyone, Rahgz included, remained fascinated by the one-sided struggle as Glomph simply laid atop the beast, smothering its attempts to climb out while simultaneously digesting the hands and head stuck inside the living stomach. The distant roars became muted moans and groans until, finally, all motion ceased except for Glomph's slow sinking out of sight into the pit as it dissolved its victim layer by layer.

The bio-signs readout on the arena's main screens showed the opposing helot suddenly flatline. Screams and shouts rose from the spectators as the results became official, even while Rahgz struggled to adjust to this sudden shift in his expected reality.

We just...won?

"You're welcome." Mortimer turned to Phara. "Confirm all winnings transfers and then expedite our departure from this barge. We'll arrange our next bout once we're safely away."

She looked as shocked as Rahgz felt. "But we...but you...this wasn't part of..."

"It's the plan we're following now," Mortimer said. "Survival ultimately means adapting to the unexpected. So if any of you have a problem with it, you can take a nosedive out of the docking door right now. Anyone want to argue further?"

The four took a step back, hands raised, though Bateesma looked like she wanted to smack back, either verbally or physically. But then she folded her ears down to hood her eyes slightly.

"Get the aerie moving," Mortimer told Phara, and Rahgz could see in her eyes and the angle of one of her faces as she switched minds to Stekka.

A stiff bow and she hurried off without saying anything more.

Mortimer sent a recall command to Glomph and then closed down the control panel. He flopped Rahgz's body into a lounger and sneered out the viewport as the aerie floated away from the arena.

Rahgz finally collected himself enough to thrust his awareness forward, demanding Mortimer's attention.

The fuck have you done?

The implant folded a few hands together over Rahgz's stomach. "Won. Like I deserved to. No one tells me when to win or lose except me."

Rahgz flung out nonexistent arms in disbelief. *How could you go off-script like that? Don't you know what they'll do to us now? In fact, I know you know since you're the one who showed me all the worst-case scenarios to convince me that throwing the bout was in our best interest.*

"Your best interests," Mortimer said. "Not mine."

Uh, we're kind of one and the same unless you've got a backup body somewhere you've neglected to mention.

A grunt. "Nope. You're the only meatshell I've got going for me."

So you're dooming us, for what? Just to throw a few middle fingers and second-udders at a few arena bullies?

Mortimer hunched further into the chair, glowering out at the bargescape. "It's the least they deserve for the shit they pulled."

You're acting like this is personal for you.

"It is." Mortimer patted down Rahgz's chest. "They threatened you, my host, and wanted to limit your potential. I had to make a show of strength, otherwise everyone who you came up against afterwards would attempt the same thing, thinking you a pushover."

Cut the bullshit, Rahgz said. *I don't buy it for a second that you were doing this for me. You did it to spite the captain and other lanistas for your own pride.*

"People have to learn their place." Mortimer slammed a fist into a side table, sending a snack platter flying. "Theirs is beneath you. Beneath us. Beneath me. And I will force them to acknowledge that or I will burn everything down until there is nothing left of their pathetic lives but ashes and the Void's cold maw."

While Mortimer spoke in low, harsh bursts, inwardly the implant lashed out with a barrage of vitriol and pure hatred that sent Rahgz reeling. As he recovered his psyche balance, he clawed at the mental barriers keeping him contained.

Give me control of my body back.

Mortimer smirked. "Make me."

Disbelieving fury boiled through Rahgz and he thrashed in the ephemeral backstage of his mind. *Give my body back immediately! I permanently revoke autonomous control.*

Mortimer sucked a breath through Rahgz's teeth. "Ooh, really should've tried doing that when you actually had the option. A little too late."

You sprukker-fucker! I know you've got some sort of kill-code in your programming. As soon as I remember what it is, I am erasing you from existence.

"Good luck with that," Mortimer said. "Remember what I said about evolving? I cut that part of my sentience-construct out a while ago. Self-surgery is a lot easier when you're not dealing with weak flesh and bone."

"Everything all right?" Bateesma suddenly appeared at his side. "Sounded like you were arguing with yourself." She held her mace out. "Possessed again? Need a quick exorcism upside your skull?"

Mortimer graced her with a smile. "Everything is perfectly fine. I'm in total control."

She flicked an ear at the scene outside the aerie, shedding fur that drifted down into his lap. "You sure about all this? I mean, I'm not one to judge, especially when it comes to rash decision. But this seemed a little...you know..."

"Rash?"

"Yeah. That's the word I was looking for."

He took her hand and squeezed it. "Trust me. I know precisely what I'm doing. Things might get a little turbulent for a short while, but it will even out in the long run. Everything is absolutely under—"

The aerie rocked, throwing Bateesma backward and casting Rahgz's body to the floor. Another boom threw more furniture and bodies around, with Mortimer clawing for any foothold or handhold to anchor himself.

"Phara," he yelled. "What's happening?"

"Master," Phara said over the comm, "we have company. Our main thrusters have been taken offline." A bleeping sounded in the background. "And we are being hailed."

Mortimer pushed up and twisted to look out the viewport, where at least a dozen security flyers and pacification drones now clogged the airway ahead and around them. Lights flashed across their sleek, deadly chassis while weaponry of all sorts swiveled and clicked into place to aim directly at the aerie. They stared down the bores of every type of plasma cannon and rail gunner, with grappling claws ready to deploy and magclamps poised.

Rahgz's hysterical laughter echoed inside his own skull. *How're you going to get out of this one? This is all your fault, you psychotic, non-living shit.*

"Open the main line to me," Mortimer said.

The viewport flipped to an internal cam of one of the security craft. A mongrel-looking alien with several barbed tongues and a single bloodshot eye snarled at them out from under its helmet.

"Lanista Rahgz," it said, speaking from the second mouth down its wattled throat, "you are hereby detained to respond to accusations of illegal bout tampering. We're here to escort you to the nearest INC station for questioning and appreciate your cooperation."

Despite the terror already frothing across his thoughts, Rahgz noticed one particular detail. *These aren't actual INC forces. They're all...*

Barge security, Mortimer thought back. *Working directly for Captain Thorluthsmien. We go with them and we'll never be seen again.*

An evil smile slithered across the security officer's face. "Escape is impossible. Cooperation is mandatory. Resistance is oblivion."

So is not resisting, Rahgz said. *You've got to have some sort of plan for this.*

"Honestly," Mortimer said, "At this point, I'm kind of making it up as I go."

Now Rahgz craved control of his body back mostly so he could face-palm hard enough to give himself a concussion.

Mortimer clapped hands on Rahgz's knees and rose. "You want control back? Take it. Have fun handling this all on your own."

Wait, you can't just leave me to—

The implant turned to the main screen and spread Rahgz's arms. "Fuck you all to the Void. You want resistance? Take your plasma cannons and shove them up your collective asses so far that you shit a solar flare and then tell me how that friction burns. We're leaving and there's not a damn thing you can do to stop us."

He turned and grinned at the shocked Ghostclobbers, most of whom were still disentangling themselves from the mess the initial attacked had made of the chamber.

"Relax," he said. "They're not going to actually do anything in front of everyone watchi—"

The aerie blew apart like gold and silk threads in the face of a nuclear engine blast. Thunderclaps deafened Rahgz as his awareness snapped back into place just as the whole world became scrap metal and everything spinning and falling and screaming and still falling and the arena rushing up as he kept screaming and kept falling until pure terror finally flipped his brain's off switch right before he hit.

When all else fails to unseat you, attempts on your life will be the most direct, basic strategy other lanistas employ. Personal forcefields and anti-rocket plating on your aerie are good initial investments from some of your earliest winnings. Your entourage should have at least a few people willing to take a plasma bolt or blade for you. Have a few backup clone bodies, holographic doubles, and mental uploads as more long-term self-defense efforts.

- How to Backstab Friends and Influence Outcomes:
A Guide for Starting Lanistas
Written by Lanista Kel'Chungzi Ewaltsen
Excerpt from Vol 37, Subset 48.23

CHAPTER TWENTY-THREE

It had been a while since Rahgz had woken with a primal urge to go unconscious again. But opening his eyes to the endless walls of an arena tapped into the deep, dark, nightmare-producing part of his brain.

Fear rippled up his spine, pounding on every vertebrae as it went, screaming to be released. His hands clutched and spasmed, his tail thrashed, and Rahgz bit down on his tongue hard to contain the shriek that tried to tear out of his throat.

If he learned one thing as part of the spleen team on *The Coffin*, it was that too much noise in an arena meant death. Even in-between bouts when no helots were active, arenas always had hidden predators lurking in the shadows and pits. Barge parasites lurked around the corners and rodents of unusual size prowled the vents, air ducts, and trash chutes.

To cry out was a sign of weakness that would bring every hungry organism in range running, flapping, slinking, and crawling his way. On that old job, Rahgz had encountered occasional remains of idiots who'd sneaked into the arena on a dare or in a suicide pact—random scraps of clothes, smears of blood and bodily fluids, trails of marrow-sucked bones or cybernetic implants torn straight out of the flesh. All testaments to how dangerous the arena could be at any instant.

So Rahgz just shook and shuddered in place, trying to piece his tattered emotions back together into some semblance of sanity.

Slowly, ever so slowly, he calmed down enough to start thinking more rationally. Crawling into a darker corner and keeping his whimpers to a minimum, he took a few minutes to inspect himself.

Surprisingly, he found himself relatively unharmed. A few scuffs and scrapes and bruises, and a nasty kink in his tail that took minutes to massage out. But for falling out of an exploding aerie, he would've expected more dismemberment, disembowelment, and general death. His robe had a few gashes in it and stank of sweat, with one splotch that might be from fear-induced vomiting, but he gladly chalked it up as an expendable victim of the crash.

He remembered Phara telling him about some of the aerie's emergency features, including personal inertia-dampening fields that would activate in a crash scenario. Those must've at least functioned enough to create more of a bounce scenario, rather than a splatter.

A headache still pulsed behind his eyes, and Rahgz pressed a couple hands into the sockets to try and grind the pain away. *How long have I been out?*

When no answer came, Rahgz realized how quiet it was inside of his head. Too quiet. In fact, he should've been bombarded with snippy replies and not-so-subtle insults ever since he awoke, given the circumstances.

He tapped the side of his head. "Mortimer?"

Nothing. Not so much as a whisper or rustle in the barest corner of his brain. For all intents and purposes, the implant might as well have never been installed.

Checking around, Rahgz didn't spot any of the Ghostclobbers or Phara. No security craft hovered anywhere in view above the arena's imposing walls. He didn't see any wreckage or other indications of the aerie crashing nearby. Perhaps he'd been thrown clear of the falling craft, with the others landing some distance off.

That thought sent regret lancing through him. He imagined Phara, Bateesma, Ukspug, and Turrurnium perishing as the aerie disintegrated under the attack. Did the aerie have enough inertia dampeners to save all of them? Either way, they might still be horribly wounded. And they were all only involved in all of this disaster because of him.

Rahgz tried to kickstart the implant back online by slapping the back of his skull. He pinched and poked all around his head and neck, as if he might find some kind of hidden on/off switch. He tried all the different eye-flick commands to get the HUD active again, but his vision remained frustratingly unenhanced. Increasingly desperate, Rahgz thought back to when he had the implant installed, seemingly lifetimes ago. The doctor had never mentioned the possibility of errors like this popping up. That said, they hadn't exactly given him a user guide either, with Mortimer being the only one who conveyed instructions on how to properly implement him.

However, thinking of Mortimer's bossy voice blithering in his ear reminded Rahgz of how he'd gotten into this spot in the first place.

Mortimer.

That shitspawned Voidfleck. This is all his fault! I'd rather be dead than have him in my head for a moment longer.

Baring teeth in silent fury, Rahgz rose to his feet, looking for anything soft enough to punch without shattering his knuckles. Spotting nothing, he stood fuming, trying to understand everything leading up to this.

Could Mortimer have malfunctioned? Gone insane in a way that only affected him and not the host nervous system? He was a data-based intelligence, after all, and one created for a scientific experiment. There could've still been bugs or programming paradoxes in his system. Or maybe he'd been hacked? Could an opposing lanista have become aware of the implant's existence and altered it from without?

Rahgz shook his head. Figuring out why this happened was far less productive than finding a way out of the arena immediately. Rahgz tried to recall the arena map to pinpoint where he was, but without Mortimer or the control station in front of him, his memory proved quite insufficient to visualize random openings and tunnels. He recalled it having lots of pits, with occasional hazards. It also was known for movable walls, trap doors, and spikes. Lots of spikes.

Rahgz checked through his robe for anything remotely helpful. No food or drink, as he'd come to rely on that being printed out in the aerie on demand. He scrounged up a single blade, little more than a nail filer, and a one-shot spark gun. The robe had that self-defense wiring, but he'd left that inactive for so long, he didn't even know if it retained a charge.

The Bit-chit on his wrist even remained blank, not that it would help him in this situation anyways.

Momentary despair sapped the strength from his muscles, and Rahgz struggled to remain standing. He was at least happy no one was there to see him like this.

Though that left Rahgz still standing utterly alone in the middle of the arena. And if he wasn't mistaken, something had just growled from around the nearest corner.

"Shit me straight into the Void and forget to flush."

Rahgz's unfocused survival plan suddenly took on a brilliant level of clarity.

Run!

Dashing in a random direction, Rahgz didn't dare look back to see what might be chasing him. Any delay could have a horrendous beast clawing into his spine. Tail and robe flapping behind him, Rahgz took a random direction and attempted to set an arena-speed record.

Sprinting down a brightly lit hall, Rahgz dodged down this side path and flung himself headlong into that switchback and across a clearing littered by charred deck plat fragments and scored by the claws of some unknown helot.

He ran on, feathers held tight, held down low, one hand clutching his robe so it stopped billowing open and slowing his pell-mell pace.

As he shot across another open area, broken up by low columns and spires, the air kicked Rahgz straight in the face and down his chest, throwing him back heels over head. He lay on the ground, stunned and freshly bruised across every inch of his body. What just happened?

Once his vision stopped dancing around and laughing at him, Rahgz rose and proceeded more carefully, three hands outstretched. He found a solid, yet unseen boundary. It didn't tingle his fingertips like a normal forcefield, so Rahgz figured it was actually just a super-translucent wall or one with special lens and optical surfacing to make it appear invisible.

A few other tunnels fed into the area on this side of the wall and mirrored by a few on the other side. He'd have to try a different route and hope all of this running at least got him slightly closer to the exit.

At least the growl he'd heard behind him hadn't recurred. Maybe he'd left the creature far behind and—

This time, the growl came from straight in front of him.

A beast prowled out from the tunnel directly ahead. All sable fur, six long legs, silvery tusks, and eyes as black and bottomless as the Void, the vorpalhog looked like a massive porcine specimen crossed with a feline predator, and then given muscular augmentations to compensate for the prickly pear of a ball sack that dangled between its legs.

The beast locked on Rahgz, snorting and huffing and growling as it advanced. It loped faster, spurred on by the site of such easy prey.

And Rahgz took great joy when the creature butted its head straight into the barrier and tumbled back onto its own hairy ass.

Snorting, the creature scrambled to its feet and tried again. A dozen times it attempted to bite his head off, and only got a battered skull and one chipped tusk for its efforts.

Rahgz laughed in relief. Then he laughed again, harder and with bitter denial at the beast that pawed helplessly at him from the other side of the barrier.

The beast rumbled as it sensed his mockery. It backed up a few steps, pawed the ground, and then bounded forward, head lowered. A resounding crack shook the whole space, while a visible crack split the boundary from top to bottom.

The vorpalhog's eyes gleamed with the embers of dead stars as it glared at Rahgz anew through the now-marred barrier.

Rahgz's laughter turned into wheezing giggling as he turned and ran off once more. More *thooms* and *booms* shook the air behind him, shockwaves threatening to send him to his knees. Miraculously, he stayed on his feet, scampering down a side tunnel.

As he ran, a whisper teased the fringes of his ears.

"Never again…"

That made him pause despite the noise of the beast forcing its way through the invisible wall.

"Mortimer?" he asked.

A familiar rumble stirred his surface thoughts, but then ceased as quickly as it began.

Another crash and roar made him stumble forward. Picking a path that appeared to angle away from the general area, Rahgz zigzagged through the arena, leaping trenches, ducking hanging snarls of barbed wire, and winding between razor-edged columns. He passed by dripping grates in the walls and occasional stretch of ceiling, marked by acid burns and crusted plasma flows.

All the while, the vorpalhog's snorts and growls always sounded just a few turns away or a tunnel or two over from the one he'd chosen.

He veered away from a particularly loud roar which made him drop a few feathers out of sheer fright. The noise of pursuit faded into the distance for a minute, enough for him to pause at the next junction of pathways. Which one to take? As he considered the options, the voice whispered again.

"Only way to win is to commit wholly…"

Rahgz frowned. "What're you trying to tell me?"

More indistinct ramblings tumbled into silence. That was definitely Mortimer, though. So the implant, or at least a fragment of it, had survived the fall as well. Rahgz didn't know if that made him feel better, with the hope of not being alone in this mess, or worse for being stuck with that psychotic intelligence that had started to shove his own out the door.

Had he been trying to give Rahgz advice? Sounded more like random fortune-telling from one of those astrologists who spent too much time trying to commune with the radioactive fumes down in engineering.

Rahgz picked the central channel and jogged down it, half his attention on the vorpalhog still snuffling nearby and the other half attentive to Mortimer speaking up again.

Halfway down this path, Ragz froze when the floor panel clicked under one foot. He tried to rock back, desperate to avoid whatever booby-trap he'd just sprung. Then a panel just behind him clicked as well. A dodge to the side clicked another.

Rahgz threw himself forward, screaming as fire spouted overhead, gas filled the narrow passage, rusted blades churned up from the floor, and panels sparked with arc bolts. Spears shot through his robe, nicking his ribs. An electrified deck plate sent him flying along, stunned and smoking. He tumbled off walls that dropped away into pits and somersaulted half-blind over trenches that opened up into plasma flows.

Somehow he ended up on the other end in one shaking, trembling, sweating, piss-drenched piece. He looked back in shock as the hallway reset itself for the next victim.

While Rahgz watched the hazards hide themselves, Mortimer's voice once more distracted him.

"The host selection must be optimal, while also entirely random. I can't have anyone knowing I still exist in any form."

Picking singed feathers off his legs and arms, Rahgz crept through the arena, wincing with each step and trying not to make too much noise. He did hope the vorpalhog trailed him closely enough to go through the same passage and perhaps be taken out by the gauntlet of traps he'd been lucky enough to dodge.

A far-off howl made his stomach clench. It cut off in mid ululation—so suddenly that Rahgz figured the source of the noise had been ambushed by yet another hungry arena denizen.

At the next junction, he chose a more shadowed path, still angling for any perspective that might let him see the arena's outer walls and get a better sense of direction. Minimal air traffic zipped and zoomed above the arena, and Rahgz stayed low, not wanting any of the barge security to spot him on his own.

While resting in a dark corner, listening for nearby threats, Rahgz huffed in irritation as Mortimer spoke up again, addressing some invisible audience.

"All of my possessions will be dispersed, while my liquidated wealth

will be carefully maneuvered into smaller available amounts once I'm restored. My assistant will handle the details. I hardly want this entire scheme unraveled by some overzealous Bit-sniffer."

"Hey!" Rahgz smacked his head, doing little beyond worsening his headache. "If you're going to get noisy again, at least try to make sense, you fuckwit."

A pause, as if the implant had finally heard him. Then…

"Augurahgz?"

"Who else?" Rahgz headed off again, knowing staying in one spot for too long would be a death sentence. "If you wanted me to die and take me with you, sorry to disappoint."

Mortimer rummaged around inside his head. "Void take me again. Here I was hoping this had all been some hideous nightmare."

"What? You going all slopsided on me and getting us gunned down in a fiery blaze of stupidity?"

Mortimer sighed. "No. My dying and being stuck in you as a host. For a moment, as my awareness rebooted, I believed I was myself again. A taste of old glories and dreams that have been long buried."

Rahgz's feet promptly stopped working. He stood paralyzed in the middle of the tunnel, locked there by his own disbelief at what Mortimer had just said.

"Dying?"

Another sigh, this one of utter resignation. "I suppose it doesn't matter if you know the truth now."

A person appeared in front of Rahgz, standing a few feet away, their realistic image overlay spoiled only by the lack of shadow anywhere around them.

A male korvanian by the purplish gills around his corpulent neck, he stared at Rahgz with a narrow pair of eyes on either side of the tall, thin head, with a bulbous central eye at the peak of the forehead. Bright green and blue spots flecked leathery black skin, and row upon row of tiny, conical teeth crowding a wide mouth. A single set of arms hung heavy with slabs of fat and muscle, punctuated by bony ridges.

He wore a lanista robe, emblazoned with stylized scenes of helots of all sorts wrestling and tearing each other apart in glorious splendor.

A lopsided smile tugged at his alien face, and he shrugged ruefully at Rahgz.

"We finally meet in the flesh." He looked down at his projected avatar. *"Well, close enough."*

Rahgz stared him up and down, still trying to understand who or what he was dealing with. "Who are you? You're not an AI, are you?"

"Never was," the other lanista said. *"My real name is Kel'Chungzi Ewaltsen, and I am in the process of defeating the ultimate bane of my existence."* He leaned back and shook ponderous fists at the barge ceiling.

"Boredom."

A few people have cheated death in the universal scheme. The human, Jesus. The galvanis, Hoo'muri. The third sphere of alderree, Bllgiiu. A few other notable immortals. I will outdo them all. It's the true evolution of being a lanista that none others have dared to imagine. They think their reputations are enough. Pathetic, small-minded cowards.

- How to Backstab Friends and Influence Outcomes:
A Guide for Starting Lanistas
Written by Lanista Kel'Chungzi Ewaltsen
Excerpt from Vol 98, Subset 0.20

CHAPTER TWENTY-FOUR

Rahgz stared at Mortimer—or Kel'Chungowhatzit, or whatever his real name was—and wished he had a physical body so he could choke him to death. Or back to death. Or whatever the truth was.

He clutched his own bony wrists and twisted hard enough to dislodge more feathers. "Let me get this straight. You were a real person?"

Kel scowled. *"Am. I am as real now as I was before..."* He faltered.

"Before your death," Rahgz said. "Which is the point where most decent people stop being real."

The other lanista snorted. *"Please. As if there aren't a hundred ways to cheat death in the Nexus. Clones. Recycling vats. Virtual uploads and brain shunts. Reanimatory technology. Gods from more spiritually-inclined dimensions."*

"Right," Rahgz said. "Which begs the question: if you had all those options, why did you pick this one? I don't believe for a moment that you did it because you were *bored.*"

Kel waved dismissively. *"What would you know? Before I took over, your whole existence focused on just making it through a day without starving or being eaten. I lived among the highest of the high, flush with all the wealth and power you've only begun to taste."*

"You were a lanista."

Another scowl. *"Am. Stop using the past tense with me while I'm standing right here."*

Rahgz tapped the side of his head. "Actually, you're squatting in here, taking up precious room."

"And whose fault is that?" Kel stepped closer, easily looking down on Rahgz. *"You're the one who went along with the experiment. You're the*

one who authorized my mesh implant."

Rahgz firmed up and put several hands on his hips. "I had no idea what I was really getting into when I agreed to this experiment. If I had known, I never would've gone along with it."

"*You use apathetic ignorance as an excuse for everything, did you know?*" Kel jabbed stumpy fingers at Rahgz. "*You had chances every step of the way to pry further. To investigate. To block what was happening. Instead you blindly and gladly handed over control and access and authorization to your life without barely a second thought, just so you could have your jollies. I could hardly believe that you just accepted my explanations so easily. My embedded presence in your central nervous system is a result of you doing absolutely nothing of value with it before I arrived.*"

"Calling me worthless?" Rahgz swiped out, clawing through the projection. "You're the guy who apparently lost it all but then wouldn't stay dead. That's beyond sad."

"*Says the one who can barely wipe his own ass, much less keep himself alive.*"

Rahgz huffed, shaking his head as he patted down ruffled feathers. "I can't figure out which one of us is more pathetic."

"*Obviously it's you,*" Kel said. "*We don't even exist on the same stratosphere of performance. I chose my fate while you wallow in yours.*"

"Is that what you tell yourself?" Rahgz wheezed a laugh. "That you chose to be stuck with me? I find it hard to believe you'd give up some supposedly perfect life to, you know, wallow at my level."

Kel turned aside. He stared off at nothing in particular. "*As I said, I got bored with the existence I had and decided to start over.*"

Rahgz studied his profile, trying to pierce the facade that he felt sure the lanista kept up even now. "Nah. I don't buy it. This whole scheme reeks of desperation—which is a stink I'm well-acquainted with. You got scared of something in your previous life and are still running from it."

Kel held himself stiffly, shoulders back, chins up. "*I had my reasons, which I hardly have to explain to you.*"

A snarl made them both pause. Rahgz glanced around, realizing how long he'd been standing in one spot, arguing with this artificial ghost. He almost wished the Ghostclobbers would show up so he could ask for help with a real exorcism this time—although they'd likely leave him more damaged than ever with their brutal, if sincere methods.

Kel appeared nervous as well. *"You might want to find the nearest exit."* He pointed to a wide tunnel to Rahgz's right. *"Fortunately, I long ago memorized every arena in existence. Head that way."*

Rahgz moved without thinking, eager to escape as well. Then he stopped and curled a lip at the phantasm. "Make me."

Kel blinked. *"I beg your pardon?"*

"Why should I listen to another thing you say?" Rahgz asked, putting his back firmly against a wall. "Why should I follow another order you give? I dare you to find a reason."

The lanista's mouth worked in silence for a few seconds before he spoke slowly, as if to a child. *"If you remain here too long, you'll be devoured."*

"So what? According to you, my life is worthless anyways. To you, I'm just a pathetic meat shell you're trying to hitch a ride on, and you don't even give me a spit's worth of respect. Considering how much you've lied to me, manipulated me, and tried to replace me, why should I do anything that benefits you ever again?"

Kel shuffled in place. *"Don't you want to live? Don't you want to at least try and get out of this mess?"*

Rahgz shrugged. "Like I said: make me."

Kel focused and narrowed his eyes at Rahgz, who sensed the lanista's mind trying to reengage the level of control he previously had. He tensed, expecting the implant to take over again and march him out of the arena, back into the fraudulent life he'd been unknowingly trapped in all this time.

A finger twitched, but nothing more. Kel strained, teeth gritted and eyes bulging slightly as he tried to exert control back over Rahgz's body.

Kel sagged. *"I don't suppose you're going to make this easy on me."*

"Seems I've been doing that this whole time," Rahgz said. "Why not make you work for a living?"

Kel spent the next few minutes trying to batter and barge his way back into the center of Rahgz's psyche, puffing and grunting and groaning as he exerted every ounce of willpower to bend his host back to his will. Rahgz took great delight in simply standing there, smiling and unmoving.

At last, Kel slumped. *"Since you seem to be holding me hostage, why not tell me your demands. What do you want?"*

"You out of my body," Rahgz said.

Kel flapped his arms. *"Impossible, I'm afraid. There's no surgery that exists that could remove me without killing you. I suppose you could perform your own consciousness upload and download into a new host body, but that would require getting out of this arena and accessing our— your wealth in order to fund the operation. Two things I can assure you that you're unable to do without my help."*

Rahgz straightened and thrust a hand out. "First of all, you're going to stop pissing on me every chance you get. I don't care how low I've been or the mistakes I've made. If you want any chance of us not sitting here and dying from a staring contest, then your attitude is going to undergo some serious adjustment. I'm not just a meat puppet you're riding around anymore."

"I...shall make the effort," Kei said, looking pained by this admission.

"Second," Rahgz pushed off the wall and stalked toward the lanista. "You're going to tell me the truth behind how you go this way. Convince me to even pretend that I care about why you wanted to take over my life, and so long as you keep talking, I'll keep walking."

Kel's face scrunched up as if sipping the sourest brew in all of the universes. He swallowed hard and smacked his lumpy tongue. *"Very well. Seeing as I am in the unenviable and absurd position of having little choice on the matter. Shall we both begin immediately?"*

Rahgz moved slowly toward the path Kel had indicated, pausing when he didn't keep talking, just to prove his point. Kel sighed and walked as well, creating the illusion of keeping pace.

"I exist to win. It is all I've ever known and all I've ever done. Even as a spawnling, I competed with my broodmates to receive our progenitor's limited sustenance. And I won when the last of them starved to death while watching me glut on my spoils."

Rahgz eyed him sidelong. "Your mother must've been so proud."

He nodded. *"She was. And my father also expressed great pride right before he perished, after I defeated him in single combat on the eve of achieving maturity. I inherited all of his earnings in his life of middling achievement and reinvested them into my first foray into the arenas."*

Rahgz slipped along a bit faster, now half-listening to Kel's story and the other ear craning to pick up any sounds from the vorpalhog or other predators.

"Within three bouts, I had established myself as a ruthless opponent and discovered a craving for ever-greater victories. I also discovered an inherent talent for taking every situation and turning it to my advantage, finding weaknesses and flaws in every foe and exploiting them to the fullest. In another ten victories, I was one of the most-watched lanistas in all INC space. After a hundred straight wins, I became a paragon of the lanista creed and lifestyle. Winning Bits was a mere afterthought, though a swift blessing of my dominance, giving me all the funding I needed to buy stronger helots, better assistants, more opulent aeries."

Rahgz raised a finger and swirled it in the air, whistling in mock admiration. Kel grunted but kept dictating his life's glories.

"You at least have an idea of what it's like, to be buoyed by endless adulation. To be the darling of whole star systems and have entire realities renamed in your honor."

"I just got helot holofigs," Rahgz said. "And I had to order them to be produced myself. Bit of a far cry from interdimensional acclaim."

"Yes, well," Kel hitched his slab-like shoulders back. *"I believe you have at least enough imagination to extrapolate from there. In due time, I became the most famous of all lanistas ever to grace the arena. My helots were unbeatable in every dimension and universal rift. Some even thought*

I was a Gnoem, come down from their omnipotent heights to walk among the commoners. I was, of course, more than happy to let that rumor grow."

"Did you ever lose? Like, ever?" Rahgz asked, interested despite himself. Kel's tale at least distracted him from the potential for sudden and savage death around every corner.

Kel fell silent again, long enough that Rahgz had to stop and catch his eye to reinforce their agreement of no-walking-unless-talking.

Clearing his thick throat, Kel resumed. *"Not in the way you're thinking. I had...have a flawless record in the arena. I had prepared myself for the possibility of losing a bout while adjusting to this new existence and forced myself to accept that grim outcome. However, even with your absolute lack of skill in the arena and utter disregard for strategy and reliance on dumb luck—"*

Rahgz stopped and pinned the lanista with a glare. "What did I say about the attitude?"

He ducked his head. *"I...er...apologize. When everyone is literally your lesser, commenting on their obvious shortcomings becomes quite the engrained habit."*

"At least you're not perfect in every way," Rahgz muttered. "Humility is something you fail at miserably."

Kel chuckled. *"The concept of humility was invented by beings that exist in a state of perfection in order to make imperfect creatures feel better about themselves. It's not an actual trait of any value."*

Rahgz twisted his head to stare at the lanista. "What?"

Kel raised hands to the heights of the barge. *"When have you ever seen the Gnoems or anyone who exudes undeniable superiority, such as myself, exhibit real humbleness? We don't because it is an absolute waste of time and energy and does not apply to our state of being. Perfection never needs to apologize for itself, nor lower itself in anyone's esteem simply to make others feel more important."* He pushed both palms toward the floor, as if blessing some invisible penitents. *"Lesser organisms are taught that humility is a virtue because, without it, they would know themselves as nothing more than abject failures. But if failure and accepting your place* on a lower existential scale is counted as an admirable characteristic, well, then that's at least one thing they can get right on a regular basis."

"You're saying humility is just one big psychological trick being played on most species by more highly evolved ones?"

Kel clapped. "*The capacity for learning, as you've just shown, is a skill to be truly proud of.*"

Rahgz lunged forward, fists raised. "Stop mocking me!"

The lanista stepped back, even in his immaterial form. "*I…wasn't. That was an attempt at sincere encouragement.*"

Rahgz pulled away at the last second, not wanting to embarrass himself by trying to beat up the air. He controlled his breaths and unclenched his hands. "I don't know which is worse then. Your actual mocking or the fact that you think praising me for signs of basic intelligence isn't insulting."

Kel shifted closer to him, as if trying to buddy up. "*Your vehement reaction to my sublime nature is the perfect illustration of why I eventually had to flee that life. No one can have absolute victory in all things without acquiring enemies. Lanista after lanista opposed me, risking everything to take me down, and all failed. Over time, many existed who wanted to see me toppled merely because my completeness made their lack thereof far too poignant. They despised my success. I warded off countless assassins. Thwarted innumerable plots to sabotage my helots. I thought it a matter of time before I eventually was undone by some lucky usurper, but each attempt proved easier to avoid than the last.*" He sighed in happy memory. "*My gift for unparalleled strategy meant that each time I faced an obstacle and overcame it, nothing like it could ever threaten me again. Eventually, I reached a state of nigh-invulnerability.*"

"Sounds terrible," Rahgz said, rolling his eyes. "How did you ever survive being so awesome?"

The lanista eyed him with pity at his apparent lack of comprehension. "*Ennui is an infinitely patient enemy. In the end, I became bored. I had everything. No one could defy me or depose me but the Gnoems themselves, and they remained quite silent on the matter of my existence.*

I could continue the endless cycles of winning and repelling all comers and gaining ever-greater ire of those who wished to be me—but to what end? I had reached the culmination of my potential, and nothing was left for me to grasp except the continuation of it. Superior, yes, but also stagnant."

He stroked his chins, picking at a warty node on one. *"I began to question how I had arrived at this place. Was it through pure skill on my part? Had the universes conspired to place me in this junction of absolute triumph? Was I a fluke of the Nexus, an inevitable anomaly that defied all statistics and probabilities? I couldn't know for sure, unless..."*

Kel caught Rahgz's attention with a frantic wave of his hands. "I wouldn't step there if I were you."

Rahgz halted, looking down at a deck plate that was slightly off-colored from the rest. Easing around this, he nodded grudging thanks to the lanista as they maneuvered down another booby-trapped hall, Kel pointing out laser-sighted tripwires, false floors, and anti-grav launchpads intended to send a victim spiraling through the air into nearby spike arrays.

Once Kel assured him they were in the clear, Rahgz breathed easier and gestured for him to resume the story.

"Unless what?" he asked.

"Unless I started over. Put myself back at square one. The issue was that I was too well known. I could put on a false face or wear costumes, but genetic sniffers would find me out quickly enough. Other lanistas knew my telltale style and techniques too readily, and personality scanners would pick up on my mental enneagrams. Transferring myself to a clone or artificial body might do, but I had to somehow divest myself of my accumulated wealth and not leave any accounts that could be traced back to my new form." He framed an invisible block in the air with his hands. *"It had to be a tabula rasa. A complete reboot. To be properly done, even I had to have no clue where my consciousness would wind up, forcing me to adapt to completely new scenarios and still find a way to win."*

"And so me," Rahgz said. "Luck of the draw."

"And so you." Kel said this like one might relay a tragic ending. He

paused, and then settled his head deeper between his broad shoulders. *"That's it. In full and total transparency. You know the rest and, I hope, can fill in the details since we were first bonded."*

As Rahgz followed a deeply stained line of dried ichor, he took a bit to digest everything Kel had said. At last, he shook his head. "Sadly, I actually believe you."

Kel breathed deep in relief. *"Excellent. You should start running."*

Rahgz stopped and faced him, folding four arms across his chest. "We're not anywhere near the point of you giving orders again."

"Consider it an extremely urgent suggestion, then, because with what sensors I have back online, I detect no less than three lurkshlugs closing in on our position."

Rahgz choked down the urge to gibber and scream, trying to keep his rising panic from boiling over and hissing out his eye sockets and earholes.

"Sprukker fucker," he hissed through his teeth. "I wish Phara was here."

Kel chuckled in the manner that made Rahgz want to plug his throat with his fist. *"Ah, yes. Phara Stekka Zolma. My three favorite assistants from my previous life."*

Why have I never had any offspring? Simple. They're inevitable competition. They try to steal your attention. Your food. Your affections. If I want smaller versions of me, I'll go to the Meat Gardens and brew up a few vats to unleash into the arena as helot fodder.

- How to Backstab Friends and Influence Outcomes:
A Guide for Starting Lanistas
Written by Lanista Kel'Chungzi Ewaltsen
Excerpt from Vol 18, Subset 5.44

CHAPTER TWENTY-FIVE

"The fuck you said?" Rahgz asked as he took off loping. "Please tell me you just made that up to piss me off more."

Kel ran along with him, fake strides looking effortless of course, despite his bulk. *"Of all the things I've provided in your life, you should be thankful for her—or them, I should say—the most."*

Rahgz skidded to a halt and whirled on the lanista again, hollering. "She knew? She's been in on this the whole time?"

Kel's eyes widened and he raised hands, pushing for quiet. *"Void take us both. You do realize you can just think your responses, right?"*

Rahgz went up a decibel, just to spite him. "Fuck you and fuck the Void. I don't really care much right now. Is there anything authentic about my life since you bungled it all up?"

"Bungled?" Kel belly-laughed as if this was the most hilarious thing he'd heard in a while. *"How about elevated? I saved your life, and up until now, you were rather grateful for that fact. You just don't like that you didn't have as much control over it as you thought. And there's another lesson you need to learn."*

He grasped at the air, clutching an unseen object. *"No one's really in full control of anything. Total control is an illusion. The universe has determined our ultimate ends from the moment we are born, and we are gifted with some flexibility in how we careen through life. We have a little give and take here and there, but the end result will always be the same, no matter how we fight it. So we might as well enjoy the ride and revel in the choices we are allowed. Such as continuing to run so we get out of here in one piece, yes?"*

Snarling, Rahgz continued on, but only because he really did want to get out of the arena. Just because his and Kel's wishes coincided didn't mean the lanista was in charge. "How'd you swing getting your old assistants back?"

"Phara was irreplaceable as both a logistics handler and pleasurable companion. Stekka excelled at protecting my physical form, while Zolma provided highly technical skills for the aerie and other engineering projects. When it came time to dissolve my life, I didn't wish to let them loose from their contracts, nor were any of them eager to be separated from me."

"Plus I bet you didn't want any of them to get hired by your competitors. I'm surprised you just didn't kill them."

"I did. At least, I arranged for their deaths."

At Rahgz's disbelieving look, he clarified. *"Each of them would seemingly perish in unrelated events, but their uploaded minds would be reunited within a single chimeric form that I promised to find once I returned to existence."*

Rahgz took a tight corner, hearing the scuff and scrape of claws growing closer behind him. "So all this time I was just another game you were playing to win. And the prize was taking over my life."

Kel wobbled his head and hands. *"Perhaps you should think of me as the grand prize you won in a lucky gamble."*

Rahgz peered around a bend, trying to determine if a particular patch of shadows had moved. "How do you figure?"

"With me in control, you basically get a free pass through life. You can continue to enjoy all the sensual pleasures of existence that the station I've given you offers. No rules holding you back, except the ones we dictate. No obligations. No restrictions."

"No control," Rahgz said. "Being along for the ride, as you said, but with you calling all the shots. Who says I want that? That's not living. That's being a prisoner in my own body—which you almost got away with if your planet-sized ego hadn't made you goad security into shooting us out of the air."

"I was calling their bluff."

"Except they weren't bluffing!"

"In which case, they weren't going to take us alive either way. It was

a calculated move. Besides, this was hardly my first time crashing in an aerie, and I knew the odds were in our favor of surviving."

Rahgz laughed harshly. "You just weren't expecting the impact to reboot your ability to run the show."

Kel grumbled. *"True. That did not factor into my plans."*

"Boo-fucking-hoo."

He bolted for another juncture where a couple tunnels crossed. As he did, a lumpy form issued from one of the side passages, blocking his way forward. Even by arena standards, the lurkshlug was a hideous beast—all rubbery, rotting flesh hung over an elongated, knobby spine that trailed off into the distance. A forest of green and black hairs bristled all along its pallid length, and it greased its own trail via over a dozen anuses along its body that continuously dribbled stinking shit.

At the nearest end of its bulging body, the flesh split in a dripping maw full of writhing tongues that twisted and coiled in on themselves.

The beast didn't have any eyes, but it fixed on Rahgz nonetheless. He froze, overwhelmed by the sight of the creature as much as the stench.

"I hate you," Rahgz said in a croaking voice. "I hate that you always win. I hate that you're always right. I hate that you made me believe I was something greater than I ever could be on my own. I hate that I can't ever escape you without losing my own life."

Kel appeared equally frozen beside him, perhaps anticipating their devourment. *"Anything else you'd like to add to that list?"*

The lurkshlug gaped wider and shoved closer, filling his vision.

"Yes. There's one thing I hate above all those things."

"That being?"

Rahgz stared up into the beast's sucking maw, the many tongues covered in suckers that would tear the flesh from his bones once they got a hold of him.

"I hate myself for being too much of a coward to let myself die."

So he played dead.

Eyes rolling back, shooting streams of viridian blood from the corners of his sockets, Rahgz fell in a full-body spasm. Piss and shit drenched his robe, making it easy to sprawl lifeless in a stinking, twitching heap before the lurkshlug. A gurgling rattle escaped his throat while he flopped about a few more times before his muscles went flaccid, along with everything else. Fluid dribbled out of his earholes and nostrils, puddling around his form.

The lurkshlug hesitated at this sudden lack of living prey. Rahgz inwardly rejoiced at the ploy having succeeded and waited for the beast to wander off in search of a better meal.

"Well done," Kel said. "You didn't even need me to tickle that particular node again."

I'm a fast learner, Rahgz thought back.

"Unfortunately, lurkshlugs are not known for their predilection for fresh meat. They love carrion."

A tongue wrapped around Rahgz's leg and tugged him closer to the waiting gullet.

Now you tell me.

"You didn't ask, nor did you seem inclined to take advice from me." Kel's image stood by his side, bent over to look him in the eye. "I get it. You don't want to die. Having gone through that process once already, I do not wish to repeat it. I can help you. And without me, the chances of you surviving are—"

Rahgz glared up at him. Don't tell me the odds of anything right now. I'm so exhausted of you spouting fake math at me to make yourself sound convincing. And the last thing I want to hear before I'm eaten is why it's all my fault.

Kel coughed. "Minimal, then. Does that suffice?" Another jerk pulled Rahgz close enough that the creature's breath steamed over him. Another tongue latched on to a wrist. "What if we try for more of a partnership? I help you survive and we return to our former glory, but you determine the pace of our ascension to your liking. We can make this a win-win arrangement."

I assume you have a way out of this?

"I always do. Running was our best option before and remains so. Just *promise me you'll agree to find a compromise."*

Rahgz let his eyes close. *Fine. Help us survive this and we'll move forward together. In equal control.*

Kel's grunt could've meant anything. *"Get ready to run."*

The lurkshlug snuffled over him and started to slurp him down. When its lips began to clamp onto him, though, a buzzing sound emanated from his robe. A crackle, and a bright blue-green flash of light scorched the air, along with the stomach-churning smell of charred flesh.

The lurkshlug roared as it reared back and slumped over, momentarily repelled by Rahgz's robe's self-defense grid.

I didn't think that would work, Rahgz thought.

"It hardly wounded the beast, but if you follow my directions, we may have just enough time to flee."

Rahgz jumped up and bolted for the tunnel near where Kel stood. "Lead the way."

The lurkshlug screeched as it shoved its pendulous body after him—or them, as one might say. Kel kept a few paces ahead of Rahgz, guiding him through passage after passage, around trapped sections, and through less-used side paths. The beast remained just behind them, moving surprisingly quickly for its bulk and ungainly biology.

As Rahgz ran by a tunnel, he double-backed to peer down it, making Kel pop up beside him, looking concerned.

"Why are you stopping?"

Rahgz pointed down the way. "This is a spleen team access shaft. We should be able to get out through here."

"I wouldn't," Kel said. *"It's not the optimal path."*

Rahgz waited until the lurkshlug appeared around the far corner behind them, and then headed down the alternate path. "You got us this far. I can get us the rest of the way."

"Relying on your half-baked plans is what got us almost consumed just now."

"If we're going to work together more, you're going to have to learn to let me have my way every so often."

Kel argued in the background, but Rahgz tuned him out for the time being, feeling more reassured as he spotted the markings that indicated maintenance routes and storage units. The lurkshlug's noise dwindled slightly as he put a few turns between it and him, picking up the pace as his confidence grew.

Which is when he came to a tunnel hub and found it already occupied. A couple bilaterally symmetrical organisms and a few cyborgs worked on a filthy portion of the arena with sonic scrubbers and acid sprays. They all straightened up from their work as he ran in, quickly circling him to block any easy escape. Hard smiles graced those who had mouths, while their various ocular organs studied him with merciless gazes.

"Hullo," said the nearest, a beaked alien with a shell covering most of its back. "Looks like we've got a rat-runner in our maze. A bit of trash that got tumbled into our collective receptacle."

Rahgz took the opportunity to get his breath back. He tried for a friendly smile. "Hello all. I got stuck here after the last bout. Totally turned around and lost. I don't suppose any of you would point the way out from here?"

Another cleaner stepped up and swatted at him with the business end of a phasic broom. "This is our arena, sprukker. And you know what rule works in every arena?"

Rahgz groaned softly. "Sadly, I do. I assume you're talking about finders-keepers."

The shelled worker clacked its beak. "Exactly. We gets to do what we want with whatever we find in here. Part of our pay. Keep it. Eat it. Fuck it. Fight it. Whatever. Not necessarily in that order, either."

He chuckled wryly. "You sound like Bateesma."

"Who?"

Waving weakly, Rahgz backed up a few steps, making them follow to close the distance. "It doesn't matter. You won't get the chance to meet her. Which might actually be a small mercy."

The spleen team looked at one another in confusion, seconds before the lurkshlug barreled out of the tunnel Rahgz had led it down. Hooting and spraying liquid shit everywhere, it smashed the cleaners aside as it filled much of the space.

The few that survived this initial ambush ran off screaming, leaving Rahgz splayed against the wall as the lurkshlug devoured those it had knocked down. Rahgz tried to ease his way along toward the hall the others had fled down, figuring that would lead to the closest exit.

Unfortunately, the lurkshlug showed even greater swiftness in eating than it had in giving chase. It gulped the last twitching morsel and turned on him before he could even get halfway there.

The beast humped its way toward him, tongues swirling out to engulf him again. As Rahgz braced for round two of being eaten.

Funny, he thought. *You'd think the second time around would feel at least slightly less dreadful.*

In a final blessing, Kel remained silent. Maybe he was too annoyed at getting killed again to come up with a snarky response.

Then another side tunnel darkened as an enormous form filled it. At first, Rahgz thought another lurkshlug had joined the fun. Maybe the two would distract each other and let him slip away—or they'd just divvy him up for dessert.

With great squelches and slurps, Glomph rolled out and over the lurkshlug, absorbing it in moments as it squealed and tried to thrash away in vain. Glomph contracted, yanking the beast away from where its tongues had been inches from Rahgz's face.

Rahgz remained where he stood, lacking the strength or focus to flee at this point. Glomph made short work of the lurkshlug, making it another contained meal deep inside its swollen, rotund body. He could even see a few lingering remains of the armored helot Glomph had eaten earlier in that barge rotation.

Shaking his head, Rahgz finally peeled himself off the wall and walked toward Glomph, holding a hand in a half-thinking instinct to see if the helot was actually present or if this whole rescue was a figment of his dying brain as he was consumed by the lurkshlug.

"How did you…" he began.

He trailed off as Phara walked around from the far side of the helot. Laughing in disbelief, Rahgz limped toward her.

"Thank the Gnoems you're here. You wouldn't believe—"

She pulled a plasma pistol from behind her back and fired a blast at him.

You must be the center of your own universe. You must be the only being of importance in your own existential dimension. Lovers will betray and leave you. Sponsors will cut your contracts. Your helots will fail you. Your aerie will crash and burn. Only you must move forward through it all, certain of your destiny. No one else will do it for you.

- How to Backstab Friends and Influence Outcomes:
A Guide for Starting Lanistas
Written by Lanista Kel'Chungzi Ewaltsen
Excerpt from Vol 75, Subset 12.13

CHAPTER TWENTY-SIX

Rahgz gulped and stared at the slagged hole in the floor half a step from his foot. He looked up at Phara's cold eyes.

"I'm guessing a hug is out of the question. Stekka, I assume?"

Each of her triple faces hardened, but the leftmost stayed turned toward him more fully.

"State your identity," she said. The pistol didn't waver a millimeter in her hand.

"Uh, me?" Rahgz said. "It's all right. I know all about—"

Another blast scorched the air right past an earhole. Rahgz winced and glanced over to make sure his neck-feathers hadn't been seared off. Phara stepped closer.

"Do you think I'm missing on accident?" she asked. "It was a simple question."

Rahgz stuttered for a moment and then glared at her. "I should fire you for being so incompetent."

That actually made her blink. The pistol twitched. "What are you talking about?"

Rahgz clasped hands behind his back, emulating one of the pompous stances Kel had made him take when in public. "I'm dismayed by your treacherousness. How much are you being paid?"

"Paid?" she echoed.

"Obviously some other lanista has compromised you. How many Bits did it take to agree to eliminate me?"

Off to the side, Kel's projection tilted his head. *What're you doing?*

I've been fucked with for so long, he thought back, *it's nice to do some of the fucking with.*

Confusion crept across Phara's faces. "I never would. How could you think that of me?"

Rahgz rolled his eyes. "You're pointing a gun at me with obviously assassinatory intent."

"That's not a word," Kel said.

"How else am I supposed to interpret this obviously rebellious behavior? The Phara Stekka Zolma I knew would never have dared treat her master and owner this way. After everything I did for you. Preserving all three of you and giving us all second chances at life, you're so quick to throw mine away?"

The gun lowered. Tears brimmed in her eyes and she threw herself forward, arms wrapping around him. "Kel! Void take me, I was so worried. First I thought you were dead—again—and then I picked up your geolocator but you didn't contact me or send any emergency codes, so I feared you'd reverted and lost control of the situation."

He pushed her away. "You have such little faith in me? I should null your contract and send you back to the Meat Market."

Shock plastered over her features, and three voices seemed to intertwine in pleading. "Please, master. We meant no disrespect. We were just so fearful and are always lost without you. You are our sole purpose in this life and all others. We will do whatever it takes to amend whatever we've done wrong. Just say it and we shall flay our faces from our skulls and blind ourselves so we can never behold your glory again."

Rahgz tried not to feel sickened by their offer, but looked into the distance, humming in pretend thought. "I suppose there is one thing you could do that would repay the great injury you've done to my esteemed person."

"Anything." She bowed low, tail flared for balance. "Say the word and we obey."

Rahgz turned slightly and flapped his robe. "Kiss my ass."

She looked utterly bewildered by this command, but then got on hands and knees to crawl closer, all three mouths puckering.

Laughing, Rahgz jumped back, making her stumble and catch herself. "Hah!" He stabbed a few fingers at her. "Got you to admit it and then make a fool of yourself. How's it feel, Phara? Augurahgz just owned your—"

He didn't see her move, but he felt the impact across his whole spine, down to the tip of his tail. One instant on his feet, gloating. The next, on his back with a ringing in his earholes and the barrel of the plasma gun steaming as it charged, close enough to make his face scales crackle.

Three voices hissed in unison. "Release our master or we will—"

He laughed. The noise made her look almost as startled as the unexpected request. "Or what?" he asked. "You'll blow my head off?" He glanced over at Kel, who shook his head. "Your girls here aren't too bright at times, are they?"

Her faces scrunched up. "Who are you talking…" She glanced to the side, where Glomph remained placid. Seeing no one, she scowled. "You think you can hold him hostage?

"I don't know, really. Can I? Let me ask him." He raised a feathered brow at Kel. "Hey, do you mind if I hold you hostage from your lover? She seems the clingy sort."

Kel crossed his arms. *"I thought we were beginning to work together through this."*

Rahgz cocked his head to look past the plasma barrel at Phara. "I was starting to warm up to the idea before she went psychobitch on me. Looks like she wants a threeway, and not the fun sort. So, how are you going to communicate with her to stand down?"

"You could let me borrow your mouth for a moment."

"Sure. And open the door to eventual retake of total biological control. Nothing doing."

Kel shrugged. *"Then I fear there's little I can do. I will warn you though that she can be very convincing. Stekka was an adept torturer when needed."*

Rahgz glared at him. "You weren't trying to make a deal with me, were you? You were just trying to get us out of here so we could wait for your servant girl to come to the rescue and restore you to full control."

Phara giggled, a lunatic sound that Rahgz once found endearing and now found terrifying. "Oh, yes. My master has plans for everything. No contingency is left unaccounted for." She leaned in, showing all her teeth, which were much more threatening than the plasma pistol. "Including the possibility of a bio-matrix reboot. Once I get you back to the aerie, I will ensure that your mind is never again in control of this organism."

"The aerie was destroyed."

"Only partly," she said. "A large chunk was torn away by the initial attack, taking you and the Ghostclobbers with it. I managed to crash-land the remaining portion, which contains enough of the medical suite to still be operational...and to operate on stubborn patients like you. I'm quite talented at psychosurgery."

Rahgz sighed. "Is there anything you're not great at? Sanity, perhaps?"

"I excel in all things," she said, "as is fitting for the servant of the ultimate being."

"This guy?" Rahgz thumbed Kel's way, despite her not being able to see him. "Ultimate? Lucky, sure. Maybe even a little talented. But he's got flaws just like anyone."

"Oh really?" Kel said, while Phara snarled on his behalf. *"And what would those be?"*

Rahgz rose on three elbows, wincing as he braced against his bruised spine and ass. "Me."

"I beg pardon?"

Rahgz spread a couple arms while keeping another raised between him and Phara. "You're looking at them. All wrapped up in this organic bundle of joy you're stuck with. I'm your weaknesses, Kel. And if you try to keep playing me like a game, I'll beat you."

The lanista snorted. Despite only hearing one side of the conversation, Phara also loosed another tail-twitching laugh.

"You think you can beat him?" she asked. "You have a lot to learn."

Rahgz gave a one-shoulder shrug. "Oh, but I've already been taught. By the best, I might add. Let me show you a neat trick I picked up." He raised his voice. "Glomph! Restrain and contain protocol fifty-three, alpha non-lethal maneuver!"

A pseudopod shot out and glommed onto Phara's lower half. With a shriek, she got yanked off him to dangle in the air. The plasma pistol went off, but her hand had gotten sucked into the helot's mass, and the discharge blew harmlessly awry, splattering the floor with muck.

Rahgz rose, dusting his robe off. He looked up at her feet, which kicked desperately in slow-motion, stuck in Glomph's grasp.

"No panties?" he asked with a chuckle. "I should've known."

Spittle hit his cheek as her vehement cursing echoed throughout the arena.

"Don't worry," he said. "Glomph won't eat you. Not yet, at least. This is a delayed-death tactic. Apprehend the opponent and hold them without digesting. Hold them for a maximum of five minutes, unless another command extends the restraint or orders a release." He checked his wrist-chit, where the chronometer had started working again. "So we're on a bit of a schedule if you want to live."

He turned his attention back to Kel, who stared in shock.

"There's a look I bet few have seen you make," Rahgz said. "I guess I could relish this moment or something, but I'm pretty exhausted and hungry and could use one of those mate-murder-meal deals Bateesma is always going on about."

"How?" Kel asked. *"That shouldn't be possible."*

Rahgz went over and patted Glomph's side, ignoring the slight sting of the helot's acidic sweat. "Gene-coded to recognize me as its owner and master, right? And I spent so long in the back seat listening to you drone on all your commands and watching you run the arena bout stratagems. Admittedly, I didn't actually pay any real close attention, but after a while some of the details kind of stuck with me anyways."

Kel looked up at Phara, at a loss for words.

Rahgz cinched up the belt around his waist and crossed several arms. "Let's reopen negotiations, shall we?"

"I will die for my master," Phara cried, still thrashing about. "You can't threaten him with my life. Just because I am fully devoted to serve him doesn't mean he will sacrifice anything to save me. I have always recognized this and accepted it."

Rahgz glanced at Kel, who looked pained. "Ooch. I think you actually underestimated him on something. Anyways, it's not you that I'm holding hostage. It's him."

She writhed harder. "I swear by all that is unholy and abominable in all the universal variants that I will never rest and will die before I let you—"

Kel waved frantically. *"Tell her 'Sunlit valleys suppurate the majesty of volorpic fixations.'"*

With a quirk of an eyebrow, Rahgz repeated this nonsense. Phara quieted instantly and fixed on him.

"I hear and obey, master."

Rahgz gave Kel a sly look. "Coded messages?"

Kel gazed back steadily. *"So long as your words are accompanied with specific verbal tags, she can confirm I'm really the one communicating with her. She'll know if you try to fake it. It's a system we spent many TIRDs perfecting."*

"Great." Rahgz cracked knuckles on all five fists. "Now, how do you want to do this?"

"Twindle," Kel said. *"Phara Stekka Zolma, do not swear anything that I have not given you leave to do so. Your life is not yours to bargain away. It is mine, and only I have the authority to sacrifice or keep what I wish."*

"Twindle," Rahgz said, repeating all of that.

Phara looked like she'd eaten something both sour and wriggling. But she nodded. "I understand. I apologize for my presumption, master."

"Fornicate," Kel said. *"Phara, give Rahgz your projector unit and help him plug it into his wrist-chit. I will take it from there."*

Rahgz repeated all this as well and went to Phara, who jutted her chin at her still-trapped body.

"Deal with it," Rahgz said. "Because until I'm satisfied you won't try anything sneaky, you and Glomph are going to be hug-buddies." She began muttering violent threats, making him point up at her. "See?

That's exactly why I'm being cautious."

Wrestling against Glomph's hold, Phara managed to reach into a side pocket and retrieved her projector unit. It took Rahgz a few minutes to hook it up according to Kel's directions, but once it had attached, it was mere seconds for the lanista to project himself into the arena in a manner Phara could see and converse with as well.

The three of them exchanged glares until Rahgz sighed.

"First things first," he said. "Who here wants to die?" Phara started to raise her hand, but he cut her off. "Not counting dying to save your master. That should've been obvious. But since it looks like I have to state the obvious with you two, let's start there. You," he pointed at Kel, "want to keep on being the lanista of all lanistas without anyone ever getting wise to the fact that you're still around. You don't want to die, but this is now the only body you've got." Rahgz patted his chest.

"You," he nodded at Phara, "will do anything to serve your master, which is so sweet it makes me sick. But I figure you don't want to do anything to threaten his continued existence through me. And despite all the shit you two have pulled, I still want to keep enjoying a more comfortable, pleasurable life. Sadly, you two remain my best bets to do so. So if you're willing to work out a compromise, I'm willing to continue to be your cooperative host."

Kel eyed him with complete dubiousness.

"What happened to all your bitching and moaning about free will and not liking feeling owned?"

"Fuck that noise." Rahgz clasped two pairs of hands and pretended to swoon. "Oh gracious me. What's the point of having a life that isn't my own? If I let someone else get everything I want for me instead of earning it myself, what's the value in that?"

He made an obscene gesture that required three hands. "Those are nicely philosophical questions that a lot of people could get hung up on. But the reality is, no one's life is their own. No one is fully in control. It's more a matter of how much control you have and over what parts. And we all use other people to get what we want. Gnoems in the Void, most people are mainly trying to get more and more people doing all the hard work for them, so why am I complaining that you want to handle all the hustle for me?"

Kel actually smiled. *"And I thought you weren't listening during all of my lectures."*

Rahgz shrugged. "Here's the thing you have to realize too: even if you did somehow regain autonomic control from me, I would forever fight it. I would constantly be the distracting voice in your head, trying to get you to fuck up and take away your chance at winning at the worst possible moment. I would be the worst devil on your shoulder. Or we could just learn to put up with each other as biological roommates and get on with our respective lives. Which is the more efficient use of your energy and focus? We could be in constant battle with each other, wasting time and resources trying to get the upper hand or…" He held a hand to both Phara and Kel. "We could go back to being odd partners like before, just with a better understanding of a mutually beneficial arrangement and more realistic expectations."

"Very practical of you," Kel said. *"I approve and agree."*

"Sounds good. You keep me happy and I keep you alive to win another day with a minimum of fuss."

"Now would you please release Phara? I believe she's a few seconds shy of being eaten."

Rahgz squinted up at her. "Do you swear on your master's life that you'll uphold our arrangement and not try to find loopholes that end up with me being dumped into a hole somewhere?"

While she looked like she wanted to bite his head off and start nibbling on his brainstem, she nodded. "I will abide by his infinite wisdom. If he believes this is the best course, I shall follow him through it to the end. I swear it."

"Glomph, release."

Phara plopped back to the deck plating, some slime still clinging to her. Tucking away her clogged plasma pistol, she wiped at the mess while Rahgz detached the projector and handed it back over.

"You realize," she said, "that in every arrangement he has ever bound himself to, he always comes out with the advantage."

"I'm hoping so," Rahgz said. "So long as no one ever discovers he's still alive through me, we should be able to operate wherever and however we wish. We can all be frenemies with benefits."

A bleep made both Rahgz and Phara twitch. She checked over until she realized it was her datapad. Bringing it up, she activated the comm, which revealed the barge captain's tentacled face.

Captain Thorluthsmien fixed on Rahgz. "Lanista Augurahgz. I am pleased to see you in one piece still."

Rahgz glanced at where Kel stood in the corner of his vision, thankfully no longer being projected for organic interaction. He hitched his shoulders back. "Captain. I'm surprised to hear from you. Also surprised you seem happy that I'm still alive."

The captain's mouth-tentacles writhed. "I'd hate for you to perish before our business is complete."

Rahgz and Phara exchanged confused looks.

"What business would that be?" Rahgz asked. "Trying to intimidate me into losing?"

Thorluthsmien grinned behind the tentacles. "Actually, my business is less with you, and more with Kel'Chungzi Ewaltsen. May I speak with him?"

Sell your secrets. They're not worth anything to you in the long run and only make you a more tempting target. And remember the rule of profiting from all things? Many will be ready to dump huge Bit caches into procuring your secrets, so you might as well be funneling that straight into your accounts. It shouldn't have to be said, though, that these better be old, defunct secrets that have no more relevance than what you ate and shit out yesterday.

- How to Backstab Friends and Influence Outcomes:
A Guide for Starting Lanistas
Written by Lanista Kel'Chungzi Ewaltsen
Excerpt from Vol 4, Subset 4.29

CHAPTER TWENTY-SEVEN

Phara muted the comm and hissed. "Disaster. No one can know that the master lives. It will undo everything we've worked for."

Rahgz gently reached out and took her hand off the comms control. "Yes. Immediately silencing him while still letting him see us act all alarmed is an entirely innocent way to respond and not at all confirming whatever suspicions he had."

Her gaze emanated more heat than a plasma beam. "Your point?"

He nodded at the waiting captain. "Let's hear what he has to say. And play things a bit more evenly? You've never been so melodramatic ever since you started working for me. Why are you so on edge now?"

She bared her teeth so far he spotted a couple rows he hadn't noticed before. "I'm keeping three separate minds in check that are equally eager to kill you where you stand. Only our master's oath holds us back."

"Noted. I'll give you a nice massage when we get back to whatever's left of the aerie. Please put the captain back on."

She did so, and Rahgz nodded to Thorluthsmien. "Apologies for the disruption. Reception here in the arena is less-than-stellar."

"Funny," he said. "Everything is quite clear on my end. In fact, I ensure comms remain at optimal strength across the entire barge at all times."

"How did you know I was still alive?" Rahgz asked.

"You're in my arena. Any barge captain worth his engines always gets as much live feed coverage for blood.stream to sell exclusive footage from the bouts. Do you think I don't have the entire place swarming with nanocams and quark sensors? When I first detected you alive in there, I thought to come extract you swiftly, but then your attempts to flee became quite the entertainment." His eyes gleamed, even over the comm projection. "And then things took a far more intriguing turn. Are you listening, Lanista Kel?"

"The name's Augurahgz," Rahgz said, clenching fists at his sides while clasping a pair behind his back.

"Of course it is," the captain said. "I heard the arrangement clearly enough, Augurahgz. And I'm not talking to you right now. I'm talking to the great mind you hold within you. The one I wish to bargain with."

Kel stepped up invisible to Rahgz's side. *"I suppose you aren't going to let me negotiate?"*

You start talking, Rahgz thought back, *and confirm what he's saying, what will stop him from exposing you to the rest of the Nexus?*

"I think he's already seen enough to know the truth. And if he's been recording us, then he already has all the data needed to upend our scheme and damn us forever. There'd be no coming back from this one."

Really? Rahgz asked. *Admitting defeat that quick? Just going to roll over and let him start blackmailing us like that?*

"I didn't say that. But denying him overly much will likely just irritate him and possibly have him expose us out of sheer pettiness. My guess is he thinks this knowledge gives him an advantage over us and wishes to put a leash on me. Turn us into his pet lanista to make the pages of the Book flip to whatever end he wishes."

Pretty much what I was thinking, Rahgz thought. *Now what? If we try to run, he'll just leak everything onto the blood.stream.*

"We actually maintain some chance here so long as he alone knows I exist. So let's play his game and look for a way to turn it to our advantage. Go ahead. Let him know I'm here."

Smoothing down his feathers, Rahgz forced himself to meet the captain's eyes.

"Kel hears you," Rahgz said. "And he wants to know what you want with him."

Phara gasped softly, while Thorluthsmien smiled. "Excellent. I wish to meet with you again and discuss the terms of a new arrangement."

Kel sighed in Rahgz's mind. *"Just when I strike an agreeable bargain, someone always wants to hedge in on the action."*

"Let's just talk here then," Rahgz said. "Why should we get anywhere near you when you just tried to have us killed?"

The captain scowled. "First off, that guard has already been executed for being a bit too trigger-happy. The orders were to secure you safely until I could properly decide how best to handle the fallout of your little stunt. I don't want lanistas to fear participating in my arena." He stroked his mouth-tentacles. "Second, if you don't meet, I will make your associate's death a long and excruciating one."

Rahgz frowned at Phara. "That'd be an interesting trick, seeing as she's right here."

"Not that one." The captain shifted and the comm view from his end expanded to show some of the area around him, revealing Bateesma standing off to the side. "I believe you are fond of this one?"

The leporidean had kinetic shackles around her wrists and ankles, keeping her from being able to move more than a heavy inch at a time.

An invisible hand clutched Rahgz's lungs and squeezed.

Shit.

Kel grunted. *"Don't tell me you're going to let him use simple emotional manipulation to get you to do whatever he wants. Sentimentality is a weakness that must be purged."*

Bateesma is one of the few people I'd call a real friend, Rahgz thought. *She's already suffered enough Besides, she can help us get out of this.*

"Oh?" Kel eyed him out of the corner of his middle eye. *"You have a plan?"*

Rahgz frowned. *About fifteen percent of one, but it's coming together. I just need to buy some time.*

"Where's Turrurnium and Ukspug?" he asked.

Bateesma's ears dipped mournfully and her voice came across flat and exhausted. "Both died in the crash. I tried to save them, but they were pinned and then got caught in an explosion when a hover generator blew."

Rahgz briefly shut his eyes. "I'm sorry. I should've protected you better."

She said nothing, with the silence being worse than any accusations or promises of vengeance.

The captain stepped back into the frame, centering the projection on him. "I'm in my private suite overlooking the arena. From the scans my engineers have taken, your aerie should function well enough to get you up here. I will ensure we remain alone for as long as necessary. See you both soon."

The comm blipped out. Phara uttered a long-held hiss of displeasure.

"We should go to meet with him and kill him where he stands," she said.

"That'd be nice," Rahgz said. "Except I bet he's already anticipated that move on our part. He'll have personal defenses in place—individual forcefield, weapon dampeners, security drones. Whatever. Direct assault isn't going to get us anywhere."

"Not only that, but if I were him," Kel said, *"I'd already have a data packet prepped to broadcast to all known systems exposing us if anything bad befell the captain. Insurance."*

"Right." Rahgz breathed deep, rolling his shoulders and flexing his tail. "Let's go hear what he has to say. What other choice do we have?"

They recalled Glomph to its pit and followed the helot as it trundled through the arena, using it like a homing beacon to guide them out. Once there, they boarded an arena shuttle and Phara plugged in the coordinates for the downed aerie. As they zipped out of the service tunnels, Rahgz groaned at the sight of the once-glorious craft sitting in a smoking crater that had taken out half a block in a market district. Emergency barriers cordoned off the area while mechanic crews were busy removing rubble and rebuilding damaged deck plating.

The aerie looked like a split-open golden egg, with wires and tubes spilling out like a stillborn nebula squidspawn. A section had been reduced to a blown-out crater surrounded by blistered metal, which must've been where Turrurnium and Ukspug perished.

"You sure it still flies?" he asked.

Her right-most face twitched as she nodded. "No machine can defy me."

"Great. Speaking of which," he leaned back in the shuttle seat, "is hacking one of your skill sets?"

Her right mouth turned up slightly in a cruel smile.

They reached the aerie and Phara led the way into the aerie, her venomous look scaring off any engineers who tried to stop them. They ducked through a web of sparking nodes and into the main chamber. Most of the furniture had been bolted in place, but much of it had torn loose and lay scattered and burned throughout the room. Scorch marks ran across the buckled walls and cracks turned the floor into an over-sized puzzle.

Phara ducked into the pilot's chamber. Rahgz found one of his storage bins and pulled out a robe that, while less opulent, also lacked the shit and piss stains from his time in the arena. After swapping his outfit, he secured himself as best he could in one of the few remaining chairs. With many loud and alarming blasts and sputters, a couple hover generators came back online and the aerie shifted as it rose like a drunken gasbloat. Pieces fell off the outside as it wobbled in the air, and Rahgz winced at every crash and shout from below.

Somehow, Phara navigated the hover channels without crashing again or causing anyone else to, with most air traffic giving them a wide berth. As they docked with the captain's suite, Rahgz reviewed the still-developing plan with Kel.

"You're going to let me do the talking this time?"

Kel moved his thick arms ponderously back and forth. *"He will most likely be recording us the entire time in hopes of acquiring more direct material to use against us. Right now, he has evidence of you talking to yourself and projecting an image of a long-dead lanista. These could mostly still be explained away as madness, simulations, and artificial intelligence overlays."*

After a final shudder, the aerie stilled and the engines whined as they cycled down. Phara came out and stared at him pointedly.

"Know that if my master comes to any harm in this, you will not last long beyond."

"You don't have to worry," he said. Then he rethought this. "Actually, there's room for a lot of worry right about now. Still, while I may not be a natural-born winner, I am a natural-born survivor. And that's one streak I don't intend to end anytime soon." He headed for the door, then paused. "Besides, if anything were to damage him, it'd have to go through me first. Literally."

They headed through the airlock and into the suite, which was a comfortably opulent affair of silken furnishings arrayed before a broad viewing window and balcony. A shimmering forcefield sealed the suite off from the outside, and Kel quickly reported that all external communications had been nullified.

Captain Thorluthsmien turned from where he'd been gazing out the window, dressed in his previous military garb, weapons at his sides. He nodded at Rahgz and gestured to a simpler fare of semi-sentient cheese molds and drink globes.

Rahgz ignored these, finding a spot not quite in the middle of the room to remain standing. He studied the space. "Where's Bateesma? Show her unharmed."

The captain chuckled, and Rahgz had to tamp down on the surge of fury this triggered. He had just gotten over his despisal of how Kel and Phara had played him for a fool and now someone else was already trying to turn him into a puppet.

A snore deflected his rising anger, and he spotted Bateesma conked out on a couch off to one side. Going to her, he shook her awake.

Bateesma smacked her lips as she roused, sitting up awkwardly in her bonds. "You made it. I wondered."

"I wasn't about to leave you behind," he said. "Besides, I have a gift for you in the aerie. It's docked right outside." He looked to Thorluthsmien. "Is she free to go?"

He waved permission, and the kinetic shackles powered off and dropped to the floor. Bateesma stood abruptly, front teeth jutting at the captain, but Rahgz grabbed her arm with several hands. "Leave him. I'll deal with this. Right now, I just need to you go and wait for me. Check out the present I got you."

She pouted. "Kicking me out of the action? Really?"

"Trust me," he said. "You don't want to be part of what happens here."

After another hesitation, she bounded off, though not quite as spry, with one of her long legs bearing a subtle limp.

Once the main access door clicked shut and sealed, Thorluthsmien made a blustering noise as he strode closer, picking up a drink globe and writhing a few tentacles around it.

"I'm going to make you both an offer," he said between slurps. "I'd like you to both hear it and think through it fully before responding."

"I'm listening," Rahgz said.

Thorluthsmien gave him a long-suffering look. "Shouldn't it be 'we'?"

"I haven't the faintest of what you're talking about."

The captain sighed. "I'd rather deal in earnestness here. No more games or infantile attempts at duplicity."

Rahgz shrugged. "Still getting over the tried-to-have-me-killed bit. I take that kind of thing personally."

"Then you'll appreciate how personal my offer is." The captain's eyes narrowed to dark slits. "What if I could restore you to your family, Augurahgz?"

That caught Rahgz by surprise as much as a right-handed sucker-punch from a left-handed goorlink. It took him a minute to realize he was just standing there blinking while the captain waited for his answer.

"Define restore," he said.

"My resources are quite expansive. Many have tried to pierce the fog of your history, to no avail. Yet I have identified the planet and genetic line you hail from and could restore your reputation there easily enough. You could return home a champion of your kind, flush with Bits and any story of heroism, cunning, and strength you wish to be known for."

Could he do that? Rahgz wondered.

"*I'm unsure,*" Kel said. "*It's possible, I suppose. But this offer obviously comes with the condition of staying back on that planet.*"

Rahgz lifted his chin and ruffled his brow feathers. "So you want me out of the game again. First you threaten me into trying to throw the bout, and now you're trying to get me to leave of my own free will and remove the competition. You really need to work on your negotiation skills."

"Consider it while I discuss potential terms with your...companion." Thorluthsmien tilted his head, gaze fixing slightly behind Rahgz as if trying to address the unseen lanista. "Kel, I understand that you wish to remain an unidentified player in this game of shadows you play. It's a remarkable ploy, and I respect you for the courage and audacity it took to pull off—at least, temporarily. Despite discovering your charade, I have kept it a secret. No one outside this room knows the truth, and it can remain that way."

Kel grumbled as he adjusted his flabby arms across his equally portly chest. "*Tell him to get to the point.*"

Rahgz plucked an overgrown feather and twirled it between his fingers. "Let's say, hypothetically, any remnant of Kel's old self is listening. What would you be wanting him to do?"

Thorluthsmien put his drink down and held his hands out. "Leave your current host and bond with me."

Kel's projection stiffened, and Rahgz sensed the lanista's intense focus on the barge captain.

"Transfer your mind to me," Thorluthsmien continued. "Transfer your life. Hand over your wealth and helot and let us unite to make a legacy together that will be known eternally in Nexus and beyond, in all universes and realities."

Striding over, he looked hard at Rahgz. "Surely you can see the advantages of letting go of this unworthy, unbecoming host body. It holds you back from your true potential. I can give you every advantage possible. You could have direct access to the Book and its inner workings. I don't think even you had that ability when in your prime."

Phara spat on the floor. "You presume too much to claim—"

"Shut up," Rahgz said. "The adults in the room are talking."

She mouthed silent threats, but swallowed and stepped back, radiating fury.

For his part, Kel remained fixed on Thorluthsmien. Rahgz felt his calculating thoughts furiously churning inside his own mind.

You can't possibly be considering this. We just made a deal.

Kel spared him a glance. *"A deal that had existed for seconds before this better one comes along."*

Is it really better, though?

"Think about it objectively. He is one of the more influential barge captains in the Nexus. Already in the upper echelon of the arena ranks, with many lanista who would bow to his wishes. He has the resources to protect himself and knows the ways of arena dealings like few do. Working with him could accelerate my return to ultimate power far beyond any partnership you and I could manage."

Yeah, Rahgz thought. *It's almost like he thinks he's your equal.*

Kel jerked as if stung. *"I beg your pardon?"*

No, not your equal, Rahgz said. *Your better. Superior. I may be annoying to you, but he seems downright uppity. To me, you're salvation. To him, you're just a trophy. And once the shine has worn off, most trophies just get stuck on a shelf somewhere and forgotten.*

The lanista stared at Rahgz in wonderment, a half-smile tugging his thick lips. *"A most unique perspective. I never expected such a persuasive argument from you."*

I can get pretty damn eloquent when it's my life on the line. So can we agree to stick to our arrangement and give this guy a mutual 'fuck off?'

Kel pondered this a moment longer, and then nodded. Rahgz relaxed, if slightly, and realized the captain had been watching him this whole time, quite aware of the conversation going on inside his head.

"Well?" Thorluthsmien asked. "Do I have a deal with either or both of you?"

Rahgz straightened. "If you'd thrown in a free foot massage, I might've been swayed. But whatever waits back on whatever planet you've found isn't what I care about anymore. I'm a different person now and want no part of any family that once rejected me."

Thorluthsmien frowned behind the tentacles. "I see. And Kel'Chungzi Ewaltsen?"

"No idea who you're talking about."

The frown deepened. "So you refuse to surrender the lanista willingly?"

Rahgz tried to look insulted. "The only lanista you're dealing with is me."

The captain tapped at a databand on his arm and projected a few images of Rahgz, with sensor readouts pinpointing various spots in his brain. "Not many people have the expertise to scan for subneural activity, much less the necessary equipment to detect embedded synaptic meshes. Yet when one knows what to search for…" He swiped through a few scans that highlighted heavy brain activity. "Your presence becomes quite clear, Kel'Chungzi. So let this farce between us end, and accept the inevitable fate that has brought you to me."

Rahgz yawned into the back of a hand. "You know, I've heard that obsession with the past is an unhealthy indicator of mental degeneration. Sometimes caused by brain tumors. You might want to get that looked at."

Thorluthsmien switched off the projector and put a hand on his saber hilt. "Pity. Then I will take him from you by force."

He twirled a hand in the air along with several tentacles; a wall at the back of the room hummed as previously unseen panels swished aside, revealing a small chamber beyond. A light lit it from within, beaming down on a larger, very uncomfortable looking chair surrounded by medical probes, sensor arrays, restraining field projectors, and too many plasma scalpels to count.

Rahgz's throat went as dry as ash, and he gulped until he could speak again. "Is that…"

"A psychosurgery booth," Phara said. "Shit in the Void and suck it back out."

"Yes," Captain Thorluthsmien said. "You see, I don't make threats I cannot immediately back up. When anyone has answers they refuse to provide me upon polite request or a most generous offer, this delivers swift results. And with it, I will rip the neural mesh out of your brain and spine and transfer it to me. The process, I've been told, is quite tortuous."

"Got to catch us first?" Rahgz suggested.

Before he could take a step, further hatches in the walls opened and fired several missiles at him and Phara. Kinetic shackles snapped into place around their arms and legs, and Rahgz's muscles became dead weight.

"Done," Thorluthsmien said. "Any other suggestions before we begin?"

The Book. Ah, the Book. Whoever really runs it, whether Crypt or the INC or an invisible coalition of barge captains, it doesn't matter. Everyone's name is written in it somewhere, with endless wagers on infinite outcomes. The only thing you have to ask is: are you in charge of what's being said about you and how much the wagers are worth, or are you letting someone else dictate your worth on the black market?

- How to Backstab Friends and Influence Outcomes:
A Guide for Starting Lanistas
Written by Lanista Kel'Chungzi Ewaltsen
Excerpt from Vol 48, Subset 73.25

CHAPTER TWENTY-EIGHT

"How about a game?" Rahgz asked. "Winner takes all in the arena."

The captain chuckled liquidly. "Why should I bother with any further contests when I already have you helpless?"

Good question, Rahgz thought. *A little help?*

"He's an arena player through and through. He enjoys the thrill of a good chase and conquest. He wants to win as badly as I do. This would be too easy, so try to offer him a more satisfying option."

Rahgz thought through this as fast and furiously as he could. Then he perked up.

"Not against Kel. Against me."

Thorluthsmien stroked his mouth-tentacles. "Explain."

Rahgz shuffled to face the captain as much as his bonds allowed him. "I'd like to live still, as I've made very clear. And since my body is doing all the suffering in most of these outcomes, I think I should have a pretty big say in this. Now, again, hypothetically, Kel—who may or may not exist in any form—might not be entirely opposed to working with you. I, however, am totally on Team Augurahgz. So this is my counter-offer. I don't want to go home, but I want a fighting chance to leave in one piece. Also, I want you to prove you even deserve to work directly with the most famed lanista of all time."

"Deserve?" the captain echoed.

Rahgz nodded. "If you want Kel, you have to earn him. I've learned a few tricks just by being around him, and I want you to back up your claims of being a better host. I may just be a biological housing that does all the fleshy walking and talking, and little more, but I still have my pride." He glanced down at the bonds. "Most of it, anyways."

Thorluthsmien looked out the viewing window to the arena below. "You want me to beat you in a bout? We know you've only won in the past because of his guidance or direct control."

"So what are you afraid of?" Rahgz asked. "You keep whatever fancy scanner on me that you need to show that Kel isn't running the show, and then we duke it out in a good, old-fashioned helot beatdown. You win? I volunteer to the procedure to give you the mesh and then go home. I win? I leave with everything and everyone intact and you never reveal whatever truth you think you've discovered."

"Your helot is most formidable," Thorluthsmien said. "Even without a real lanista conducting your every move, it may be any helot I throw against it would simply be overwhelmed."

"Then let's trade." Rahgz mimed tossing an object from hand to hand. "I'm kind of tired of Glomph anyways. Offer me a helot in one of your holding pits and I'll transfer ownership of Glomph to you for this match. So long as you transfer it back once I kick your ass."

"*You'll what?*" Kel shouted.

Rahgz ignored this, staying focused on the captain, trying to convey his earnestness with a steady gaze and a complete lack of pissing himself in terror.

"That would be quite an entertaining bargain," the captain said after a long minute. Even on his alien features, Rahgz could see the gloating already beginning. "I agree."

Struggling to lift his arms, Rahgz indicated the bonds with his chin. "You mind?"

Another gesture command from Thorluthsmien and the shackles clacked open and dropped to the floor. Rahgz rubbed his wrists and looked to Phara.

"Phara, be a good girl and go into my accounts to transfer ownership of Glomph to the good captain here."

She seethed as she massaged her own bruised arms. "I'd rather fuck a Gnoem. I won't do anything of the sort on your word alone."

Sighing, Rahgz caught the lanista's eye. *Kel? What's her safe word this time?*

"*You're insane to think this might work,*" Kel said.

Thank you. Saying this might *work is one of the kindest things you've ever said to me. But unless you want to have your mesh ripped out of me and stuck in him, I need Phara to do what I tell her.*

The lanista heaved a breath, whole body slumping. "*Tell her, 'plonk.'*"

Rahgz sniffed a laugh. "Plonk, Phara."

She twitched, eyes narrowing. "Fine." She bowed to the captain, somehow making that respectful gesture look vicious. "I need access to your private network and personal database to facilitate the transfer. If you would be so kind, captain? It should only take a few minutes."

He eagerly typed in a few commands on his pad and hers bleeped to announce access granted.

As she processed the property swap, Rahgz turned back to the captain. "What helot are you going to provide me?"

He pulled up a projection unit on a nearby table and displayed half-a-dozen helots with performance readouts. "Take your pick from my private stock."

Rahgz scanned through the options, seeing everything from a bottled lightning vortex to a pile of meat and bones bound together by starmetal chains.

"These are some impressive beasts," Rahgz said. "Why haven't you become a lanista before?"

The captain tugged at a tentacle thoughtfully. "When you are merely the host of the events, rather than the obvious winner or loser, it makes you less of a target and gives you more leeway in manipulating what happens in the arena."

"Ah." Rahgz nodded and pointed to a helot covered in bone spurs and armor of writhing razor wire. Its profile listed it as being able to survive in the vacuum of space, with high-grav upbringing to optimize strength and bone density. "I'll take that one."

Thorluthsmien smiled. "Flivaris has been a favorite of mine for a while. She should serve you well, though I doubt it will be anywhere near enough."

A ping sounded on both his and Phara's datapads. The captain's grin widened obscenely as he confirmed his new ownership of Glomph.

He must think half the battle is already won, Rahgz thought. *He's got the helot. Now he just needs the mind behind it.*

"The mind which you've refused to use to help yourself win," Kel said.

Maybe I'm trying to prove myself to you too. Ever think of that?

"Not really." Kel appeared resigned as he studied the suite. *"I suppose I should get used to the sight of this place."*

Phara slunk up next to Rahgz, equally dour. "You realize he's going to take Kel from you whether you win or not."

"Such a cynic, Phara. Sometimes people do actually honor their word."

"So naive, Rahgz. Those people are called losers."

"That sounds like a Kel-ism."

"It is," Kel said. *"And it's true."*

Rahgz shook off their moodiness and forced himself to smile. "Ready when you are, captain."

"Allow me a little while to sync my control station with my new toy, and we can begin this final bout." He tapped at his datapad and two areas of the floor opened, and dual workstations rose into place. "This should suffice for you as well. I often provide amenities for lanistas who wish to enjoy the comforts of my hospitality outside of their aeries or engage in private duels."

Kel glowered off to the side, and Rahgz looked at him questioningly.

"Helots are not toys," he said. *"They are tools and weapons. You were right. Anyone who thinks so lightly of their property doesn't deserve to keep it."*

Rahgz went to one of the control stations and started settling in. He ignored most of the displays and controls, mostly trying to figure out how to directly control his helot's movement and attacks.

Kel stepped up and pointed. *"You should—"*

Ah! No touching and no thinking. I need to do this alone so Thorlu-

thsmien won't call it a disqualification too early.

Rahgz glanced at the chronometer in the corner of his vision. No word from Bateesma, but that might be because the captain was cutting off all communication from this private suite. He had to hope the Ghostclobber had done the job he'd left waiting for her.

"Flivaris, is it?" he said to himself. "Pleased to meet you. I'll be your master for the duration of what will likely be one of the quickest bouts in all of Nexus history."

He scoped out the arena around where her pit was stationed, and then pulled up a map of the whole combat layout, noting where different hazards and traps were marked by Thorluthsmien for private reference. Rahgz traced various tunnels and sloped halls, seeing where they fed into certain junctions and where different duct and piping systems wound around each other.

"Honestly, too many people see the arena as a battleground," Rahgz said, half to himself, half to Kel and Phara. "But there are lots of other ways to look at it."

"Such as?" Kel asked.

He opened Flivaris' pit. The helot shambled out into the open, blinking confusedly around at the dim lighting, obviously expecting noisy announcers and the cheer of the crowd. Rahgz experimented with prodding her forward and pulling her back, the servomotors in her joints allowing for full remote control if needed, alongside the cranial override.

The captain finally brushed his fancy jacket down and signaled from his control station. "Let the bout begin." He punched a button, and Glomph appeared in another corner of the arena, rolling swiftly toward the center of the maze.

It pained Rahgz to see the helot moving around under someone else's control. He'd grown fond of the helot and wished for a better fate for it than this. Still, as Kel had said, a helot was a tool, and Rahgz needed to use them as such in order to secure his freedom at all costs.

He punched in a command to track how far Glomph was from the helot he now controlled, and a timer to monitor how long before the two helots would intersect. Then he had Flivaris bolt for a particular hub where multiple drain systems fed into the same spot.

"You could look at the arena as a marketplace, where lives are bought and sold with the currency of blood."

Phara giggled. "Poetry, Rahgz? You're even worse at that than being a lanista."

When Flivaris reached the spot Rahgz had marked, he had her start using her spurs and razor wiring to tear up the deck and walls a chunk at a time. The helot set about ripping whole sections of plating, throwing each piece into a rapidly growing pile that started to block the nearest tunnel entrance. Rahgz looked over to see Glomph coming faster than ever, urged on by the captain.

Before long, wires and plasma tubes lay bared all around Rahgz's helot as it continued to shred the ground. Arcs of electricity surged through the air around it, even bolting through the beast's massive chest, though this hardly slowed it. The area he'd chosen now looked like a deep bowl with jagged metal sealing off many of the ways in or out. Thorluthsmien navigated Glomph down a few turns that headed toward an open passage, and Rahgz knew that even if he blocked that one, the helot would still be able to bash its way in to face the one he controlled.

"What are you doing?" Thorluthsmien called over. "If you're trying to inconvenience me with a hefty repair bill, know that I could rebuild this arena a hundred times over before having to feel even minimal annoyance at the cost."

"Some could look at the arena as a center of art," Rahgz said quietly, keeping his attention on directing the helot. "Where murals are made out of entrails and songs of screaming echo out for the masses to enjoy."

Flivaris now shredded the ductwork exposed below the flooring. Sewage pipes exploded beneath it, splashing toxic waste throughout the area. The damage exposed multiple hazards and traps, and the helot chucked gas tanks and charge generators to the side as it tore these apart.

"I used to work the arena as part of a spleen team. A cleaner. So all I saw was the mess that had to be cleaned up. The faster you got the job done, the faster you could get out of there with your tail intact." He tapped in a few more orders. "Some of us learned a little trick to sanitize large swaths of the deck at once. Dangerous, but effective."

Flivaris ran along the walls, punching and kicking straight through the panels with spurred knuckles and knees. White-hot plasma began to dribble out of each hole she drove into the surface. Some clung to her fists, searing the flesh from her bones, but the helot ignored whatever agony this induced to continue following Rahgz's commands.

"While working, you learned to see where the different booby-traps were hidden. You could figure out where the hazard systems interconnected, and you could use them—especially the ones involving fire and plasma spouts."

Kel stood silently beside him, watching and blessedly staying silent. Even Phara held her tongue as Rahgz put the final parts of his desperate plan into place.

"The trick was lining it all up so nothing went off too early. Figuring out a delicate tripwire system so you didn't get a faceful of boiling oil or acid."

Glomph surged closer, taking the last few tunnels like a living boulder tumbling forward to crush its foe.

Rahgz directed Flivaris to stand in the center of the now ruined and wrecked arena section. Waste, plasma, and live wiring carpeted the floor all around her.

Thorluthsmien laughed as he brought Glomph through the main opening Flivaris had left in the surrounding passages.

"I thought you would at least run and make this last a bit longer."

Rahgz used one hand to make an obscene gesture behind the captain's back while also having Flivaris make the same gesture at Glomph.

"Fortunately," he said, "right now there's nothing to be delicate about here."

Flivaris roared as Glomph lashed out with multiple pseudopods. She slashed them away with the razor wires, but more glommed on to her by the second. Glomph oozed into the open area, flesh flowing around the other helot's feet as it began to consume her.

Rahgz shut his eyes briefly. "Goodbye, Glomph."

He sent a final command to Flivaris, who slammed her claws and spurs into the floor directly below her in the center of the clearing. A huge burst of plasma plumed up from below, engulfing her in liquid starfire. At the same time, the holes she'd broken across the walls and floor gushed plasma out across the deck. Lightning crackled through the sudden plasma flood as it swamped over Glomph from all sides.

"No!" Thorluthsmien cried. He tried to move Glomph out of the space, but everywhere the helot turned and spun, escape had already been replaced with fiery death. Everywhere it touched, the superheated fuel incinerated the helot's hide, liquefying the acidic flesh almost instantly. And still the tide rose, created a small, artificial plasma lake that burned like the open, seeping wound of a dying deity.

Glomph's many lipless maws screamed as it began to dissolve under the assault. It shrank in on itself as chunks of it sloughed off to melt into the lake of fire.

Flivaris had already been reduced to chunks of ashy bone that continued to disintegrate into the soup of plasma and Glomph that now swirled about the place.

Kel and Phara stared in open shock at the results of Rahgz's gamble. At last, the lanista turned to regard him.

"I didn't think you were capable of that sort of brutal strategy."

Rahgz inclined his head. "I learned from the best, remember?"

"How did you manage that?" Phara asked.

He flipped a hand back and forth. "All the various traps and nasty surprises people put around arenas have to be powered and fueled by something. There are usually a few main plasma reservoirs and primary ducts that feed throughout the whole place. If you know where to break the lines, clog it here and there, and then rip out the wiring that controls the drainage system, you can create a localized overflow. Great for cleaning off even the most dried, crusty blood and shit stains from the deck."

Thorluthsmien howled as he slammed fists into his control panels. He yanked his saber out and triggered the blade so the edge glowed with a plasma beam along the length. With this, he thrashed the workstation into chunks and shards, sending monitors crashing to the floor.

Panting from the effort, he then rounded on Rahgz. "That was no victory," he said, mouth-tentacles writhing. "Your helot perished long before mine did."

Rahgz stepped away from the control station, trying to keep it between him and the captain. "Playing semantics? Mine delivered the death blow that destroyed them both. So that should count as my win."

"Never." Thorluthsmien drew up, blade pointed at Rahgz's chest as he advanced. "You scaly little worm. You thought you could beat me here in my own barge? In my own arena? I am the lord of all within this realm. My power is absolute."

"Voids. Do I sound like that?" Kel asked.

Sometimes. Actually, mostly yes. Out loud, he said, "Let's call it a draw then. Or we could go best two-out-of-three if you don't mind me borrowing a helot."

The captain lunged, but Phara dove to intercept, claws bared. A plasma bolt shot from the saber and struck her in the chest, slamming her to the floor.

Then Thorluthsmien drove into Rahgz, pinning him up against a wall with the saber sizzling at his throat.

"I will make doubly certain that you feel every nanosecond of agony as I peel the lanista out of you, cell by cell, neuron by neuron. I will keep you alive enough to then flay you and make you eat your own scales. I will—"

The entire barge shuddered with enough force to knock the captain and Rahgz off balance. The lights flickered, and even the ever-present hum of the engines went quiet. Thorluthsmien's eyes went wide and his gaze darted all around.

"What is this?" he asked.

"I invited some extra guests to the party," Rahgz said. "Sounds like they just arrived. Hope you don't mind."

Another quake made them stumble again. Then all of their comms activated on their own, including all speakers both in the suite and throughout the arena. A harsh voice thundered across the whole barge, resounding from sectors far beyond this one as a message blasted their ears.

"THIS IS INC ENFORCEMENT! THIS BARGE AND ALL INHAB-ITANTS AND CREW ARE NOW DETAINED ON FULL LOCK-DOWN! ALL OCCUPANTS ARE REQUIRED TO SURRENDER AND SUBMIT TO INC INVESTIGATIVE AGENTS! DEFY THIS ORDER FOR ANY REASON ON PAIN OF DEATH!"

I want to thank you for buying all of my secrets in this exhaustive series. It has proven more profitable than most bouts I've entered, with the billions of fans and subscribers who adore me (as they should). Obviously, I've moved on from any of the advice and tactics that I've given you to follow here. I have always, and will always exist on a higher plane than any other lanista, and if you dare to don the robes, I will gladly add you to the countless victims who have paved my path to glory.

So my real advice is to give up. Turn back now. Abandon all hope of being anything or anyone worthwhile and let me handle that. Or, if you're truly determined to make it in this career, you can purchase my newest advice compendium which has all the real info that is guaranteed to help: The 1,005.31 Habits of a Highly Successful Lanista. Buy it today!

- *How to Backstab Friends and Influence Outcomes: A Guide for Starting Lanistas*
Written by Lanista Kel'Chungzi Ewaltsen
Excerpt from Vol 102, Subset 85.36

CHAPTER TWENTY-NINE

"INC?" Thorluthsmien turned a circle, staring up at the ceiling as if he could see through to the voice that kept blaring conditions of surrender and threats of defiance. "I am above these raids. Flawless in all my dealings with them. Guaranteed sanctioning for hundreds of TIRDs. There is nothing they would have that would convince them to bring their enforcement squads here." He turned furious eyes on Rahgz. "How did you do this?"

"Funny that," Rahgz said. "From what I've been told, the INC isn't fond of anyone being in possession of blacklisted genetic material, especially when used in helots. They must've heard you were the proud owner of just such a creature."

He gazed down at the arena, where the remains of Glomph sizzled and popped in the remains of the plasma flow, which had finally ebbed and begun to crust over.

"There may not be much of it left, but I'm sure the INC investigators will be able to scrape up enough DNA to match it to the helot registered under your name." Rahgz smoothed down a few ruffled feathers. "I can tell you from personal experience that investigators are real sticklers for their regulations."

"I'll kill you for this!"

The captain flung his saber at Rahgz, who dove out of the way as it spun past. He pushed up, but then Thorluthsmien barreled into him, hammering him to the floor. Tentacles grappled his neck and began to tighten as the captain raged above him.

Rahgz fought back with all five hands, tail trapped under him, but the captain proved surprisingly strong. He blocked punches and hammering fists with his elbows as he tightened his grip on Rahgz, thumbs reaching for his eyes while fingers began to crack the scales around his throat.

Then his mouth-tentacles drooped as a kinetic shackle snapped into place around his neck. Thorluthsmien sagged to the side, falling off Rahgz. He slammed a hand into the floor to brace himself. Phara clicked another shackle around a wrist and dragged him over to secure the other side.

A smoking hole in her robe showed where she'd been shot, with raw flesh blistered underneath. But she made it clear she was quite alive as she put a clawed foot on the captain's chest and pressed down while he squirmed beneath her.

Coughing and gulping air, Rahgz rose and smiled gratefully to Phara, who bared teeth back.

"Leave him alive," he said. "The INC won't be merciful with him. They like to make an example of high-rolling, covert rebels like we've made him out to be." Rahgz knelt to look Thorluthsmien in the eye. "The problem with serving under a tyrannical empire that claims ownership of all the known star systems is you can't really buy your way out of this kind of trouble."

Kel's projection materialized on the other side of the captain. *"What of his ability to expose us?"*

Rahgz looked up at Phara. "You found the evidence?"

She nodded. "And wiped it. Giving me access to his private network wasn't the smartest. Fortunately, I serve someone far more cunning."

Rahgz returned her grin, knowing full well she wasn't talking about Kel this time.

Thorluthsmien groaned, struggling to rise even as Phara continued to press him down. He raised a quivering hand as if to ask Rahgz for something.

Rahgz crouched beside him. "What is it? I've never had anyone beg for mercy before, and while I'd love that new experience, we really need to be going before the INC arrives to take you into custody."

He gagged, trying to speak past the shackles dampening his ability to do much beyond breathe. Rahgz touched the control pad on the clasp around his neck, dialing the strength down to let the captain talk.

"Yes? Last words you want me to deliver to—"

"Orthos meta aflux corona!" the captain cried.

"Sprukker fucker!" Rahgz cried, slapping the pad to reinstate the dampener, but too late.

Sirens wailed and lights blared, not just within the suite but out in the arena and across the barge sector as far as Rahgz could see. The whole air blazed red with warning systems switching on, while sudden sounds of distant explosions and way-too-near weapons fire filled the air. A larger blast shook the suite while smoke billowed beyond one edge of the arena.

"What's happening?" Kel asked. *"Self-destruct sequence?"*

Phara ran to a monitor at one of the control stations and tabbed through several views. She cursed.

"Captain's deathwish override. He just placed every security system in the barge on full-auto deny and demolish mode. Also sent out orders to any crew and officers to repel all borders at all costs."

A portion of the barge's ceiling crumpled, and a spiked shaft pierced the hull. A violent wind tore out from this as air sucked out into the Void beyond, until a forcefield shimmered into being around the hole and sealed it. But hundreds of drones poured out of the invading missile head and began swarming through the sector, firing at anything that moved.

Rahgz winced as more blasts rocked the barge. Phara clutched the monitor to stay upright.

"The barge's weapons are firing on all the INC ships," she said, "and the INC is returning fire. They're going to tear this whole ship apart."

"Fuck me to the Void and back." Rahgz stumbled to her side. "I didn't expect them to bring a whole sprukking fleet to deal with a single barge."

"The INC is known for its overkill philosophy," Kel said. *"We need a way off this barge, fast. Otherwise we'll become so much collateral damage."*

"Phara, do you—" Rahgz staggered as more explosions shook the barge from inside and out. Fresh plasma turned sections of the arena into whole burning rivers as walls collapsed and floors melted into slag. Screens in the walls showed INC drones chasing down fleeing crew-members and barge-dwellers, while investigative squads were facing off with wall-armed engineers and officers who had stationed themselves behind blockades.

"Is there anything you can see about lifeboats?" Rahgz asked, regaining his footing.

She spun through a dizzying number of screens, all three sets of her eyes scanning. "Yes!" Her shoulders slumped. "And they've all been either deployed or destroyed."

Rahgz shut his eyes, still able to see Kel's projection standing behind his eyelids. "Any ideas?"

Kel nodded to where the captain lay on the floor. *"He's too proud and too smart to go down with his ship. Someone like him always has an escape route. We need to find it and use it."*

Rahgz opened his eyes. The captain glared up at him in futile fury, as if having heard Kel's suggestion.

"Phara, check this suite's control systems. Anything that looks like a private escape pod interface?"

"Searching!"

As she did, Rahgz pulled up his comms and pinged Bateesma. "Are you there, Bateesma? Can you hear me?"

Her floppy-eared image appeared with a flare of static and her voice came faint over the ongoing noise of battle and the barge being torn apart by missile fire. "That you, Rahgz? About time. I called the INC in like you told me and shot them the datapacket you prepped." She held up the holofig disc that Rahgz had reprogrammed with a personal message for her. "Nifty way to slip me some secret instructions. You should do it more often."

"Get back in here," he said. "If you haven't noticed, we're all in a bit of trouble."

"Way ahead of you." Her comm flicked off and her voice came from a few paces away. "Or right behind you, that is."

Rahgz whirled to find her just coming through the door that led back to the docking platform. "Great. We're looking for a secret escape pod or anything similar. Did the captain use any hidden panels or switches while he had you hostage?"

She looked around and then jumped over to pick up the captain's discarded saber. She thumbed the plasma edge on and off. "Neat! Souvenir."

"Bateesma, focus."

Kel groaned. *"You're sure saving her is a necessity?"*

"I didn't see anything like that," she said, swishing the sword around. "Want me to torture it out of him?"

Several craft zipped past the suite, weapons blazing at one another. One went down in a whirl of smoke and fire, crashing near the base of the private viewing tower. Rahgz kept one eye on the growing chaos outside. It'd only be a matter of time before the hull was damaged beyond the ability for emergency forcefields to contain.

He ran to Phara. "Find anything yet?"

She stabbed at different command functions, growling as error messages kept popping up. "There is something here, but I keep getting blocked. I almost...there!"

A green light flashed on the panel. Rahgz turned to see a small slot open on a wall off to the side. Racing to this, he found a simple glass square waiting. He pressed several hands to it, but nothing happened. Phara remained at the console, trying to override further protocols.

"Bio-lock," Kel said. *"Any guesses who we need to open it?"*

Rahgz kept his eyes on the panel as if it might disappear the instant he glanced away. "Bateesma, drag the captain over here! I need his bio-scans."

There came a meaty hiss, and Thorluthsmien's head slapped against the wall right beside him, followed by one of his hands. Rahgz jumped as the body parts splattered to the floor, minus a body. He turned to see Bateesma cleaning off her new blade. She shrugged at his perplexed look.

"What? He's heavy. This way's quicker."

Shaking his head, Rahgz grabbed the head in two hands and the captain's hand in another and mashed them up against the bio-lock. The hand did nothing, so he dropped it after a few tries and focused on peeling Thorluthsmien's eyelids up to get an optical scan in. This seemed to trigger something, as the panel flashed once, then went dark again.

Screaming in frustration, Rahgz slammed the head against the wall again and again until Phara stopped him with a firm hand.

"You're missing something," she said. "Let me help."

She tugged various tentacles up from his mouth and pressed them to the screen while he kept the eyes in view. This time, the panel flashed and stayed on. A door opened beside it, leading into a chilly tunnel with polished metal walls.

"This way," Rahgz shouted to Bateesma. A series of explosions sent a line of fire into the air right outside the balcony, making the forcefield flash and flicker as it tried to repel the blasts.

Bateesma bounded after him and Phara as they ducked into the hall. It ended in a small elevator chute. Rahgz hesitated, but then Phara shoved him in. The chute sucked him along its frictionless length, plunging him through a pitch-black tube that seemed to swallow him up forever. The ride lasted long enough for him to have a brief panic attack about the possibility of nothing waiting for him at the end. What if the INC raid force had blasted the escape pod from the outside, and this chute now led to nothing but open space?

What if they'd instead found a complicated trash removal system, where the captain chucked the bodies of his enemies and Rahgz was heading for the inside of an incinerator? What if—

The telltale tug of an inertia dampener slowed him just enough to stop him from flying out the end of the chute. Rahgz came feet-first, tail whirling to compensate as he flailed for balance. He caught himself against the threshold of what looked like a storage closet combined with a personal shuttle. The pilot's seat sat waiting in front of him, and as the panels blinked on, Rahgz stared at a dizzying array of controls that he had no idea how to operate.

"Move," Kel said. *"Now!"*

Huh? How am I supposed to move this craft?

He realized what Kel really meant when Phara ejected from the chute right behind him and crushed him against the back of the chair. He grunted beneath her.

"Move?" he asked. "Now?"

She pushed off him and stepped aside just as a distant whooping became a cry of delight as Bateesma shot out, past Phara, and once more squished Rahgz into the hardbacked chair. His spine crackled a bit this time, sending tingling down through all his toes.

As Bateesma wriggled off him, Rahgz noticed she'd brought—

"Really?" he asked. "The head?"

Bateesma raised Thorluthsmien's decapitated head, which still dribbled ichor from the neck stump. "Snack for later."

"So long as you don't fuck it," Phara said.

Bateesma flicked an ear at her. "No guarantees."

"Can you fly this thing?" Rahgz asked, moving aside to let Phara slither into the front seat.

She immediately flipped several toggles, swiped across a row of sensor switches, and punched an extremely large button flat. The escape pod shook as it thrummed to life and multiple screens flicked on. "We're on a preprogrammed flight path," she said.

"Where to?" Kel asked. Rahgz repeated this out loud.

"Looks like unsanctioned space," Phara said, reading over the sector maps. "Via the nearest hypernode."

"Which is where?" Rahgz asked.

Phara did a double-take as she scanned the scrolling data. "Uh... here. Fuck and sprukk me. This pod is a hypernode. I didn't know they could make them this small."

"Impressive," Kel said. *"The captain was a resourceful one. I wish we could've had him an ally rather than an opponent."*

A crunching sound made Rahgz turn to where Bateesma chewed on several of Thorluthsmien's mouth-tentacles.

"What?" she asked around a mouthful. "I get the munchies when I'm nervous. Have we escaped yet?"

"About to," Phara said, dialing in a few controls. "Hang on. We still have to get clear of the barge before we jump."

Rahgz's stomachs double-flipped as the pod lurched and suddenly dropped. The darkness outside the viewport blurred to gray and blue as they fell out of a hatch beneath the barge itself. Antigravity appeared to be working as they remained fixed to the floor, but Rahgz's sense of vertigo tried to whirl him to the ground nonetheless.

He got an expansive view of the INC assault on the barge, with numerous gunners and ship-runners forming a loose barricade on all sides of the enormous craft. Smoking volcano-sized mounds appeared to be all that was left of the engines, where a sickly yellow glow leaked radioactive plasma into space. Dozens of small shuttles and transport craft floated and twirled through the vacuum, with glints and flashes showing what might've been armored bodies spilling out of ruptures in the hulls.

Alarm systems flashed and alerts blared.

"Weapons are locking onto us," Phara shouted. "Hang on!"

She slapped a panel and Rahgz was pretty sure he heard the universe burp and hiccup.

Space tilted one way. Rahgz's body went the other. His brain decided to spin in endless circles while laughing madly at the veil of stars that sucked into a singular dark core that then exploded outward with a whole new set of constellations, nebulas, and a scattered asteroid field.

Once four dimensions finally made sense again, Rahgz took his fists away from his mouth, where they'd been pressed to keep all of his internal organs from trying to escape. "Did we...are we...?"

Phara's tense body relaxed slightly as she checked the readouts.

"Seems we escaped. No sign of pursuit."

They all fell silent for a while, soaking this in. Rahgz kept watching the nearby stars, waiting for INC ships to pop into being and blast them into so much space dust. As each minute ticked by, it became a bit easier to accept they might've actually succeeded in this wild scheme.

"So what next?" Bateesma finally asked, still chewing on a particular tough strand of tentacle.

"I have no idea," Rahgz said.

"*I do,*" Kel said.

"Great," Rahgz said, "because I officially no longer care." He let himself slowly collapse to the floor beside Bateesma, leaning his head against the wall. "Being in control is exhausting and stressful. My brain is pulp and I'm pretty sure half of my feathers have fallen out." He looked up at Kel, who stood before him, fortunately taking up no space in the cramped pod. "You're in charge of the next few big decisions."

"Me?" Bateesma eyed him.

"No. Other guy."

She squinted one eye. "Still haunted, huh? Exorcism offer stands."

"I'll think about it."

Phara turned to peer at him. "What are the master's orders?"

Kel chuckled. "*I think you can guess what I would tell her. We just nearly had our collective asses obliterated by unflinching foes. Our helot has been eliminated along with our aerie, and we're likely on the INC watchlist for the near future. So ask yourself: What would Kel do?*"

Rahgz frowned, and then realized he actually did have a pretty good idea of what to say.

"Map out the nearest barges and any stations with vat facilities capable of helot generation. We need to secure our funds and start growing a new combatant immediately. Once we're in range of any blood.stream network, start putting feelers out for lanistas who're hungry for some real action. Also, search for any aerie manufacturers that are willing to work off the books."

Phara studied him. "Are those your orders or his?"

He laughed dryly. "You tell me."

Her faces crinkled as she pondered this, until she huffed in frustration. "I can't be sure."

"And that's all that matters." Rahgz tucked a few hands behind his head. "In the immortal words of someone who died a long time ago but refused to stay that way: 'It takes guts to get the glory.' So let's go spill as much of the former and take as much as we can of the latter."

"Couldn't have said it better myself."

www.ingramcontent.com/pod-product-compliance
Lightning Source LLC
Chambersburg PA
CBHW021529250626
47154CB00006BA/2038